Redemption's Lady

Redemption's Lady

L. T. Clark

Country Oak Publishing

Clarksville, TN

Edited By: AA Editing

Cover Design By: BetiBup33 Studio Design

Library of Congress Control Number: 2021912776

Printed in the United States of America

For Malcolm—

May you pursue your dreams and see the world with wonder.

And for those who believed in me and pushed me—

Without you, this would never have happened.

Prologue

All she could think to do was run. The villagers would not give her refuge and her husband had betrayed her. He had tried to turn her in to the men who were hunting her. Elaraine was considering her options as she headed for the outskirts of her village. She came to the quick conclusion that to stay would mean death and fleeing may be her only chance for survival; so, she decided to risk being captured by the Rischiaks rather than being imprisoned or burned alive for her crime. The Rischiaks were rumored to have reached the borders of the next village, but no official had confirmed the rumor, and she thought being caught by the enemy army was better than being caught by her own people. There was at least the slim chance of mercy in the hands of the Rischiaks.

A cousin of the royal family was dead, and the only two witnesses who came forward pointed their accusing fingers solely at her. Guards had come to get her at a family dinner and had given her a day to get her affairs in order. She begged to be able to explain what had happened, but her pleas fell on deaf ears. Someone had to pay for the man's murder, and she was the one chosen to do so. She had spent her given day preparing to go to her sentencing like a good citizen, but when she saw the men coming into the fenced yard, her husband told her how her family thought of her as a liability. She had believed him. She was a young, impetuous wife and her outspoken nature had gotten the Hedri family in trouble more times than she could remember. Her husband told her that they had decided that if someone should die for the crime, then she should so at least one nuisance would be out of the way. What remained of her heart broke; the remaining courage she had to face judgment fled her; and she ran from the armed guards chasing after her. Lightning lit her way, and as she sprinted through the tall grass, she thought back on that fateful night.

It had not been her idea to visit the tavern that evening, but her husband had gone to his parents' village for a few days for a festival, and her sister-in-law, Moraiah, suggested they go and have a nice night without cooking. Elaraine's brother, Moraiah's husband, had left the village a while before and had not returned yet. She knew how distraught Moraiah was over Orin's absence, so Elaraine acquiesced after some light persuading from Moraiah. She had thought it would be a good distraction for the other woman. Instead, they had been accosted by Dalun Shrevelt and Elaraine had fought back. When the trouble had started at the beginning of the evening, Elaraine had begged Moraiah for them to leave, but Moraiah had refused and Elaraine was not going to leave without her. The men in the tavern had been rowdy that evening, and no one was standing up in defense of the women. One man in particular was being persistent and was steadily becoming violent when the women tried to ignore him.

When Dalun Shrevelt grabbed her and would not let her go, Elaraine grabbed a knife from the bartop and stuck it deep in Dalun's stomach to save them both. She could still remember the warm blood hitting her hand and trying to wash it off later. She remembered the panic that made her grab the knife. She had been so scared. Both women ran back to Moraiah's home, praying that no one would blame them for what had happened and that Dalun would recover. But it was a false hope as everyone in the town feared Dalun and his family. If it had been any other man, it would have been fine as self-defense, but this man was related to the king, who had to take care of even the most heinous of his relatives. Elaraine knew of three attacks by Dalun on members of the village that the king had pardoned, even when one of the men died from the fight. Any hopes she had were dashed when Dalun died later that night of his injury. She had been living in fear ever since and it did not take long for the villagers to turn on her.

Elaraine neared the tree line and turned east towards the mountains. Her dark brown hair whipped behind her as she ran. She had heard of a hermit who might give her a safe shelter for the night, but he lived deep in the woods. She had to reach him soon if she stood any chance of not sleeping in the storm thundering in the hills before her or in a cell. She could hear the men following closer behind her. Their yells were getting clearer, and her legs were quickly tiring under the strain. She felt a last surge of energy and tried to run faster. She splashed through a large puddle, not caring about the noise, only that she got far enough away for the men to not bother looking for her anymore. She knew it would be a few days before the next village got word of her escape, but she also knew the news would still beat her there and that her husband would let his old friends still in the army know where they could find her. She kept up her flight for as long as she was able, but the voices behind her kept getting closer and closer.

She didn't see the creek before she fell face-first into the muddy bank on its far side. It was so shallow from the recent drought that it hardly made a noise as she crossed it. She sputtered for air as she scrambled back to her feet. Someone grabbed her shoulder in a tight grip and she frantically shook it off, more terrified than she had ever been in her life. She was still too far away for the person holding her to be the hermit. The hand was on her shoulder again before she could get back to her feet. She pulled the dirk from her boot and sliced at her attacker, missing him completely. When she finally managed to wipe the mud and grime from her face she realized she was looking at one of the most beautiful women she had ever seen in her life. The dirk fell, forgotten, from her fingertips, and she crumpled in a heap on the creek's bank. The world faded to black as she felt herself being lifted from the mud.

Chapter One

When Elaraine awoke in Ranci's cabin the day after she had been rescued, Ranci told her that she had two choices: learn to survive or return to her village. She told Elaraine that if she worked hard and trained for hours each day, she would be able to leave the woods as good as any man in the King's army and if Elaraine waited long enough to leave the safety of Ranci's land, no one would remember the way Dalun Shrevelt had died, least of all that she had been the one responsible for his death. She would be free to live her life as she wanted. Her husband would remarry and would move on with his life thinking she was dead. No matter what they had done that led to her ultimate flight, it saddened her to think that her family would forget her. She would be a lost daughter of the Hedri, and that made her heart hurt worse than her husband's betrayal.

Elaraine chose to stay with Ranci and her son to learn to survive on her own. As the days went by and no one came to get her, she relaxed more and more into her new life. She had found peace in Ranci's home and thrived in their company. Ranci was a hardened woman and demanded the best from her son and Elaraine. For the refuge she was given, Elaraine was happy to give it.

Dayn, Ranci's son, was Elaraine's pillar of strength during the year she spent with them. He would sit with her when she needed to cry and would listen to her when she wanted to talk. He endured her wrath when her anger overwhelmed her and she lashed out. Dayn never judged her and was the most patient man she had ever met. He was the first true friend she realized she had ever had. They would discuss for hours on end the Rischiaks sending their army past the Swennian-Rischiak border and Dayn's dreams of joining the army. He would meet her by the creek each day and teach her what she would need to know in order to survive later, like self-defense and weaponry. He made a worthy opponent as he was a good head taller than her and many times stronger. She looked forward to her time with him each day. She was finally beginning to match him in skill when her training ended abruptly.

The men were waiting in the cabin with Ranci when Elaraine and Dayn returned from their sparring lesson. Ranci was standing in the door, frowning and looking stern, as usual. The only difference from any other day was the loud voices coming from the house and the cloud of unhappiness that seemed to hang over the little cabin. Ranci descended the steps and came slowly towards Elaraine. Dayn placed a comforting hand on Elaraine's shoulder and went to the porch after a curt, dismissive glance from his mother. The woman placed a cold hand on Elaraine's shoulder where her son's had been.

"Elaraine, I couldn't ask for a better ward. You're obedient, quiet, and hard-working. You have worked hard to be useful around here. But you came here fleeing. We never discussed where you were going that night I found you, but you must have been looking for my husband, the renowned hermit. But instead of reaching him, I found you." Elaraine nodded. "I told you that you could stay here for a while and learn how to survive on your own."

"Ranci, I've done everything you've ever asked of me. I've worked hard, I train with Dayn for hours on end every day. I've done nothing but try to make you proud while I've been here." Elaraine's voice cracked with frustration. She jerked her chin toward the voices. "Who are you giving me over to? Why are you making me leave?"

"If I had it my way, you'd stay and live here forever. I'd give you this little cabin when I died because I know Dayn doesn't want it, and I would let you do whatever you wanted. But some men have come for you from the village. The three of us can't keep them away and I can't endanger my family anymore. You have to leave with them."

"What do you mean?" Dayn yelled and he ran towards them. "You gave her your word! You told her she could stay! You said she was safe here!"

"I know what I said!" Ranci snapped at her son. "But I can't allow those men to take you away, too, and we cannot beat them in a fight. It's for the best, Dayn!"

When Dayn looked ready to argue further, Elaraine held up her hand to stop him. "No, I understand. I said I would stay until you said for me to leave. I'll honor my part of the bargain. I'll just go and get my things and leave." She offered Ranci a short bow. "Thank you for taking me in and keeping me safe this past year."

Ranci held her head high as her son passed her. It always amazed Elaraine how stolid the other woman could be. She was so beautiful and always so unhappy. Elaraine knew the story behind the sadness, though.

Ranci's husband, Dayn's father, left them when Dayn was born, saying that he could not be the father of the child. He claimed that a wizard sired the boy. Both parents became hermits in the woods, forcing Dayn into a life of solitude as well. Ranci's husband refused to ever meet with his son, and Ranci wore her anger and disappointment like a cloak.

"Your things are packed and by the door." The small amount of pity Elaraine was able to detect in Ranci's voice snapped her attention back to the situation at hand. "Please get them and leave quickly and quietly."

Elaraine nodded and shuffled past her, resigned to meeting her fate. Dayn was already sitting at the table, his head in his hands and looking miserable. The village guards were standing in the corner talking amongst themselves. Elaraine knew better than to run away again. It had been a year since she had killed Dalun, a year since she had run the first time. Her husband had made it painfully obvious before she had even left that he did not love her and was going to leave her. Her parents were probably still feeling the betrayal of the shame her killing Dalun would have brought upon them and their loyalty to the royal family being questioned. She hated herself. She could honestly, whole-heartedly, admit that she hated herself. It was her fault she was now going to be taken away because it was her fault that she had killed Dalun. It had taken a long time to realize that she was the only person she could blame for her circumstances.

She walked past Dayn, her loyal friend, and stooped to pick up the sack in which her meager belongings were already packed haphazardly. She noticed him raise his head as she passed him. His green eyes were red and swollen. He was her age but looked much younger. He grabbed her hand as she walked back to the door and knelt on the floor in front of her. He placed her hands on his face and began to tremble. She wiped at the salt trails on his cheeks without thinking about it.

"Elaraine, don't go! We can leave, just the two of us, and survive on our own! We can outrun the guards and live as travelers. You don't have to go with them!" he whispered urgently.

Elaraine dropped her belongings and knelt in front of him, embracing him. "Dayn, I stayed here too long. You know as well as I do that I would have been caught eventually. I killed a man...I don't even deny it! I must go back. I have to face judgment."

"No!" he rasped. "I've seen these men training! They are the most pathetic of the village guard. With me to help you, I know you can get away!" He shook his head. "Fine, don't take me along with you, but you...you just have to get away!"

Elaraine patted his shoulder and stood up. "Quit crying, Dayn. Don't encourage someone to be a coward when you wouldn't be one in the same situation."

"There's no life for an ill-begotten son here," he hissed bitterly. "My one chance is to get away to where no one knows the shame I have to live with, where I can create a new life for myself. Let's do that together."

"The only 'shame' is that you're crying for something you have no control over. And if there is really 'shame' to be had with your birth, it lies with your parents." She turned toward the guards and held out her wrists to them. "I'm ready to go now."

The head guard approached her, a length of rope held loosely in his hands. He was a hard man and looked tired. She remembered him from when he was younger and couldn't remember a time that he didn't look haggard. The three younger guards were close behind him, their hands on their sword hilts. Elaraine didn't even bother to pick up her belongings and held her wrists out for the man. They were tied tightly with the rope, and the other end was tied to one of the guard's belts. She was led outside and placed in front of the guard on a horse. She knew this younger guard very well.

His name was Nox, an orphan of the village. He had grown up alongside her and had once been one of her closest friends. They had been in constant trouble together throughout their childhood. He had become a very handsome man; most of the young girls had their hearts set upon him. He was such a good man, but he didn't have any interest in the women of the village; not that the girls' fathers would allow them to marry him anyway. Marriage to an orphan with unknown parents would not be advancing their families in society, after all. The girls would need to marry someone with land or money, but preferably both, for their families. Elaraine had had her eye on him at one time in her life and those had been the arguments her father had given her. She pitied Nox, in a way, even though she knew it was by his hand she would be handed over to the judgement of death or imprisonment. He was destined to a horrible fate that she was fortunate to have avoided: eternal loneliness.

Nox whirled his horse around and started off toward the village at a fast trot, with two guards in front of them and one behind them. The head guard talked to the guard riding beside him and they seemed to laugh the entire ride back to the village. Elaraine just bowed her head under the weight of her troubles. She had so many questions to ask Nox, but she could not bring herself to break the solemn silence that had settled between the two of them. The quiet and depression that insulated her seemed fitting, in a way. She knew all the young men there and she could tell they were not happy at having to bring her into the town. They gave her pitying looks and bowed their heads when they looked her in the eyes. They had all grown up together. Two of them had even been in the tavern when Dalun died.

Nox had the horse jump the creek where Ranci had found her that day almost a year before, jarring her from her thoughts. She cleared her throat and fiddled with the ropes on her wrists.

"Is my family all right?" Her voice sounded small and foreign to her.

It took him a few moments to answer. "Your parents, brothers and sisters are fine, the last time anyone heard anyway. They moved to the capital. I suppose that was to prove their loyalty to the crown. A messenger came to question them about the Dalun Shrevelt incident." She felt his eyes boring into the back of her head. "Their loyalties were questioned, you know." He sighed heavily. "Moraiah and her son still wait in the village for Orin to return. Staur remarried and is happy enough. I'm not sure how that is, though, since you're not dead." He thought for a minute. "You couldn't ask for more, you know."

She nodded, thinking about her family for a time and hoping they were no longer in trouble because of her. Then she shivered and looked around.

"Nox, I'm in trouble, aren't I?" He didn't answer her. "I thought you could understand why I did it, Nox. You were there! Can't you talk to Rochstaff on my behalf?" Still no answer. "I don't expect to not be punished. I just want the punishment to fit the crime! Rochstaff will not give me a chance!" She felt herself getting angry at his silence. "Nox, please answer me!"

"What answer do you want? You already know how much trouble you're in! I can't believe you ran away, Elaraine! Why couldn't you just stay and face the consequences? If you had stayed, maybe my talking to him would have helped...maybe. But it's too late for that! Your running away made you look guilty in everyone's eyes! People that even saw it happen have been changing their stories, saying you plotted to kill him from the outset! Everyone in the village knows that he had attempted to win you before you married your husband and that he held a grudge. Everyone knows he treated your family unfairly. Besides, Dalun Shrevelt was a nobleman, a cousin of the King. Someone must pay for his death, even if he may have deserved it. Maybe if Rochstaff is in a good mood when we get there, you'll have a chance."

"That's a lot of 'maybes,' my friend."

"Being a friend to you has nothing to do with this, Elaraine, and you know it!"

"Nox, quit talking to the prisoner!" the head guard yelled back to him. "You don't want to look like an accomplice of hers, do you?"

Elaraine knew that it was no use to argue her case to these men. If Nox wouldn't help her now, or even speak on her behalf, then her hope for a fair punishment was utterly lost. She grudgingly understood why he would not speak for her, but it still felt like a betrayal. She just hung her head and prayed for a quick death. The prisons of the kingdom had a horrible reputation for excessive cruelty and for forgetting prisoners in their depths.

She noticed the trees thinning around her. The boundaries of the village were painfully clear, letting her know that the time was fast approaching for her to meet Rochstaff's judgment. The villagers were lined up along the only road into the village. No one said or did anything as they rode past. The eerie sight sent a shiver up her back. It made her think of a funeral, and she didn't think that was far off from what would be happening once the judgment had been made.

Elaraine risked a few glances into the crowd and saw Moraiah near the fringes of the villagers in the back. Her head was held high, and she was staring at Elaraine as she rode past. Elaraine's heart sank seeing her at the back. No one had accused the beautiful Moraiah for that night out of respect for her husband, Orin, and Elaraine doubted that she had spoken about what really happened. Elaraine was left to take all the blame for Dalun Shrevelt's death. She hoped that Moraiah had told the truth if she'd had the opportunity, and that's all she could expect from her friend. Moraiah looked tired, but proud. She had always been unbearably proud, but it had given her the reputation of being strong and reliable in the community. Next to her was Elaraine's nephew, Josi, watching her with pity and something akin to hate in his eyes. He looked small and betrayed, like the world was weighing him down. He was only fourteen years old, but he looked ten years older in that moment. Near them was Staur, Elaraine's husband. His arm was wrapped around a tall and lean blonde woman next to him who was whispering in his ear. Elaraine knew the woman and had always disliked her. She thought the pair suited each other. Leaning against the execution platform in the center of the village was the judge, Rochstaff, chewing on a long blade of meadow grass. Nox pulled the horse to a stop near the platform.

"Is that her?" Rochstaff yelled, breaking the silence. He straightened and stretched his back. "If it is, bring her over here."

Nox steered the horse towards the judge, another kinsman of Dalun and the King. He untied the rope from his belt, knowing Elaraine would not be able to escape with the entire town waiting in the square for her judgment. Her spirit was broken, and everyone knew it. Rochstaff just sneered at her as he recited the list of her offenses: murder, fleeing judgment, treason against the King, and theft. Elaraine just groaned when she heard Rochstaff explain the theft charge. Staur had filed it for the necklace she was wearing when she ran. Nothing had ever truly been hers. Dayn had told her about the charges after he had visited the village for supplies a few months before, but the theft charge still hurt her. Just one of those charges would have meant a certain death sentence. Being charged with all four offenses should have sealed her fate. She expected to be taken up the steps to the execution platform but, to her surprise, Rochstaff began to laugh.

"After a year of hiding, do you really expect me to kill you?" Rochstaff laughed. He waved his hand around. "No, no. See, I'm not that nice, and the royal family is not so generous to criminals. You obviously wanted a death sentence, Elaraine Hedri. If you didn't want to die, you would not have come so quietly with the guards. So, instead, you are sentenced to a life of imprisonment in the Dungeons Ussal. If you are so desperate to live, see out the rest of your days there. If you are desperate to die once you get there, which I am sure is what will happen, as murderesses and traitors are not shown any mercy there, I am sure they will be more than happy to accommodate you in your death wish. But I will not have your death on my hands today. I won't be giving you an easy way out of your actions." He turned and spat in the dirt and tossed the blade of grass aside. "Now, before I go and eat dinner, is there anything you want to say?"

Elaraine stared at him silently for a while, but then she noticed Rochstaff prepare to leave. "Please, you did not let me plead my case. My side of the story has been left untold. I am sure once you hear it you will grant me some reprieve."

He cocked an eyebrow at her. "Your husband pled your case a year ago when you ran away. He said you claimed to be guilty of Dalun Shrevelt's murder and that is why you left." He looked at her like a wolf looks at prey. "So, you see, things have been settled for a year. We just needed the person to put into the dungeon. Nox! Worrin!" Nox looked up at him warily. "Take her to the Dungeons Ussal. They are waiting for her there. Do not stop until you get there." He looked at Elaraine with disgust. "You should have just killed yourself when you killed my cousin. You could have saved a lot of people a lot of trouble. It has been significantly more trouble than what your life is worth."

Nox rewrapped her wrists with rope and placed her on her own horse this time. They had to travel quickly to get to the Dungeons Ussal before nightfall, and his horse would not have been able to make it to the destination with two people on its back. Tears sprang to her eyes as Elaraine was thrown onto the horse by two men of the community she had known and trusted her entire life. Worrin had even been friends with her father.

There was a stirring in the crowd that caught her attention. Her nephew came to the edge of the crowd towards her, his hands balled into fists.

"Aunt, why did you do it?" he said softly. "Why? They came after Mother. They threatened to send her to the Dungeons Ussal if they didn't find you soon. Father hasn't returned and I would have been left alone. Aunt, why is it that you committed the crime, and my family is the one that suffers?"

"Josi, I did not ever mean for you or your family to suffer, and one day you will understand," she said to the child, raising her voice so that the people around her could hear her. "It doesn't matter what I have done. Grow to be a good man, like your father. He will return home, don't give up hope." Nox began to lead her horse away slowly. "I love you." Her nephew walked back into the crowd, his head lowered and his shoulders shaking so slightly she could have sworn she had been imagining the sobs. "Josi! You believe me, don't you?"

He turned and looked back at her as her horse went away from the village back toward the trees. "I don't know," he yelled. She saw the grief and confusion in his face, the expression completely breaking what remained of her shriveled heart.

The familiar forest was surrounding her again, but she did not notice.

Elaraine was allowing herself to wallow in her pain and embarrassment. This was truly the first time since she was a child that she had felt sorry for herself. When she had been with Ranci, she had been angry at the situation, but had not felt sorry for herself. It would have been so easy for her to blame her current predicament on Dalun or Moraiah, or especially on her husband and Rochstaff, but all she could think about was if there had been another way to get out of that situation to begin with. She still couldn't see any, but there had to have been one. No one ever had to die. She had let her fear rule her that night and a nobleman was dead. She had only meant to protect herself and Moraiah. She hadn't even realized the knife was in her hand until it was in Dalun.

Nox and Worrin were talking to each other over her head about problems in the village. Apparently, most of the villagers had fallen on hard times with the drought that year. The grains just weren't growing that year and it did not seem like rain was going to come before the end of the growing season. Their livestock were withering away without their feed. Worrin's father had had to sell his farm and move to another town.

The sulking woman just ignored them for a while and wallowed in her own self-pity. However, the topic soon changed and Elaraine began paying close attention to their conversation when Moraiah's name was mentioned.

"What happened to her?" she asked, interrupting their conversation. "Is Moraiah going to be all right?"

Worrin glared at her. "Before this mess, she and your brother were happy together. But rumor has it he's staying away so his loyalties aren't questioned like your parents' loyalties were. I think he's dead. Maybe you'll see him when you die, and you can explain to him why you destroyed so many lives and ruined his family."

Nox coughed. "Worrin, that's not fair and you know it! She didn't have a choice. You were there! Dalun tried to attack them! It was all in defense against the wrong person in the wrong way."

"There's always another way! She didn't have the right to kill anyone!"

"Then what should I have done?" Elaraine whispered as she felt her dark tendrils of hair baking in the summer sun. "Believe me, I keep thinking that there had to have been another way, but I haven't been able to see it. He would have followed us home, gotten us alone, and he could have done any number of things. I had to protect us. None of you stood up to protect us, so I did what you should have done."

Worrin glared at her and then at Nox. "Why couldn't you just have walked away?" he croaked. "If you had just walked away, Nox and I could have done what was right. If he had followed you home, you both had husbands that would have sought revenge. If he had gotten you alone, you could have yelled, and the villagers would have come to your aid and defended you. But we would have been able to uphold the law without anyone dying!"

"Why couldn't you have done that when he had his hands on us in the first place?" she snapped. "I would think if you were truly committed to your duty over drinking with your friends, you would have done something then. Protecting your friends and their wives should have been pretty high on your list of priorities if you hadn't been so drunk!"

"Will the two of you just stop it?" Nox groaned. "A lot of different things could have been done. But there's nothing that can be done about it now. Dalun Shrevelt is dead. Too many lives have already been destroyed over this. Let's just get to Dungeons Ussal and separate ways still as friends."

"We were friends, Nox, but that doesn't make us friends now." Worrin kicked his horse into a faster trot. "The three of us may as well be strangers at this point. Let's just get there and leave this whole episode behind us and forget about each other the best we can."

"He's right, Nox," Elaraine whispered. "You and I were friends, Worrin and I never were. It takes a man to stand up to a noble and neither of you did, forgetting your oaths in the process." She took a deep breath and let it out slowly. After a while, she added, "So I suppose we'll all be parting ways as strangers after all."

"Elaraine! Please, this is my job! I should have stopped him, I know that! But I can't go back in time any more than you can and with this war coming we can't afford to make enemies within the imperial ranks. The king would be an awful man to cross right now, and it was his cousin that was killed. Another of his cousins sentenced you. If I have any chance whatsoever of getting a rank in the army when I need to join, this is my chance! This could be my one and only chance!" The desperate tone of his voice was gone and an undertone of sobriety was added. "I can't marry well, or even hope to be happy, if all I amount to is a village guard with no parents, glory or title. I am tired of this lonely life. If I am to fight to be happy, let this be the first step."

"So instead of being chivalrous and righteous, you lost your courage and became the worst kind of gutless coward." She raised her tied hands to her forehead and tried to calm her temper. "You became a selfish and unrighteous man without friends. You get only what you deserve in this life. I have the kind of life I deserve through my actions. I wish you luck living the kind of life you have shown you deserve. Maybe you are lonely because that is your punishment."

"That's not right, and you know it!" he growled. "Don't judge me when I never judged you."

"I'm not going to fight you on this, Nox. Maybe after a few decades in the prison I'll be able to forgive you for not standing up for me. Maybe I'll be able to think things through enough and maybe people will have forgiven me for what I have done. But, until then, you're going to have to realize that you two are the ones taking me to imminent torture and eventual death. No friendship can survive that particular betrayal."

"That's a lot of 'maybes,'" he said, repeating her earlier words with dripping sarcasm, but gaining no response from her. "So...that's it, then?"

There was a drawn out and awkward silence. Worrin began to cough and wheeze in his saddle. Nox and Elaraine gave him worried looks as their horses weaved between the trees. Worrin didn't seem to notice their concern and kept grumbling to himself as his coughing steadily grew worse and it became harder for him to catch his breath.

"I can't think of any way for us to get past this," Nox admitted at last, looking away from his sick comrade. "But if I think of one, I'll let you know," he added, laughing nervously. "What? Not even a snicker? I'm giving this all I possibly can to lighten the situation! You can at least pretend to appreciate my efforts."

Elaraine looked away from him in dismay. "Please forgive me if I just can't find the humor in the situation." She saw him shudder from the hate in her voice, making her regret her tone immediately. "Nox, that's not to say—"

"Would you two just be quiet?" Worrin yelled as he began to sway from side to side atop his horse. "It's like being with an old married couple and I am tired of listening to you argue." He began to pant. "Besides, who really cares if you two part as friends or not? The Dungeons Ussal will end any relationship she has in the world beyond its cages."

"Worrin, are you all right?" Nox asked the other guard. "You aren't looking very well at all."

Worrin began to cough uncontrollably. "Why do you care? It's just a little cough! I'm fine."

Nox straightened his shoulders and took an authoritative tone with Worrin. "Do not speak to me like that. I care because in the past few moments alone your condition has become drastically worse!"

Nox wheeled his horse over to Worrin's and took the man's reins. Elaraine's horse just followed Nox's against her deepest wishes that it would just bolt and take her away. Soon the three of them were dismounted by a large elm tree, Elaraine tied securely to the trunk. Nox crossed his arms over his chest and stood in front of Worrin, who was slouched against the tree, his head between his knees, coughing into his tunic.

He growled, "Worrin, how long have you been sick?" He kicked the man's boot when he didn't get an answer.

"It's been months, really," Worrin said, giving up the fight. "Just let me sit here for a minute and I'll be ready to ride again. These bouts always pass in a few moments." He glanced up at Elaraine worriedly. "Nox, maybe you should go on ahead with the prisoner. Rochstaff will skin us alive if we don't get her to the prison soon, and I am only hindering you."

Nox shook his head and laid a hand gently on Worrin's shoulder. "No, Worrin. Rochstaff won't really care that much if she's delayed slightly as long as she eventually gets there. He'll be much more upset with me if I leave you behind sick and alone. We can't afford to lose a guard because he's sick. What if an animal or a Rischiak were to get to you?"

Worrin pushed him away. "You're saying that for your own sense of loyalty! But admit that your sense of duty says for you to leave me right here."

Elaraine edged herself closer to Worrin and knelt on her haunches. "Worrin, if I were going to try to escape, I would have already tried to do so. I've been nothing but the most accommodating prisoner you could have possibly asked for. Now quit worrying about my escape and let Nox help you!" She softened her tone a bit. "If he can help you get better then you will be able to return and help your family come out of this hard time. Isn't that alone worth accepting his help?"

Worrin shook his head, ignoring every word she said as he was struck with another coughing fit. When it subsided, he was pale and shaking. "Nox, we both know that I'm too sick to finish this. I can't do this anymore. If I get even close to the Dungeons Ussal, I'm dead, and we both know it. They have too much sickness already there and I can't afford to get anything else on top of this!" he added softly as he settled back down further into the trunk of the tree. "I'd leave you if the roles were reversed, don't think for a second that I wouldn't." Another spasm of coughing wracked his body, and this time, when he pulled his hand away, there was blood all over his fist. "I'll go back to the village and see the healer."

"If you're coughing blood, Worrin, there's nothing he'll be able to do," Elaraine said somberly. "That's a sign the sickness is too far gone to help."

"Do you think I don't know that?" he spat at her sourly. "I've known I have been at the edge of death for a while. I promised your husband I'd get you and now that I have, I guess my body is saying that I can let go now. My business is finished."

Nox sighed and sat by Worrin, pulling his friend's head to rest on his shoulder as more blood-infused coughs wracked his body. "Well, lucky for you, I'm not you and I'm not going to leave you."

Chapter Two

Nox and Elaraine stayed with Worrin until he coughed his last and slumped to the ground to rest eternally in peace. His tunic was stained red down the front from the blood he had coughed in his last minutes. Worrin's death really put things into perspective for Elaraine. Seeing a man slowly slip away while he suffered was much different than just seeing the body fall to the floor. Death had become very palpable to the young woman. Suddenly, she cared whether she died or not. She vowed to herself that if her god let her live and escape from her imprisonment, she would never kill another Swennian. The look of pain that crossed Worrin's face before he closed his eyes for the last time made her choke back tears. The blood dribbled down his chin uncaught.

Nox left her tied to the tree with Worrin's body while he walked away to be alone for a while. Elaraine understood his need for solitude, but it was more than a little disconcerting for her to be so close to the body. The sun was setting and shadows were lengthening when Nox finally returned. The birds singing merrily in the trees were ignorant in their bliss of his utter misery. Elaraine felt her heart hurt for him when he sat next to her on a tree root. They just sat in silence, one thinking about the other and the other thinking about the dead.

Nox stood up at long last and walked over to loom over Worrin's body. His fists were clenched and his face was clouded with grief as he looked down at his fallen friend. "What kind of man am I, Elaraine? I had two friends I could truly count on in this world. One is now dead and the other I have to deliver to the Dungeons Ussal." He took a calming breath and closed his eyes. "What kind of man am I? You were right." He punched at the tree futilely. "I am a coward. I am an insufferable fool and a terrible friend. What kind of person does that?" He turned to her. "What kind of person puts their own wants over the lives of friends? If I hadn't, Worrin could have been home right now seeing a healer and you would be at home with your family. Was it my life's path that has changed everyone else's?"

Elaraine moved as close to him as the ropes would allow. "Nox, how long have we known each other? Since we were first wobbling about outside without hanging onto other people's fingers. In that time, I have never known you to be manipulative, for you to have betrayed anyone, or even for you to have said a bad thing about anyone. You generally put everyone else before yourself." She watched him heft Worrin into his arms in one quick motion. "A lot of people would have just left Worrin behind to finish their duty like he asked you to. A true friend stays behind in their hour of need like you did." She squared her shoulders and became resolute, willing the shake in her voice to stop. "But Worrin would want you to finish what you started and were ordered to do. Bury him, honor him, and do what is right; but then you need to take me to the prison before you get in trouble." Nox frowned at her. "You are a good friend and a good man, albeit an inconsistent one." She tried to put on a smile for him, but could tell she was failing miserably. "I'm so sorry about Worrin, Nox."

Without a word, he walked into the woods with Worrin held close. Elaraine wasn't sure how long she waited at that tree, but it was a wait she didn't mind. This was time Nox needed to deal with his grief, something that the man did not want to express with company. It was completely dark when he returned, muddy and desolate. He sat down by her and stretched out his legs, flexing a fist and grinding his teeth. Elaraine just remained quiet, letting him have this time to himself and thinking about things herself.

Finally, he let out a garbled moan and she heard him stand back up. "It's too late to get you to the prison tonight. I know you said I needed to go ahead and see this through, but continuing tonight just the two of us is more dangerous than the risk is worth. One more day in my captivity may not be too disagreeable in comparison to what may happen tonight if we continue on. I'll deliver you there tomorrow, but at least you'll have another night to put that off."

"You mistake what it means to be in captivity, Nox," she said softly. "In one form or another, I have always been a captive. To duty, to family, to my mistakes... it seems to me that being a captive to the law is the best one I have been so far. It is far better, in my opinion, to be the prisoner of society than of a domineering husband or growing up unable to become what you truly wish. You never had that problem. You wanted to be a guard and then join the army if the time ever came. Your birth status would not matter if you moved to another village, so you cannot count that as a true burden. But I never wanted to be a farmer's wife, Nox, let alone Staur's."

He turned his swollen face towards her. The moonlight streaming through the trees made the tears running down his cheeks glisten. "Then what is it that you wished? You had a husband who provided for you, a family that loved you. What more could a woman ask for? What more could you possibly have wanted?"

"Leave it alone, Nox," Elaraine said, her mood suddenly changing. She no longer felt in the mood to console him. She was frustrated that he couldn't understand her. "You don't know what a real family is, so how can you judge me and what I have done?" She felt a growl start to rumble in her throat but checked herself. "Whether reaching the Dungeons Ussal is put off until tomorrow or not, I don't care. It will be you who will be punished for my being delivered late, not me." She glanced over at him and saw his mood darkening once again. She sighed heavily. "Nox, I'll make it out of this all right. I'll live out my sentence if I can. What is done is done. If I can live with this future, why can't you accept it as well?"

"It just doesn't seem right," he ground out. "I could let you go free, but then my future will be in shambles. Can I do nothing else for you, then?"

She smiled gently and sadly at his sudden concern. "What can you do? Take me to the prison, live a long and happy life, join the army like you wanted, win glory and a woman's heart. But don't get in trouble on my account, I beg of you. I don't want anyone else to get in trouble because of me. So, take me to the prison now. Let's risk all the danger." She stood up as well as she could while still being tied to the large tree and prodded him with her foot a few times. "Nox, you have done enough for me for a lifetime already by showing me this bit of kindness. Maybe at least your future can be preserved out of this whole ordeal. That would be something good that could come out of all this. Now stand up, wipe off your face, and let's just get this journey over with. Quit trying to please everyone else and start thinking about yourself for once!"

He laughed bitterly, wiping his face with his filthy sleeve. "If I did that, I wouldn't take you to prison. I would merely let you go out here in the wilderness and give you a chance at life." He stood up and untied her from the tree and then re-tied her hands in front of her. "I've thought about how I'd do it, you know. I'd claim you knocked me out and killed Worrin in an escape attempt." He walked her over to the horses and helped her up on one. "But that would be wrong," he sighed as he tied her to the saddle. "That would just send out more men after you, as though you and your family weren't having enough problems right now. But it would be the happiest moment of my life to know you were free."

She watched as he mounted his own horse. "Nox, just finish your job and return home without feeling regret. How many times must I tell you that I am ready to live with what I have done?"

He shrugged morosely and looked straight ahead as his horse led hers in a walk. "I suppose I just don't understand how you can be so calm about this. Most people I have to take there are kicking and screaming the entire way there."

She cracked a wry smile. "You have to admit that I have never been like 'most people!'"

He laughed in agreement as he kicked his horse into a trot and pulled her horse to follow suit. They did not say another word as they rode through the night, nor did they stop or rest. Their minds were both lost in their own thoughts and turmoil.

Elaraine was surprised that she was actually looking forward to getting to the prison. Her positive anticipation sickened her, but at least it would end her dread of the unknown.

Nox was filled with shame, torn between his own morality and his duties, not wanting to hand his friend over to the warden when they got there but also not wanting to anger Rochstaff and ruining all chances he might have of being commissioned when it came time to be drafted for the royal army. He had always been the dredge of society because he could not prove any family ties of social standing. He was seen as a burden to the small village when he had been brought there, only to be left by the man who had delivered him there shortly thereafter as well. Orin had helped mentor him in the fighting arts when the older man had returned from the last war and had always been a guardian to his younger sister's friend. The guard position and future it could provide him had been his first real chance at a life, and he knew he owed this chance in large part to Orin.

All too soon, the quiet ride turned tense as the prison's outer garrison came into view. Nox straightened his back, and Elaraine felt her entire body tense. For a moment, Elaraine contemplated escape, but quickly squashed that idea when she saw the guards riding out to meet them.

The guards' silver armor was glistening with a golden hue in the dim torch light they bore. The sight of the four guards made a foreboding first sight of the Dungeons Ussal. Nox dismounted and took a crumpled and sweat-soaked scroll out of his tunic. He handed it to the first guard when they reigned in next to the two of them, their horses skidding a little to stop and whinnying their compliance. A horrible stench followed the group and quickly enveloped Nox and Elaraine. Elaraine stayed straight in the saddle as a couple of the guards began talking about her as though she wasn't there. She felt herself flush when they started taking bets on when she would kill herself. If either of them were correct, she would not be alive for long once she arrived at the prison. Nox heard them too, and she could feel the air tense as he put a hand on the sword at his side, throwing a panicked look back at her. Elaraine shook her head at him and mouthed for him to just let the guards be. She watched as his hand slowly slid to rest on his thigh.

"Now, just to be sure I have this straight," the guard reading the scroll said, breaking the glare Nox was giving the other men. "She is accused of murdering the king's cousin, treason, stealing from her husband, and evading the guards by hiding in the woods for a year?" Nox nodded. "So why, may I ask, is she here and not headless or swinging from a tree branch? Why do we have to bother with her? Could Rochstaff not contend with this prisoner, either? It seems he is losing his control over your village. Soon all the Hedris will be here for a little family party."

"She is here because that's what Rochstaff said we should do with her. If you don't want to uphold his judgment, then may I recommend you go to the king? I'm sure he would be most interested as to why his cousin's decrees of law and order, especially as they pertain to the murder of another of his cousins, are not being upheld by a few dense prison guards," Nox spat out. He looked at Elaraine out of the corner of his eye and set his jaw. "I know you must do your jobs, but at least do her the courtesy of not hurting her until she is within the walls of the prison. Until she is within the prison walls you cannot punish her."

The guard walked up to Elaraine and spat in her face as he dragged her off the horse. She wiped her face with her sleeve and urgently fought the urge to vomit in her disgust. Nox stalked over to them, ready to fight, when the other guards held him back. The guard tugged Elaraine around and tied a new, stronger and rougher rope around her wrists so tight she felt it instantly rubbing her skin raw.

"I can see you're her friend, Nox, and want the best for her. But let me give you some friendly advice. We're the guards of this prison and we don't like being told how to do our jobs. Not by those within our own ranks and certainly not from a mere village guard. So, about your opinion on how we should treat her, we really don't give half a—"

"I know you don't," Nox shouted and tried to break the hold the other guards had on him. "But at least treat her as a woman before you condemn her to a hell unlike any else in this world. The horrors should start in there," he pointed wildly at the stone walls beyond them, "and not out here! The least you can do is let us part ways with some form of dignity."

"She lost that chance when she killed Dalun Shrevelt," the guard snarled as he threw Elaraine to the ground and kicked her in the ribs. The other guards restrained Nox as Elaraine picked herself up after some difficulty. "Now, leave, young guard, before you join your friend here in the 'hell' you just so kindly referred to."

Nox held up his hand to the guards, pleading to be released from their hold. "Please, just let me say good-bye to her... for that's what it's surely going to be." The head guard hesitated but eventually nodded his consent, and Nox went over to Elaraine slowly, like he might spook her if he walked any faster. He held his arms out to her and embraced her. "Please, Elaraine, forgive me for doing this. I wish I didn't have to and I'm regretting having joined the guards, but I'm bound by the law in this case."

Elaraine pushed away from him firmly. "I do not blame you for bringing me, Nox. I don't know how many times I have to tell you that." She looked back at the imposing stone walls that would imprison her. "But I don't think I'll be able to forgive you."

"I'll find a way to make everything right," he whispered softly in her ear so low it could have been mistaken for a breath if she hadn't been listening or so close to him. "Somehow, I'll make this right."

Elaraine turned back to the guards and lowered her head. "Might as well get this over with," she told them. She refused to look behind her at the man she had grown up with. "Good-bye, Nox."

"Let's go," one of the guards growled as he grabbed her arm and started to drag her away.

"Elaraine, I'll find a way!" Nox yelled after her. "I promise you, I'll figure this all out and make everything I have done right."

She didn't take her eyes off the stone walls that would soon be her new home. She heard Nox yelling his latest promise right before she heard his retreating hoof beats. She kept following the guards, who dragged her along the winding path to the dungeons as they walked their horses back. The sun was just coming up over the horizon as she stepped onto the old, slimy drawbridge. She silently enjoyed the first few rays of sunlight for the briefest of moments before being drawn roughly into the prison by the guards.

The cold and dankness hit her senses like she had run into a wall. The overwhelming smell of death and decay shook her soul and churned her stomach. Tears welled in her eyes from the horrible stench. She stumbled over the slimy stones only to be dragged past racks with men hanging on them and other torture devices to a small cell in which she was thrown in unceremoniously with such force that she skidded across the filthy floor until a wall stopped her progress, her body making a muffled thud with the sudden impact.

She could hear blood curdling screams emanating from down the dimly lit hall. Guards paced the halls, their footsteps resonating in her ears. Listening to the sound of boots was the only thing that kept her sane in those first few moments. Listening to the screams would have driven her as mad as the other prisoners.

She could see nothing; her eyes had not yet adjusted to the dimness of the dungeon or the darkness of her cell. The slamming of the bars and the squeal of a guard turning a key in the lock behind her made a panic set in that focusing on the footsteps couldn't deter. She rushed to the bars and threw her still tied wrists out between them. She yelled for someone to come back. She just wanted to see someone else, make sure she wasn't dreaming and to make sure she was not ultimately alone. Her heartbeat was the only thing that she could hear as panic consumed her. It drowned out even the screams.

Then torchlight was rounding the corner. She saw the guards dragging someone who seemed to be dead, and they stopped in front of her cell. The man looked up, and she saw the dark trails of blood running down the side of his face, his head shaved to the scalp and bleeding, but what hit the hardest was when those piercing green eyes looked at her in the torchlight and she felt herself grow cold under their severity. Before her eyes, they softened and turned away from her.

The man was hung by his wrists on the wall opposite her cell, shackled by his wrists with his toes barely touching the ground. He looked so frail she doubted that his body weight would hurt his wrists too much. He stared towards her cell for a time, their eyes never meeting from the shadows, but they could feel the other's searching gaze. Another torch was lit and placed in a holder outside her cell, which was pushed into darker shadow, but it allowed her to study her new neighbor more.

The keeper of the prison walked by then and opened her door. He came in and closed it behind him with a loud clang. Elaraine backed toward the far wall of her cell, her hands guiding her as she slowly stepped as far as she could away from him. He paced the cell front, twisting his leather gloves behind his back and whenever he turned he would slap them against his leg.

"As you know already why you are here," he began at last, "I don't feel the need to waste my breath reiterating your charges. While you are here, you will be subject to the same rules as the men. I am not going to fool you, Elaraine Hedri; you are the first woman we have had here during my long time as keeper of this prison, and I am not going to adjust my policies to accommodate the fact that you are a woman. So, you will be fed twice a day if we remember you are in here, punished for any disobedience, and you will be here until the day you die, which hopefully won't be too far away as I already grow tired of you and am tired of hearing about you." He went back to the cell door, went outside to the hall and locked it behind him. "I do hope we understand each other, Elaraine Hedri. I am a busy man and need to leave, but feel free to refrain from making any requests. Have a nice stay," he sneered over his shoulder at her as he left. "I will see you when they carry your corpse out of this cell to be burned."

When the sounds of the keeper's footsteps had completely disappeared, she felt herself relax minutely for the first time since she had left Ranci and Dayn the day before. She walked back towards the cell door and looped her arms around the bars. The man the guards had dragged in was still looking towards her. He shifted his body against the wall and she could see him heave a heavy sigh. He looked so familiar! She considered for a while how that face looked almost too familiar for comfort. Then it hit her painfully. Her poor brother was looking at her, those green eyes penetrating the darkness suddenly as she came to the horrific realization. His face was swollen almost beyond recognition, but those eyes could not be mistaken.

When she had heard that Orin was there, she hadn't expected for him to look so pitiful and hopeless. He looked beaten and exhausted. She reached out for him desperately. It was her fault. If she had not run away, she could have explained that Moraiah had not laid a hand on Dalun and should not be held responsible. The guards then would not have gone for Moraiah and then Orin would not have had to take Moraiah's place in the Dungeons Ussal. Having no one to blame but herself, Elaraine started to cry as her hands continued to only grasp the empty air right outside her cell.

"Orin? Orin, please, please tell me you are all right!" Tears were spilling over her cheeks in torrents and landing at her feet. He looked up at her, squinted harder into the shadows of her cell and frowned. "Orin?" She could hear the quaking desperation in her own voice as she called for him.

He seemed to strain in the dim light for his voice. "Elaraine?" he croaked. "Elaraine, is that you?" Her sobs confirmed it for him. "The Dungeons Ussal were the last place I thought I would ever find you, little sister," he said somberly amidst her sobbing breaths. "Don't cry, Elaraine," he murmured, his tone softening and mollifying her. "We will see each other through this trial just as we have others. Everything will be all right. We are together, so please don't cry."

Elaraine thought that he was trying to convince himself more than her, but she didn't care. His words were soothing her. Leave it to Orin to make her feel all right by just talking to her. He had always been her protector, her mentor, and one of her best friends. Her tears still ran but her sobs were subsiding.

"Orin, how long have you been here? You are so thin!"

He thought for a few moments before he looked completely crestfallen and allowed his head to fall to his chest. "It's truly a sad thing when you can't even remember how long it's been since you've seen your wife and son, isn't it? The days run together here and too soon you forget how to keep the time correctly."

It was torture for Elaraine to be that close to her suffering brother and yet utterly unable to comfort him. It was one of those rare moments when she knew she could be his pillar of strength, but, try as she might, she couldn't get to him. She was completely pressed against the iron bars by now. Both of her arms reached for him futilely. His head was still lowered, consumed in his despair, but she had to give up on trying to reach him. Instead, she lowered herself to the floor and looked at him with pity.

"Orin," she groaned, "this is my fault. If I hadn't run away, you wouldn't be here."

He snapped his head up and she could feel the anger radiating off of him. "Elaraine, I never want to hear you say that! Unlike some of the family, I know you couldn't have done things differently. If it hadn't been for you killing Dalun, who knows what could have happened to you and Moraiah." After a minute of silence, he added with a laugh, "Two of my favorite ladies are worth a little pain, Elaraine."

"But—"

"You aren't the one who got me put here," he reminded her. "They came for Moraiah. What kind of husband, or man, would I be if I let them take my wife without a fight? She did nothing wrong. You did nothing wrong. I'm here, Elaraine," he looked at her, "because I did the right thing and actually spoke up for the two of you. I am here because of things I did, not because of what you did."

"It was the first time I ever defended myself, Orin," she ground out. "I lived my whole life for other people and now I'll never know what it's like to truly live for myself."

Orin looked at her with sympathy. "You will know what it's like one day."

She shook her head. "We both know I'll die in here, Orin, and I'll die without knowing what I could have been in this world."

"You've been lost since I first went to war and you never found your way back."

"I think I was on my way back when..." She trailed off and shook her head to block her tears from falling. "And now things will never be the same."

They shared a companionable and sad silence. Elaraine was getting used to these long pauses, something that before she ran away would have driven her crazy within a few minutes, but Ranci and Dayn often went a day or two without speaking at all and she had been forced to adapt to the silence. In recent weeks she had found herself reveling in it.

Orin eventually faded off to sleep and Elaraine scooted to the back of the cell until her back rested on the wall facing her brother. He was not a believer in anything he could not see, and she hoped she was far enough into the shadows that his darkness-adjusted eyes wouldn't see her as she knelt and folded her hands in a silent plea.

It's not that she particularly believed in something intangible watching over her. She believed in tangible things and she had never seen proof of the existence of something unseen watching over her, but sometimes she just got the feeling she was being protected by something. She figured that now, in her time of dire need, she would try to talk to whatever that protector was, as she sometimes did when she was a little girl. She did not ask for help for herself. Instead, she prayed for Orin, that he might escape and find Moraiah and Josi again. She wished only for his health and happiness.

When she was finished, her exhaustion from the trials she had endured in the past day finally overwhelmed her. She sank reluctantly down to the putrid cobblestones and laid there. Her cheek was laying in something slimy with the worst kind of foul smell attached to it. She thought it might have the consistency of blood, but it lacked the smell of iron. She forced herself to block the thought of what it might be from her mind and closed her eyes, noticing that there wasn't much difference between having her eyes open and closed. But she was thankful her eyes had adjusted enough for her to recognize her own flesh and blood. A rat was scurrying around her cell looking for the leftovers of a meal she had not yet received. It scurried over her booted feet and she futilely tried kicking it away. Orin was somehow still sleeping as she cried herself to a land of flowering green meadows and forested hills.

Worrin and Nox were there with her in her dream. Ranci was sitting on a boulder she passed by with the two men, both of whom were holding one of her hands like old friends. They seemed happy. Worrin was well and alive and Nox did not seem so worn and tired. When they reached the top of the hill, Dayn was there. Dayn reached out for her, but her feet seemed to cement themselves in the leaves. She shook her head at him as Worrin and Nox placed restraining hands on her shoulders. He smiled at them sadly and then jumped off the rock he was on, sending himself careening off the cliff. Elaraine tried to jump forward to reach him, ripping herself out of Worrin's hand, but not Nox's. Nox held her too tightly for her to get away from him to get to Dayn. Her feet were finally able to move, but it was too late. Ranci was standing suddenly where her son had been seconds before. She smiled eerily at Elaraine before she came sprinting towards the threesome. Elaraine braced herself for the collision of their bodies when she saw the woman wasn't slowing down. But the collision never came. The next thing Elaraine knew, Ranci was screaming as her body was passing through hers, but it was not Ranci at the same time. This woman passing through them looked like a corpse with sallow skin and carved out features. Skin was hanging off her limbs like her robes should have been. The disturbing image is what ultimately woke Elaraine from her slumber.

She felt eyes on her back, boring holes into her. With a heavy sigh, she turned over and stretched her aching limbs. When she opened her eyes, Orin was awake and staring at her in the gloom. She wiped her face as she sat up and felt whatever had been on her cheek become stuck on her hand too. To say she was disgusted would have been an understatement. She crawled back to the door and sat on her haunches.

"Are you okay?" her brother croaked. "I haven't heard yelling like that since the last person got tortured." He cleared his throat. "It scared me, Elaraine. Are you okay?"

She nodded and wiped the perspiration off her forehead, then rested her head against the cold bars. "Yes, Orin, I'm fine. You don't have to worry about me."

He shrugged minutely as he hung there on the wall. "I'm your older brother, Elaraine. It's part of my job." He moved his hands a little bit to create some more blood flow in his arms and groaned. "I must admit, though, that it's just a bit strange to me that I'm having to look after my 'good' sister in a prison. I'm supposed to be looking after you in the village, making sure your husband treats you well, helping you harvest your fields when your husband is away, that sort of thing. You are supposed to be living a quiet life."

She shrugged back, feeling the anger welling once more in her breast. "I'm not supposed to be seeing my brother hung up in iron shackles instead of being with his family, so I guess we're both a little out of our elements here." He looked as though she had hit him. She sighed and berated herself. "Orin, I didn't mean for that to come out the way it did. I didn't mean to sound so hateful. I'm sorry."

He made a wry face. "I understand. It's pretty easy to get angry and frustrated here." After looking around himself suspiciously, he lowered his voice so it wouldn't echo off the walls as much. "So, how are we going to get out of here?"

Even though she had been thinking of the same thing, Orin stating it so bluntly startled her. She had to take a moment to compose herself. "What do you mean?"

"Come on, you're smarter than that, Elaraine! I mean 'escape.'" He just looked at her for a long time. "You truly don't think I mean to let you stay here any longer than I have to, do you?"

She felt herself begin to tremble as she shook her head, partly due to the excitement of the idea of an escape and partly from the fear of what could happen if they were to be caught. Her attempt at a laugh came out as a harsh cough. "Orin, I'm locked up in here and you're attached to a wall there. I'm open to suggestions as to how to get out, but I'm at a loss here."

He thought about it for a while. "Well, we're going to have to do this quickly," he sighed. She just cocked her head to the side and waited for him to explain himself. "If they don't kill me here soon then they're going to take me back to my cell and then either way we will have no chance of leaving here alive." He moved his legs as much as he could. "And considering that I haven't exactly been the model-perfect inmate here, I would say the former is more probable than the latter." He settled back down and closed his eyes. "It will all be okay, Elaraine, you'll see."

Chapter Three

Elaraine wondered at how Orin could be so sure of himself, how he could sleep moments after discussing escape plans with her. How he was more concerned with her own safety and comfort than his own made her more aware of how terrible his condition was. It truly touched her, this love and protection he never failed to give her. All either of them could think of was getting the other out of that jail and back to their family safely. Elaraine vowed not to let Orin down. She would devise a plan to get out of there so they would not have to learn which of the options he had mentioned would come to fruition. She could lose everything else in her life now, but not her brother. She wasn't intrinsically a dramatic person, but she knew deep down in her heart that should Orin die because of all this, then she would die too, whether by her own hand or by driving the guards to do it. The guilt would be too overwhelming if she lost Orin.

She believed she had thought of everything for an escape by the time Orin awoke. She had considered sawing through the iron bars, digging out of the cell through the floor inch by inch, pretending to be dead...what she considered to be everything. She wracked her brain again and again but could not think of anything that could also save Orin. She knew that that would not matter to him, that her getting out would be enough for him to die in peace. He had gone to prison to protect his wife and son and would die to protect his sister. He saw it as a moral duty as an older brother, but it would not be enough for her. She had grown up in the past year. A year ago, maybe she would have taken the chance to escape without him, but now she wasn't going to allow anyone to take the slightest fall for her, even if it was claiming that they did it in her stead just to keep an "accomplice" out of the prison. She would find a way for the both of them to escape with their lives.

Orin had been thinking about how to escape as well. It was all he could dream about these days and now that he saw that his sister shared his same fate, the thoughts intensified to where no other thought could permeate his mind if it wanted to. He had the perfect plan, but he wanted to see what his little sister had come up with. She needed to learn how to get out of worse situations than this if she wanted to make it out in the world by herself. He had opposed her marriage, but could not go against his parents in the matter. After all, he had been in the army at the time and away from home, not to mention that his family needed to better their status in society. They had always had bigger dreams than just being poor farmers but did not have the means to turn those dreams into reality. They had encouraged her marriage, but had not forced her into it. Elaraine understood all that, he knew, but he also knew that she knew her duty was to her family before her own desires. He hated it for her, but that was just the way it worked, so that was how it had to be.

Elaraine knew Orin could have gone anywhere after he was released from his military duties. Moraiah would have followed him to the stars if that's where he decided they should be, but he chose instead to remain in Gegernen to keep an eye on her and start his family. His friend had been her new husband and while he loved his friend as he would a brother, he also knew that Staur was not good for any woman, and would never be good enough for his little sister. It surprised everyone, though, how much Staur had changed while Orin was away. He had turned from a warm and kind person to being cold and ruthless. No one knew why he had changed, and no one particularly tried to find out, either.

Elaraine adored her brother. He was able to do whatever he wanted and yet he had stayed to watch over her. Now, in the hour when he needed her most, she was failing him, and that depressed her. She made a promise to him, albeit he had been asleep when she had made it, that she would get him out of the prison alive. She had come up with a rough plan to keep her promise, but she had realized within a few seconds that she would need the cooperation of a guard or outside help to make it a success. Seeing as how she could not get word to anyone outside the prison's walls to come assist them, she would have to find a way to befriend a guard and she knew that that could take a while, time they probably did not have. Despite the downfalls of her plan, she remained excited about it while she explained it to her brother.

Orin just listened to her talk about her plan: how she would talk the guard into letting Orin walk around for a few minutes to get his circulation going again. How Orin would then wrestle the keys from the guard and free Elaraine. Elaraine would unlock a few other prisoners to create a diversion and then they both could escape in the resulting chaos. Orin nodded occasionally and felt himself grinning to himself. She was so proud of herself for a plan she admitted was doomed to failure, but he could tell all she wanted was his freedom, and that touched him deeply. She became so animated at the part about him escaping that he had to remind her to keep the volume of her voice down in case a guard should walk nearby. When she finally finished, she sat cross-legged like an excited child and seemed jittery waiting for him to tell her he liked the plan. He let himself laugh a little. She frowned, but that just made her look more like the child she used to be.

"Elaraine, I think that's a very good plan. But there are major flaws in it. No guard is going to let me off these chains for any more length of time than it takes to kill me or move me, whichever they feel like doing at the moment." He smiled when she put her face in her hands to think a little more. "However," she looked up at him, hope written all over her face, "I think we can use your plan and some of one I've been working on for a while, all right?" She just nodded. "Do you trust me, little sister?" She nodded again, this time more eagerly. His gaze softened as he watched her transform back into that happy girl he knew years ago, even if the transformation was only for a few seconds. "We're going to get out of this, Elaraine. You will be all right." He could see her face clouding and she ducked her head under an arm. "If I could give you a hug right now, little girl, I'd be over there."

"I know," she whispered.

"Just pick up your head and be proud you came up with that plan, Ela."

She tried to maintain a stolid face but failed. "You haven't called me that in forever. I really missed you when you went away to war, Orin. I couldn't help it how every morning when I would wake up, I would cry because I knew you were far away. I just didn't see why the Rischiaks should get to see you more than I did. Then, within so short a time of your coming home to your wife and son, you are away from them again." She held up a hand to stop him when he made a motion to interrupt her. "No, you listen this time. People keep telling me that your being here isn't my fault, but I know it is. So, please let me get us out of here, Orin. Let me get you out of here. Just let me do this one thing for you."

Orin rattled his chains to catch her attention. "Now, you listen to me," he said with venom. "I am here and you are here. There is nothing that can be done to change the past. So, now, let's just figure out a way to get out of here and then you don't ever, ever blame yourself for this again, do you understand me?" She nodded, startled at his harshness with her for the first time in a long time. "Now, go to sleep, Elaraine. We're leaving in a few hours, and you will need the rest." He saw her confusion. "No questions right now. Sleep. I'm not going to let you stay here long enough to get beaten for the first time."

Alas, as soon as the words left his mouth, they could hear the thuds of the footsteps of guards coming down the hall and the clanging of the keys on their belts. She cast her brother a fearful glance as the prison keeper rounded the corner, rolling the sleeves of his blood-spattered shirt up to his elbows. He handed the guard on his left his black robe and stopped in front of Elaraine's cell. He commanded the guard with the keys to unlock the door and went in the small cell, the door locking behind him and the guard. The guard began unrolling a length of chain from his arm and wrapped the shackles around her wrists, attaching the other end of the chain to the wall.

"Now, Elaraine, it came to my attention some time ago that you killed the king's cousin. While the Gegernen judge may have deemed the Dungeons Ussal a worthy punishment, I have determined that it is not. The three of us lost a beloved cousin that day. I have been sitting in my chamber trying to think of a more suitable punishment for you. The mere idea that you had the audacity to overstep your place is enough to curdle my blood, but then you had the idea to kill a noble." He raised a booted foot and struck her in the stomach, making her fall to the ground with a pained grunt. "However, I am generally a generous man. So, in that spirit, I am going to give you a generous punishment from the bottom of my heart."

The beating she received on that third day was worse than anything she had ever experienced before in her life. He beat her harder when she cried for mercy. A boot in the face finally knocked her unconscious for the rest of the beating. Orin told her later, though, that the prison keeper stopped soon after she lost consciousness, as though without hearing her cry out he had lost interest in her pain. She had heard ribs crack, could feel her body swelling under the intensity of the attack. The guard only moved in on the attack to move her back away from the wall so that the prison keeper could beat her better. The chain and shackles kept her securely unable to defend herself.

It didn't matter to Elaraine how many times beatings like that happened, how many ribs were broken, or how many black eyes she received. Elaraine realized that he was just an allegory of the royalty she despised. She now had an outlet for all the hate she had been feeling for herself. She blamed that family that got away with everything under the sun merely because they shared an iota of royal blood in their blue veins. She had welcomed the unconscious euphoria that enveloped her with the boot in the face.

It was a dreamless unconsciousness, without pain or fear. It was a time when she couldn't hate herself or anybody else. When she came back to reality, it was to a shout from Orin. He was yelling her name over and over again and it was not just the stone walls that made it echo in her head. Her whole body was in pain. When she tried to move her arm to push herself up, she started to cry and saw white hot with pain at the smallest motion of her right arm.

"Elaraine?" he yelled again when she cried out. "Answer me! Are you all right? What's wrong?" He thought about it for a moment. "Okay, I didn't think that question through well." He laughed wryly, futilely trying to lighten the moment. "Elaraine, please, just tell me if you're all right!"

She felt the tears rolling down her cheeks but just grinned and bore it to keep from scaring her brother again. She took a few heavy breaths of the putrid air to gird herself to look brave for Orin. He was looking at her with a set jaw, clenching and unclenching his bound hands. She tried to put a blank look on her face, knowing he would not be fooled into believing she was entirely fine even in the flickering torch light.

"I'm fine, Orin, really. I couldn't feel half of it!"

"How's your face? He kicked you pretty hard there." He groaned. "I couldn't stand it, Elaraine. I had to look away. I haven't seen the prison keeper get so angry before. That was the worst beating I've seen since the war."

"Well, it's nothing I can't take care of. I'll be good in no time at all, just you wait and see! Maybe he knocked some sense into me." She tried to sound cheerful for him, not wanting him to suffer so much.

"I highly doubt that, Elaraine. I know you and I know how you lie. I was there when you lied to Mother and Father about sneaking out from the house at night to take care of that sick pony. You just batted your eyes and sounded so sweet when you claimed you hadn't. They didn't see through it and neither do I. You're acting happy, even though the events leading up to this happiness make it impossible to believe. You cried in pain a few minutes ago and now you act like nothing could hurt you more than my being unhappy." He paused. "Correct me if I'm wrong, Elaraine."

She groaned. "I admit it. But what's wrong with trying to put your mind at ease while I take care of myself? I'll make a deal with you. If I promise to quit faking how I feel, when I start to get better I'll go along with your escape plan, no questions asked whatsoever. In return you have to have a little faith in me."

He sighed. "No questions whatsoever?"

"I promise!"

"Then I suppose this is the best that I will get from you, considering I can't take care of you from over here. But you also have to promise me that I can take care of you when we do get out of here."

"Orin, you really don't have to—"

"I do, Elaraine. I left for too long. My little sister had to grow up without me there. At a tender age of twenty-seven, you're already in prison with a husband on the outside in Gegernen. If I'd been there, maybe I could have had Mother and Father call off the wedding because Staur was no good for you... or anybody else."

"Staur is remarried, Orin."

He jerked his head towards her. "Staur is remarried? To whom?"

"A blonde with...assets. At least now I know I can live my own life now, right? Who cares about him anymore?" She sighed. "But I'm not going to lie, Orin. I don't want people thinking that I am a horrible person like Staur is going to tell them I am."

"Staur may be a dense, egotistical character, but he isn't cruel."

"You weren't married to him."

"Was he ever mean to you?" he growled.

"No, no!" she said firmly. "Nothing like that. He just wasn't ever there. He always stayed away, flirting with the other women of the village, in front of me as often as he did it behind my back. He shamed our marriage, Orin. I'm really rather happy about the marriage being essentially dissolved. I can live my life if we can ever get out of here!" She heard his chains rattling. "I'd like that, to be able to do what I want for once."

"What would you like to do, little sister? If you could do anything at all."

She thought for a minute. "Well, I think I'd go and see what I could of the world. I'd leave this part of the country and make a new life somewhere else. I'd try to no longer be a nuisance to the family. If I stay away long enough, then my crime could be forgotten, for the most part, and maybe one day I could return to Gegernen. I do not want to burden our family with my troubles any longer."

He thought for a minute. "Would you like some company on your wanderings?" The silence dragged on. "What I mean to say is, well, I can't very well stay around after the breakout and I can't imagine life without Moraiah or Josi. So, would you mind if we sort of tagged along and kept you company?"

She smiled and saw him smile back at her "Do you think Moraiah and Josi would mind going with us?"

"I don't see why not! It would be like an adventure they always talk about wanting and they would be able to see everything I learned to love in the war."

"Well, if it's all right with Moraiah, then it's all right with me!"

He laughed. "Elaraine, I wish for once you would think only of yourself and nobody else. But seeing as how that's never going to happen, my family and I are going to accompany you. Maybe we could go east!"

She laughed. "Whoa, there, brother! First we have to get out of this hell hole!"

"I hope you don't mind breaking this up soon, you two. The prison keeper is asleep and the guards are away... might I recommend we get this thing started now?" A body turned the corner of the corridor and looked at them. "Unless, of course, you two want to stay here and bond some more, in which case I'll come back at a later time that is more convenient to you."

Elaraine gasped and clutched the bars, blinking disbelievingly in the dimness at the newcomer. "It can't be!"

Orin winked at her. "I told you it was all taken care of! You didn't think I was just playing a trick on you to make you feel better, did you?"

The man came over and unshackled Orin from the wall without saying another word. While her brother fell in a heap on the floor, the blond-haired man turned and smiled at her. She could hear the mechanisms turn in the lock of her cell as Orin got his arms and legs working again and Nox just stood there, looking at her.

"I wasn't about to just let you rot in here, you know," he whispered. "Half a week is enough time for you to have been seen and yet not missed when the next guards make their rounds. They would rather forget you were here at all."

"But— but how did you get in here?" she stuttered when she finally overcame the initial surprise at his unannounced appearance by her cell.

Orin was by her side and trying to lift her up, but he was too weak to hold her. He crumpled to the ground, not letting her go. He felt along all her bones, feeling for breaks. He seemed dismayed at what he found as he began to curse and mumble under his breath. Finally, he looked up at Nox.

"I can't carry her, but she can't walk," he explained, his pain resonating in his voice. Nox knelt beside them and took Elaraine in his arms. "Please be careful," Orin croaked. "A few of her ribs are broken. The prison keeper beat her hard."

Nox nodded as he cradled her gently against his chest. "Orin, just trust me, will you?" Orin just looked at him skeptically. "I know how to be careful when I need to be! But right now we have to get moving!"

They could hear someone coming swiftly down the stone hallway and Elaraine began to tremble against Nox. She bit back a yelp as she was jostled when he had to move her so he could hold the door for Orin. They locked the cell behind them and skulked in the shadows until the guard rounded the corner. The guard looked into her cell and cursed loudly when he saw that it was empty. He took the torch from the wall and held it through the bars to see into the far reaches of her cell to make sure. He spun and looked at where Orin was supposed to have been hanging up and she could see his hand holding the torch begin to shake. When he replaced the torch in its holder, she could have laughed at the fear she saw on his face as he faced where they were hiding.

He started to yell for help and Orin leapt forward, tackling the surprised man in a flurry of limbs. Elaraine was astonished at Orin's sudden burst of energy despite his frail looks. Nox covered her mouth with his hand to hide the yell he knew would come as Orin broke the young man's neck. Just one twist, one torque of the wrists, and the man was dead. Orin was breathing hard as he turned back to look at them.

Nox uncovered her mouth and wiped her face off with his sleeve. "I don't know what you were rolling around in, but it really reeks and it's all over you!" he whispered with disgust. Then he added with a groan, "Now it's all over me!"

She looked up at him and whispered back, "It's not like the keepers here condone clean accommodations, you know."

Orin was still panting, but the way he stood there in the corridor told them it was time to go. He waved Nox forward, who moved surprisingly fast considering the extra weight he was carrying. He soon passed Orin. They ran quietly along the cobblestoned corridor, the torches along the walls becoming blurs in their haste. Orin was panting heavily, so Nox slowed the pace slightly to accommodate him. Prisoners they passed yelled and cheered and begged for help as they passed the cell doors, making Orin and Nox curse.

As they rounded a corner, they came face-to-face with the prison keeper and quite a few guards. The guards drew their swords and advanced while the prison keeper just laughed hysterically from the shadows he had backed into. Nox never took his eyes from the guards as he placed Elaraine on the floor well away from where the prison keeper had disappeared. He shoved her into a dark recess and rolled the sleeves of the shirt he wore under his tunic up to his elbows. Elaraine held her breath as she tried to get up to help, but Nox put a foot on her shoulder and pressed her back down to the floor gently but firmly, his back to her.

"Nox," she protested, "I can help!"

"You're too hurt," he fussed back. "You'll only get in the way!"

"Orin's hurt, too!"

"Stop, Elaraine! Orin can fight because he's trained to fight his entire life. If you want to argue with me about it, might I recommend bringing this up again once we're out of here?"

That's when the guards began their brutal onslaught. Nox and Orin were fighting for their lives as well as Elaraine's. Nox tackled the guard nearest him and wrestled the sword from him, slitting the man's throat in the same motion. Blood spurt all over the floor as the dying man writhed. Orin was backing away from one guard deeper into the shadows and the fool followed him. When the guard was out of her sight, Elaraine heard the tell-tale popping snap that betrayed his death. Orin raced back into the dim light with the soldier's dirk.

Their chances were a little better now that they were both armed. Though hurt and scarred, Orin moved with a fatal grace. Nox fought beside him with an intensity that scared Elaraine. Sweat ran down Orin's bare back while Nox's face was completely drenched and his shirt clung to his arms.

The fight had moved back down the hallway into the full light of a torch. The prison keeper moved with the fight and was illuminated in the flicker. Orin was fighting with his back to the prison keeper. Elaraine did not like the gleam in the man's eye as he watched her brother kill a guard. She struggled to her knees when she saw him fumbling in his robe for something. Elaraine glared into the dimness as she saw something in the prison keeper's hand reflect the torchlight. She lurched through the darkness at him, ignoring her protesting bones and the pain the slightest movement spurred across her nerves. The prison keeper heard her coming and turned on her.

He raised his dagger to her chest, but adrenaline pushed her on. Nox and Orin were too busy in their own struggles to realize what was happening behind them. Her chest hurt, her knees were giving out under her, but she still pressed on. His fist landed on her temple, but it was not something she had not felt before. Her good leg kneed him in the groin, but she lost her balance. Nox tripped over her in a maneuver of his own and was sent careening across the floor, but that created enough of a distraction for Elaraine to scramble back to her feet and make another lunge for the prison keeper. He had turned his back on her and was looking at Orin and Nox again, not expecting for her to have regained herself so quickly. He never saw her coming.

Chapter Four

She tackled him, ignoring her protesting body. Orin had just killed his last attacker and Nox was quickly dispatching the last of the guards. The prison keeper hit his head on the floor as he fell and cried out for help. Orin turned and started towards them, but Nox was holding him back and telling him to let Elaraine take care of the keeper herself.

When the prison keeper lay there motionless, Elaraine clawed at the floor around her, looking for anything that would finish him off, knowing that she could not do it with only her bare hands. A man behind her moaned in his final moments of life, but the metallic clanging sound that reverberated around her told her that Nox had helped his soul to depart. When she looked behind her, still looking for something to kill the prison keeper, she saw Orin looking more hopeless than she had ever seen before. Nox was back beside him, holding him back. Elaraine saw the chain by their feet and Nox noticed her gaze. He stooped to pick it up and tossed it to her. The merry jingle it made in the air was eerie to her ears.

The prison keeper had awakened and was starting to wriggle under her body, trying to escape from her weak grasp. She grabbed his hair at his forehead and smashed his head against the ground a few times as hard as she possibly could, trying to subdue him a little. He stopped flailing and began searching for the dagger he had lost when she tackled him. Elaraine did not want to kill the man, but she knew she had to. She wrapped the chain around his neck and pulled the ends as hard as she could. She could feel his struggles becoming fainter and fainter under her.

"You won't get away with this!" he garbled, blood foaming from his mouth.

She spat down at him like his guards had done to her. "Maybe not," she growled, "but you should have known you wouldn't get away with hurting my brother!" She leaned down and whispered in his ear, "But at least I fight fair and don't go trying to stab people in their backs!"

With that she tightened the chain one last time and held it taut until he stopped moving for good. She held the pose for a few more seconds. She heard Nox and Orin coming up behind her slowly. A hand was laid firmly on her shoulder. A bell was ringing in her ears but she heard someone tell her to let go, that he was dead. She did as she was told. As she felt the chain slip between her fingers, she also felt herself slipping away from consciousness. The last thing she remembered was hitting a cold and slimy floor.

* * *

She woke up warm, listening to the men nearby. A fire was crackling merrily next to her head. She could smell the difference between where they were and the Dungeons Ussal. The question was: where were they? She sighed and rolled over to her other side when a branch in the fire snapped from the heat, but the pain as she did so was so unbearable that she screamed.

In an instant, Nox and Orin were by her side, trying to hold her down. Tears were seeping from her closed eyes, much to her embarrassment. A cool hand was placed on her head.

"Elaraine?" Orin was whispering soothingly. "What's wrong?"

"I can't turn over," she ground out between closed teeth. "All I wanted to do was turn over. But my side is going to kill me."

Nox began to laugh in relief. "Elaraine, you can't do that when you have broken ribs on that side!" he explained. "Please, just lay still!"

She opened her eyes to glare at him. "Well, this side is tired and going numb, so what do you recommend I do?"

Orin cursed under his breath in frustration, but Nox ignored him. "Just lay there! You need to stay off the bad side until the wound heals a little more!"

She looked between the two men. "What wound?"

"The one the prison keeper gave you...." He raised an eyebrow at her. "Elaraine, how did you not feel his dagger? The blade broke from the hilt. We had to pull it out of your side when we got here."

She frowned and thought back to the fight. She kept going over the events again and again. She became convinced the prison keeper did not even know he had stabbed her because he kept looking for it as she was strangling him. The thought of him struggling beneath her brought to mind his face, slowly deadening. It turned her stomach.

She dry heaved, having had nothing in her stomach for a few days. She felt her brother gently hold her up until she finished, patting her head hesitantly until she was done. Nox moved to the other side of the fire and sat down, looking at her expectantly as she leaned back against Orin. She closed her eyes against the pain of moving. When she opened them again Nox was still watching her.

"What?" she asked grumpily.

He shrugged. "I was just wondering what we're going to do now. I mean, killing eight guards and a prison keeper is not going to go unnoticed for very long. Men are going to be sent out to hunt us down." He motioned toward her brother. "Orin said you wanted to go exploring for a while until people forgot your name and your crime." She nodded. "So where do you want to go?" He paused. "After we get Moraiah and Josi, that is."

"I can go and get them here in two days' time," Orin chirped from behind her. "We can find a place for the two of you to hide and I'll get my family and come for you."

"Go to Gegernen alone?" Nox sounded concerned. "The villagers know you and they know you're supposed to be in prison. Seeing you sneaking around the village is bound to raise a lot of questions and a lot of attention that you're not going to want or need. You will be doomed to failure before you even begin."

"What do you suggest, then?" Orin was angry and gripped her more tightly. "I'm not going gallivanting about the country without the family I haven't seen in a year! I won't abandon them!"

Nox thought for a minute and then stood up. "I'll go and get them."

"They won't go with you," Elaraine spoke up. "They'll blame you for Orin being in prison. You guards aren't in good favor with the family right now, you know."

"No, he's right," Orin said reluctantly as he let his grip on her ease. "He's the only one whose presence in the village will be accepted without a second thought. Moraiah trusts Nox and Josi looks up to him like an older brother... they'll follow him. They may not like it at the outset, but they will give him the respect of listening to him and then they will follow him." He still sounded unsure when he looked down at his younger sister. "He is the best choice to go. We can't both go because then you'd be here by yourself."

"I can take care of myself for two days," she told him resolutely as she patted his hand. "Please, go and get your family. I'll be here when the two of you get back. I'll find a good hiding place and wait for you." Orin just shook his head. "Orin, please... let me do this to prove to myself that I don't need someone else to look after me... that I can survive on my own!" She looked up at Nox, pleading silently for his help.

Nox blinked and looked from her to Orin. "She can do it, Orin. One of us can get supplies and the other can get your family." He looked up at the sky. "It'll be dawn soon. We can find a place for her with the sunrise and set out once we're sure she'll be all right."

Elaraine felt Orin draw a deep breath from behind her. She had to cut him off now before he talked the two of them out of it. "Orin," she whispered. "Please, just go with Nox. Don't put off seeing your family for another day. I'll be fine. Leave me with some water and I'll be fine." More hesitation. "Just grant me this request. Get your family and return quickly."

His resolve to stay with her was failing and the other two knew it. It had been so long since he had seen his beloved wife and son. The decision was made and Orin laid Elaraine back on the ground so she could get some sleep before it was time to go. Nox was on watch and Orin was soon fast asleep on the other side of the fire. After an hour or so, Elaraine still could not fall asleep and she watched Nox at her side, who was picking at the ground with a stick, deep in his own thoughts.

"Can't sleep?" he whispered, not wanting to wake Orin, who needed the most rest after his long ordeal.

"Nope," she sighed, blinking a few times. "I think I've slept too much already today."

He laughed softly. The glow of the flames outlined his form. He was slouched over and never looked at her. He threw his stick to the ground. She wiped a hand across her face and inhaled the sweet air surrounding her, willing herself to relax so she could sleep.

"Can we talk?" he asked suddenly, surprising her out of her reverie of freedom.

"Sure. What do you want to talk about?"

"I need to tell the full story about everything." He looked up at her. "I want to tell you the whole story, and then you can talk, all right? I'm afraid," he inhaled sharply, "that if you start talking, I'll lose my determination and I won't be able to tell you everything that I need to tell you." She nodded her encouragement, and he continued animatedly. "I had always been in the background of your life, Elaraine. Your family was nice enough to accept me even though I was an orphan and had no family. When we were old enough, I knew you had had your eye on me but your family chose another. We both accepted it and moved on. I was there whenever you needed to talk about the latest thing Staur had done to disgrace you and your relationship. Orin was away or I know you would have gone to him first and Moraiah couldn't have understood because she had a perfect marriage.

"That night, in the tavern, I had been so surprised to see you there. You hardly ever went to the village anymore. You kept away from people. Worrin and I were celebrating his engagement and we were talking about Rochstaff hopefully giving us his recommendation when we enlisted. The Rischiaks were not as close as they are now, but we were already thinking about it. Worrin wasn't sick yet and he was so happy.

"We were both watching what was going on. We knew Dalun was completely drunk when he approached you. Then he put his hands on you, and we did nothing. For a year, I did nothing but think about what I could have done differently. I relived it every time I went into that tavern. Worrin's wife became sick and died suddenly a few months after you disappeared, and then Worrin quickly went downhill. I tried to ignore it," he remembered with a tinge of despair in his voice, "and you saw the results of that. But you had been seen by the river near Ranci's cabin and I knew that a group would be sent out to find you.

"You have to believe that I never wanted to go hunting for you with the intention of taking you to prison. I knew you would go anyway. I merely did not want one of my colleagues to find you and handle justice in their own way. I thought I could keep you safe if I went. Besides all that, we grew up together; some of my earliest and happiest memories have you in them. When Orin couldn't watch over you, I did. At least I tried. I had grown to think of the two of you as I would my own siblings." He laughed wryly. "It took longer with you. So, when they were taking Orin away last year and you were gone, I volunteered to take him to prison.

"It wasn't right and I knew it. An innocent man just standing up for his family had no reason to be in prison, but there was nothing I could do about it. Orin, he understood. He said the same thing you did about it not being my fault. I made a promise to him then, Elaraine. I regretted it for almost a year until we found you.

"I promised him that if you were found I would be the one to take you, that I would be the one to deliver you to the Dungeons Ussal, so the last face you'd see on the outside of those walls would be a friend's. The judge had already made up his mind about your punishment, you see? And I could do that without my conscience being any worse for the wear, but I took it a step farther than I should have. I don't regret it now," he said hastily, "but I made it. I told Orin that I would get the two of you out." He took a deep breath. "I should have been punished, too. I didn't do anything when Dalun accosted you and Moraiah and then I didn't do anything after you killed him. I just stood there. You and your brother may have forgiven me for it, but I haven't. I doubt I ever will, to tell you the truth." He tossed a stick into the fire. "I did want to advance my position in society, better my chances for an officer's standing when I joined the military, but when I saw you being led away... all that just disappeared. All my ambitions and hopes faded away as you disappeared into the Dungeons Ussal. I knew then that I would uphold the entire promise I made to Orin. I chose my friends over my future."

He looked at her sadly. Elaraine could not think of anything to say to him. She only blamed him for taking her brother to that hell, but with the story she was hearing, she could not even be angry with him over that now. Of course, she couldn't be sure that the entire story was true, nor would she discuss what had been said with her brother. She held back tears as she thought about what it must have been like for Orin: knowing that he may never see his family again and thinking of people other than himself in his hour of dire need. He had always done things like that, and she did not think there was any way she could ever possibly come close to repaying him.

"Nox," she said softly, trying to keep her emotions in check. "What are you trying to say you want from me?"

Her question seemed to take him aback. "Your forgiveness or condemnation," he stuttered wildly. "I just need to know where I stand with you. Orin has already said that he never blamed me, but you said the day I handed you over to those guards that you blamed me for what happened to him and I just wanted you to know the whole story." He patted her arm tentatively when she continued in her pensive silence. "Please believe me," he pleaded. "I've told you the whole truth."

She was moved by his speech. She just did not know how to answer him. On the one hand, it would have been so easy to tell him that all was forgiven and they could go back to being the friends that they had been as children. On the other hand was still that nagging voice in the back of her head that told her that he was still the one who betrayed her brother despite his words of friendship. She held a hand up to him when he opened his mouth again.

"Just give me a moment, if you don't mind. This is all rather sudden and I'm not exactly sure what to say," she explained.

She went back to studying the sky. The stars were so vivid and the treetops were clear. She watched a shooting star cross the sky. It was hard for her to believe that she could miss the outdoors so much after only half a week. It made things around her so much more real. She could feel the dirt on her tunic sticking to her in a way that in any other situation would have made her bathe immediately.

Orin snorted in his sleep and began to toss and turn, drawing her attention to him. He looked so peaceful over there, but the past year had aged him past his thirty-five years. She wondered if Josi would understand this change. How could a boy understand the horrors his father had endured to save his mother? She could not comprehend it or even conceive how that topic would be broached with Josi.

Josi. The young boy who had brought light to her own life. Twenty-seven years old and it took a nephew to make her happy. Josi brought laughter back into her life. It had made her die a little inside when he confronted her on the day she was sentenced in the village. He looked so much like his father had at his age.

Nox had stopped moving around nervously and focused all his attention on her, trying to study every movement and facial expression she made. Elaraine knew she should hurry and tell him how she felt. She could never possibly truly hate the man. He was like another brother to her. He had saved her life and, more importantly, her brother's life.

She took a deep breath and tenderly massaged her side, trying to form the right words in the right order. She had so many things to tell him, and so few words would actually formulate themselves into sentences that held any meaning whatsoever. His eyes seemed to penetrate her mind and read her thoughts because they softened in the firelight, and a small smile curled his lips.

"Nox, you're like my brother. A very stupid, ambitious brother," she laughed softly. "But you've always been there for me, and for that I will be eternally grateful. But how can I lie here and hate you when you helped us escape? You may have put my brother into the hands that tortured him, but you saved his life too." She reached over and patted his hand, trying to hide the wince of pain the movement caused. "Nox, you don't have to ask for forgiveness. That was given when you came back to help us."

"So you truly won't mind if I join you in your wanderings?" He seemed overjoyed at her answer. "You won't leave me behind?"

"What about joining the army? Becoming an officer?"

"That can wait. I'm still young and we will always be at war with one country or another. I can come back after a while and join after everything here has come to a head and blown over."

"No one will know you helped us escape, will they?"

He frowned and shook his head slowly. "No."

"Then you don't have to wait for anything to happen here. You can go ahead and go to the capital. Even if you're not made an officer right away, your charisma and charm, not to mention your leadership, will easily get you that nicer rank and uniform."

He scoffed at her words. "What would you know about it?"

She became defensive despite herself. "Do you know anything about running from the law? No, you don't! You *are* the law. So stay here. Or, better yet, since you think that, as a woman, I would have no idea what I am talking about, talk to Orin about it and do what he tells you to do."

She closed her eyes and felt the tic in her jaw working away furiously. She absentmindedly picked at the ratty bandages that covered the dagger wound under her tunic, trying to get the feeling of his staring out of her mind. She had saved his life in the escape, and she resented his superior attitude.

"If you weren't going to treat me as an equal anyway, then why did you even ask for my forgiveness?" she whispered, knowing he had not yet moved away.

"It's different to hear it than to know it," he retorted coldly. "And I am treating you as an equal. You just really have no idea what you are talking about when you talk about the army."

"Have you ever been in the army?"

"Obviously not."

"Then how much more do you know than me? At least I heard from Orin what it was like."

"True, but you don't exactly have the personality to want to enlist like some women do and you don't listen to the stories told in taverns. So all of your supposed 'knowledge' comes from a brother who isn't going to tell his sister everything."

"Stories told by old drunk men willing to say anything for another tankard of ale doesn't constitute a trustworthy source of information on anything that isn't just stories. At least I had a brother, and he is trustworthy."

"That's not fair."

"Neither is treating me with the condescension of a superior, like I know nothing. You are most definitely not my superior, Nox," Elaraine said with venom.

"Then what am I?"

She felt herself go bug-eyed with anger. She forced herself to close her eyes and swallowed hard. "I thought you were my friend."

Chapter Five

Nox cursed at her and went back to the log he had been sitting on before coming to talk to her. Elaraine was livid. Things had been going so well until Nox had treated her with more condescension than she had ever known. She had been treated that way by every man she had ever known except for Dayn and Orin. Nox had shared their company until now.

Elaraine thought about her future plans the rest of the night. Both men had asked her where she wanted to go on her adventures. She did not really know anything past the woods surrounding Gegernen and all she knew was that she wanted to see things she never had before. She wanted to see the mountains where her brother had fought so many battles. She wanted to go to the capital eventually, probably in a few years when her face was long since forgotten.

A couple of times Elaraine risked a glance at Nox. He looked gloomy and furious. He kept closing his eyes and his jaw kept clenching. She thought for a while that he was not taking enough care of keeping watch, but who was she to tell him how to do his job? They made eye contact a few times but both remained resolutely silent. Finally, it seemed Nox could not take the silence anymore.

"Elaraine, why would you even offer an opinion on something you know nothing about? When I correct you on something like that, you can't just get mad and blow up at me like that!" he growled.

"That's not what I got mad at you about," she mumbled just loud enough for him to hear her as Orin stirred at Nox's outburst.

"Then what did you get mad at me for?" He stood up and began to pace. "I really can't understand it! I tell you the escape was planned all along, that I regretted my ambitions, and then wham! You tell me to leave and join the army anyway like you didn't appreciate it!"

"So all this was so that you could feel appreciated?"

"You know that's not true!"

"Then tell me what is true!" she growled. "I'll tell you what I do know. I know that you had no right to talk to me like you're better than me. You had no right to say you think you're better than me."

"I can't voice my opinions?"

"Say whatever you want, but you can't expect me to like everything you have to say! I won't be silent on everything!"

"Then maybe I shouldn't say anything at all if I just want to keep the little princess happy!"

"If you truly thought that I was acting like a little princess then you wouldn't be here right now trying to talk your sense into me."

"I don't know why I even bother," he grumbled as he plopped back down on the log.

Elaraine turned her head away from him and toward her brother. "Neither do I."

She was still frowning as she watched her brother toss and turn on the ground. Orin was restless in his sleep. His sister's argument with Nox had not gone unnoticed, but he tuned them out and attributed the whole thing to sleep deprivation. The fire barely gave off enough heat to be felt by the three of them. There was something rotting nearby, but they were all just thankful the smells were not those found in the prison.

At dawn, the tension was palpable between Nox and Elaraine. Orin pretended to be oblivious to what had been said the night before, but he couldn't pretend not to know that Nox had been a fool about something and that harsh words had definitely been said by both parties. Nox knew absolutely nothing about dealing with women, and the older man knew that. Elaraine refused Nox's offered help to move her to the hiding spot, opting instead for Orin's plan, even though it meant moving slower and more painstakingly. It was painful for the siblings. Elaraine looped an arm over her brother's shoulders and shuffled along, all the while trying to keep as much weight as she could off her brother's scarred and marred back.

It was difficult finding a hiding spot good enough to conceal her for a couple of days. She needed to be within crawling range of a water source, which greatly decreased their options. They settled on a rock outcropping that was in the shape of a cave with bushes in front of it that hid the entrance. It had a way out on the side and was close enough to water that she could drag herself to it. The rocks would provide her with enough protection from the elements without her needing to light a fire, and it was still warm outside at night. It was not ideal as it was not completely hidden, and she would still be within a close searching range of the Dungeons Ussal, but it was the best that they could find in such a short amount of time.

Orin lingered by her before they left to go back to Gegernen. He kept changing his mind about whether to go with Nox or stay behind with his sister. On the one hand, he had not seen his family in a year. On the other hand was that overprotective instinct he had over his now injured sister. Having to choose between families right then was tearing him apart. She made the decision for him during another one of his brotherly embraces when she saw Nox stomping back and forth in front of the rocks checking the sun overhead.

"It's time for you two to get going if you're going to get back in two days like you promised," she said as she pushed him gently away towards Nox.

He shook his head. "I'm not sure this is such a good idea. Someone should remain with you."

"Orin, I'll be fine!"

"But you're hurt."

"So are you." She smiled at him, knowing she was going to win this argument. She so rarely won in an argument against him.

"It's different."

"Like hell it is."

"I can protect myself when I'm hurt."

"What do you think I did? I killed the prison keeper, didn't I?"

"It's different when you're talking about maybe having to fight off animals or the men that are coming out to look for us. In the Dungeons we were nearby had you needed us."

"And if you're here with me that means you're having to fight for two people while worrying about my being safe at the same time and while wondering about how Nox is faring at smuggling your family out of

Gegernen. That would lead to certain disaster, and what makes you think I would let you do that?" His crinkling his nose told her she had finally won. She gave him a peck on the cheek and a slap on the shoulder with her good side. "Now, get going so I don't have to stay alone for too long."

Elaraine just waved the other man away; it was not like Nox was going to bother to say good-bye to her. He did not apologize, and neither did she. It would not have done any good anyway as neither person was in the mood to accept any apologies. Instead, all they received from each other were glares, arms being folded over chests, and grunts under their breath when they thought the other could not hear. Orin looked from one to the other and sighed. He just shook his head as he went to Nox and took one last look over his shoulder at his sister.

"We'll be back in two days," he called as they started to walk away. "Stay safe and stay here!"

"I will!" Elaraine waved and gave him the best smile she could muster.

He stopped and stared her down. "I mean it! Stay here unless you absolutely have to!"

Elaraine rolled her eyes and smiled back at him, nodding her consent. "Get going!"

Their departure made her feel very isolated, and she did not know what to do with herself. She could not exercise. She could not even move enough to go foraging for any other food than what few berries and other plants they had left her with. She just looked around her at the rocks and created stories for herself, imagining people long lost to the ravages of time roaming through these woods and sitting where she was now.

The sun was approaching noon when her imagination finally ran out. The birds singing just reinforced her aloneness. She wondered if Orin and Nox had reached the village yet. She laughed bitterly to herself. Of course they would not have reached Gegernen yet. They probably would not be there until nightfall. The going would be slow with Orin not in his peak form and having to stay out of sight.

Elaraine decided that the best thing she could do would be to get her injuries to heal as soon as possible. With that thought in mind, she began to stretch her legs. She refused to crawl to the creek for her water. She would walk, even if it had to be slowly. She groaned when her stretches put strain on her chest. But she was just happy they had escaped with their lives.

When she thought her legs could support her, she braced her good side against the rocks and breathed heavily, trying to calm herself, knowing that she was about to experience a lot of pain. She kept her left arm tight against her side, hoping that the pressure might ease some of the discomfort while she used her right to help push herself up. A white-hot pain spread across her body, but she refused to crumple back to the ground.

She bit down on her tongue and closed her eyes, waiting for her body to adjust to the pain. Her chest felt like it was on fire, and the rest of her felt numb. All she knew was that pain. She leaned her head back to rest against the cool rock, feeling the sweat running down her back under her light tunic. It made her shiver involuntarily, and that just created even more problems for her than before.

Finally, the worst of the excruciating pain subsided, and she just stood there, supporting herself on wobbling legs. She wiped her face with her sleeve. She took first one step, and then another. She found the pain bearable and took a third step, then wrapped her arms across her body and stood there, looking at the breathtaking scenery surrounding her. She had been too busy trying to get up the small hill to the rock formation to even notice where she was.

From her vantage point, she could see the Dungeons Ussal in the distance, but there was also a dark beauty to the fortress when she looked at it, despite all the pain associated with it. It looked bleak and foreboding, but the towers rose high over the trees and through them in the distance was a tall mountain too far away to be seen clearly. The blue sky made the green landscape all the more vivid.

The birds singing in the trees above her brought so much joy to her life right then. An eagle screamed as it soared over her head as she stood there. It took her back to her childhood when she would play with her friends in the woods by her home in Gegernen. She and Nox could lose themselves for hours in the woods playing. Her petty squabble with Nox seemed all the more unimportant as she considered her surroundings.

After a while, she realized that she was extremely thirsty. She could hear the creek but she had no idea how she was going to get there. Walking down the rocks would be precarious on her wobbling legs, and crawling was just out of the question now that she was standing up. Her pride would not allow her to crawl.

With that thought in her mind, and that thought alone, she grabbed a dead branch leaning against a rock near her and used it as a crutch as she started down the crags and pebbles. She slipped quite a few times on moss and loose stones and had to wait for the searing pain to subside again each time before she started back on her way to the creek. The going was slow and hard, but she was determined to get to that creek. She refused to think of the trip back up the slope.

She glanced behind her at the path she had just come down. She risked the pain of laughing when she saw the little chipmunk following her. The little plump animal was just like a shadow. He stayed far enough back to not get underfoot but close enough to obviously be following her. She tested him by facing him and moving backward. She smiled broadly as she saw him move toward her hesitantly and stop when she stopped. His little eyes just looked at her so hopefully she could not help but let her guard down a little.

She turned back to the route she was on and shuffled along, step by painful step. The little scurrying from behind her told her that her little friend was still there. She saw the creek come into view. She looked behind her and saw that she had not travelled that far. It was disheartening, but at least she had not crawled. Looking at the bank to get to the creek though, she realized she would have to abandon her makeshift crutch and crawl down to that sparkling haven.

When she got down on her backside and began to slip and slide down the bank, she looked back over her shoulder to the chipmunk. She held a hand out to him and he scooted over to her shyly. He nosed her finger and she was surprised by how friendly he was being to her.

"Do you need water, too, little guy?" She smiled as he backed away from her at the sound of her voice but came back when she cooed to him. He came back and nuzzled her hand again. "Are you alone, too?" she sighed as he stood on her hand. "It's not like I mind being alone. I enjoy my own company. But I just got my brother back and now he's gone again." She looked back up at the creature settled in her hand. "Do you have an older brother? Mine is the best I could ever ask for. He has a family, you know." She began to scoot her body down the hill, distracting herself from the pain by talking to the chipmunk. "His son, Josi, blames me for his father going to prison." She hit a rock on her bad side and gasped. She had not expected for it to hurt that badly. "I blame myself, too, to tell you the truth. But what's done is done." Her feet touched the bank and she looked up. "Do you think I'll be able to make amends to Orin's family?" The little animal just looked at her, giving nothing away. "Are you going to stay with me until Orin, his family, and the idiot return?"

She put the small animal back on the ground and maneuvered so that she was able to drink from the creek more easily. The chipmunk just stayed right next to her, watching her get her fill. A minnow swam along in the shallow water. After her thirst was quenched, she just lay there on the sandy bank, drinking in the sunlight. She was tired but refreshed from the small trip. Never did the chipmunk leave her side.

* * *

The sun was getting low on the horizon when she opened her eyes again. She felt slightly guilty at having been out of her shelter for so long without her guard up. The chipmunk was sleeping soundly on her hand. Something moved in the bushes but it turned out to be a rabbit venturing from its hole. She was happy. She felt at home there.

She sighed, regretting already having to leave this place. She lifted her hand and the chipmunk jumped off, running in front of her back up to the path she took to get there. She turned around and crawled back up the bank to where she left her branch, then made her way back to the rock outcropping and settled on the floor, her new friend sitting near her.

She set about naming the little guy. She went through names like 'Buggy' and 'Monk,' but there was something agonizingly familiar in his eyes. It took her back to Ranci's cabin to a young man teaching her how to defend herself. Those lucid green eyes were smiling at her as she fell yet again trying a new sword trick, holding back a laugh. That same look was in the chipmunk's gaze now.

"Come here, little guy," she encouraged. The little mammal ran over to her and settled in her lap. "I'm going to call you 'Daynny.' You remind me of one of my best friends. You two have the exact same eyes." She picked up a berry and offered it to him. He turned his nose up at it so she ate it herself, making a face at the bitterness. "I know it's not much, but it's all I have."

She lay down and grunted as her broken ribs made their presence known once more. She changed the bandage on the dagger wound with considerable difficulty, but that task was soon done and night came on swiftly. She was too restless to sleep and so she instead opted to tell the story of her life to Daynny. Elaraine believed it to be around midnight on that cloudy night when Daynny fell asleep and she was left to her own thoughts once again. But she eventually faded off to sleep herself and had a dreamless night.

The next morning started off like she had pretty much expected it to. The only difference was that Daynny was gone. That made her heart sink slightly, but she soon remembered that he was not a pet but a wild animal. She got down to the creek more easily than she did the previous day and partook of that sweet water. She kept an eye out for Daynny, but he never came to her.

It was around noon, with the sun hidden behind dark clouds, when the noises began beyond the rocks of her cave. She cowered in the back of the small cave, not moving, hardly breathing. She tried hard to remain quiet, but soon her position became too painful to bear and she had to move. She thought for a moment that it was probably just Daynny coming back, but the sounds were too loud to be a mere chipmunk. A human-shaped shadow crossed the formation's entrance and the bush that protected her cave began to rustle wildly. Someone was coming in, and Elaraine was alone, unarmed, and in no condition to fight anyone off.

She felt each bead of sweat run down the nape of her neck. She felt around herself and found a loose rock the size of her fist. She saw the man come into the cave and she knew that she had been found and unless she acted right then she would be dead. She raised the stone as the man came over to her and stooped near her. He was on his haunches when she hurled the rock at him, hoping and praying it would not miss his head. It did. It veered so far to the right that he did not even have to duck.

He laughed at her and sat down. He extended a hand to her and she swatted it away from her. His features were still hidden in shadow. She just trembled where she was, waiting for her life to be ended by this stranger. It was scaring her even more that he did not attack her or say anything at all to her. He was just making himself at home. Finally, she could not take the silence anymore and broke it.

"If you're going to kill me, I wish you would just go ahead and do it!" she yelled. "I can't stand this waiting for it."

The man raised an eyebrow at her and set his jaw. "What do you mean? I'm not here to kill you." He cocked his head. "I thought you'd be glad to see me. You were so glad to see 'Daynny.'"

"What do you know about it?" She was so confused. The voice, the shadowy profile— it was all so familiar and yet all so impossible.

"I know everything about you, from the time when you were three and set your fence on fire to the time when in the prison you had a nightmare that involved me jumping off a cliff, which I find very disturbing, by the way." He looked at her for a moment longer and then sighed heavily. "Do you still have no idea?"

She just shook her head and scooted herself closer to him to get a better look at him. "It's impossible. I told you to stay with your mother."

"I told you once that I wouldn't let you get hurt anymore. I couldn't do that when you first left, but I can do it now while it's within my power to do so. I know you're leaving with your brother and Nox. Can't I come, too?"

"Why would you want to leave Ranci?"

"Why wouldn't I? I'm old enough to leave home if I want to, and I do! I really do!"

She thought to herself for a moment and nodded. "Wait, how did you know about Daynny?"

"I am Daynny!" he chuckled. "How dense can you be?"

"So I wasn't ever alone?" Tears sprang to her eyes. "I wasn't ever on my own?"

He shook his head. "Why would I let you do this alone? You're hurt! I didn't get in your way at all. I just wanted to keep an eye on you! I wasn't going to change unless you needed me, but then I thought you knew me so I didn't think you'd mind." He looked at her curiously. "You don't mind, do you?"

She could only shake her head and click her tongue in thought. "No, I don't mind. I was proud of myself up to now for taking care of myself out here alone, so I just wish you had told me it was you from the beginning."

"I did!" He eyed her curiously. "My eyes, remember? I made them look like my eyes! You recognized me!"

She grinned with acceptance and recognition. "Fine, you can go, but if you ever sneak up on me like that again, I swear to everything I hold dear in my life that I will kill you and bury you somewhere deep in the woods where no one will ever find you."

They sat there talking for hours as though they had not seen each other in years instead of just days. The dark clouds eventually blew away and let the sunshine in and cast away the shadows. When the sun began to set, they sat in a companionable silence waiting for Orin and Nox to arrive.

Then the light that was let in by the entrance was blocked suddenly and an angry voice began to growl. "Why aren't you alone?"

Chapter Six

Elaraine and Dayn raised their heads in surprise with a jerk. The next thing she knew, Dayn was on his feet with a small knife clutched tightly in his hand. Elaraine struggled back up to her feet, grunting in pain, and stood between the men. Orin had his sword at the ready and Nox had an arrow pointed at Dayn's head.

"Everyone, please, just calm down! Just take some slow, deep breaths," she cooed. "Orin, Nox, this is Dayn. He and his mother took me in when I fled from Gegernen. You remember, don't you, Nox? He was there when you came to get me. Dayn, this is my brother, Orin, and the proverbial thorn in my side, Nox." She grasped hold of a rock to support herself as the pain continued to shoot through her body. "Now that all of you have met, can we all settle down, put our weapons down, and just talk for a minute?"

Nox and Dayn relaxed their stances after another tense moment, but Orin did not lower his sword. Instead, he took a step closer to the newcomer of the group and glared, shaking his head at his sister. He puffed his chest, his back straight and tall, as he turned back to Dayn.

"I need to know why he's here, first," Orin said gruffly. "I'm not bringing Moraiah and Josi in here until I know at least that much. I think it's a reasonable request to make." He looked expectantly at Dayn, still not easing his defensive stance. He softened his tone a bit when he received a reproachful look from his sister. "You may have befriended my sister, but you haven't befriended me."

Dayn arched an eyebrow in a small show of defiance to Orin. "I believe you're under the impression that I owe you an explanation when, in fact, I do not. I have explained myself to Elaraine and she can tell you if she sees fit. Otherwise, might I recommend you lower your sword?"

Orin would not stand down. "Seeing as how you are coming in late to the situation, I highly recommend you take the opportunity I'm giving you to explain yourself before we," he motioned to Nox, who raised his bow and arrow again, "make it so you'll never be able to answer anyone again."

Dayn looked from one man to the other. "So unless I spill my personal life's secrets, the two of you are going to take the cowardly way out and kill me? My family took your sister in when she needed help when she either could not go to you or when she did not think she could go to you, risking our own lives, and you are really threatening me right now? Does that not already prove my loyalty to at least her? If I were going to hurt anyone, I would have hurt Elaraine when you had left her here alone and would not have been here when you got back!"

Nox scowled. "It's not considered cowardly to be suspicious and protective when you're being threatened on all sides. It's called being responsible."

Elaraine sank back to the ground from the exertion of standing for so long. She had not stood for such a length of time without help for about a week. "You're all acting very childish. You should all be ashamed."

"We should be ashamed?" Orin sputtered incredulously. "What about him?" He pointed his finger accusingly at Dayn.

Elaraine rolled her eyes as she lay down. "All three of you are being foolish and should be walloped."

"You're comparing us to this whelp?" Nox sounded disbelieving. "That is hardly fair."

"I think a good spanking sounds like a good idea, Elaraine. After all, when you act like a child, you deserve to be treated like one, do you not?" a musical voice chimed in from behind Orin. Moraiah pushed her way in, dragging Josi in behind her. She turned to her husband, placing her hands on her hips and knitting her eyebrows together. "And just how does acting this way help us raise your son, Orin? Lower your weapon and just trust the man. He did, after all, take care of Elaraine while she was in hiding, like he said. The least you can do is trust him now!"

Elaraine studied Josi while her brother tried to justify himself to Moraiah. Her nephew looked confused, but in awe of the situation, looking everywhere at once. His gaze swung continuously between the three men. He was extremely thin, but tall for his age. She had not noticed it before but he greatly favored his father in appearance the older he became. Then he looked back at her, matching her stare for stare. Finally, with jerky movements, he crossed the small space and stood over her.

"Aunt Elaraine," he said flatly, "I'm glad to see you are still alive."

She raised an eyebrow at his cool formality. "Thank you. I see you and your mother are both well. I bet seeing your father was a nice surprise."

He scowled and bent to her ear. "Don't pretend you suddenly care about my family," he hissed lowly. "Just because my mother and father have forgiven you doesn't mean I deem you worthy of my forgiveness."

She frowned and felt the muscle in her jaw ticking. "Josi, you don't know what you're talking about."

"What doesn't he know about?" Orin asked from his spot on the defensive, trying desperately to change the subject away from his actions toward Dayn. He looked from Elaraine to Josi and back again. "What does my son not know about that makes you so upset, Elaraine?"

Moraiah looked like a mad woman as she pulled Josi over to her. She was a puny five feet in height, but she made him look small in her fury. Josi shuffled his feet in the dirt as his parents glowered at him. He crossed his arms on his chest and refused to say anything. Orin waved Moraiah off as she tried to stop him from walking right up to their son. Everyone could see Orin trying to keep his patience.

"I'm not used to having to ask so many times, son. Now I want to know what you said to your aunt that made her upset," Orin said softly, but Elaraine could plainly hear the anger in his tone.

Moraiah patted Josi's shoulder, then stood beside her husband after a moment's hesitation and pulled him away. "Orin, we need to talk."

He took her hand from his arm softly and shook his head at her. "In a moment, please, my dear. Right now I want to hear what he said."

"That's what we need to talk about," she whispered. "I think it's best if I tell you what's been going on with our son before you become angry at him within only a day of seeing each other again. Maybe if you hear about it from me neither of you will say something you will come to regret."

With that, Orin allowed himself to be pulled out beyond the bush to speak with his wife in hushed tones. Nox came over and sat on his haunches by Elaraine as Josi went and sat on a small stone near his parents to try to listen to their quiet conversation. Dayn just fiddled nervously with his hands after returning his knife to its hiding spot, not quite sure what was going on. Elaraine had to admit that it was all rather confusing.

"Elaraine, I need to apologize," Nox began. "Orin explained to me why what I said the other night was wrong. I never meant to offend you. I wasn't trying to belittle you."

She turned her eyes away from her nephew and frowned at him. "Well, you did offend me, Nox. Multiple times. I stand by what I said about your being a coward and a fool. We grew up as friends, we are friends. But I don't have to like you right now. Just let me be angry for a little while."

He nodded slowly, sadly. "I understand that. But I just wanted you to know that I truly am sorry."

She bit a lip. "Are you coming with us?"

He cocked his head, confusion written all over his face. "Where else would I go?"

"To join the royal army."

"My place is here amongst my friends. You and Orin are the only family I have ever truly known. I'm not leaving you two now."

"Then let's put this whole thing behind us and pretend like it never happened," she suggested. "It takes too much energy to be angry."

"I'll try and do better."

"You better," she said, surprised at her own boldness at the moment to speak the truth, "or you'll be lucky if 'coward' is the worst thing I call you."

He cringed. "Your words feel like a whip. I don't like you to be angry with me. I've only ever tried to be your friend. I can't help if I was raised to think that men are more able than women to do a lot of things. It never occurred to me that you were different. But I'll try to do better all around."

She frowned and rubbed her temples in an effort to control her temper. "You may not be able to control how you were raised by Rochstaff, Nox, but you sure can help how you act now if you know it's wrong and start fixing how you think."

They both became distracted by Moraiah and Orin coming back into the cave. Orin was frowning and Moraiah was looking at the floor and twisting her hands in front of her. She came and sat next to Elaraine, dismissing Nox from them with a sideways glance. Orin was pacing in front of Josi. As the two other men watched Orin and Josi, Moraiah took Elaraine's hand in hers.

"I never got the chance to thank you," the woman told her meekly. "You defended us that night and now you have helped get Orin back to me."

Elaraine shook her head and patted the woman's hand. "It's my fault Orin was taken in the first place. I shouldn't have run away. I should have stayed in Gegernen and cleared your name from the beginning. Rochstaff never should have gone after you."

Moraiah smiled down at her pityingly. "No, Elaraine. I wouldn't have let you do that anyway. It's both our faults, what happened that night. I may have killed Dalun if you had not. We've both had to pay for it in our own way. But now we can have new lives! Just think of it: we can move somewhere where nobody has heard of our names and shame and be happy once again! Josi can grow up without the stigma of being related to us and you could remarry. We can send for your parents later."

Elaraine laughed. "I don't think I will be remarrying for quite a while, if at all. I have tried my hand at it and have found the entire institution disdainful." She added hastily, "Unless, of course, one is lucky enough to find one's soulmate like you and Orin."

The mentioning of her husband's name made the woman snap her head up to look at him again, still pacing in front of the sweating boy. "I hope he'll go easy on Josi," she whispered so only Elaraine could hear her. "This past year has been extraordinarily difficult on Josi. He has had to contend with bullying and relentless teasing from the other children in the village and hasn't had his father there to help him with anything. He had to help me on the farm. He had to grow up too fast and is not a child anymore. I would blame the two of us, too, if I were him."

Elaraine patted her sister-in-law's hand softly. "I blame myself, too. Orin will keep his head, don't worry. You know my brother," she laughed. "He acts like the big bad wolf sometimes when he is truly just a lamb."

Moraiah laughed with her. "True. He's always puffing his chest at the other men and acting tougher than they do. It is really quite irritating at times, but other times it is too endearing for words. You can truly feel safe falling asleep next to a man like that every night."

"I can't believe you said that to your aunt, son," Orin was starting, drawing their attention back to the situation at hand. Dayn and Nox quietly excused themselves from the enclosure to escape the tension swirling in the air. "It is not her, nor your mother's, fault I was sent to the Dungeons Ussal. I went there to save you and your mother. I went there willingly. I would do it again. It is a sad thing when a man dies, Josi, but to blame your mother and aunt for something they did in a state of fear and panic is not right." He put a large hand on his son's shoulder. "Forgive them, son. In my eyes, they did nothing wrong. Your aunt regrets what happened every day and will probably do so until the day she dies, if I know her. Your mother has had to suffer being by herself to raise you for the past year, bringing the crop in by herself because you were sick and unable to rise from bed for a few weeks. You had to step in and help take care of things while you could, and I appreciate that. It is something I wish you did not have to do. I have no doubt it will take time to fully forgive, but you have to try," he said urgently, gently shaking the young man. "Start to heal the relationships hurt by this whole ordeal."

"But it is her fault that I must leave Gegernen and my friends," Josi said softly with the venom clear in his voice.

Orin's voice clouded over. "It was my decision to take you and your mother from Gegernen," he growled. "Do not talk about things you know nothing about. You don't know what is best for you, we do. And as for your 'friends'...people who tease you and bully you, as your mother says all the children were doing, are not your friends."

"They were my friends until they killed Dalun Shrevelt and you went to prison. No one wants to be friends with a relative of a murderess," he spat out.

The yell resounded in the cave as Moraiah stormed to Orin's side. Josi had tears cascading down his cheeks. Moraiah had turned a bright red and was shaking visibly in her anger. Elaraine stood up to handle the situation calmly, a state Moraiah and Orin no longer seemed to know existed. Moraiah clenched and unclenched her fists several times before she spoke.

"How dare you speak to your father that way!" she growled. Elaraine had never seen her so angry. "He has been gone a year and all you did was talk about how you wanted to see him again. Well, he's here, isn't he? He's alive and well and wanting to be with us, too. And you have the audacity to speak back to him like that? You do not have the right to take that hateful tone with him!"

"I have never committed a crime!" Josi yelled. "I am a better man than he is because I have not been to prison! I wanted him back, not for him to take us away! Gegernen is my home! All of my friends are there!"

Orin lay a hand on Moraiah's shoulder and led her away so she could calm down. He nodded to Elaraine with a wry smile as they passed her, allowing her to speak and take control of the argument. Josi was just glaring at her, hate emanating from him like smoke from a fire. Elaraine set her jaw and crossed her arms over her chest.

She started off slowly, calmly, trying hard to remain in control of her tone and emotions. "Your 'friends' are miscreants, and you believe our sins are what ran them off? Well, I have news for you, Josi. They were never nice children." She put a finger in his chest and began to jab him with it. "Your father was protecting his family when he was taken away. That is a man. Your mother and I stood up for ourselves when no one would step up and protect us and for that you condemn us? Who are you to be our judge and jury? You are too young to know anything of the world outside of that perfect little fantasy world you so obviously live in! You didn't have friends in Gegernen. Friends are not so fickle as to leave you like they did. Your parents are good people, and so am I! I don't need your forgiveness, Josi, because you don't determine my fate! Our sins are between us and whatever god we choose to pray to. You can hate me if that is what makes you happy, but I never want to hear you speak to your parents that way again. Do you understand me?" He just glared at her. She straightened up taller, ignoring the pain that radiated through her. "I guess you may be a little hard of hearing after all the yelling tonight, so I'll repeat myself: do you understand me? A yes or no will suffice."

He looked a little shaken at her hardened demeanor. He nodded slowly. "Yes, I understand."

As she began to walk away back toward where she had been lying down, she heard him mumble something under his breath. Whatever it was made Orin grimace and Moraiah blanch. Dayn and Nox came in and stood near Orin, who was motioning over at his son.

"Son, I'm disappointed in how you have treated your family. We are all you have left," he said solemnly before letting Josi storm out into the night. He looked at the other adults and shrugged. "He won't go far. He doesn't know the way back to Gegernen."

Moraiah was kneeling next to a sack. Items were scattered next to it and she was muttering something to herself, looking for something. Elaraine tapped her shoulder and looked at her apologetically.

"The imp deserved it," Moraiah said flatly. "My son often does not know when to hold his tongue. He should not have said those things and he needed to see that there are consequences for his actions. Just because his father was away and he was the man of the household for a time does not mean he is a man." She gave a delighted trill with her tongue. "I found it," she squealed happily, handing Elaraine a small pouch.

Elaraine smiled at the woman's excitement. "What is it?"

"A rub for your ribs," Moraiah said, busily returning everything back to order in the sack. "It will heal the bones more quickly and make it easier for you to ride a horse."

She stood and took the pouch from Elaraine. One glance from her told the men it was time to give the women some privacy. She had Elaraine lay back down and soon she was rubbing a putrid concoction over the woman's ribs. Moraiah changed the bandage covering the knife wound and calmed Elaraine when the dried blood was torn and reopened the wound a bit.

After a time, the men returned, and there was some amicable conversation about the journey to and from Gegernen. Both trips had been relatively uneventful. The only thing Orin thought worth mentioning was that he had scared Moraiah while she was in the kitchen and she had struck him in the head with a water jug, thinking him an intruder. That story gave everyone a hearty laugh. Orin was looking healthier than he had before he left and even clapped Dayn's back and shook his hand, saying "I'm sorry for what had happened earlier."

"I understand," Dayn replied. "If she were my sister or I were bringing my family back and saw a stranger, I would have been worried, too. And I should not have been so defensive." Orin laughed and all was forgiven by both parties.

A few hours passed this way before Josi finally came back. He did not ask for a place to sit in their circle, nor was one offered. The conversation continued like he was not even there. Orin and Moraiah looked up occasionally to make sure he was still there with them, but every time they looked he was still standing against the back wall watching the adults talk.

Finally, he sidled up between Dayn and Nox. Nox quirked an eyebrow at the boy but said nothing as Dayn continued telling one of the many stories he had involving Elaraine, a sword, and her falling into the river by his mother's house. Elaraine could only grimace while the others started laughing. When they all finally stopped laughing, Josi cleared his throat softly.

"I've been thinking about what you all said," he said softly. Everyone was nodding, encouraging him to continue. "I'll try and act more grown up."

With that said, he walked away. Elaraine watched as her nephew spread out on the ground near the brush to sleep. Soon, they all followed suit and were all lost to their own dreams.

Elaraine had the same nightmare she had in the Dungeons Ussal, with Dayn throwing himself from the cliff and Ranci passing through their bodies. She woke up in a cold sweat, but no one else had been awakened. She was glad she had not cried out this time and had not disturbed anyone.

She stood up very slowly, noticing the pain in her side had dramatically decreased since the night before. She attributed it to Moraiah's salve. She made her way through the sleeping bodies to the entrance and from there to the creek, where she drank heartily and looked at the sky, lavishing in the innocence of the early morning. She heard some stirring from the small camp so she decided to turn around and head back to it. The sun was just peeking over the horizon when she returned to the rocks and her friends and family.

Moraiah was already up and packing the few things that had been unpacked the night before while Orin and the other men saddled horses. When she asked Moraiah where Josi was, Moraiah smiled and pointed back inside the cave. Her nephew looked so untroubled in his sleep that Elaraine really hated to wake him, but wake him she did. When he finally woke up from her gentle shaking of his shoulder, she smiled down at him.

"It's time to go, Josi," she murmured. "It's time to go and find an adventure!"

Chapter Seven

The morning was clear and warm with a slight breeze as they began their journey. The horses were all eager to depart and made no protests at the hands of their riders. Elaraine was on a white mare with a black mane and tail. Nox and Dayn were both on roan mares in front of her. Behind her, Orin rode a black charger with white socks. He was holding his wife's small hand in his. Moraiah rode a beautiful black pony she had named "Tix." Josi was nearly falling asleep behind them on his gray speckled pony. Elaraine smiled to herself. At last, their adventures could begin. At last, she could be herself without any qualms of maybe upsetting her family's plans for her. She soaked up and radiated this elation that surrounded her.

Elaraine considered their progress that first day to be excellent considering they did not have the foggiest idea of where they were headed. She was just happy in her freedom. By Nox's reckoning, they had only gone a few leagues, slowed down by the rocky terrain and Elaraine's and Orin's injuries. Her chest and his back made it difficult to ride for too long at one time. But both would have been completely happy to continue without stopping if it were not for Moraiah demanding breaks so the two of them could rest.

"If you two don't rest more, you won't be able to recover as quickly," Moraiah was saying to Orin that night as they were bedding down.

Orin had been grumbling about their slow progress as he poked the fire with a stick. He tossed the stick into the fire with a resigned sigh. Tonight would not be a night he would argue with Moraiah. Elaraine was glad he was starting to choose his battles with her. Moraiah was a hard adversary to beat. By not arguing, Orin was just saving himself and those within earshot a lot of aggravation and irritation.

"I agree, but it is still disheartening," he said, finally having decided what to say. "I knew the going would be slow at first, but I wasn't expecting to go this slow. I thought we would be further south than this by tonight."

While Orin had been disgruntled with their progress that first day, each day their progress improved. They still did not have a notion where they were headed, each knowing only that anywhere was better than prison or Gegernen right then. Orin's back was healed completely with miraculous speed in only a couple days after they left the cave. Elaraine's chest and stab wound took longer to heal, but, then again, she had always been a slow healer.

Moraiah rubbed her salve on Elaraine's ribs every evening and every morning there would be an obvious improvement. The riding would jar her ribs, though, making Elaraine feel like for every two steps forward she took in the healing process, she was forced one step back. She was becoming discouraged with the progress she was making, even though everyone else was quite pleased with it. She wanted immediate relief from the pain, but that relief was not coming.

Every day Josi would become slightly happier. He began to question the men about how things were when they were growing up, especially focusing his questioning on Dayn, who seemed more than happy to accommodate the young boy. Josi learned everything, from who Dayn's father was to what Dayn was, from why Dayn wanted to join the little troupe to why he and his mother had taken Elaraine in. That they had lived in relative isolation in the woods practicing some magic fascinated the young boy. Nox just frowned at most of the stories, muttering negative and disparaging things. It took Orin telling him to stop for Nox to finally allow Dayn to tell Josi stories in peace. The stories remained a point of contention between the two in private, however. To Nox, sorcerers were an impossibility of nature, like a mountain made of glass, so he could not keep himself from thinking of Dayn as a liar or as insane.

Josi and his relatives were slowly beginning to regain their old relationships. He still did not say much to his parents or Elaraine, but he no longer glared at them like they were the causes of all his troubles. Elaraine thought it must be because of the fresh air every day because she knew it was doing wonders for her own disposition. She felt healthier and they were all laughing again. It was a sound Elaraine had missed dearly in the past year. Ranci had never laughed while she had lived with them. Dayn rarely laughed either, though when he did his laughter sounded like music in its pure happiness.

As they headed south and east toward the border with Rischiak, the land became flatter and greener. Wildflowers bloomed everywhere. There were more birds here than there had been in Gegernen. At night, they could hear the wanderings of the nocturnal animals that prowled the forests. It was here, after two weeks of travelling, that Elaraine finally completely healed from her injuries from the beating and stabbing and was able to move around with the ease she had been able to before her brief imprisonment.

Orin and Moraiah were thrilled that she was once again the healthy and vivacious woman she had been before everything had gone so horribly awry. Her renewed health meant decisions could be made. It was there in the eastern regions of Swennia that they all decided on where they would go.

They did not want to be vagabonds on the run from the law anymore. However, they did not want to be given over to the law. From a man they had passed travelling the other direction on their path, they learned that a band of Rischiaks were encamped on Swennian soil on the Swennia-Rischiak border. The band was said to be ransacking nearby villages to feed and shelter their troops. Their killing many men a night was not a rare occurrence, and Swennians were flooding northward to escape the slaughter. They discussed going to the border to help the army protect the small villages for redemption.

"I'm all for it," Dayn said eagerly.

Josi was off watering the horses at a nearby river they had been travelling parallel to for the past two days, and Moraiah was cooking dinner for everyone. Elaraine had been allowed to sit in on the discussion with the rule that she could not argue with the results if they did not go her way. This discussion would be treated as a civil council would, with everyone having an equal vote in the matter. Equal voting power had been Moraiah's rule when Orin had called the meeting, and, although he had agreed with his wife initially, he grit his teeth as the conversation surged on to keep himself from taking control and making the decision for everyone else.

"We can't just rush in there, swords drawn and swinging," Nox countered. "The Rischiaks won't take kindly to our being there, and the Swennian army will have a lot of questions about our being there." He suddenly seemed scared of going anywhere near the royal army.

"They won't know why we're there. We could just say we moved there. That far away from Gegernen, they probably will not have heard what has happened," Dayn suggested. He seemed all too ready to play a hero.

"Nox is right," Orin said, trying to pacify both men. "We will need a plan if we decide to do this."

"'If?'" Moraiah called over. "We all know that we are going to go there and take care of those poor people. You just need to decide on how."

Orin grinned sweetly back at his wife. "Of course we do, but everything must be decided in its own time, darling." He turned back to the group and raised a hand when Nox opened his mouth to speak again. "Let's just decide on if we're going before we start making plans we aren't going to use," he suggested. Unanimously, they agreed they should go to the villagers' aid. "Okay, then, does anyone have a plan as to how to protect them?"

Elaraine cleared her throat, drawing their attention to herself. "I want to go and help the villagers, too," she started. "But only Orin and Nox are professionally trained to do this sort of task. Dayn would be able to hold his own, but that leaves Moraiah, Josi and me. We would only become burdens to all of you. What good would only three men do in this kind of situation?"

"You know how to fight decently," Dayn reminded her. "I taught you, so you'll be more than adequate to be of use."

"Moraiah and Josi will need to stay in one of the villages nearby those in trouble," Orin thought aloud. "I can't risk them being there when we attack the camp."

Moraiah looked up sharply. "Orin—"

"It will be what they least expect we low Swennians to do," he reasoned with her. "Let alone only four of us."

"Four against dozens," Elaraine said to no one in particular.

Nox looked askance at her. "More like four against hundreds."

"And just how does someone suggest we do that?" Elaraine said, her mood suddenly changing. "I am more than willing to help those people, but I still want to live through it. And Nox is right that the army will have questions we can't afford to be asked."

"This is why women should not be involved in matters like these," Nox groaned.

Moraiah threw a stick at his head, narrowly missing him. "Nox, don't let me catch you talking that nonsense again," she warned, "or I will throw something a little heavier than a stick next time."

Nox mock-saluted Moraiah, making her smile for the briefest of moments before she sobered once again.

"Yes, Moraiah." Nox said mid-salute. Josi came back and began to help his mother with the dinner. Nox began to tease him. "Learning to be a good housewife there, Josi?"

Josi turned bright red but ignored him. Elaraine felt anger well up inside her for the embarrassment Nox was causing her nephew. Everyone remained silent for a minute.

"Well, you've learned the first lesson well," Nox continued lightly, oblivious to the tension he was causing. "A good wife never speaks unless spoken to."

Elaraine just could not take it anymore. "Some men in this world are secure enough in their masculinity that they don't have to speak their minds to everyone every minute of every day. I believe that someone who does that is so worried about their masculinity being diminished that they forget what being a real man is. And a few shorts weeks ago you said you would stop spewing all this nonsense. Leave him alone or we will leave you alone!"

Orin and Dayn both hid their faces as they tried to contain their laughter. Josi had his back turned to her, but Elaraine could see that he was laughing silently. Moraiah just smiled at her over Nox's fuming head. It was hilarious to her that Nox had nothing to say back to her now. Without calling him any names, Elaraine had successfully silenced the never-ending fountain of opinions. He just stood up and stalked off into the woods without speaking or looking back at the others.

Dayn let his laughter out with a howl. "I can't believe you actually said that to him!"

"I can't believe it actually got him to be quiet," Orin agreed.

Elaraine shrugged, happy to finally have a moment's peace from Nox and his mouth. "Well, I don't mind hearing people's opinions, but he is just insulting!"

Moraiah wrapped her arms around her husband. "I agree! I'm only glad Orin is so open-minded about having a wife like me!"

"I'm just lucky to have a wife to put up with me," Orin laughed as Moraiah danced back to the fire cooking the dinner. "So, does anyone have any ideas on how four of us can fight the Rischiaks?"

"The odds are highly stacked in their favor," Dayn said soberly. "But if we could get some help from the men of the villages we may just have a chance."

"We would need to be able to kill a majority of them without the rest of them knowing we were even there," Elaraine piped in. "Or just a way to kill a lot of them at once and then it wouldn't matter if they knew we were there or not."

Dayn was really excited now that he felt he was contributing. "Like a distraction?"

"What kind of distraction?" Orin asked cautiously. He liked watching the amateurs discuss tactics, but he felt the weight of making the final decision weighing heavily on him.

Elaraine shrugged, the extent of her impromptu military stratagem exhausted. "I honestly have no idea. I thought you all would have some ideas, but definitely not me. I'm new at this, remember?"

Orin just nodded as Dayn became despondent and sighed. "I am, too," Dayn finally said. "I only know how to hunt and sword fight. Otherwise, I'm pretty much useless until you give me something to do."

Orin just smiled and shook his head. The time for his decision was at hand. "And as much as Nox is going to be loath to admit it, he has no idea what he's doing either." Moraiah snickered behind them. "Okay, so here is what I was thinking. We need a very large diversion, so we're going to need more than just the four of us. I vote we go to the villages and enlist help. We're too close to the border for anyone here to be overly concerned with the dealings in Gegernen, so I highly doubt they will have heard of our problems. However, just in case they have, I further my vote to include Dayn being the spokesperson and the only one seen in the village." Dayn seemed to glow with being given an important job. "We will have to see what kind of camp the Rischiaks have there, so I'll do that. We'll work out the other plans once we get there and know exactly what we are dealing with. Right now, though, we need every man we can possibly get. Agreed?"

They all agreed, and Moraiah set their dinners in front of them. It may have been only a scanty dinner of soup made from roots and other plants they had found that day, but the weary travelers considered the meal to be fit for a king. Nox eventually came back, still looking gloomy. He took Josi aside and spoke to him in whispers. From Josi's content face when they came back, everyone knew that Nox had probably apologized for his embarrassing comments to the young boy and everyone just left it at that.

They were all in visibly higher spirits that evening. Jokes and stories were told. There was laughing all around. It was hard for Elaraine to believe that only a short time ago, two of them were probably to be executed, one was a law-abiding guard, two were merely subsisting, and the other was just leaving his home for the first time in his life. Elaraine was constantly amazed by the turn in their fortunes. When it was time to bed down for the night, Josi approached Orin, who was busy trying to ready Moraiah's bed for the night.

"Father?" he asked quietly. "May I please keep a watch tonight?"

Orin chewed the inside of his lip and looked his son over. "I'm not sure," he said at last. "Are you sure you're up for it? You have to stay awake the entire time you are on watch."

The boy just nodded enthusiastically at his father. "We're far enough away from Gegernen and the borders where there shouldn't be any enemies lurking around or looking for us. It's the perfect time for my first watch! Please, Father!"

The men all exchanged skeptical glances with one another. Elaraine just frowned. She understood the need Josi felt to prove himself to Orin, but this probably was not the best time for mistakes. What if he fell asleep on his watch?

"Why doesn't he just stay up with the person who takes the first watch tonight?" Moraiah suggested. "They could tell him what to watch for and listen for and it could be like a training session for his taking a watch tomorrow night."

Orin flashed Moraiah a brilliant smile. He would not have to disappoint his son as much as he thought he would have to when his son first asked him for a watch shift. "What an excellent idea!" Elaraine did not like where this was going. Orin was looking at the faces around the campfire, all frozen in whatever activity they had started. "Who is supposed to have the first watch?"

Elaraine reluctantly stood and finished unfolding her blanket. "I am," she answered.

Orin frowned, probably remembering what had been said that first day before they left the cave and wondering if Josi had forgiven his aunt yet. Elaraine just nodded at him, knowing that was what was on his mind, accepting the responsibility of training Josi. She studied Josi for a long moment, unable to read his face for signs of resentment or of any other emotion. Orin understood and somberly told his son to obey his aunt and learn what to do. With that, the man continued with his task without another word on the subject.

Elaraine may not have had the experience of a soldier like Orin or the experience of a guard like Nox, but she had sat watch like everyone else in the family had when they would travel from village to village when she was growing up. She knew how to keep watch as well as Orin could from that experience. She had sat out by the fires through storms, snow, and summer nights. Josi would be in good hands, and Moraiah and Orin knew that.

As everyone else fell asleep, Elaraine took her post on a log nearby, just outside of the fire's glowing range. She looked up at the sky, still thankful every time she saw those stars to be free. She probably would have been dead by now if she had stayed in that prison. She was not quite sure where Josi was. She was beginning to think he had changed his mind about keeping watch when she heard the leaves and twigs crunching behind her under a light and hesitant walker. She smiled inwardly as he sat on the other side of the log, as far away from her as he possibly could and still be on the fallen tree.

"Who do we wake for the next watch?" he finally asked.

She looked over at him from the corner of her eye. "Nox, but that won't be for a few hours."

They sat in silence for a while. An owl hooted occasionally, and the bushes would shake from the movements of the night animals hunting for their meals. Josi was startled a few times by nature, making Elaraine just shake her head in the darkness.

"You don't have to listen to everything, you know," Elaraine finally advised. The boy looked over at her. "For example, the birds will not harm us. The small animals in the bushes aren't going to hurt us. You're just listening for the big animals and people. You will jump at everything if you listen for everything. You're free to sit out here and enjoy the evening and time to yourself for the most part. You just have to pay attention to things that don't belong."

"But how do you know which sound is which?" he asked, his want to prove himself overpowering his need to hold a grudge.

"Most sounds you hear are natural. The birds hooting, the trees swaying... those sorts of things. What you're listening for is anything that doesn't sound natural. If there's growling nearby, or clanking, footsteps, talking, hoof beats... anything that you don't usually hear in your surroundings at that time of the day or night, you need to wake everyone up, all right?"

Josi nodded. They settled back into their silence. Elaraine was thinking about the looming journey to the border. She was scared out of her mind about facing the Rischiaks, but she found herself looking forward to proving to the men that she could be just as important an asset as them. She was so consumed by her thoughts, she barely noticed Josi moving closer to her on the log.

"Aunt Elaraine?" he finally asked her. She turned to face him, a small smile touching the corner of her lips at his saying her name without any malice for the first time in a long time. "Are you angry with me?"

"I thought you were the one angry with me. I've just been trying to give you your space."

"I was angry with you."

"But not anymore?"

"No."

"Why not?"

He shrugged. "Father and Mother explained to me what happened. It was easier for me to blame you for what happened to my family than it was for me to blame anyone in the village. You ran away. You should have stayed to help us, but you ran away."

"I had to."

"I know. I know that now."

Elaraine held the bridge of her nose as she leaned on her arms. "Josi, if

I could have been there, I would have. But I would have been of no help to you dead."

He nodded. "I know that, too. I just wish none of this had ever happened."

She smiled at him. "We all do. But, Josi, this was the hand we were all dealt. Fate led us here, to this spot in time and to this place. It may not be fair, but whoever told you that life was fair was a liar."

"I never said that life was fair," he protested.

"I know you didn't, Josi. What I'm trying to say is I never meant to bring such harm to your family. They're my family, too, you know. If I had seen another way to handle the situation with Dalun Shrevelt, I need you to believe me that I would have done it that other way. In my panic I did not see any other way."

He sighed and put his face in his hands. "Of all the people to run into you that way, it had to be a noble. It had to be the king's cousin."

Elaraine laughed as she looked back up at the sky. "Maybe it's not such a bad thing, though." Her nephew just looked at her like she was crazed. "We're out here on the cusp of something greater than ourselves," she said. "We are communing with nature, becoming better friends, making stronger bonds, and appreciating life for everything that it's worth. Maybe all this can be worth that painful year?"

Josi just shook his head. "I can't agree with you about that," he said softly. "I'm not going to lie to you. I still don't like what happened, and a part of me still blames you and Mother for Father being taken away." Elaraine nodded, growing sober but understanding his point of view. "But I have hated it, seeing you walking away from me and knowing that I've caused you pain like that. I never should have said what I did, Aunt Elaraine. Please forgive me."

Elaraine smiled over at him. She patted him gently on the back. "Josi, you were forgiven the moment you said those words. You were an angry young man, and you had every right to be. Just think about what you say before you speak the words from now on, if you don't mind. You have to learn to be happy with your situation or you will always be miserable."

Josi just nodded at her forgiveness and released a relieved sigh. He turned with her to look back up at the sky. Finally, he turned back to her.

"May I ask you a question?" She nodded over at him, not taking her eyes off the clear night sky. "How are you so cheerful, Aunt? Even after only two days out of the prison, you were so happy!"

She looked at him from the corner of her eye again. "It takes too much energy to be angry. I need my energy for other things."

He did not understand, but he let it rest. Right then he needed to learn what else to watch for, not expend energy trying to understand his father's sister. Soon, it was time to wake Nox, and the two of them faded off to sleep, one thinking about making his father proud and the other of distractions and traps for the Rischiaks.

Chapter Eight

Josi kept a good, uneventful first watch over them the following night. It was made more difficult because a wind had picked up, carrying sounds away from them, but he managed to do his job well, and Orin was immensely proud of his son the next morning. It was nice having two people getting a full night's sleep at night. Moraiah and Dayn were the lucky ones that night. When Josi woke Elaraine for her watch, she could see a visible change in him. He was maturing faster than they had thought he would as their journey went on. He was growing up and acting much older than his fourteen years.

Travelling to the villages that were being harassed and attacked by the Rischiaks was difficult. The terrain they had to cross had many barriers and was hilly. They made hardly any progress each day as they tried to maneuver their horses around the worst parts of the rocky outcrops. Between the rocks and the heavily forested woods they had to go through most of the time, Elaraine and her companions could have sworn they only travelled half a league each day. Tix was being extraordinarily temperamental most of the time, making it necessary for them to walk most of the way, leading their horses around trees and briars.

For a long stretch of the journey, a sheer cliff face was on one side of them that dropped until it met a river far below them. Orin looked down at the river at one point and had gotten dizzy, needing to sit down for a short spell until he felt he could walk safely once again. He blamed it on too much breakfast to help keep some of his dignity, but his fear of heights wasn't a secret.

After the pathway along the cliffs ended, the fires from the Rischiak encampment served as a beacon, leading them toward their destination. During the day black smoke from the fires wound into the blue sky, polluting everything. When the wind blew their way, they could even smell the smoke. Moraiah cursed when she first saw all that smoke, thinking that patches of the forest they were travelling through had caught fire. It earned a few chortles from the men in the group, but the two women exchanged wary glances. Josi was too happy that his father was teaching him about military strategies to even notice that the women were worried and that the men were becoming even more cautious than before.

"Do you think they've moved any?" Nox asked Orin the third day since they had seen the fire, his gaze never roaming from the smoke.

Orin just shook his head and pointed. "No. Their campfires are staying steady. We would have noticed if their camps would have changed because our course would have changed. We have been travelling due east for the past three days."

That settled some worries the travelers were feeling. At least the enemy had not yet realized there were strangers in the woods. They had yet to pass signs of any watch guards in the woods. They were probably too focused on the nightly raids to care if a half dozen wanderers were getting close or not. But they could also tell that the camp was enormous for the small group to handle, with troops numbering in the hundreds or thousands.

They literally stumbled onto the ruins of a small village when Orin fell over a crossbeam he had not seen or been looking for. They had been surprised to see a clearing ahead of them, but had thought it to be a meadow, not ruins. No one came to greet or confront them. Some of the rubble was still smoking from a recent fire. They scoured the site, looking for anything telling them where the people had gone, or if they had gone at all. They found a few corpses here and there, but nothing like the massacre they had expected when they had seen the smoldering ashes.

Nox held up an arrow he had found near the edge of the forest. Moraiah and Josi were staying near the tree line, holding the reins of all the horses. The mother refused to allow her son to go into the ruins to see any unnecessary carnage. Dayn covered the body of a young girl and slammed his fist in one of the remaining posts left standing over her, sending cinders cascading into his hair. Orin touched his shoulder, only for it to be flung off.

"They killed the children!" Dayn shouted at him. "I haven't seen any adults here, not even the old. Have you?"

Orin just shook his head. "No," he said at last. "They've all been children."

"Then don't stand there and try to act like everything is all right. Their parents should have been here! They should have protected these whelps with their lives! Instead, they run away? What kind of parents are those?"

Nox came up to them and tossed the arrow aside. "Parents run away every day." His tone was bitter. "A child dying like this or dying at the hands of the Rischiaks isn't much different. At least their parents could offer them mercy this way. At least this way they won't be tortured by the Rischiaks until they are finally allowed to succumb to death."

Moraiah led Josi away from the scene so he could not even hear what was being said. Until they were both gone, no one spoke. Finally, Elaraine turned to her friend.

"You can't possibly mean what I think you do," she whispered, keeping her voice low so Moraiah and Josi couldn't hear her. She was looking at the arrow Nox had cast aside.

"I can and I do," he said. He motioned around them with a sweep of his hand. "Do you see anything that shows any signs of the Rischiaks? Anything at all? I don't. I've looked. I've scoured the remains looking for anything that would say the Rischiaks did this. I've only found Swennian arrows and butchered Swennian children. That means this was done by the parents."

A tic started working in Orin's jaw. "Are you sure? I mean, absolutely sure? We cannot have any doubt if we are to accuse the parents."

Nox looked offended. "I may not have been a soldier, but I've trained with them and I have studied our own country's crafts. There is nothing foreign here. How many children do you think were in Gegernen when we left that could not do adult things like the farming and fighting? There were around two dozen. Look around. I bet there's about that here, meaning that the parents killed the little ones. The oldest I've seen here was probably in their eighth year. It happens occasionally. I remember hearing about it last year at the capital. Some old soldiers were talking about something like this along the Swennian-Rischiak border. It happened here, I'm telling you!"

"How could parents do something like this?" Dayn asked, his voice strained.

Orin sighed and kicked the post next to his boot and cursed. "They were misguided."

"Where do you think they went?" Elaraine asked after a short silence. "Is there any way to tell with this fire?"

"The Rischiaks are a little further south from here," Orin pointed, "so I think the best bet we have is to go North and East. We may not find the villagers from here, but at least we might find someone who knows what happened." He stooped to pick up the arrow Nox had tossed aside and turned away.

They started to walk out of the clearing slowly. Elaraine stopped for a moment and looked behind her at what would serve as the graveyard for so many innocent children. They did not have the time to give them all a proper burial and would have to leave them as they had found them. Nox stopped beside her and let her think for a moment in silence before he put a comforting hand on her shoulder.

"They didn't suffer," he said simply. "If it was their loved ones who did it, like I'm sure they did, they wouldn't have let the deaths drag on or they would have just let the Rischiaks do it themselves. The children would have died quickly."

Elaraine nodded as she continued to stare at the scene around them. "It's heartbreaking, Nox." She looked up at Nox with tear-filled eyes.

He just steered her away to where the others were already waiting for them atop their horses. The terrain was smooth enough now to ride their horses and they all eagerly took advantage of that.

After a while Nox broke the silence between himself and Elaraine once again. "Do you want to know what the secret is?"

She glanced sideways at him. "What do you mean? What secret?"

"The one that allows you to move on from something like that without thinking too much about it." He said it so smoothly, without a hint of condescension and with all the care he could muster.

She nodded, feeling more tears springing to her eyes. "Please."

He nodded. "Well, the first part is to look at it objectively. You didn't know them. There's no reason to mourn, so you only have a reason to be angry. The second is to not think about it too much. Things like this happen all the time, unfortunately." He laid a cool hand on her shoulder. "Take comfort in the fact that we're going to kill the Rischiaks that made the parents do this."

She looked at him through puffy eyes. "But it wasn't the Rischiaks who killed those children."

"No, that's true." He sighed and looked back at the trail ahead of them. "But if you think about it, if it hadn't been for the Rischiaks, the parents wouldn't have done what they did."

She just shook her head at him, surprised at his calmness. "Nox, there is always another way. The children are dead because their parents gave up."

"If you truly believe that, then why did we march on that camp?" He looked at her and smirked. "We could send in diplomats and allow them a hand at peacemaking, but even you supported this plot to help defend the villages. You have never helped people who have given up, so if you genuinely believed that those parents have given up defeating the Rischiaks you would be turning away and calling for diplomacy to be used instead."

"Diplomats have been tried," Dayn said, falling into pace with their horses. "If they hadn't, then armies wouldn't be marching this way, too. From what I understand, the king has been trying to be very diplomatic about this conflict."

"Kings always say they don't like conflict," Orin chimed in. "Yet every reign seems to have war and evil."

"What is with all this negativity?" Moraiah growled. "Did that sign back there teach any of you anything?"

"Children younger than me." Josi could be heard whispering. He glanced over at his parents, wondering if they would have done the same thing.

"We'll need all the allies we can get," Nox finally said.

"We'll need to hurry before this happens in more villages," Orin agreed.

"One is too many," Moraiah said plainly. "That one behind us was too many."

"I know, my love, but there is nothing we can do about that one."

"We can only make sure it doesn't happen again," Nox agreed.

The men kicked their horses into a gallop to catch back up with Orin.

Moraiah was lost in her own thoughts and did not notice Josi was steering his steed away from her and towards his aunt. The two rode in companionable silence for a while.

"Would they have done that?" he finally asked, his voice cracking in anguish. "Would Mother and Father have done that to me?"

Elaraine looked at her nephew and thought for a few minutes. She did not see a reason to lie to him. "I honestly don't know, Josi. I can tell you that they would try their hardest to make sure you are safe and loved and that that is all they care about. They would not have done anything lightly, and you can bet that the parents of those children didn't do that without a lot of soul searching too."

"But then the parents ran away."

She nodded. "Yes, but if they hadn't, what would have become of them?"

"They've become murdering cowards," he spat. "Defenseless children!"

"Yes, but that is the tragedy of war, is it not?"

He thought about it for a minute. "I don't want us to go to the Rischiak camp."

"The Rischiaks are our country's enemy." She was surprised at him. "What have they done to deserve our mercy?"

"What have they done to deserve our personal hate?" he countered. "We don't even know why it is we're at war! Gegernen is too far away to be affected by a war with the Rischiaks! The king says things and we must obey? It is nonsensical!"

"It's the way of the world, Josi." Elaraine was getting tired of this conversation. She knew it was not her nephew's fault that the situation was aggravating her. The plan had had her mind reeling for a while, too. She had no idea why they were at war, but they were. "It's our duty, and that of our countrymen, to protect our lands," she tried to reason with him. "If we don't, then who will?"

"If we don't sanction peace, who will?" he countered, steering his horse back to his mother.

Elaraine thought about the situation the rest of the long way to the next village. She went over every argument she had ever thought of again and again as to why what they were doing was justified, trying to convince herself that a sneak attack was warranted and not cowardly. The slaughter of the children helped her internal argument. The trees thinning around her was what snapped her back to her companions and the situation at hand.

The men dismounted and Elaraine followed suit. Moraiah and Josi stayed in their saddles and took the reins of the other horses. Orin put his hand on the hilt of his sword. They walked past the tree line, each praying in his or her own way to not have another scene like before. Each sighed heavily with relief when they heard the daily noises of a village. Orin looked over his shoulder and gave a comforting gesture and a smile to his wife and son.

Elaraine was still nervous as they walked into the village amidst the villagers, drawing many a wary and curious glance. She kept wondering if maybe news of their escape and crimes had reached these people yet. No one approached them, and she felt slightly comforted. Orin took control of their group and assumed leadership with only a glance at his companions. He walked down the main road like a man who had been there before and had already been accepted by the community.

"Who is it that comes in like he is king?" a man shouted from a doorway at them. He leaned against the door with his arms crossed.

"One who has vowed to save these outlying villages from the Rischiaks," Orin shouted back. He drew a deep breath. "One who would speak with the village leader."

"And what if the village leader is not here or does not wish to speak with you?" the man retorted. "What if he refuses to speak with those who are insolent strangers?"

"Then I would tell him that these 'insolent strangers' may be his village's one chance right now in defeating the Rischiaks."

"The king's army is on their way!" another man yelled.

Women were starting to hide their children in houses while the men were starting to gather around the village's center, around the strangers amongst them.

"We have been on the road for a while," Orin said, keeping his voice even and strong, "and we have yet to hear a single word about the king's men. They will not be here in time to save you."

"And what can three men, two women and a child do to help?" the first man hurled back at him, looking past the small party at the sound of hooves.

"Three men and a lady," Moraiah called out as she and Josi galloped thunderously into the clearing with all the other horses in tow. "The 'child' and I will not be going."

"But—" Josi started to protest, but a sharp look from his mother silenced him instantly.

"You did not want to march on the Rischiaks anyway," Elaraine whispered up to her nephew. "And your mother is right, Josi. You should not come along for this battle."

They turned their attention back to Orin arguing with the man who they deemed to be in charge of village affairs, the first man to call out to them. Elaraine was frustrated at the slow progress they were making, but she tried to quell her impatient nature and let her brother take care of obtaining an ally or two. Finally, Dayn could not take the speed Orin was using to gain their trust anymore and jumped into the conversation.

"Please, sir," Dayn said, stepping forward. "I'm sorry to interrupt your verbal battle with Orin, but the situation at hand demands speed, not dilly-dallying around trying to ascertain whether or not we will be true to our word and see this through to the finish."

"Forgive me, sir," the man replied. "But I am in charge of this village and I will be the one to determine whether or not to follow you to battle or wait for an army that was promised me by the king."

"Was the army promised to a village about half a league from here to the west?" Nox spoke up. "They didn't arrive in time to help."

The man just nodded at him. "What do you mean?"

Orin looked around at the villagers murmuring loudly amongst themselves and cleared his voice. "Please, allow us to speak to you in private about this matter. It really is too sensitive a topic for the ears of your children and women."

The leader nodded tensely and showed them the way to his home. It was small but comfortable with obvious signs that it lacked a feminine touch. Orin and the man took seats at the table while the rest of the travelers stood behind them, along with a few of the higher ranked men of the village.

"We started off on the wrong foot," Orin offered after a few moments of silence. "I am Orin." He then began to point to the respective people in his group. "That is Nox, a village guard; Dayn, a sorcerer's son; my sister, Elaraine; my wife, Moraiah, with my son, Josi. We have travelled a long way to come to your aid."

The man waved his hand as a dismissal. "Orin, let's end pretenses. We know each other well and I know it. But only these men know I am a prince. I told you before I grew up in a village and not in the capital. I came here for a respite from the army." He clapped Orin on the back and told him he was glad to see him once again. Then he turned to the other travelers in the small cottage and extended his hand to them. "I am Prince Shep. What news do you bring from our sister village?"

"It is burned and the children were killed," Orin said softly. "The Rischiaks were not the ones to blame, though," he added quickly. "It was the villagers themselves."

Prince Shep thought for a moment. "The villagers said that it was the Rischiak army."

"The Rischiaks were not at fault there," Nox said adamantly.

"What do you mean, 'the villagers said'?" Orin cocked an eyebrow at the prince, his casual tone with the prince surprising everyone but the prince in the room. "They are here, then?"

The prince nodded, undeterred by Orin's easy manner. "But you say it was these parents that killed their children? It is pretty unbelievable. And, if true, it is unforgivable."

"More unbelievable things have happened, have they not?" Moraiah chimed in.

Prince Shep held a hand up to tell her to wait a moment. "And you also say that you will help us against the Rischiaks?" Orin nodded. "I am not sure how much help three men and, as you say, a woman, can be, but I will make a deal with you."

They all listened, rapt in the exchange. Elaraine looked at her nephew and sister-in-law. Moraiah was holding Josi close to her. Elaraine thought that it was probably embarrassing the young man, but if it was he gave no outward indication.

Orin started speaking again, so she turned her attention back to her brother.

"And what kind of deal is that?"

"Prove to us that it was the parents, and we will join you without waiting for the army my father has promised us."

Orin held his hand toward Nox, never taking his eyes from Prince Shep. "Nox, the arrow, if you please." Nox handed him the arrow Orin had given to him when they left the scene of the slaughter. Orin handed it over to the prince in his turn. "Nox found this at the village. There weren't any signs of anything from the Rischiaks there, so the Rischiaks obviously did not do it. There were no dead adults, only children. And the children were young. Send your own men out there if you wish. They will see the same thing we did."

Shep just fingered the arrow delicately, running his fingers at the end and testing the point of the stone, making sure to avoid most of the blood stains. He shook his head at Orin grimly and swallowed a few times. "No. The first step in an alliance is trust." He handed the arrow to the men from the village behind him for their own inspections. They looked disgusted and nodded their acceptance at the prince, but everyone in the room knew the prince would not need their acceptance to form the bond with Orin and the rest of the group. The prince extended his hand to Orin and they shook firmly. "We'll join you!"

Chapter Nine

It was hard for Elaraine to believe the quick turn of events. Without much difficulty at all they had their first ally. That he was a prince sounded dangerous to Elaraine given the troupe's history, but she could not deny that he was powerful. The men in her company seemed thunderstruck in his presence as well. When Prince Shep, his men, and Orin left the small house, Elaraine and her friends remained rooted to where they stood. Moraiah and Josi were the first to regain their composure and they were the first to follow Prince Shep back to the village center. One of the prince's men still carried the arrow clutched in his hand, his knuckles were turning white with his tight grasp.

Elaraine studied the prince as she followed him. Prince Shep was close to her brother's age, she guessed. The world visibly weighed heavily on his shoulders, but he stood tall and proud as he addressed the crowd of people. He did not recoil from the glares as he stated the evidence of the filicide. He did not back down when the refugees cried their innocence as the people in the prince's village began to cast them from their ranks. He was firm and proud like a royal should be. Elaraine was awestruck by the way Prince Shep handled the ugly situation. He easily had the men of the village expel the other village's members from their borders. To her eyes, Prince Shep was obviously a well-trained prince.

It went much more smoothly than the new arrivals had expected. They had expected a fight, but the parents had just hung their heads after initially declaring their innocence then accepting their guilt, and then they all left. Josi watched the procession in amazement before swinging his gaze back to Prince Shep, his jaw slightly ajar in his admiration.

When the last of the ruined villagers had left, Prince Shep gathered his own people around him. He stepped onto the platform in the middle of the village, his trusted men following him. He looked around until his eyes fell on the weary travelers. He smiled encouragingly and waved them up to join him. Orin and Dayn led the way to stand behind their new ally. Elaraine stayed behind Nox and stood near the back edge of the platform, hoping not to attract more notice than was absolutely necessary.

"These people have travelled a long way to help us fight the Rischiaks," the prince said, gesturing to Orin and his company. "We all know their close proximity and we all know that the threat is imminent. They have offered to join us and attack the Rischiaks, but the king has also promised to send us an army to help us. We just need to decide what to do," he said for all to hear. He cleared his throat. "I have decided to join these people and ask that every able-bodied man join me. It is entirely up to you. We will be outnumbered, out-armed, and out-experienced, but no one will have more heart than those who go. After all, if we don't fight for our families and our land, what else is there to fight for? But there will be no hard feelings against anybody who decides to stay behind. There will be no punishment for those who do not join us."

His speech was simple, barely a minute long before he was walking off the stage, his men following behind him and the travelers after them. The line of men waiting to join them was already forming in silence. Elaraine was bewildered by how the prince could inspire so many men to follow him to a battle that almost certainly would mean their deaths. He had given them the choice of joining, but most of the men were there, already arming themselves and preparing for the departure. Prince Shep went up to a few of these men and spoke to them in soft undertones. The men he spoke to ran off like the flames of hell were lapping at their heels. Then he sauntered over to Orin, Dayn, and Nox.

"We need to get word out to the other nearby villages for more men to join us," Dayn said. "Otherwise, all our efforts will be for nothing."

Prince Shep just smiled at him. "Word has already been sent. The other villages will have men being sent to the lake by twilight."

"How can you be sure?" Dayn asked rudely, forgetting his place as a respectful guest and subject of the crown.

All of Dayn's companions shot him looks of dismay for his tone, but no one around the prince seemed to notice. Prince Shep just shrugged and smiled even more genuinely at his guests, throwing his arms open to include the entire village.

"Because I'm Shep. Anything that happens here falls under my jurisdiction. If I tell the men to come, they will come." He lowered his voice, adding, "And because most of the people here do not truly know of my birth, their following me means more to me than anything, so please keep that a secret."

"They will come just because you said to?"

Prince Shep clapped him on the back. "When you're a good leader, you have good followers."

Orin cleared his throat. "And what is the significance of this lake? Why not just tell the men to come here?"

Prince Shep raised an eyebrow at the query and waved his hand around them, encompassing the entire village with the gesture. "War is men's business, not for sensitive ears to listen to." That seemed to make him remember something because he dropped his hand from Dayn's shoulder and looked between Moraiah and Elaraine. "Speaking of which, you said that the young one would not be joining us and that one of the women would be?"

Orin nodded as the other two men in their group scowled. He motioned Elaraine forward. "My younger sister, Elaraine, will be coming with us. My wife will stay behind with my son."

Prince Shep regarded Elaraine with a long stare. "Are you sure she'll be able to fight and not get in the way?"

"She's proven herself before," Orin said carefully. "She fights with heart but shows no mercy. She has watched Nox's and my backs in fights before."

"How has she proven herself?"

Nox stepped in front of Elaraine defensively. "She saved Orin and me, and that is enough."

Elaraine had expected another blown-out-of-proportion argument with Nox over her going to the Rischiak encampment to fight with them, but here he was defending her right to go. She looked at him thankfully, feeling in her heart how much he had raised in her estimation, but the look he gave back to her was not supportive but resigned.

Prince Shep just nodded slowly and began to circle her, judging her worth with close scrutiny. She straightened her spine and lifted her chin. Elaraine was more than slightly irked with this kind of treatment, but she held her tongue, knowing that insulting the prince would not win her any favors and would probably mean that she would not be allowed to go. Finally, he stopped walking around her and pushed Nox out of his way so he could look her in the eye. She met his gaze unwaveringly.

"Your brother and the others can defend your bravery all they want, Elaraine," he said softly. "But they can't see what's buried deep within your heart. I want to hear it from you: in the heat of battle, with men screaming and dying, will you be able to stay on the field until victory is gained or death comes to find you?"

His words were more than a little daunting for her. She had not thought about the situation in quite that way before. His words conjured images she had not experienced yet and did not particularly desire to experience. Her mind flashed to an image of Dalun Shrevelt writhing on the ground after she had stabbed him, but she knew even that would not prepare her for what lay ahead of her. The fight at the Dungeons Ussal would be the only thing she could truly look to as an experience in battle. Looking at her brother and Nox, those men who had risked everything to save her life, convinced her. How could she possibly let these three men, the men who had travelled through dells and over mountains with her, ensuring her safety, go into battle without her? She took a deep breath to steady herself before turning her attention back to Prince Shep.

She squared her shoulders and raised her head. "Sir," she began.

"Shep," he corrected, trying to hide an amused smile, but the annoyed look he gave her with a slight shake of his head towards the villagers behind him did not escape her.

She nodded, acknowledging she understood his hint. "Shep," she corrected, "if I did not think I could do this without endangering other people by my being there, I would ask to stay behind. But I promise you," she met Orin's eye, "I will do everything in my power to gain the victory and support those with whom I go into battle."

Orin just smiled at her as Prince Shep threw his head back and laughed again. Nox and Dayn looked downhearted at her declaration of going into battle with them, but they kept silent. Elaraine knew they had secretly hoped she would remain behind with Moraiah and Josi. Moraiah grasped her hand and squeezed as Josi just sighed heavily beside her. The prince called for four horses to be brought for them before he headed off to arm himself.

Orin took Moraiah aside and spoke quietly to her, telling her to stay in the village with Josi, promising her a speedy return. Nox and Dayn went about loading the horses with arms and supplies that the four of them would need for a few days. Elaraine looked at her nephew, who had turned a pasty white.

"Josi, are you all right?" she asked, turning to face him.

He swallowed hard and turned to her. His eyes pleaded with her. "Please, Aunt, don't go with them."

She tilted her head to the side. "Josi, I'm going to go with them. I have to go with them."

He embraced her tightly. "No, you don't!"

"Josi, I need to breathe!"

He continued unabashedly. "Shep even asked if you wanted to go. You could have said no!"

"No, I couldn't have," she ground out breathlessly, patting his back. "Your father, Dayn, and Nox risked their lives to save mine and I would do the same for them without a second thought. How can I stay here and let them go without me?"

He released her and held her away at arm's length. "My aunt shouldn't have to go to battle."

"My nephew shouldn't have to live during a time in the kingdom when there are battles and invasions," she countered. "But such is life."

"So you would lay down your life for this foolhardy plan?"

Elaraine shook her head. "I would not lay down my life for a plan, but for people I would. In a heartbeat." Josi bowed his head. "You would follow your father to the death, too, Josi, and you know it."

"But you're not following him! You're following Shep!"

"I both am and am not. Your father wouldn't be following him unless he trusted him, Josi!" Moraiah said, rebuking her son softly as she came up behind him, her eyes betraying the worry she was fighting to conceal. "As it so happens, he trusts Shep implicitly." She looked up at Elaraine. "Though he won't tell me why."

Elaraine threw her hands up in the air. "He has not said a word to me about it, either." She turned and shrugged into the heavier tunic Dayn was holding out to her. She turned back to her sister-in-law. "Just trust him. If he says Shep is a good man, then he is."

"I know that," Moraiah said defensively. "But I just got him back, and now he's leaving again."

"It's not like it's for a year this time," Dayn said gently. "We'll be back in only a day or two. Three at the most. You can take comfort in that."

Moraiah glared at him, not appreciating his comfort. "When you have a spouse who is gone for such a long time, then you can come back for me to tell you to take comfort in their leaving for battle."

Dayn was backing away from her slowly, looking contrite. "I didn't mean to be callous, Moraiah. I'm sorry."

Elaraine grabbed him and led him away. "She knows that, Dayn. Just give her some time to calm down. She is only worried."

"I didn't mean to upset her," he whispered.

"Just get up on that horse and don't say another word to her until we get back. It's safer that way."

He frowned down at her, pausing in the middle of mounting his steed. "'Safer'?" She just raised her eyebrows up at him, willing him to understand. It hit him like a brick. "Oh! I see! Safer! Got it!" He finished climbing up on his horse. "Orin says you're to ride Tix," he pointed over his shoulder.

"Tix?"

"He's gotten stronger than the one you were riding before. He's faster than that old mare. You need a younger horse for this." He looked around at the men already mounted around them. "You better hurry and mount up; it looks like we're getting ready to head out."

Elaraine took the reins from Nox and mounted with ease. She noticed a sword and long knife had been attached near her saddle, and her bedroll with a change of clothes was behind her. She would have to thank Nox and Dayn later for getting Tix ready while she had been busy arguing with Josi.

The column of a few dozen men and Elaraine rode silently from the village, the women and children standing stolidly in the roads to see them off. They did not protest the departure or the reason for their leaving. They all just held their heads high and did not say a word. Prince Shep led the way back into the forest down the well-travelled road. Dayn and Nox moved their horses to either side of Elaraine's. She just looked ahead of her to where Orin was now talking with Prince Shep.

"Are you scared?" Nox finally asked.

"I'd be a fool not to be, would I not?" she said softly.

"That's true," he said. "But if you're that scared, you should have stayed behind."

"You supported my coming when you were talking to Shep," she reminded him.

"I didn't support your coming. All I did was say that you were an able-body who could fight."

Elaraine took a deep breath, willing herself to calm down. "You just got back in my good graces, Nox. Let's not go and ruin that so soon."

He shrugged. "It was your choice to come. You won't be able to blame anyone but yourself if you leave the battlefield scared and crying."

She looked over at him, her self-control slipping fast. "And when was the last time you went to battle?" His silence was enough. "For someone who hasn't been in a battle like this either, you sure do talk a lot. Do not presume to know what I will do. Think instead of what you will do yourself."

Dayn snickered loudly. "She has a point, you know!" he called to Nox, who had kicked his horse to trot along the column to go to Orin to get away from them. "He sure does follow Orin around a lot, doesn't he?"

Elaraine glared at Nox's back. "He can't hide his arrogance behind my brother for long." She turned and smiled at Dayn. "He probably just doesn't want me to come along so that I won't see him scared out of his own wits and crying."

That made Dayn laugh, and they talked amicably for most of the ride to the lake. Elaraine had never seen him so at ease, and she wondered why. Why was he so at ease on their way to battle and he was always so tense every other time she had known him? Finally, as the lake came into view, Dayn's mood changed completely.

"You know, I didn't want you to come either," he said flatly. She just looked at him without a word. "Not because I think you can't handle yourself," he added quickly. "But because even though I know you can handle the situation, I won't be able to handle the situation with you there."

"How do you mean?" she asked carefully, trying not to show the anger roiling within her.

"I'd be worried about you if you had stayed back at the village, too," he said softly. "At least at the village, there isn't a lot of the enemy swarming around trying to kill you."

She nodded as she calmed herself down. At least his reasons for her not tagging along were purely because he cared, not because he doubted her courage or skill. He looked at her worriedly, unsure of how his confession would be welcomed.

"I understand," she said to put his mind at ease. "I appreciate your concern, I do. But just trust in me and worry about yourself if you can." He looked at her doubtfully. "At least try."

He nodded. "I'll try." He smiled sheepishly at her. "I can't make any solid promises, though. I'll be sticking close to you whether you like it or not. I'll find you in the battle."

They both laughed as they rode into the clearing. They got a few grudging looks and glares from the men around them, but they did not care. In a time of turmoil and tension, the two friends were able to find comfort in each other and that was all that mattered to them. Orin and Prince Shep just smiled when they saw them, but Nox glared. Elaraine just ignored him and focused all her attention on Dayn, the loyal friend she knew would not betray her.

Men from other villages were already gathering about the shore of the lake. The crimson sunset was reflecting off the lake, giving the scene a surreal feeling. Prince Shep dismounted and gave the reins of his white stallion to a tall man in a green tunic. They talked for a minute before Prince Shep motioned for his followers to dismount. Dayn and Elaraine made their way to Orin's side and stayed there, not wanting to be separated from him in the chaos of the men finding their friends and reorganizing.

Orin laid his hand on Elaraine's shoulder as a man jostled them as he passed. It reminded her of market day in Gegernen in its hustle and bustle. Commotion and noise surrounded them. Prince Shep and the men from his village who seemed to be his guards were talking in hushed tones near the edge of the group. They would immediately become silent and glance up when a man would venture too near their conversation. Finally, the prince walked to the edge of the lake and called for everyone's attention.

"I'm going to keep this short. We all know the Rischiaks are close by and are harassing the villages. We're going to separate into groups. One is going to be in charge of a diversion, namely setting the Rischiak tents on fire. Another group is going to be the archers. The members of the third group are going to enter the camp from the east and the fourth group will enter the camp from the west. Please do not separate yourselves in groups with your friends. Seeing a friend fall in battle is one of the hardest events to move on from and we cannot afford for you to grieve in this battle. We leave in an hour."

His speech was short but to the point. Friends parted ways with words of encouragement and promises of meeting at the end of the battle. Nox moved to join the archers after saying his own words of encouragement to his friends. Dayn and Orin just looked down at Elaraine.

"Which group will you be joining?" Orin asked, his brotherly protectiveness coming out.

"Which group are you joining?" she asked flippantly.

"The group attacking from the east."

"Then I will join that one, too." The words were so easy to say, but in her mind she was plotting a way to make her move.

Dayn cleared his throat. "Then I had better join the west. All three of us can't be in the same group." As he started to move away, he threw a torn glance back at the siblings. "Take care of her, Orin! I'll join the two of you during the battle!"

Orin nodded as he handed his sister Tix's reins. "I will, Dayn! Take care of yourself and we'll see you at the end!"

Elaraine mounted Tix and patted his neck. She put her wrist guards on while they waited for Prince Shep to tell them which way he wanted them to go and what time everything would start. She could feel the adrenaline pumping through her veins; sweat was pouring down her forehead. She wiped the sweat from her brow with her shirtsleeve. Orin tied a small chest plate to her from his saddle. When he was satisfied that she would at least be partially protected, he moved amongst the rest of the men.

Finally, Prince Shep mounted and gave the orders that the attack would commence at midnight. The men entering from the east and the west would start their onslaught amongst the confusion of the distraction and the archers would cover the retreat unless they could get clear shots of the Rischiaks. As the respective groups called out to one another as they went their separate ways and started to ride out to their different destinations, Elaraine took the chance and made a break for it.

She wheeled Tix around and sprinted over to the end of the distraction group's column. It took a while for her friends to realize her change in column, but she heard them when they did. Orin and Nox called out to her, unable to reach her from their spots in the lines. Dayn tried to wheel his charger around, but the men behind him shouted to get back in formation and he was forced to continue on with the men he had assigned himself to.

"Elaraine!" she heard them yell over and over again. Orin told her to get back in his line, but she ignored him. She felt a tinge of guilt at her disobedience, but she was focused on doing her part. A hand grabbed her reins. She looked up and saw Prince Shep looking down at her.

"Why did you change columns, Elaraine?" he asked softly.

She hesitated before answering him. "I'm not any good at archery," she said humbly, "and I'll only get in the way of Orin and Dayn if I join their groups. They will worry about me too much and that will only endanger them. I think I'm small enough to slip into the camp undetected with this group and I can do the most good here."

He let go of her reins and smiled down at her. "In that case, I'd be more than happy for you to join us." She just looked at him as they started to catch up with the rest of the group. "I'm in charge of the distraction," he explained. "And I'll take care of you." He laughed at her worried expression before sobering suddenly. "Besides, if I don't make sure you come out of this all right Orin will have my head on a stake."

Chapter Ten

As they drew closer to the enemy's encampment, the men became more and more solemn. None of the men spoke, but no words needed to be said. From this point on, their success was going to be based almost purely on luck. The problem was, Elaraine had never had much luck. Orin did, and Nox certainly carried more than his fair share, but Elaraine was left with the dredge of the luck. She began to curse herself for choosing to go along with the distraction group.

"You nervous?" a gruff voice asked beside her.

She glanced over at the man who seemed to be Prince Shep's personal guard and nodded under his scrutinizing eyes. "Who wouldn't be?"

"I wasn't thrilled when I heard that a woman would be joining us on this little venture," he admitted. "But the stories your friends have told, I think, pretty much sealed your fate." He smiled warmly at her. "It looks like you're with us 'til the end!"

She smiled back. "I'm not sure yet if that's a good thing."

"Trust me," he said softly, nodding at Prince Shep's back, "with him with us, we'll be all right. He won't leave anyone behind."

"Why would anyone be left behind?"

He just looked at her patiently. "In battle, there isn't time to look after fallen comrades. You protect them while you can, but sometimes you have to leave them to save yourself. You can come after them when the battle is over, but too often it is too late to save them."

"So why bother staying with them to begin with? Why 'protect them while you can'? If I am here, I am one less distraction for them there."

A look of shock spread across his face. "If Orin fell, wouldn't you stay by him until you couldn't any longer?" She nodded. "The same is true for these men. They ride to battle with brothers, cousins, and neighbors. To every man is owed the livelihood of another. By riding with us, we have become your temporary brothers and friends and we all protect each other.

Our lives are interconnected for this time."

"I just don't understand why you would leave them, then."

"You'll learn, in time," Prince Shep spoke up in front of them.

His tone was soft and kind. His presence seemed to strengthen the men and his words seemed to give them hope. It had been true: because he was Shep, men came to the lake. It had not mattered if he was a prince or not because it was not a fact he broadcasted. They had come because he was a leader amongst men and he had earned their respect and drew their attention when he spoke. His dark auburn hair being caught by the wind every once in a while was enough to catch her attention. She blinked her eyes a couple of times.

"Probably just because he's someone new to look at," she whispered to herself, guiding Tix between a couple of saplings.

"I didn't catch that, sorry," Prince Shep said from beside her.

She jumped in her saddle at the shock of him riding right beside her. "I was just grumbling to myself," she admitted hastily, but unwilling to say anymore.

He just grinned at her. "You are truly a woman, Elaraine." He held up a hand to silence her when she opened her mouth to protest. "No, listen." She closed her mouth. "Now, that was not meant derogatorily. I meant it to say that you are hard-headed, warm-hearted, spirited, and a genuine thorn under more than one man's saddle." He frowned again at her glare. "I'm not explaining this too well, am I?"

She sighed and shook her head, returning her attention to Tix's path. "You are truly a man, Shep." She grinned back at him. "And that was meant derogatorily."

He laughed as he galloped back to the front of the line. "I would expect nothing less, Elaraine. I would expect nothing less."

She started to think about the events ahead. She was in a group of maybe a dozen men, one of whom was very distracting with his witticisms and inability to keep his mouth shut. She looked at him again. She mentally added his looks to that list of distractions. Shep's guard beside her had begun to try explaining how he foresaw the battle going. He seemed very hopeful.

"If you're this optimistic of victory," she asked at last, "then why did these villages not unite before and turn on the Rischiaks and drive them out?"

He thought for a moment. "I'm not sure, to tell you the truth. It seemed a few times that we might. But Shep always seemed to be waiting on something. He'd told me of a dream he'd had once in which these travelers came to save us all. He thought it a sign to wait for the travelers. He said we were waiting for an army from the capital, but he always talked about this dream, too." He looked sideways at her. "At least, that's my theory as to why we waited so long: he was waiting for your company."

She would think about that later. "You and Shep are close, eh?"

"I've seen him grow up from a tot. I taught him how to fight and I was told by his father to watch over him. It's been history ever since. I promised I'd never leave his side and I do not plan to."

"You're a good man."

"I try to be."

He patted her shoulder and they continued on in silence a little longer. Then Prince Shep held up his hand and made a motion for them all to dismount. Elaraine did not tie up Tix like the others were doing with their horses; she did not want him to be restrained if something went badly. She had traveled with him long enough between riding him herself and Moraiah riding him to know that he would not stray unless something bad happened nearby, and then he was as good as gone until he was called for.

The small troupe made as little noise as possible as they crept through the brush and bramble closer to where the voices and noises of the jollities of the Rischiak camp were coming from. Elaraine gripped her knife on her belt and the veteran that had ridden beside her motioned for her to put it away.

"We're only meant to distract," he whispered almost silently. "Do not be bothered with something already in your hands. It will be easy enough to grab when the time comes. You don't want to lose it during the distraction." He put his arm around her shoulder in a fatherly gesture and wiped the sweat from her brow. "Stick by me, missy. Stick by old Andell and I'll keep you safe."

"Andell, I've never been this scared in my life," she whispered back, despite a few glares from her comrades.

She could feel him shaking from silent laughter as he replied. "Neither have most of the fellows we're with, missy. It's natural. I'd be more worried if you had been this scared before."

She nodded and watched as Prince Shep began to act out with his hands what their distraction was going to be. From what she could gather, they would separate into pairs, take the campfire, and spread it to the shelters. Their long stay in this valley had meant that tents had become less desirable than a more stable shelter and buildings had been constructed in their place. She noticed the wood and smiled. The entire camp was made of wood. She forced the smile inward, feeling for the first time an assurance of victory.

Andell jabbed her in the ribs as he made his way to where they would begin their assault. He pulled her along like he was leading a cow to a field. He was acting like it was just another day for him. Why he had chosen to be her partner instead of being Prince Shep's puzzled her until she saw that Prince Shep did not need any partner.

He was built like a bear, tall and strong. He carried a shield that covered his body from his shoulder to his knee. He was the only man with a shield in the distraction group. She stared at the shield for a moment. It was beaten and battered, but the image on it was still as good as new. It had a picture of a wolf howling with an arrow going through the animal's snout. She watched as he smeared the metal with dirt to cover its shimmer in the firelight. He was tense as he knelt and the others crept closer to him. She knew why he did not need a partner: every man there was his partner. The men followed him as they would a king and she knew that these men would protect the prince until they drew their own final breaths.

Almost too inconspicuous to notice, Prince Shep gave a nod of his head, indicating that they were to commence the assault. Andell led Elaraine through a briar patch, tearing her heavy tunic in a couple places when it would snag on the thorns. She did not care for the small pricks she could feel all over her body, but the responsibility she felt to see her duties through pushed her onward.

It had been almost too easy for them to get into the camp unnoticed. A sentinel had had to be silenced, but a group to Elaraine's left had made short and easy work of that problem. Andell motioned to the nearest fire and drew his sword without the metal scraping against the scabbard. When she went to draw her sword, he stopped her and motioned that he would protect her while she took care of the fire.

She took a deep breath and crawled in the shadows to the crackling branches. She reached as far as she could until she grasped hold of a smoldering branch and crawled back to Andell with it, unnoticed by the nearby Rischiaks. She breathed deeply on it, spurring the embers back to life to a flame. Andell nodded his approval to her and pointed at the shelter they were next to. They braced themselves because they knew as soon as it was lit the camp would erupt into chaos with most of the Rischiaks heading directly towards them.

Before she could set the shelter on fire, yells and the clashing of steel sounded to their right. A shelter had gone up in flames. There was no time to lose, so Elaraine jabbed the branch at various places on the shelter to start a blaze. Andell was covering her back as he had promised when the Rischiaks discovered them.

His long sword swinging, Andell kept the swarming enemy at bay. Elaraine threw the branch back into the fire and pulled her own sword out. She was not as skilled as the men in her group and nowhere near as strong, but she suddenly felt a surge of power course through her veins. She did not wait for the first Rischiak to get within striking distance of her. Instead, she went back-to-back with the veteran soldier and began to hack through the bodies advancing on them.

Her first kill stunned her. She sliced right through his arm and still he fought on, his arm flopping to the ground like a fish. She had to cut his throat with the knife from her belt to finally bring him down. The gore of it all made her gag. She had not known what to expect, but it most certainly was not this. She had to stay focused, though, as more of the enemy were coming at her. Andell was yelling at her to go and find Shep, to start making their way to the southern end of the encampment. But Elaraine was so turned around she had no idea which way that was.

"Elaraine, go!" he yelled at her again.

She kicked a Rischiak foot soldier in the groin at the same time she gutted him. "I'm a little busy right now, Andell!"

He finished another soldier off with a thrown knife to the brain. "Listen to me! You have to get to Shep! It's no good here! There's too many!"

"Then we'll go together," she yelled back, gaining the first sight of some of the men they had come with fighting just as desperately. "I'm not leaving you!"

"You have to! I can take care of myself! But you have to get word to Shep that we can't hold out over here!"

"What happened to the optimism?" she grunted, trying to parry with both the enemy and Andell.

"It's changed into realism." He turned to her and finished the man she was fighting off. He kicked her in the butt and sent her sprawling to the ground. "So go!" He engaged another man. "I'll be right behind you!" he promised.

She nodded as she sprung to her feet and sprinted to where she thought the south of the camp was. She stopped to help one of the men from Shep's village with a giant of a Rischiak. She managed to knock the Rischiak to the ground and then she watched in disgust as the villager hacked the giant's head off and held it up by the hair for his comrades to see. Then she was off again, sprinting towards Prince Shep to deliver Andell's message. She glanced behind herself a couple of times and was reassured when she could see Andell slowly following her.

Her own sluggish pace was aggravating her. Everywhere she went, bodies were pushing against her, and fighting and swearing erupting all around her. She cringed a few times as she saw one of her allies fall to the ground, obviously fatal wounds gushing blood.

Up ahead, she could see Prince Shep. He was fighting back-to-back with Orin. Dayn was nowhere to be found. They were surrounded, and their situation looked grim. Some of the Rischiaks facing them were wielding flanged maces with deadly force. She cringed as a mace missed Prince Shep's head by a hair's breadth as he ducked just before it made contact.

Andell caught up with her. His size alone had helped him push people out of the way as he had made his way to Prince Shep. Elaraine was too small for that and had had to duck and weave for most of the short race to this spot. Also unlike Elaraine was his inability to just wait and watch for the result of Orin and Prince Shep's struggle. He raced headlong into the fray and stopped an axe from making contact with his beloved leader's head by grasping the axe handle and wrestling the Rischiak for control of it. Elaraine rushed to her brother's side and they fought side-by-side, working on the same enemy until he fell, and then they would move on to the next one.

Suddenly, the camp seemed to go silent. It was eerie, really. Like Elaraine was the only one living, or like she was looking at the scene from the outside. The Rischiaks immediately retreated behind a newcomer to the scene, this ugly behemoth wielding a broadsword he could handle with one hand and a battered and rusty shield. The large Rischiaks were a rare breed of man she had only heard tales of. They were the Schralls who were said to live in the mountains in western Rischiak. His leather tunic was marred with mud and blood and was torn in multiple places. His leggings were equally worse for the wear.

It was a scene from a nightmare. Prince Shep's followers went and stood behind him silently. Neither side made a rush at the other. Dayn came and found Orin, who was leading Elaraine away by the cuff of her tunic. He held Elaraine's face close to his chest. She could feel her brother's heart racing beneath his sweat-soaked tunic. Dayn stood in front of the siblings, his sword drawn and ready, as Prince Shep and the Schrall circled one another.

"Donnelly, you know you should not be camped here," Prince Shep growled as he shifted his weight yet again.

"We have every right to be here," Donnelly roared back, his voice echoing in the silence.

"Go back to Rischiak! Your presence won't be tolerated here anymore!" His shouts were becoming angrier by the second.

"And what do you propose to do about it?" Donnelly sneered. "So far all you and your men have done is circled around like bugs around a mule—irritating, but not threatening. So you lit a few fires? We can rebuild our camps."

"Besides having admitted to being animals, you are mistaken about what's going on here."

"Oh really?" the man laughed. "And what might I be wrong about?"

"You're going to leave. Tonight."

"And what makes you think that you can make me? We have taken a liking to this area. We're staying." He spat in Prince Shep's face.

Prince Shep did not back down. "Women settle arguments with words. They're smart."

"I prefer to settle it the hard way."

"Thus, my point is proven."

Putting words aside, the men crouched, their shields brought up to be ready. The wolf on Prince Shep's shield shone in the moonlight. Donnelly made the first swipe with his sword, but Prince Shep jumped back a few feet to avoid it. The Rischiak captain kept advancing as his men fell into an ill-formed arc behind him. Prince Shep's men followed their suit. The loosely made circle formed a boundary the two men kept pushing against in their struggle.

Donnelly lost his footing on a blood-soaked rock and fell to the ground. Prince Shep saw his chance and pounced, pulling a knife from his boot. Donnelly merely flicked him away like he would an insect. Prince Shep flopped onto the ground in a dusty roll. In the flash of an eye, he was back up, his own sword flashing in the firelight.

The Rischiak was breathing heavily, unused to such prolonged close combat. Prince Shep, on the other hand, was tired from having to battle such a monstrous man. He was on the offensive now, however, and he refused to let Donnelly get the upper hand again. He kept beating the man further and further back into the ring of waiting Swennians.

Orin pushed Elaraine behind him toward the shelter of the trees. She did not understand the reason for his urgent prodding, but she knew he wanted her to get back toward Nox and the other archers. Dayn noticed her reluctance and pushed her away, impatient with Orin's gentle urging.

"Elaraine, go!" Orin hissed. "You don't want to be here for this next part."

"I've been here for the rest of the battle," she hissed back. "Why should I not be here for the end?"

Orin groaned. "Please, Elaraine. I've allowed you to come this far! Just humor your brother just this once?"

Elaraine barely heard him. Her attention had been drawn once again to the two men struggling for their lives in the center of the ring. They were grappling on the ground, both too tired to hold up their swords and shields any longer. She felt herself tense up when Prince Shep was flipped onto his back, but she let out the breath she was holding when he pulled another knife out and held it up to Donnelly's neck. Both sides were merging on the pair, the air growing even tenser as neither group knew quite what to do. The only sounds were the sounds of Prince Shep's and Donnelly's punches and their grunts as hits made contact.

"Elaraine, this is not going to be good. It's no place for a person new to battle like you!" Orin was trying to move her again, not taking his eyes from the Rischiaks across from them.

"With that argument, then if I have to go, Dayn should have to go, too," she countered, feeling like she was being treated like a child more and more every minute.

"This isn't the time to argue with me," Orin growled, giving up on his good-brother demeanor. "Now go!" he yelled as he shoved her roughly away from himself toward the trees.

She cowered from him. She had not been afraid of the battle. Disgusted, tense, stressed— all of these she had felt during the battle, but not afraid. She had always been afraid of Orin when he struck that tone with her. She turned her back on the crowd to go to Nox like Orin wanted her to when she heard a general uproar of the men around her. She spun on her heel to see a Rischiak trying to sneak up on Prince Shep with a knife in his hand. Prince Shep was oblivious to his new attacker, as he was still concerned with Donnelly. Without thinking, Elaraine rushed past Orin and through the throng of Swennians to the Rischiak and pinned him to the ground. He spat in her face and cursed her.

She ground out as she wiped her face in disgust, "At least I've proven I'm no coward! Sneaking up on a man like that is not being a man!"

Suddenly, behind her, Andell began to scream. Elaraine turned to see what was happening when she felt the man's knife enter her side. She groaned and rolled from on top of him. She closed her eyes and let her consciousness fade from the world around her.

"My prince!" Andell was yelling as her eyes closed. "Prince Shep!

Please, don't leave me now!"

Chapter Eleven

Elaraine was slow in coming around back to consciousness. Her stomach was throbbing and hurt her acutely, but she had endured intense pain when she had broken her ribs, so she had only momentary qualms about moving about with a knife wound. After all, she had had a knife wound before and it had not been as bad as she had thought it would have been. There was a slit of sunshine coming in her tent through the tent flap, but it was pretty dim. Elaraine guessed it was either overcast or just beginning to dawn.

Orin was lying on a bedroll near hers. He had an arm flung across his chest, the other resting on her hair. She could not help but smile at this older brother of hers. He looked worried, even in his sleep. But, at the same time, it was the only time he was ever peaceful and not moving around. He was an old man in a young body and everybody knew it if they knew him.

She could feel the compress knotted tightly around her stomach. It was too tight, but she deserved the pain after forgetting about the knife that man was holding. She mentally kicked herself for interfering. She should have listened to Orin when he had told her to leave. It was a fight that was supposed to have been between Donnelly and Prince Shep, but at the same time she knew that the other man was interfering just as much as she was, if not more.

She reached down and felt the cloth under her fingertips. It was wet and sticky. She sighed as she tried to sit up, but her stirring woke up someone behind her and she was pushed back down. She looked up to see Prince Shep looming over her, his eyes searing holes into her soul.

"You're not supposed to move," he whispered down to her.

"I just want to sit up," she countered. "I need to change the compress."

"Then let someone else do it. Your brother would kill me if he found out I'd let you move around at all."

"He would never have to find out," she groaned softly, trying to maneuver out from under his hand. "He's dead to the world right now."

"He only went to sleep because I said I'd keep an eye on you. I'm going to be true to my word, and you're going to stay put. You can be a pain in his neck, but please don't be one in mine." He smiled down at her. "The healers would skin the three of us alive if they found out that I was here watching you and you were moving about."

She gave up her struggles, too worn out to argue. "Fine. I give up."

He frowned. "You're too old to pout, Elaraine."

She cocked an eyebrow up at him. "I am neither geriatric nor senile yet, Prince Shep, so I'm not sure what you're meaning by 'old,' here."

He recoiled with a smile. "Uh oh. Would it be safer for me if I left the tent?" he joked. "Dayn was the last one to get in trouble this way. I hear Moraiah was quite ornery when we left," he said, settling back down. "What happened?"

Elaraine noticed his leg was heavily bandaged. She nodded to it. "Are you all right?"

He shrugged, absentmindedly picking at the material covering his calf. "I've had worse and I'll have worse. The healers were just overly concerned and I didn't feel much like arguing with them. Ironically, I like to avoid conflict."

"You were passed out, Prince Shep," Dayn joked quietly from the tent flap. "You wouldn't have been able to do much arguing unless you're equally persuasive when you are out cold."

Elaraine noticed with amusement that Prince Shep was glaring at her friend. She just closed her eyes and smiled as the two men started to bicker. She closed her eyes and listened to them. She might be too old to pout, but she knew the two of them were too old to fight like children.

"Why are you smiling?" Nox asked her, interrupting the two men. "They should be reprimanded, not encouraged!"

She opened an eye and looked at him. "It's not like they're using fists, Nox. Let the two fight it out this way and we'll have peace."

"We're not bickering!" the two men yelled at the same time.

Elaraine glared at them and pointed at her brother. "If you two wake him up, I swear the two of you will never rest in peace again." They quieted at her half-hearted threat. "So, when do we head back to the village? Moraiah and Josi must be getting worried about Orin."

Dayn knelt beside her and Prince Shep sat back down. Nox just rolled his eyes and stomped out of the tent. Elaraine watched him go with a strong urge to kick his retreating rear end the next time she saw it. Dayn called her attention back to himself by clearing his throat.

"Elaraine, we're not going back to the village. Prince Shep sent word to Moraiah and Josi to meet us at the capital," he whispered gently, trying not to wake Orin.

"Why the capital?" she asked, feeling herself getting nervous. She gave Dayn a searching look.

"Prince Shep needs the villagers to join his brother's forces to the south. The Rischiak queen has sent the Rischiaks over the border there and the Swennian army is getting overrun."

"Then why not go straight there if it's so urgent?"

"Because my father has called me back for a short time," Prince Shep said, speaking up. "It won't be for more than a day or two."

"Is he unwell?"

Prince Shep looked at her for a moment, thinking over his words carefully. He and Dayn exchanged glances. "You could say that," he said at last.

"Then do what you need to do. Family comes first," she yawned, and felt Orin stretch as he shifted in his sleep. "Why don't we head on to the southern border, then, and you meet up with us later?"

"Because, Elaraine, he's our leader." Dayn said firmly. "We can't abandon him."

"It's not abandonment," she pointed out. "He would be joining us later."

Dayn looked down at her evenly. "Prince Shep has asked the king for an audience to tell him about Donnelly."

"Of what importance is Donnelly?"

Shep cleared his throat softly before he answered her. "He's the Rischiak queen's younger brother. His being here means that there's more going on in this war than anyone originally thought. The king needs to know about Donnelly before my brother can lead a proper attack to the south. If there is more going on with this invasion, like I think there is, we need to discuss how to best protect Swennia."

"I can't go to the capital," Elaraine whispered up at Prince Shep.

"I won't let anything happen to you," the prince whispered down to her and patted her head soothingly.

"You can't stop them," she whispered back.

The prince just smiled at her and touched a finger to his lips as Dayn started arguing for going to the capital. Elaraine just nodded as the two men continued to talk about why they had to go to the capital. All she could think about was that the capital was where the royal family was— the family that would want retribution for the killing of Dalun Shrevelt. She had not thought of Prince Shep as a danger to their freedom because Orin trusted him and he had not mentioned Dalun. But the capital was another matter entirely. Did the men not realize that this was probably the most dangerous place for them right now? She would rehash the entire battle with the Rischiaks before willingly agreeing to go to the capital. Finally, she just closed her eyes and tuned them out. She realized that there was nothing she could do right now. She needed the healers for her wound and she did not have the energy to just leave on her own. She would have to trust in Orin's decision on whether they would ultimately go to the capital or not.

"I think she's getting tired again," Prince Shep whispered to Dayn. "Let's leave her alone. I need to tell the healers she woke up, anyway."

The two men walked out, leaving Elaraine to work out the situation in the silence. It felt like hours before the healers came in, but it could not have been that long. They examined her wound and rewrapped it. They told her that it could have been a lot worse, that had it been thrust into her a few inches higher, or if her brother had not gotten her to the healer so quickly, there would not have been anything they could have done for her. They rubbed an herbal mix on her wound that stung at first, but then it completely numbed her side. She just nodded and thanked them for their help.

"Stop worrying," Orin ground out beside her, surprising her out of her thoughts. "Prince Shep will keep us safe; you can trust in that."

"How can you be sure?"

Orin rubbed his eyes and thought for a moment. "I fought with his older brother in the last war. Prince Shep is a better man than his brother and has a lot more heart. I trusted his brother implicitly until... well, Prince Shep saved my life early on after I met him. After that war, I know I would follow Prince Shep over his brother. Does that tell you how much I trust him with our lives?"

"But we're going to the capital?" she nearly squeaked. "If they find out what I did—"

"They know what you've done. Prince Shep knew from the outset. He didn't say anything because it's not his place. Dalun was his cousin, but he knew his tendencies."

"But Dalun was the king's cousin!" she nearly yelled. "So naturally he's going to get angry! We're talking about family here!"

Orin just looked at her for a moment. "You don't remember, do you?"

She just looked at him. "What am I forgetting?"

He just shook his head. "When they were here, you weren't just feigning ignorance?"

She sighed and adjusted her compress under her heavy tunic. "You're being very evasive, Orin."

He just shook his head incredulously. "I'm not meaning to be. It just amazes me that you can forget something like that."

"So tell me now." She could feel herself becoming aggravated very quickly with this conversation.

He frowned and shook his head. "No, it's not my place to tell you another person's secret." He put a hand over her mouth to cover her protestations. "Prince Shep will tell you in time if he chooses to. Suffice it to say that he holds no love for Dalun. There is no love lost between him and the rest of his family." He slowly removed his hand.

"Is something wrong with him?"

He laughed. "A lot of people would argue that there are a lot of things wrong with him, but no; everything is just fine as far as he is concerned. He just prefers his status to be kept a secret."

They just lay there in silence for a few moments. Elaraine was trying to figure out a way to get from the tent so she could get some fresh air while Orin was trying to sort out his thoughts. They both refused to look at the other until their thoughts were sorted out.

With the sound of a man passing the tent, Elaraine turned over to face Orin. "What if the rest of the royal family finds out that I am the cause of Dalun's murder?" Elaraine asked at last, giving up on moving around idea on the basis that she did not want to get caught and be made to walk back to the tent in shame, or, even worse, be carried back.

He blinked a couple of times, coming out of his own thoughts. "Elaraine, Prince Shep is going to do everything he possibly can to keep us safe. You can trust him. The rest of us sure do." He paused. "He's given me his word to help us, partly because of what you did with that Rischiak sneaking up on him. I trust him with our lives to do right by his word."

"But the rest of you did not murder a royal!" she rasped, losing her voice from all the stress. "I am not automatically given immunity just because the prince has promised to keep our group safe! He is obviously not in good standing with his father if he was in that small village as the village leader!"

"He will keep you safe." He seemed adamant, making Elaraine lose some of her distress.

"He owes me nothing to warrant such a favor."

"You saved his life at the battle. To him, you are the most noble of people and deserve a second chance. To him, you are the ultimate friend. You risked your life to save his."

"How do you know that? He could just have been being polite to you so you could finally get some sleep."

He shook his head at her. "Elaraine, he knows me because after the last war I went with his brother to the court and I guarantee you that the royal family is more amiable than the public hears about."

"We both know that if Prince Shep fails at protecting me, my life is forfeit."

He tucked a lock of hair behind her ear. "Of course it's not!" he laughed. "Red tunics would do nothing for your complexion!" He hastily added, "At least, that's what Moraiah would say!"

"I do not think I would be condemned long enough before my death to be given the red tunic, Orin!" She eyed him from the corner of her eye. "Are you sure he can keep his promise?" Orin nodded gravely, so she finally sighed and resolved herself to this new twist of fate. "Then, fine. I will trust you. And I will trust Prince Shep, too. To the capital city we go."

He sat up and patted her leg. "I'm going to go and get us something to eat." He stood up and straightened his tunic and leggings. "Will you be all right and stay still until I get back?"

She was nodding when a shadow blocked the meager sunlight coming in from the tent flap. Prince Shep was leaning against one of the posts, his arms across his broad chest.

"Do you mind if I speak with Elaraine by myself?" he asked Orin.

Orin waved in her direction as he headed from the tent. "She's lying right there," he said happily. "Ask her if she wants to talk with you for yourself."

With that, he was gone, leaving the other two in an awkward silence. Finally, Elaraine could not take it any longer. She fidgeted with her bed sheets and looked up at him. He was still leaning against the post.

"You wanted to speak with me?" she prompted.

He nodded and walked over to a seat behind her. "We need to clear the air, you and I."

"Of what?" she asked, trying to fake nonchalance.

He stretched his leg out in front of him. "I know what you did," he said without any pomp or hesitation.

"What I did when?" She felt her chest constricting with the stress of this conversation. Her palms and forehead were cold, but the beads of sweat were still forming. One rolled down her temple until it landed on the bed roll below her.

"You killed Dalun Shrevelt. You killed the prison keeper when Nox and Orin were helping you to escape. I know what you did."

"I—"

He held up a hand to stop her. "Let me finish, please." He took a deep breath and looked deeply in her eyes. "I'm finding this difficult. Duty is telling me to find you at fault for everything: to condemn you for what you've done. But all I see before me is a young woman who risked her life for mine. You fought bravely. And you were willing to come to the villagers' aid without knowing any of them, and that shows some character, too."

"Everyone fought bravely," she said nervously. This man now held the key to her future, be it freedom or condemnation.

"Andell said that you fought more courageously and with more heart than most of the men he's seen in battle. He said he had to force you to leave his side to find me," he continued as if he had not heard her. He looked at her, a pleading look clear in his eyes. "Elaraine, I just need to know why you killed Dalun Shrevelt," he nearly whined. "I need to know why it is I have to hand you over to the king when we get to the capital. I want to hear it from you."

"Why do you need to hand me over? I thought you were going to help me," she asked, feeling bile race to her throat at the thought of palace guards taking her to the royal dungeon. For some reason, that filled her with more terror than being taken to the Dungeons Ussal.

"I am going to help," he sounded resigned. "But I need to know why I have to do this at all. I need to know why a man is dead and now the entire royal family is out for vengeance."

She just looked at him. She chose her words carefully and watched his reaction to every syllable. "It was a situation that got out of hand. He threatened Moraiah and me and no one was stepping in to help us. I did the only thing I could at the time. It was completely self-defense."

"Was there not a man there to stop him?"

She hesitated. "They did not come to our aid." She wiped the sweat from her brow. "What would you have had me do instead?"

He just sighed and wrung his hands. "I would prefer that you had not killed him." His eyes got a distant look in them. "Dalun did not use to be such a low life. He used to be a good man: fair and just." He looked down at her but did not see her. "We were friends in our childhood, you know. He was my only friend when I first went to the palace. No one really knows why he turned so mean and ugly." He laughed wryly. "We all knew it was only a matter of time until someone killed him. But who would have guessed that I would be speaking to the killer like this? That it is you makes all of this more difficult for me to handle, Elaraine Hedri." He touched her shoulder, like he was trying to make sure she was real. "I don't blame you, given the situation, but others do."

She was finding it difficult to speak. She had to clear her throat a few times to be able to formulate the words. "Orin said you promised to do what you could."

He nodded, snapping back to the situation at hand. "And I plan on fully keeping my word to him. I can only do so much, though. I'm not sure how effective my protection will be, ultimately. I do not like it right now, but it is my duty to tell the royal family that I have the person who killed our cousin in my ragtag army. I do not get to decide what happens after I give my report. That is up to the king. But I will tell him you saved my life and that may help you."

"What can you do?"

"I'm not sure, really. Maybe talk some sense to the king and my brother, like I said, but who knows if they'll listen or just turn me away like they've done to so many others?"

"It's dangerous for me to go to the capital," she nearly whispered. "Is there no other way around this? I could stay in the woods around the capital until you leave to join the border forces and then I'll join Orin, Dayn, and Nox?"

He shook his head. "You need to go and plead your case so that this will be done and over with. You shouldn't have to keep running like this." He eyed her suspiciously. "I do not condone what you did. I have accepted it and I have moved on. But that doesn't mean that the rest of the family will do so."

"What do you think you can do? You are just a man, too. Your talking to the king and Prince Arlun would probably have the same effect that Orin talking to them would have with the way you are talking. How can I trust that I will come out of the capital alive?"

They became quiet, studying one another. A bird was singing nearby and a man was singing boisterously from down the camp a ways. Elaraine could hear Orin's laugh near the tent, and that gave her comfort. But Prince Shep's nervous fidgeting made her nervous. He would tap his knee with one hand and bite the nails of the other while in the next moment he would clear his throat and look down at her. His fidgets became bigger and longer in duration as the time went on. Finally, he stood and walked to the tent flap. He looked outside and when he was certain no one would be able to hear him except Elaraine, he knelt on a knee at her side.

He looked away and then back down at her again, like a horse ready to bolt away. "Elaraine, I'm one of the king's closest advisors." He hesitated for a moment. "Andell already told the rest of the men, that I'm a prince, but only you, Orin, and Andell will know my biggest secret." He leaned down and whispered in her ear, "I'm really the king's son, Prince Shep. But what no one but Orin and Andell knows is that I was not a wanted prince, so you may be right that Orin may do as much good as I in this matter. I grew up in the village you found me with my mother until Prince Arlun, my half-brother, fell ill when I was five. Then my father sent for me, thinking he may need a new heir. Prince Arlun survived, so my father groomed me to be a military commander when I showed promise in fighting. With that, I became my father's advisor. I may be the unwanted son of the king, but I am your only hope at this point."

Then he stood hastily and walked unsteadily out of the door, nearly bowling Orin down in his retreat from the tent. Orin rushed in, still balancing the bowls of stew. He set them down and snapped his fingers in front of her face a few times.

"Elaraine?" he sounded scared. "Elaraine, speak to me! Are you all right? Do you need the healers?"

"He's really the fabled prince. Prince Shep is the fabled prince. And I have to trust in him to protect me when he doesn't even know if he can protect me," is all she managed to say before they heard the distinct sound of steel clashing upon steel.

Chapter Twelve

Orin rushed out of the tent with the first metallic clang of the fight that they heard. He stayed outside for a few moments before he came racing back inside and threw the small area apart looking for his sword. Elaraine just watched him search at first but grew concerned as he became more frustrated and frantic.

"What's going on, Orin?" she ground out as she grabbed his leg in mid-stride.

He noticed a glint of shining metal on the floor and muttered under his breath as he picked up his sword. He looked down at her, his leg still in the air. "Don't worry, it's not the Rischiaks. The men are bickering amongst themselves." He tried shaking his leg from her grasp. It did not work. He sighed. "From what someone told me, half the men want to go back to their families, which is understandable. The other half wants to go to battle for blood and glory and all that accompanies war, which is also understandable." He looked at her like she should understand. She refused to let his leg loose. "Elaraine, they might start killing each other out there over something that is only Prince Shep's right and responsibility to decide about! Now let go of me so I can go out there and help them settle the camp down! The prince is out there on his hurt leg and needs help!"

He began to back away toward the tent flap, shaking his leg as he went. Finally, she let him go and he toppled over backwards and out the tent flap, his sword grasped tightly in his hand. She could hear him curse and grumble loudly as he picked himself up. He poked his head back in the tent flap and glared at her.

"Don't you think that that was more than slightly juvenile?" he hissed, embarrassed.

"No more than you trying to keep things from me," she retorted.

"It was no secret that the men are fighting!" he yelled.

"I was talking about Prince Shep and you know it! As we went to that village and I was all scared about being killed for killing Dalun, you could have told me we were headed for a village that was led by a prince!" she yelled back. "Don't you think that that was a slightly important detail to keep from me? And why are you still standing there? Isn't there a fight to break up?"

He nodded and turned to go. "We'll talk later," she heard him mutter back at her as he strode away.

She crossed her arms over her chest and stuck her tongue out at his back. "Oh, sure! Now he wants to talk! Now he wants to tell me that Prince Shep is a stupid prince who knew about me the whole time!"

Prince Shep stuck his head in the tent flap on his way to separate the fighting parties. "Now, I really must protest, Elaraine! I am not all stupid! A little dense every now and then, but I am certainly not stupid!"

Her mouth dropped open in surprise at having been heard. She began to sputter curses as he walked away from the tent laughing. She put her arms over her face to calm down and forget that he had ever caught her saying something so impertinent. She did not hear the person enter her tent. She did not know they were even there until cold fingers wrapped themselves around her wrists and pried her arms away so they could peer into her face. She was looking into a beautiful face from her recent past.

"Ranci?" she choked out. "What are you doing here?"

Ranci just settled onto the ground beside her, obviously not caring if she got dirt all over her beautiful pale blue tunic. Her long legs folded under her easily as she just sat there looking down at Elaraine, an unreadable expression on her face.

"After all the stories I've heard tonight about you," she started softly, "the last thing I expected to find when I came in here was you hiding your little, blushing face. From what I have heard, you have finally found your self-confidence." Elaraine just gawked at her. Ranci sighed. "With Dayn leaving for battle, did you really think I would let him go without giving him a proper send off? A short, scribbled note on the table explaining himself is less than I deserve."

"He left because you wouldn't give him the freedom at home," Elaraine finally sputtered, forgetting momentarily to keep her thoughts solely to herself where Ranci was concerned. "What makes you think he would want you here now that he's finally on his own?"

Ranci frowned down at her and snapped at her. "Are you really going to speak to me like that after I took you in?" She sighed and rubbed her temples. "Well, I suppose you are right. He just walked away when he saw me in camp a few moments ago. But, I lied." Elaraine just cocked an eyebrow at her, not really surprised at this point. "The king asked me to come here to help Prince Shep." Elaraine just nodded, not knowing what else to say or do anymore. "You're not going to ask me why?"

Elaraine sighed. "Ranci, over the course of the past day, I have fought in my first real battle, I found out that I was fighting for a prince, who is, incidentally, the relative of Dalun Shrevelt, I found out that I am headed for the capital where I am perhaps going to be killed for killing Dalun, and then you show up without any pretense. Trust me when I say that you are the least of the surprises this day has offered. So while I may have questions concerning why the king has sent you here, I will not ask those questions because of the fear of getting even more surprises, which I have found too often accompany your presence."

Ranci nodded. "I can understand that. Honestly, I was surprised to see you and your brother here. I thought everyone but Dayn would already be across Swennian borders. Orin knew Prince Shep was the village leader and I did not think he would go within ten leagues of anywhere a member of the royal family resided."

It was not the first time that Ranci's breadth of knowledge astounded Elaraine. "We heard the villages here needed help against the Rischiaks. We thought we could redeem ourselves." Elaraine yawned. "I'm sorry, Ranci. I'm not trying to be rude, but this has been a rather long, hard day."

Ranci laughed sweetly and stood up. "Well, that doesn't shock me. After all, it's not every day that you find out that the family you hurt is the very one you are now sworn to protect. And you keep getting wounded! Honestly, how do you keep getting stabbed when you don't even fight that often! Your ribs are barely healed and here you are all wrapped up again."

"I didn't vow any allegiance to anyone but Orin." Elaraine chose to ignore Ranci's snide remarks about her injuries.

"You rode into battle with Prince Shep, didn't you? You chose his group over the others and even abandoned another group for his. That makes you a member of his legion." She smoothed out her tunic. "If you hadn't run from Orin's group, your allegiance would still be solely for your brother." She eyed the young woman sternly. "But you never were one to listen and do as you were told, were you?"

"What can I say? These days I find myself being a rebel." She tried to smile at Ranci to ease the new tension in the air but felt sad more than anything else. She knew Dayn would not take kindly to his overprotective mother being here. He had left home to leave her influence. Elaraine dreaded spending time with the two of them together again. "I hate to ask you to leave, but—"

Ranci held her hand up. "I need to go see what's going on in the camp anyway. Men can be so utterly stupid when it comes to their over-blown egos and misplaced opinions. I'll send Orin in when he's done bashing heads together."

She smiled warmly over her shoulder at Elaraine as she left. Elaraine sighed and closed her eyes, girding herself for the trip to the capital. The herbs did not keep her numb for as long as she would have liked, but her side was hurting less and less as the day wore on. It still ached when she moved, but she was not doing too much of that. A healer came and rubbed a new salve similar to the one Moraiah had used a few weeks ago on her wound, and Elaraine could see the wound already making progress healing. Soon after the healer left, a throat was cleared outside the tent flap. Without looking up, she called for whoever it was to enter. Heavy steps made their way to her side and sat down in the space the healer had vacated soon before.

Andell laid a hand on her shoulder. "The men are nearly settled down. Nox and Dayn are taking care of finishing it. Prince Shep and Orin want you to come and meet with them. Ranci says you have a lot to contribute to their conversation. I was ordered to carry you to them so you don't strain yourself too much. Now, I can help you get there, but I hear you have your pride. Do you think you can walk?"

She looked up at him and gave him a wry smile. "Slowly."

He smiled. "You are stronger than you look, Elaraine. A lot of men would refuse to move so soon after a wound like yours."

"Most men wouldn't have just blindly rushed a man with a knife without a plan," she smiled back. "And if they have, I think it's best that nobody knows about it so they still seem mildly intelligent."

He laughed as he picked her up. He set her gently on her feet and kept a supporting arm around her shoulders so he would be ready to help her if she needed it but gave her the space she needed to walk on her own. They limped slowly to the small fire Prince Shep, Orin, and Ranci were sitting around on the near edge of the camp. Andell helped her sit down next to Orin and took his seat next to her. Men were still fighting around them, but by this time it was primarily shouting at each other as Nox and Dayn were standing between the two groups with their own swords drawn and ready. But those already around the fire paid the ruckus no mind.

"How are you feeling?" Orin asked.

Elaraine saw a bruise forming on his temple. "I think I should be asking you the same thing there." She tapped the bruise lightly. "Did you let someone with a rock fist hit you? It's huge!"

Orin winced at her touch. "Of course not! A man hit me? Don't be silly!"

Prince Shep grinned up at them as he poked the fire with a stick and played absentmindedly with the wrappings on his leg. "Of course it wasn't a man," he laughed, "because he was too busy fighting a tree!"

"He ran right into it!" Andell joined in, slapping his knee in glee. "One minute he was going for the men fighting and the next thing we know, he's on his back on the ground by a tree."

Orin grimaced and looked away from them in a huff. "Can we please stop embarrassing me in front of my sister and continue with our discussion?"

Prince Shep studied her for a minute, narrowing his gaze slightly in thought, making her uncomfortable under the intense gaze. "You remind me of someone..." he began.

"That's not important right now, Prince," Orin hastily butted in, to everyone's surprise.

Everyone was quiet for a few minutes after Orin's small outburst. Elaraine tried to not fidget as she was apt to do in such awkward silences and was more than thankful when Ranci took mercy upon them all and broke it.

Ranci shifted her weight and adjusted her tunic. "Perhaps it would first be prudent to elucidate some things still hanging in the air." She arched an eyebrow at Orin and the prince. "Perhaps like how you two know each other so well?"

"Well, that's not a secret," Prince Shep said, slightly taken aback. "Orin fought in the last war with my older brother and I met Orin when he came back to the capital to be recognized with some award or another in the middle of the war. He had saved my brother's life a couple of times in the war. He served under me, too, though I did not know it until he came to the capital, when my brother had to leave the war. We traveled together a bit after the war and I visited him once in Gegernen. I recognized Orin when he came into the village and did not really feel the need for it to be brought up. What is the importance of our prior knowledge of each other?"

Elaraine nodded. "It still would have been nice to have known. I mean, our lives are literally in your hands, and it would be nice to know how much you know about us and how much history can be relied upon."

"I didn't know you were his sister, but it makes sense now. You are both beyond stubborn, inquisitive, and brave to a fault," Prince Shep continued good-naturedly. "I know what you did to my cousin, not that I blame you, and I know what the men who came with you did to break you out of prison and hide you. I know that Ranci gave you a haven when your own family wouldn't or couldn't. Despite what you may think, the royal family has messengers and ways of quickly knowing anything important all over Swennia." He looked at Ranci. "And, furthermore, I know that we are losing precious time discussing things that could be discussed later."

Dayn and Nox came in and sat down heavily next to Elaraine when Andell moved over to make room for them. Nox dropped his sword to the ground and sighed. Dayn just tried to get his laborious breathing under control. Both stunk with their perspiration.

"Are the men settled down now?" Orin asked them after a minute.

"For now," Nox said dejectedly. "I just don't know how to get through to them. We tried talking to them, we did, but it didn't work. Their heads are too thick and stubborn!"

"We talked until we were blue in the face, but their ears must not have holes to let sounds other than their own voices in," Dayn added softly.

"They just didn't understand until we crossed swords with them and beat them into submission. We didn't hurt anybody, but they are in their tents now tending the wounds to their pride."

"It's not going to last for long," Dayn hung his head. "So in the meantime, let's try to get this talk over with."

"Son, it is not polite to not look at the person you're talking to," Ranci scolded.

Dayn glared at her and ground his teeth. "Let's just finish this meeting before I have to go and break up more fights, Mother."

Prince Shep looked between them amusedly, but he took the hint and began to lay out the plan. "We're going to ride to the capital city. Orin, Elaraine, and Nox are going to be riding in the wagon to feign being wounded so that my father will not see them and recognize them until we are within the palace grounds. I need to tell him that I found you, though, because I will not break the law. That shouldn't be any trouble for Orin or Elaraine. I will just say that I was unable to capture you." He looked sideways at Orin. "It's not a complete lie, you know." Orin nodded. "They will not check the wounded too closely and they may not even notice that I have two Hedris in my company. Anyway, as soon as I give my full report, I will pack the troops up and we will leave to wherever we are sent, probably back to the Swennian-Rischiak border. We just need to hope we are lucky enough that you all avoid detection."

"What about that village where the parents killed the children?" Elaraine asked timidly. "Are we going to run across more of those?"

Prince Shep shook his head but did not convince her of his assurance. "Hopefully, those villagers will have been spreading the word that I will not stand for that kind of behavior and anyone who has done it will be severely punished."

They all heard the clashing of swords and they all looked in the southerly direction of the camp. Everyone except Elaraine jumped to their feet at the noise. Dayn and Nox cursed as they stood up, wiping the sweat from their palms on their leggings and Nox collecting his sword before they wearily headed off to take care of the fighting once again. The rest of them settled back down on their seats and continued their discussion.

"What happens after we leave the capital?" Elaraine asked. "I mean, you say we'll probably be sent back to the border but what happens to us?"

Prince Shep thought for a minute. "Andell is, naturally, my second in command, but I would like Orin to be in command after him. Dayn and Nox did fine where they were and you, Elaraine, you I have problems placing."

"But we are to go with you?" Her heart dropped and soared at the same time. It soared because he saw them alive and it dropped because being in his army did not necessarily mean their freedom.

"But of course!" he laughed. "I mean, we need you, you need us, and at some point you need to pay for killing Dalun Shrevelt. What better way than serving on the front lines where you very well may die anyway?" He put a hand up to stop Orin from interrupting. "I am not saying that my cousin did not deserve how he met his demise. What I am saying is that he was killed and that is a debt that needs to be paid. It was still a crime. I don't like our options here anymore than you do."

Elaraine nodded gravely. "I understand."

Prince Shep nodded in return and stood as the shouts of the renewed fight drew closer. He got to his feet with a groan. "Orin, Andell, I think we need to intervene here. It sounds like Nox and Dayn need a little help." The other two men nodded and stood beside the prince. Prince Shep looked down at Ranci and Elaraine. "Ladies, stay here. We still need to polish our plans and place Elaraine into the troops somewhere when we return."

The two women nodded, settling down in their seats with small sighs of resignation. Elaraine just stared at the older woman while they were alone, wondering how in the world Ranci still managed to look so young, putting her magical powers aside. Ranci met her stare and returned it in kind.

"Prince Shep is a kind young man," Ranci finally offered, tearing her gaze away from the other woman's. "And he has always been honest. Believe me when I say that when he promises not to tell your secret of hiding in the wagon after you murdered Shrevelt, he will uphold that promise to the utmost of his abilities. He still owes his family the truth in that he saw you." Elaraine just nodded absently. "You want to know why I'm here, don't you?" Elaraine just nodded again. "Well, aside from wanting to see my son, the king summoned me and sent me here to lend an ear to the prince and offer him my advice." She smiled. "As it turns out, he sees the worth of my powers." Elaraine just nodded. "Are you not going to say anything at all?" Ranci asked incredulously.

Elaraine sighed and lowered her gaze as well. "I never got the chance to thank you for taking me in."

Ranci blushed in her mock embarrassment. "Don't mention it." She cocked an eyebrow at the younger woman. "Would you not have done the same thing for me had it been Dayn or I in your position?"

Elaraine thought about that for a minute and then frowned. "I honestly have no idea. Now I would say 'yes' without a question, but back then I am sure I would have had a lot more questions to ask past 'what is your name?'"

Ranci smiled. "It's the only question that made sense at the time. We all already knew what you'd done in Gegernen, so that was just kind of a waste of breath. We had been expecting you to come onto our mountain. Plus, emotionally unattached women are so rare on our mountain, we knew your husband left you, and I do have a single son to think about. There's only so many women I can turn away. A mother in my position cannot be too picky in who she lets into her family's life if she ever wants to have grandchildren."

The fight was crashing closer and closer to them. The three men returned to await the fight's imminent arrival to where they were. Orin and Prince Shep were looking over their shoulders at the brawlers and began speaking to each other in undertones. Elaraine cringed as she laughed too hard at what Ranci had said and Andell was there holding her shoulder as she tried to regain her breath.

"Are we almost done?" Elaraine asked the man softly. "I know Prince Shep said we needed to discuss more things, but I'm ready to rest some more."

Andell patted her back and leaned toward his prince. "Prince Shep, she's fading fast. Are we about done, sir?"

The prince threw a glance her way just as a jumble of men poured into where they were sitting. Two men were tumbling in the dirt. Andell grabbed Elaraine as she jumped up and tried to scramble away from the fight. Elaraine recognized Nox as one of the brawlers in her rush. His nose was bleeding, but he seemed to have the upper hand in the fight. She was ready to back away even more from the brawl but she was unable to look away.

A clanging rang in her ears as she fell hard to the ground. She hit the dirt and saw a beetle scurrying along out of the way of her body. The next thing she knew, a man landed on top of her and Andell was pulling him off. White hot pain shot throughout her body. Everyone went suddenly still.

"I'm sorry about that, Elaraine. I thought the bugger would fall backwards. Most do." He was restraining the man who had hit her.

She coughed and stood back up with the help of Prince Shep. She clutched her stab wound with a hand and when she pulled her hand away there was thankfully no blood there. The other men had grown absolutely silent. Orin was dusting her off and wanting to haul her back to the tent. She kept assuring him that she was all right and not any worse off than she had been before.

Ranci was furious. "Prince Shep! Justice must be wrought for this insubordination!" She waggled her finger at the man standing limp in Andell's grasp. "There's no use in denying it! You hit her when she was unaware and wasn't engaged in the fight!"

The prince cocked his head at her. "Who said there wasn't going to be a punishment? We all saw him use the pail to hit Elaraine and Elaraine is now an honorary captain in my army while Berell is a scout with the standing of a foot soldier. There was never any doubt there was going to be a punishment, Ranci." He leaned into her. "But please, next time, don't call my leadership into question in front of absolutely everybody in the camp," he whispered so only those close could hear. He leaned back. "But what punishment should he have?"

Orin laid a hand on the prince's shoulder. "It was a rather childish act, was it not?" He winked at Prince Shep. "Remember what our fathers did when we acted like that?"

The prince nodded, thinking and smiling. "It was, and many instances come to my mind." He looked at Elaraine. "The one that stung me the most was him telling me he was 'disappointed' in me."

Orin laughed and shook his head. "No, that one hurt, but the worst was the swift swat on the butt."

"Do you think that would work here?" Prince Shep looked over at him, a mischievous glint in his eye. "I mean...the humiliation...could Berell ever get over it?"

Elaraine rubbed the back of her head, catching on to their little plot.

The new injury had soured her mood considerably. "If I can get over this headache, trust me, he can get over a little bit of soreness and humiliation."

Berell was looking disgusted. "It wouldn't hurt!" he spat. "All you'll be doing is proving to the men you all take the womanly way out! We should settle this with our fists!"

Prince Shep stepped up to him. "Kind of like sneaking up on a wounded woman and hitting her in the head from behind with a pail?" He nodded in mockery. "I can see the adult man depiction in that, all right. If you wanted to solve this like a man you should have hit someone who wasn't wounded."

Berell spat at Prince Shep, who signaled to Andell to release the man. The second Andell did, Berell received a hard fist to the gut. Andell and Ranci helped Elaraine sit back down as Prince Shep and Orin led Berell over to her, doubled over in pain and trying to regain his breath. She shook her head.

"Let Nox do it," she said. "I'm seeing him in double."
The prince patted Berell's shoulder. "Now, don't struggle, Berell. I'd hate to subdue you again." The men gathered around them began to laugh and he joined in. "Besides, if it's not going to hurt, like you say, then there's really nothing to worry about, is there?"

Nox was handed a large broadsword and he turned it so the edge was away from Berell. With a hard swing, he brought the flat side of the sword swiftly across Berell's backside. The resulting slapping sound brought hoots of laughter from their comrades and a cry from Berell. Elaraine was not finding it as satisfying as she had hoped. Nox spanked him a few more times before he tossed the sword aside and with one kick knocked Berell to the ground. Elaraine motioned to Nox and he stopped the beating, silencing the crowd of onlookers.

"Orin, where's the tent? I'm ready to rest again," she said softly as her brother drew near her. "I want to sleep."

Orin just nodded and picked her up as exhaustion overwhelmed her. Prince Shep patted her head as they strode by.

"See you in the morning," the prince said as she closed her eyes and once again drifted off to dreamland and her recurring nightmare.

Chapter Thirteen

Elaraine woke early the next morning with a ringing noise shrilling in her ears. Her head felt like it was about to explode, but she reasoned that getting hit in the head by a metal pail would probably do that to you. Orin was snoring next to her, a firm grip on his sword, which was the usual for him when he was away from home. He never liked feeling helpless in an unknown area. But her head pounded every time he snored.

The tent was packed full of people. Ranci was sleeping to her right, with Dayn in his chipmunk form on her pillow, the edge of the blanket covering him sweetly. Nox was at Elaraine's feet and Andell was lying next to Orin. The boots and vest in her peripheral vision said Prince Shep was sleeping in a cot at their heads. *No wonder Dayn had to be a chipmunk tonight,* she thought soberly, *there's not even enough room for a blade of grass to squeeze in here!*

She tried falling back asleep. From the lack of sounds coming from outside the tent, she was probably the only one awake, as it was not even dawn yet. She did not know what had woken her up, though. She had had worse headaches than this and stayed asleep, so that was not the reason. Orin was the only one snoring, and she had grown up with that sound. In fact, she found it easier to sleep these days when there was snoring than when there was not any at all.

She sighed, rubbing her eyes. Ranci murmured something in her sleep about her husband and then quieted. Elaraine just thought about the coming day and trip to the capital. She dreaded that trip and what it could mean for her. Such a trip could not bode well for someone like her. How could an errand like that possibly go well? Sure, Orin and Prince Shep seemed to have high hopes for the voyage, but they were not the ones who killed the king's cousin.

Suddenly it hit her. She was being watched. She could not find the eyes, however, and that bothered her. She tilted her head back gingerly and looked into the brown eyes of Berell, sitting still on the ground by Prince Shep's cot and picking lightly at his muddied tunic. He noticed her gaze and nodded. He motioned to the sleeping forms around them and put a finger to his lips. He made his way lightly past her and out the tent, waving for her to come with him. She struggled to her feet and followed him outside.

He was leaning against a tree, his arms crossed over his chest. He watched her approach with the barest civility. She stopped a few steps from him and stood resolutely. He laughed gruffly and walked up to her.

"Lady, I wonder if you might excuse my boorish behavior last evening. It is not in my blood or manner to usually do that sort of thing. My mother raised me better than to treat a woman like that, and my father raised me better than to sneak up on someone like that. The rush of the moment overtook me," he said, bowing, taking her aback.

"Berell, I am not sure I am worthy of such an apology. In fact, I think the spanking you received is more than enough," she whispered back.

He shook his head vigorously and frowned. "I was raised better than that, and my superiors expect better than that of me." He looked down at her. "And to speak to you, a lady, in such a manner was despicable. My conscience has gotten the better of me, you see."

"I'm not a lady, Berell." She shrugged. "By your speech, I can tell you are higher born than I am. You may be the son of a noble," she curtsied stiffly, "but I am a mere daughter of a farm family."

"Nevertheless," he ground out, but stopped himself. "Elaraine, I am trying desperately to apologize for the headache you must now be suffering because of my actions. Please accept the apology and allow me to leave, as my scouting outfit must be leaving in just a few moments." He motioned behind himself at the men lingering in the shadows of the trees.

She nodded and pointed to the scouts gathering nearby. "Now go and forget this ever happened, as I am more than happy to do."

He smiled briefly. "Then it is forgotten." He bowed once more and turned to leave. He hesitated for a moment. "You may be the daughter of farmers, but, Elaraine, you treat people with more respect and gentility than most noblewomen I know do."

With that, he turned and walked away, leaving a very confused Elaraine in his wake. He and the other scouts disappeared into the woods like a mist. They made no noise, no conversation, with their departure. It was eerie and sent a small tremor down Elaraine's spine as she watched them leave.

"He's a strange one, I'll give you that," Orin said behind her, scaring her. "But, then again, he's a scout, and I've never met a 'normal' scout."

Elaraine looked back at him. "At least he admits his mistakes. But why he uses such formality to a commoner, I'll never know."

Orin went up to her and embraced her gingerly. "My little sister, so many things you truly do not yet understand. There are good men out there... men better than even Nox, Dayn or I. Berell, Prince Shep, and Andell are just a few examples! He's formal with you because you deserve it. Had it been any number of other people in your position last night, he probably would have been beaten until their arm grew tired and the people watching laughed themselves into a stupor. But you granted him mercy and showed him respect. That is why he treats you like an equal." He looked over her head at the other men beginning to get ready for the journey ahead. "And I believe the other men will begin to do the same. The other night, you gained their trust by fighting with them, but last night you did the hardest thing someone can do: you gained their respect."

"Berell is right," Prince Shep cut in as he joined them. "I had never seen him act like he did last night, and he has served with me for years. His elder brother was a scout for my brother, and his father was a scout for my father. All the other scouts are his friends, and all of the scouts are noble born. While he has treated everyone with civility, as far as I know, this is the first time he has shown such respect to someone." He thought about it for a moment. "Well, except for Andell and myself, though those are for two totally different reasons. I'm respected for being a prince, while Andell—"

"Could kick his rear all the way home to his mother if he stepped out of line again," the seasoned veteran interrupted. "With this outfit, Elaraine, you will find that nothing is ever forgotten and, like your brother here said, the other men will be treating you less like a woman now and more like the soldier you have shown yourself to be."

Ranci coughed lightly behind them, drawing their attention to her. She was helping Dayn tie a bedroll down to a white mare. "Isn't it about time we were on our way to the capital? There's no use in putting it off any longer than we have to, you know, and since we are all awake there is no point in stalling until the day is fully here."

The prince pulled Orin aside. "The plan has had to change, I'm afraid. The healers need more of the wagon space than we first thought they would. There is no room in the wagons."

Orin nodded and helped Elaraine mount Tix once more. She groaned at the slight pain the action caused her, but it was nowhere near as bad as it had been the previous day. Orin took the reins from her and led her horse behind his. Her protests only made him laugh.

"The last time I thought you were going to follow me, you turned and ran the other direction, so now I am going to do the brotherly thing and I'm going to lead you all the way to our destination, whether you want me to or not," he managed to get out between his chortles and her arguments.

Dayn and Nox rode on either side of her, as silent as the trees they were passing. They gave each other meaningful glances over her head, but neither one spoke. Ranci rode at the front with Andell and the prince, chattering away freely at them, something that struck Elaraine as being wildly out of her character.

Elaraine could not take the silence any longer. "Dayn, I don't remember your mother being that conversational when I stayed with you."

The young man looked ahead at his mother's back. "She's not. And it's even rarer that she's happy to have left her forest."

Nox scoffed. "She's probably just thrilled that she's found her son again. Honestly! How could you not even leave her a note that says more than 'goodbye!' Maybe if you'd left a decent message for her, she would not be here!"

"Because if I had said anymore in the note I left, she would have come looking for me!" Dayn rolled his eyes at the argument.

"She came looking for you anyway! And now we're stuck with her!" Nox said, not finding the humor in the situation.

"You can't seriously believe that I enjoy her presence any more than you do, Nox."

"She is here under orders of the king," Orin said over his shoulder. "Otherwise, I am sure she was very happy that her grown son was finally out of the house." He looked behind himself and eyed Dayn. "Though I am sure a note with some sort of explanation of where you had gone would have been appreciated."

"Fine! I should have left a better note! I think we've established that little bit, haven't we?" Dayn spat back at the three of them. "Why don't we talk about something else? The weather, the scenery... anything besides my mother?"

"Your being an inadequate son is a fine enough conversation for me," Nox said sourly. "The scenery barely changes and the sky is overcast," he added, looking around himself. "So now we can get back to why it is that your mother is our new companion on this little adventure." He looked at Orin. "Why would the king direct her here?"

Orin fell back to join them, handing Elaraine Tix's reins, forgetting his earlier vow to lead her in until they got to the capital. "Is it not obvious, even to your thick head?" He sighed as Nox shook his head. "She has... certain abilities...."

"Please don't try and make it sound better than it is," Dayn sighed. "She's here because she is the strongest witch in the country. She's here in case anything were to happen that she can fix without anyone getting hurt— spells, healings, et cetera." He looked sideways at Nox, who was remaining resolutely silent. "What? Suddenly speechless? No jabs at my mother being a witch?"

"I already knew that she was a witch," Nox sighed. "I just didn't realize that she could help us with this." He apologized to Dayn for his foul mood and then added, "Anything that can help us win this war without a ton of people, particularly anyone in our group, dying in the process is fine by me. I'll even put up with your mother for that."

Dayn nodded and Orin clapped Nox on the back. "I'm glad that the two of you can talk like civilized people every once in a while without resorting to childish banter or using fists," he said, the sarcasm dripping off of every word. "Elaraine," he said, turning to his sister, "please tell me you are not considering one of these two as a replacement for your estranged husband."

Elaraine laughed and shook her head. "They are much too young, don't you think?"

Orin frowned. "They're your age. I don't understand."

Elaraine frowned and slapped Tix's neck. "You sure take the fun out of a joke, don't you?"

"So explain it to us," Nox muttered.

"Mentally. Mentally they are much too young." Elaraine laughed and steered Tix smoothly between a couple of trees. She looked over at her brother, who was finally understanding what she'd said. "Don't you agree, Orin?"

He laughed with her. "Oh, for once I do agree with your decisions about men." He looked at the two men. "Cheer up, my comrades! Somewhere out there is a catch far better than my sister." He looked over at his now fuming sister. "Of course, I meant that in jest, Elaraine! How can there possibly be a better woman out there? I already have Moraiah!"

Nox and Dayn just exchanged murderous looks. Orin kicked his horse into a gallop to catch up with the prince and his companions. Dayn looked sad and Nox just looked moody as Elaraine took her place between them once again.

"Did you mean it?" Dayn whispered, his voice trembling slightly. "Did you mean what you said about us?"

Elaraine cocked an eyebrow at him. "Orin and I were just fooling around," she explained, "and he knew it."

"It wasn't a joking matter, you know," Nox growled. "You shouldn't tread on our hearts like that."

Elaraine frowned. "Honestly, I was not aware I was doing any treading of any kind. I thought you were merely acting like brothers or friends." She swallowed. "But obviously I was wrong. I am sorry for 'treading' on your hearts."

She kicked Tix into a trot and caught up with her brother and the prince. She listened as they talked about the upcoming arrival to the capital and how that situation should best be handled. They agreed that Elaraine should stay away from the king but would still need to face what she had done. Elaraine was silent, but she agreed. Prince Shep reiterated that he would do everything he could to ensure her safety, but he decided against having them hide in the wagon with the wounded men. He decided it would be best to move the wounded men in the wagons as little as possible. Elaraine remained quiet but wondered just how much the young prince could do against the wrath of the king.

From that point on, they rode in silence, none of them truly knowing what to say that would ease the tension of the situation. Ranci continued with her one-sided conversation, seemingly unaware of the total disinterest her companions had in whatever she was saying. Elaraine knew Orin was looking forward to seeing his wife and son once more and could hardly blame him for the excited "whoop" he gave when he saw the outer walls of the capital, but all she felt was dread deep within her bones at the sight of the gray, stone walls so like those of the Dungeons Ussal.

Prince Shep put a reassuring hand on her shoulder. "When Orin and I go into the Grand Gallery to see my father, Elaraine, please stay out in the hall and out of his sight. It is far easier for him to grant mercy to someone he has not seen." He looked at her appraisingly and frowned. "You dressed as a man would not improve his opinions of you at this time, understand?" They were passing the first gates. "Elaraine, please tell me you understand that your hiding is probably the only way I can get you a fair ruling from my father."

Elaraine nodded as the second gates were being opened. "Stay in the hallway and I may be able to keep my head and my life. I understand, my prince."

Prince Shep looked over at her. "I will do everything I can for you, Elaraine."

Orin patted Elaraine's shoulder as he answered for her. "She knows that. She's just a little nervous is all." He took the reins from her once again. "Are you really all right?" he whispered in her ear.

She nodded and patted his hand. "I'm sorry, Orin. I'll be fine." She cleared her throat. "Honest. I'm just nervous, like you said."

Prince Shep smiled down at her as everyone began to dismount in a courtyard. He leaned in so close to her ear that it moved her hair as he whispered to her. "Elaraine, I swear to you, I will not let anything happen to you. You saved my life and I will save yours."

Elaraine watched as he walked briskly away as though he had never said anything to her, Orin beside him, motioning for her to follow. Nox and Dayn trailed behind Ranci and Andell as they all made their way into the huge and magnificent palace. Dayn and Nox were the only ones left in the hall to wait with her as the others were ushered immediately into the king's audience.

Dayn sat on a bench beside Elaraine as Nox paced impatiently before them. It was nerve-wracking, watching him pace a path into the flooring.

"Would you please just sit down and stop with that insufferable pacing, Nox? You are about to drive me crazy!" Elaraine growled at her nervous friend. "I am begging you!" she said, softening her tone as he turned on a heel to face her. "I'm nervous enough without having you display your own anxieties so openly."

He sat down with a hard thump on the bench on her other side. His head was buried in his hands, and Dayn was just sitting there calmly, impassive and silent. Elaraine was rather thankful for Dayn acting the way he was. It made her feel a little stronger knowing that he was being strong for her. It helped counter how the guards made her feel. The guards posted outside of the door to the Grand Gallery would cast looks their way every once in a while, unnerving her and making her wonder if they could hear something being said through the doors that she could not.

After what seemed like hours, she felt like disobeying her brother and Prince Shep and marching right into the Grand Gallery to demand to know what was being said. But, just as she made her move to the foreboding doors, they swung open, allowing the four who went in to come out. None looked thrilled or disappointed and none would offer her any explanation without some prodding.

"Well?" she nearly yelled in her impatience. "What did the king say? Do I keep my head or do I lose it?"

Orin and Prince Shep exchanged concerned looks before Ranci spoke up for them. "Elaraine, the king said, and I quote, 'I don't care what happens to her, but never let her step foot in my palace again or her head will hang on my wall!'"

"But then Prince Shep's brother stood up and made the decision for his father," Orin nearly whispered. "You are to accompany the troops to the border under Prince Shep's command to fight the Rischiaks until the end of the war. If you're alive at the end of the campaign, Dalun Shrevelt's death will not follow you anymore."

"I am to send you on every dangerous mission that comes up," Prince Shep explained. "It seems as though my brother and father have decided to allow the enemy to make their decision-making for them." He looked over at Orin. "He has never granted this much mercy to a woman before," he whispered, but not low enough.

"Who has?" Elaraine squeaked. She cleared her throat when nobody answered her for a while. "So am I a prisoner in your camp or am I free to come and go as I please so long as I am there when we are attacked by the Rischiaks?"

Prince Shep shrugged. "You will have the same freedoms as any of the other soldiers in my command. You will not be guarded and you will not have tabs kept on you or be watched. However, I expect you to be in the camp every evening, just as I do the men, and you will have to go on those missions like my brother has ordered." He laughed wryly. "If you don't, then it's my head that's in trouble. Your duties will need to be done but once those duties are done, you may do as you please."

Andell looked over his shoulder. "Your Highness, if I might suggest moving this little meeting somewhere more private... the king is coming this way and it probably would not be prudent to have Elaraine just standing here in the hallway after he has said he does not want her in his palace."

The old soldier ushered them down the hall and back outside to their waiting mounts. Orin and Prince Shep took Elaraine aside to continue their rushed and hushed conversation.

"If I had it my way, she'd be a scout, but we can't put her there," Prince Shep said to Orin urgently. "I don't want her to just be a foot soldier. She's smarter and better than that!"

"Yet she and I are mere commoners and need to be placed accordingly," Orin grimaced as he said the word 'commoners.' "We cannot be scouts, just as we cannot be in the ranks with Ranci and Dayn. We simply do not have the bloodlines."

"All I ever hear about is bloodlines!" the prince yelled, fisting his hands in his already disheveled hair. "I don't understand why, if someone has the skills needed, someone can't do whatever they want to do! Why can a smart commoner not sit in on the councils of State? Why can a commoner, like you, with a great military mind and an immeasurable amount of courage, not be a scout or an official captain?"

"It's your father's laws," Elaraine said quietly. "If we are able to accept our places, why can't you?"

"Because I don't believe in them!" Prince Shep hissed. "I believe that Orin should have his own command, but he cannot. I believe that a bad leader should have to clean out the swine pens, but they cannot. This system is unbalanced and I don't think other people see it!"

"We all see it," Orin said gently. "But we all also know better than to rise against it. The last people who dared do that were killed with their families alongside them on the spot." He looked sideways at his sister. "And, for me at least, risking my family for something like social advancement is not worth it. My wife married me for who I was and our son is being raised to respect his betters and his equals. If he turns out all right, then our jobs will have been successful as productive members of society. My sister and I are willing to be foot soldiers, Prince Shep. To fret in front of the men over not being able to promote us because of our bloodline is only degrading and embarrassing."

Elaraine nodded. "I'm just lucky to be alive, remember? I'll be happy to be wherever you place me."

Prince Shep smoothed down his askew locks and walked back to his horse. He held the bridle for a moment and sighed. "So we are off to battle without having decided anything? No placement decided for you two or Nox, no clear knowing of what is going to happen to Elaraine, and no battle plans already drawn?"

"Let Fate decide itself," Orin scoffed, waving the prince's worried comment off. Suddenly, he grinned and added, "I've found that some of the best plans are those that aren't ever made!"

They all mounted and followed their prince out of the palace grounds. Elaraine leaned over in Tix's saddle to her brother.

"Orin! What about Moraiah and Josi? Aren't you going to be able to see them before we leave?" she said softly.

His face grew hard and he set his jaw. "They never made it here." He looked over at her. "Some of Prince Shep's villagers were in the Grand Gallery and they had no news of Moraiah or Josi. They haven't been heard from since they left the village and they never made it here."

Chapter Fourteen

Elaraine could not begin to fathom the hurt Orin must have been feeling. No word from his family and they had had a couple days' head start on them to the capital. The young woman fell silently into the riding columns beside Nox and Dayn once again, riding directly behind the prince and Orin, all of them wondering where in the world Moraiah and Josi could possibly be.

"It's strange, isn't it?" Andell said at last from behind them. "Orin is always so strong and, even now, without knowing where his family is, he's still the leader we need him to be beside Prince Shep. I've known stronger men who've left the army to find their wives and children when they didn't know where they were."

"Where do you suggest I begin to look?" Orin asked softly, sounding utterly defeated. "I could search the entire country, but that doesn't mean she's even in this country. She could have been taken prisoner with my son. She is more likely to find me than I am to find her at this point."

"So what?" Dayn was flabbergasted at Orin's lack of gusto for finding his family. "You can't just give up finding them because it might be hard!"

A sad smile was given to the young man. "Who said I was giving up? I do know, however, that if I were to leave, Elaraine would feel the repercussions of my departure and Moraiah would tan my hide if she knew that I abandoned my duty. If I stay with a big group of people like this, it will be easier for her to find me than for me to find two people somewhere between the village and the capital. So you see? Staying with this group is really the only option I have left right now, Dayn."

Dayn nodded. "I suppose you're right. She's only my mother, but I know Ranci would skin my hide too if I did something like that. 'Be a man of your word' is something she drilled into my head since I was just a little child."

Orin nodded as they fell into an uncomfortable silence once again, each thinking of their own family. Elaraine was only thinking of Moraiah and Josi, though, because Orin's family was the only family she had left. Her parents were somewhere in the capital trying to show their loyalty to the crown, so she knew where they were. Nox was wondering who his family even was and Dayn was starting to appreciate his mother a little more. The thoughts of those depressed few reflected those of the rest of the men under Prince Shep's command.

"How far are we riding today, sir?" Andell called ahead to the prince after a few hours of riding in silence.

Prince Shep looked up at the treetops above them at the dusk gathering overhead. The shadows were beginning to lengthen and they would need to find a spot to stop and establish camp before it became completely dark. The dark clouds gathering were not a good sign for a restful night, but the prince remained quiet.

"Sir?" Andell tried again. He rode up to Prince Shep's side and gently nudged the pensive man. "Sir, there's a storm coming."

"I know, Andell, but we can't stay right here. There's no cover, not even brush, here. The trees are thin and short and there are no rocks to hide the horse corral behind," he sighed. "Right now, it's looking like we need to ride on."

"Your Highness," Orin pleaded, catching up with the two of them after riding with Elaraine for a short while, "most of the men are about to fall from their saddles if they don't get to rest soon. I know this isn't a good place either, but it's better than nothing, and we should still be far enough away from the border."

Andell nodded. "Sire, we're close enough to the capital that I don't think anything will happen."

Prince Shep shook his head. "It's too vulnerable." He looked over his shoulder at the men and waved Elaraine to his side. "Elaraine, since you are the woman of the group, I will ask you: do you think we need to rest right here?"

The young woman scowled at the prince. "Sire, most of the men do need to dismount and rest for a while, if not for the night. I may not need to, but some of the men do. I agree that this isn't the ideal locale for a respite, but it will have to do. Looking immediately ahead of us, it isn't getting any better."

She fell back into her spot between Nox and Dayn, still ruffled about

Prince Shep calling her out like that. She was a woman, true enough, but she believed that she had proved herself hardier than some of the men in the company. He did not need to call on her strictly because of her gender. But she was resigned to obey his every whim and listen to both his criticism and his praise. Orin steered his mount toward her and glared at her.

"You're under his command now, so stop giving him as much lip as you think you can get away with!" he whispered harshly. "A simple 'no, sir' or 'yes, sir' would have done nicely!"

"They might have suited you, brother, but that's not my style, you know that. I'm only obedient to laws and to my elders and he," she pointed at the prince's back, "is not my elder and he is not a law. He is just a prince. He was born with worthier blood than mine, perhaps, but it is just that: blood. He is a man, pure and simple, and I will treat him with as much respect as he gives me." She cast her brother a sideways glare. "I'll treat him like a normal human being worthy of a title, but if he deserves some sass, then that's what he'll get. Maybe he'll stop acting like the rest of the company is better or hardier than me just because I lack what anatomy they have."

Orin blanched at her words. "Elaraine, you have no idea what it is you're talking about so, please, just be quiet."

Elaraine was adamant, though, and would not be dissuaded. "No, Orin, you have no idea. He said 'Elaraine, since you are the woman of the group, I will ask you', word for word, did he not?"

"That's because he needed an official reason to make you an advisor so that the men don't become resentful. It justified the means to get you to a higher place in the company to help keep you safe, like I asked him to. All you're being now is plain ungrateful!"

"How was I supposed to know that that is what was happening?" she said through gritted teeth. "All I knew was that it sounded condescending! But picking me because I am a woman will just make the men resentful anyway. They will be resentful no matter what either of you do. I am resigned to being resented."

"Well, now you know," he snapped at her. "And we are doing everything we can to ease your way in the company. So now, please, go apologize!"

She rolled her eyes at the irate man. "You're so much like Father sometimes, I swear!" she groaned, but trotted back up to Prince Shep's side. She was silent for a minute, but then decided she might as well go ahead and plunge into her apology. "Prince, I am sorry for my sass earlier," she ground out. "Orin has explained why you asked me the way you did, and I regret the way in which I expressed myself earlier. To re-answer your question, yes, we should stop and rest, sir, so we are more rested for the upcoming battles. Who knows what will be happening when we reach the border once again?"

Prince Shep nodded. "It is not so much that I minded your sass, Elaraine, but please keep it to a minimum in front of the men, all right?" He smiled kindly at her. "If I didn't like your spirited ways, trust me, you would have been left behind at the capital, and not because you're a girl but because you're hurt and right now getting you healed on the journey is a dangerous liability. Understand?" She nodded. "Good. Now, I hate the idea of bedding down for the night here, but you were right, it's not getting any better up ahead of us."

Just then, Berell came racing into view with another scout right on his heels. Their horses were sweating. Andell lifted a hand to halt the columns behind them as Prince Shep dismounted by the panting men. They spoke hurriedly, needing to return to the rest of their group somewhere ahead of them.

"Sire, we need to rest here if we're going to rest at all," Berell's companion sputtered. "Tracks ahead indicate that there has been a lot of foot wear, and not just merchants going to the market. Heavy wagons have been pulled through the trees up ahead."

Prince Shep looked around them, making sure of his boundaries. "The Fief of Periborin is nearby. Could it be from his sentinels roaming through here hunting?"

Berell shook his head and bowed low. "No, sir. Periborin keeps only a few soldiers there, and the last time any of us heard, he had sent his village to the capital and his men away to the border to join up with the rest of the army." He thought for a moment. "Since Lord Periborin is in the capital, sire, perhaps we should make for his village to spend the night. It is only a league or so away, an easy ride for the sake of safety."

Prince Shep shook his head fervently. "I do not wish to intrude upon any of the lords or their ladies out here on the outskirts. They have been through enough without having to put up a company of men for an evening. I do not want to use any of their food stores or homes for even one night."

He looked around himself once more, growing grim and setting his jaw. He reached and absentmindedly rubbed the bandage on his leg. "No, Berell, bring your men back here for the evening. I'll expect your report tonight when you return."

Having been dismissed, Berell and the other scout ran to get new mounts and then raced back through the wilderness in the direction they had come from. Everyone watched their departure with mixed feelings of determination, disappointment, and expectation. No one knew what those wagons could mean. They each could take their own guesses as to what the scouts would discover in the coming days, but they were afraid to at the same time. They were the only company loyal to Swennia to pass through those woods in the last couple of months, and the heavy rainfall in the past couple of weeks would have washed the previous troops' tracks away.

Andell passed the order down the line that the men were to dismount and set up a camp for the night. There were to be no fires lit until the cause of those wagon tracks was discovered, and maybe not even until they joined the other troops at the Swennian-Rischiak border in the coming week. This made the men grumble amongst themselves, but they did as they were ordered without an actual argument occurring. Small tents were pitched haphazardly everywhere. The tent Nox and Dayn pitched for their small group was near the prince's tent, and they agonized over making the tent straight and perfect.

Orin and Nox laid out their bedrolls next to Elaraine's while Dayn left to help get his mother settled on the other side of the tent belonging to Andell and the prince. Berell and his scouts returned to the encampment covered in mud and grime. The horses were being watered at a small pond nearby by some of the younger soldiers. Ranci was very vocal in her disgust at the filthy state of the scouts, but the scouts seemed rather nonplussed about their state of filth and ignored her.

Andell had joined Elaraine and her small group after seeing to the prince's needs, finding their attention pulled away by the scouts. After Ranci started griping about how dirty those men were, Andell started to double over in laughter.

"My dear lady," he managed to say between bouts of laughter, "war is anything but clean."

Prince Shep joined the conversation and could not help his laughter as well. "They've looked much worse, I assure you, Ranci. Berell there once fell into a ditch filled with horse manure and that young man behind him, Periborin's son, Rian, once landed face first into an ant hill and had to strip to his skin screaming and yelling in the middle of a village square in front of a lot of men and a couple of ladies before the ants could bite him anymore. A bit of mud and grime is a nice change for that group there."

Elaraine laughed at the thought of Berell covered in dung. "I bet Berell was quite a sight to see!"

"Not to mention the smell!" Andell held his nose at the memory. "He did not smell great to begin with, but that was just ridiculous! We slept upwind of him for a month!"

Berell and the man Shep had called Rian were making their way toward the small gathering, their ears burning. The two scouts bowed deeply to Prince Shep and the ladies present.

"Sire," Berell began, "the other scouts and I have discussed this at great length and we have a proposition for you."

Prince Shep cocked his head to the side and folded his arms across his chest with a slight frown. "Really? A proposition?"

Rian nodded, blushing. "Yes, my lord."

Prince Shep sighed but nodded. "Let's hear it."

Berell took a deep breath and Elaraine caught him looking at her through the corner of his eye. "Prince Shep, we have been shorthanded in the scouts since the last battle and it is difficult to cover all the ground we need to so we make sure we are catching everything." Rian nodded his support to Berell. "But, sire, we believe that if we were to have just one extra person in our ranks, then we could more than adequately complete our missions to your satisfaction."

"And do you have this person already picked out or am I to choose?"

Berell nodded and turned to Elaraine. "Yes, sire, we have picked someone already. We believe that Elaraine Hedri would make a more than satisfactory member of our outfit."

The prince frowned more deeply. "She is not of noble blood and she is not a man, both of which are necessary for the scouts. My acceptance of this proposition would be an unprecedented event for the scouts."

Rian stepped forward. "Sire, it happened with the Periborin fiefdom a few years ago. A common woman named Jonni joined the scouts there and is now going to the border. Jonni is a hero in her own right."

"Elaraine could be the exact same recruit Jonni was at Periborin, Prince Shep," Berell added hastily. He lowered his voice so only their group would hear. "We have heard that as part of her punishment, she must be given the most dangerous missions. The scouts get the most dangerous missions out of all the other groups under your command. Both problems would be solved, and Elaraine would still be able to maintain her dignity, and we may be able to protect her."

"'Her dignity'?" Orin bristled. "Why would being something like a foot soldier take away from her dignity?"

Berell flushed a bright crimson in embarrassment when Andell answered for him. "He is referring to if Prince Shep had had to order her around like he would a dog like the king wants him to, not her being treated like a soldier. He meant no offense, Orin."

Elaraine thought about it for a minute and listened to her brother pleading with Prince Shep to make her stay with the main part of the company. Prince Shep and Andell just looked at each other silently while Ranci spoke praise for the plan, surprising them all. Elaraine made up their minds for them.

"If it's all right with Prince Shep, I would like to go with Berell, Rian, and the other scouts," she said, breaking the tension like a paddle through water. "I'm no noble and I'm no man, but they want me anyway and this is the best way I can serve out my punishment," she explained to the shocked faces around her. She turned to Nox and the recently arrived Dayn. "You two support me, don't you?"

"We can't go with you to the scouts," Dayn whined. "We were coming to protect you."

Nox nodded solemnly. "Dayn is right, for once." He dodged a punch smoothly. "We can't protect you out there if you go with Rian and Berell. It could be a long time before we get word you need help and can get to you."

"We protect our own," Rian said angrily. "We would look out for her as though she were our sister," he promised, turning to Orin.

"And we promise she'll return safely to camp every night," Berell added, trying to quell some of the anger pulsating from every fiber of Orin's being.

Prince Shep just looked at her, something akin to disbelief written all over his face. "Are you sure that's what you want to do? I can find a way around my father's decree if you give me a little bit of time. You don't have to become a scout and put yourself in unnecessary danger, you know. We can find you another job that would look adequately dangerous to the king."

She shrugged, trying to look calm and brave. "Sire, the way I see it is I can either ride to battle at your side and maybe get killed or I can go ahead with Berell and Rian with the other scouts and maybe keep the rest of the company from getting into a battle and getting killed until we reach the border. I also see it as a kind of adventure, which is what led us to your village to begin with."

"But this would be an adventure that could kill you!" Orin yelled.

"Just like any adventure could," Andell said in her defense. He thought about it for a moment. "May I make a suggestion, Prince Shep?" The prince waved his encouragement as he sighed heavily. "What about doing this scouting business on a trial basis? She goes out with them until noon and then rides with the rest of the company until it's time to bed down. If Berell reports that she excels at the job, then that's where she should stay, and if she doesn't excel then she remains a lowly soldier like Orin and me. No harm, no foul that way."

Prince Shep agreed to the test, and everyone went their separate ways to think about what had just transpired. Elaraine was told to be at the eastern edge of the encampment at daybreak the following morning to leave with Berell and his company of scouts. She was so anxious for the next day, Elaraine walked around in a fog, wondering what Berell would be having her do. She could read tracks and such, having been raised in the rural village of Gegernen, but she had never learned what scouts specifically did. She skipped dinner to search for Orin when he did not arrive for the meal, but she could not find him. She settled onto her bedroll to try to catch some sleep before her new duties started, but before her nightmare could grip her, she felt some drops of water hit her nose and chin.

The black clouds had rolled in and were starting to unfurl their fury on the encampment below. She groaned as the drops started to fall faster through the tent and cried out when the heavens opened. She was drenched in the cold water within seconds. Orin was over her before she knew it, his blanket creating a makeshift shelter for the two of them.

"You should try and get some sleep," she heard him mutter. "You have a long day ahead of you."

"I'm sorry I didn't listen to you when you said I shouldn't be a scout," she replied. "But one day you won't be here to look out for me, and I need to make my own decisions. I need to learn to make these decisions for myself."

He nodded, his frown not going away. "I know that, Elaraine. It's just that I'm here now, and the other decisions you've made so impulsively have ended with you getting hurt, so I'm just worried now that the same thing is going to happen. Geez, Elaraine, you're still hurt from the battle! The healers say you will be completely healed soon and shouldn't be feeling any pain right now, but I still worry about you!" He ruffled her hair. "Just call it a brother's right to worry, all right?"

She laughed and pecked her brother on the cheek like she used to when she was just a little girl. "You should get some sleep, too, Orin," she said. "I can hold the blanket up. We can take turns."

He just shook his head adamantly. "No, I can go a day or two without sleep. I have done so before and I will do it again in the future. Just lean on me and close your eyes and you'll be asleep before you know it." He could feel her stiffen. "What's wrong, Elaraine?"

She hesitated before she answered him. "I don't want to go to sleep, Orin."

"Too excited?" She shook her head at him. "Then what? Why don't you want to sleep?"

"I don't sleep well anymore. I haven't for a while. I was thinking maybe if I stay up all night tonight I might actually sleep well tomorrow."

He leaned away slightly so he could look in her eyes, frowning down at her. "Why can't you sleep well?"

She sat up, setting her chin on her knees as she drew them up to her chest. "I just keep having this nightmare. I wake up with Ranci passing through my body like we were both nothing but air. I wake up with the screams echoing in my ears."

He kissed the top of her head and cradled her like he used to. "Come now, Elaraine, and tell me all about this nightmare."

So, she told him. She told him how Worrin had died and Nox had gone to bury him himself. She told him how in the nightmare Worrin was alive and healthy and Nox looked happy once more. She told him how Dayn cast himself from the cliff when she could not get to him. Orin patted her head when she told him how Ranci transformed into this screaming banshee every night in her nightmare and how she always tried to get to Dayn, but she never could. Nox and Worrin were always holding on to her too tightly for her to save her dear friend. And Orin soothed her when she started to sob.

"Orin, I just can't take it anymore!" she cried into his shoulder, breaking down. "Every night, it's the same! I try to get to him, but I can't! Every night, he throws himself over the cliff and careens out of sight and every night Ranci passes through my body as she screams, like neither one of us is solid. Her screams are terrible. I wake up with those screams still resounding in my ears. There's only so much of seeing your friend kill himself that you can take! And it happens night after night after night." She hiccupped.

Orin just hugged her tightly, keeping the rain from her. "Ela, sometimes you have to see the bad to see the good. Dayn won't kill himself, so please don't worry. Ranci, as you know, is just like you or I, despite her magic, and is quite solid. I won't let anything happen to Dayn, Nox, or Ranci while you're off scouting. And I will certainly protect you when you are here. So please put this worry of yours away for another day and dream sweet dreams of wild horses in meadows like you did when you were a little girl!"

"But, Orin, I'm afraid what Nox or Dayn would do if I don't choose them. I keep treading on their hearts." She sped on when Orin looked like he would interrupt her. "They have told me I have, Orin! But I don't think I could ever bring myself to truly break at least one of their hearts. They have given me a heavy burden in the decision."

"Ela, do I believe you should remarry?" He nodded. "I do. But unlike the first time, this time you need to choose an honorable man who is good to you. Are Nox and Dayn great men? Yes, I think so. But if they don't make you happy, then that doesn't matter. So, forget that burden and sleep."

For the first time that day, Elaraine took her brother's advice without an argument and closed her eyes. While it took her a while to fall asleep, a great peace overcame her and soothed her.

Chapter Fifteen

When she finally did succumb to slumber, Elaraine dreamt of nothing. It had been a long time since that had happened. She had been in the Dungeons Ussal. But she quickly decided that dreaming of nothing was better than dreaming of a friend killing himself. She woke up happy with the night without nightmares and hoped it would come to her again soon.

Berell and Rian were waiting for her at the edge of the encampment at daybreak like they had promised. The other scouts were still milling around before they paired off as well to go ahead of the riders for the day. Elaraine could not help but feel elated at this new step in her life. For once, she felt like she was in the right place at the right time— that she could make a difference in the world, even if it was just a small one. If she had skills and could be used, then she felt useful. But her anxiety of the unknown still turned her stomach.

Orin had accompanied her to the edge of the camp and patted her shoulder. She looked up at him and twisted her hands nervously. He grinned down at her.

"You will do well, Elaraine, so do not worry yourself so much," he reassured her. "I will be riding with Prince Shep and Andell when you return, so come find me."

"What makes you think I can do this, Orin?" she whispered.

"Well, my little sister, you are more observant than anyone I have ever met, and that is definitely needed in this job. Besides, you have this uncanny ability to get yourself in trouble and get yourself out of it again, with help, of course," he teased. He sobered. "But, seriously, Elaraine, I know you can do this job because you know you can do this job. Have a little confidence in yourself! And, please, stay out of trouble."

She did not care if the troops saw her as she hugged Orin. That is what she had been waiting to hear. She had needed to hear his confidence in her. That someone believed in her meant more to her than she could ever explain and made her believe in herself. She looked back at Berell and Rian.

Rian smiled warmly at her and moved to greet her. "Good morning!" he sang. "It's good to see you are here early! There are a few minutes to daybreak yet!"

Elaraine was still rubbing the sleep from her eyes but smiled back at him. "Thank you, Rian."

Berell frowned at the two of them and then tossed Elaraine a brown tunic and cloak with the Swennian army emblem sewn on them to put over her green ones. "You're going to need to blend in more, I'm afraid," he explained. "Green tunics do nicely when we're in fields, but in the forests we need brown, especially this time of the year. Too many leaves are falling for you to be in so much green. I am sorry that you have to wear so many layers, but that is the way it has to be, at least for today."

She nodded and slipped the large tunic over her head and pinned the brown cloak over it, handing her green cloak to her brother. "When are we leaving?"

"In just a moment. You'll be with Rian and me until the group decides that you are up for a more traditional pairing between you and just one other person." Rian and Berell looked at each other. "We've been partners for a couple of years, and when you're partnered with someone for that long, a bond is created, and you can communicate with just an eyebrow if you have to. Silent communication can save your life as a scout. Hopefully, one day, you'll get that kind of bond as well."

Rian laughed his agreement. "I think I should warn you ahead of time, though, that now that you are a part of our little group, some of us like to prank the others when it is safe to do so, and since you are the newest member, you are going to be the new victim of our escapades."

"We're going to treat you like one of the other men because we cannot afford to treat you any differently. Just because you are a woman doesn't mean that we will expect anything differently than we would if you were a man."

"I wouldn't expect anything different," Elaraine said, looking at her feet. "But might I ask a question, milords?"

Berell frowned at her. "All right, first thing is first. We are not 'milords;' we have names and we do not wish to have our titles thrown at us. We may be nobles, but in the scouts we are all equals, no matter what our blood rank says. Many of us joined the scouts so we would not have to have our titles used." Elaraine nodded and both men sighed. "All right, what is your question?"

"If having a woman, be she a commoner or noble, as one of your number is so rare, why choose me as a new recruit?"

Rian laughed and elbowed Berell in the ribs. "And you thought she would catch on too quickly!" he jested with the other man.

Berell glared at his partner. "We chose you because you are brave yet careful; you have respect from the men, and you use it to the best of your advantage without making them feel inferior. You're observant and you read people well." He stepped over to her and laid a hand on her shoulder. "But I chose you to show you the same mercy you showed me." He waved his hand to dismiss what he had said earlier. "Those other things are important too, but they can be taught. It made sense to choose someone who already had these traits so time would not be wasted in teaching them, but you showed me the most important trait someone could have, at least to my mind, and that is mercy. If we did not take you, you would have been sent to the foot soldiers, where it's every man for himself first and other people if the soldier has time. At least out here, we are a kind of band, like brothers, if you will, and we watch out for our own all the time. That is why we chose you, Elaraine Hedri. Your being a woman does not matter one bit to us. Your being a believer in humanity does."

Elaraine nodded and followed them away from Orin and further into the woods, finally beginning to understand this brotherhood that they were trying to induct her into. They were scouts, looking out for signs of danger for the main company, but they did that to protect one another as well. Everything they did, it was for one another. They were all friends and they all believed that one day the world would not need them anymore— that they could retire knowing that good existed in the world and they could lord over their manors and fiefdoms in peace.

Berell and Rian spent most of the morning showing her signs of normality, like animal tracks and droppings, which she had known since she was a little girl. There was not any way she would have been able to grow up in a village situated on the edge of the wilderness without having learned a few of the skills they were now thinking they were teaching her. But she kept her experience in their area of expertise quiet, silently following them as they chattered endlessly on good signs versus bad signs.

She was the first to see it. Berell and Rian had just walked over it without even noticing it, but she was tired and her head was beginning to droop and couldn't seem to look anywhere but at the ground, so she saw it with relative ease. Sticking out from a couple of yellow maple leaves was a small, iron cloak shoulder pin. She picked it up and wiped the grime from its etching.

Berell and Rian had finally noticed that Elaraine was no longer following them and turned around to see what was holding her up. Berell frowned when he saw what she was holding and motioned Rian to go see what it was. Rian walked over to her, pretty dejected at having to be a kind of messenger because Berell was being too lazy to check out what it was himself.

"What do you have there?" Rian looked over her shoulder at the pin.

Elaraine looked back at him. "It's a cloak pin."

"That is not Swennian," Rian said flatly, as if it even needed saying. The pin was engraved with an owl with a crown under it, a sword within the crown.

"I don't know how it could get here, so close to the capital, though," Elaraine nearly whispered.

Rian nodded as he waved Berell over. "Intelligence has only told us of border disputes, not an actual full-blown invasion. They have been worried about this for a while, but there hasn't been any evidence to confirm the rumors were true."

"And even if there were an invasion, they couldn't get past our forces at the border," Berell said as he jogged up to the two of them. "What is it?"

"A cloak pin," Rian pointed to the object in Elaraine's grasp. "Look at the etching."

Berell squinted to get a look and laughed heartily. "It is obviously a fake, Rian. The enemy cloak pins are etched much deeper and with much more detail than this." He tapped the pin. "And this is iron. Why, everyone knows that the metal workers in Rischiak use silver."

"I did not say that there were not discrepancies between this pin and the others we have seen being worn in battle when we fight the Rischiaks.

What I am saying is that no metal worker here in Swennia would ever create a pin with Rischiak army signs upon them. So what other explanation is there?" the other scout said slowly.

"It looks old and worn," Elaraine looked up at Berell. "The detail could have merely worn off. And Rian is right: no Swennian uses the owl sign. The others, but never the owl. Our troops have a wolf on their pins."

Rian agreed with her with a single, weak nod.

"But you did not say why this is bronze, like our pins, instead of the iron the Rischiaks use. Explain the metal difference," Berell bit out. "If you can do that, then maybe I will agree with you and report this back to the prince." When the other two did not answer him, he grinned. "See? You cannot explain the metal difference away! More likely than not, this is from a child playing around with something he ought not to have been playing around with. What you both are suggesting is that a force of enemy soldiers got completely past our forces at the border without being seen." Berell laughed. "That has never happened before and is impossible."

"We can't protect the entire border," Elaraine reminded them. "And just because something has never happened before doesn't mean that it won't ever happen."

"And even if there were a mass force of Rischiaks here, wouldn't we have seen a definite sign or hair of them now?" Berell was very skeptical.

"It's a big forest," Rian spoke up. "And there's no arguing that that pin is not Rischiak. It's the sign of the Rischiak Royal Guard." He tapped the pin in Elaraine's hands. "For all we know this army has been living among us, infiltrating our ranks. And what of those strange tracks we came across yesterday?"

"Even we would notice a large group of soldiers suddenly trying to be citizens in Swennia. And those tracks you spoke of were unusual." Elaraine shook her head. "No, none of it makes sense."

"Then what do you suggest?" Berell nearly yelled at Elaraine and Rian.

"Our job!" Rian spat back. "It's our duty to report these kinds of things, whether we personally deem them real or not, and we're wasting time just arguing and yelling like this!"

That silenced the bickering. Berell hung his head and reached for the pin. "I'll run back to Prince Shep and give him the news," he volunteered.

Elaraine gripped the pin harder and pulled it out of his reach. "I can take it. There is no reason for you to go, too, when I need to report back now that it is midday and need to find Orin."

Berell made a move closer to her, raising a hand as if to strike her. Rian grabbed his arm before it could make its blow.

Rian glared at him, a warning clear in his eyes. "Both of you go. It's time for Elaraine to report back anyway. Orin and Prince Shep will have our heads if she's not back soon. If the prince gives us further instructions about the pin, Berell can bring it back to the rest of us."

The woman nodded and put the pin under her cloak, pinning it to her green tunic under the brown tunic. She turned and started to jog back in the direction of Prince Shep's army. It took a few seconds for her to hear the man hot on her heels and yelling at her to stop and stay with Rian. She looked over her shoulder and Berell was nearly upon her, his face twisted with rage. She sped her jog into a sprint. She did not feel right about his attitude about the pin. She turned and saw him still coming at her. A change had come over him since he saw the pin. He looked like a charging bull and looked ready for murder when just that morning he had been friendly and happy. Rian was running after them, his dagger already in his hand and a grim look spreading over his features. He was gaining ground on them. Rian was calling for Berell to stop and to leave Elaraine alone.

Berell did not draw his dagger and did not notice Rian trying to catch up to him. He merely caught and tackled Elaraine with his whole body weight behind the hit. She cried out and went flying into a nearby tree. The wind was knocked out of her instantly. She scrambled to her feet and tried to find her short knife hidden in her boot, but Berell was already upon her again, pinning her to a tree and searching in her cloak for the pin, a hand around her throat. She kicked and tried to punch him, but it was no use. Every time she tried to get him off her, his grip only tightened. She was still disoriented from her collision with the tree and soon had to give up her attempts at fighting back as she stopped being able to breathe from the tight constriction on her throat.

Berell was suddenly off her and rolling on the ground away from her. Two dirty brown cloaks were rolling around in the mud and the muck. Rian had his dagger to Berell's throat and was trying to subdue him. Berell spat at

Rian and got a well-deserved punch in the nose for it. Elaraine struggled to her feet and took a shaky gasp of air. When she looked back at the two men, Rian was straddling his friend, Berell too tired to throw Rian off. When he was sure Berell was under his control, the younger scout undid his own belt and started to tie Berell's hands up with it.

"I failed!" Berell screamed.

"I am sorry, my friend, but you have become crazed all of a sudden," Rian tried to smooth things over with Berell, who was not having anything to do with it.

Berell glared up at the younger man. "No, 'my friend,' I have always been this way," he sneered. "Just as you have always been the weaker and meeker of any man you have ever come across. You are just a man blind to the world around him. The only things you can see clearly are animal droppings."

Rian shrugged the insults away. "Anger is a dangerous emotion, Berell."

"Especially for the one who angered the man."

"No. Especially for the one who is angered. They are more likely to make mistakes." He got up from his knees and started to get Berell to his feet. "And such anger from a noble's son is quite unbecoming."

Berell hung his head and visibly slumped. "That pin means danger to my family."

"Mine as well, you fool." Rian was void of any sympathy for Berell. "But we were both taught to do our duty. Nowhere in those duties does it say to attack other scouts or try to hide signs we are bound to report to our commanding officer. How dare you jeopardize everyone and everything important in this world because of your anger and your fear!"

"You don't understand," Berell said, softening his tone as he began using a different tact, trying to appeal to Rian's empathy. "My entire family will be destroyed if that pin is turned over."

The younger scout threw Berell against the same tree Elaraine had been pinned to and put a hand around the other man's throat. "You had better talk fast and make sense, Berell, or my hand just might make you feel what you were going to make Elaraine feel."

Berell just shook his head, casting his gaze in Elaraine's forgotten direction. "Nothing I say could possibly make you understand my situation."

"I am not the only one who will need convincing, Berell. When I have to explain to Prince Shep why his lead scout is dead, he will understand me and my story better than a tale that was never told. So collect your thoughts and speak quickly." He flexed his hand around Berell's throat in a warning.

"I made a promise to never tell anyone," the man gasped. "Please, Rian! Please understand that what I do, I do to protect my own blood."

"Berell, you have explained nothing and yet you expect everything from me. How can I understand anything from that small bit of information? I want the whole story or you do not receive mercy from me or anybody else."

"I only ever gave you my loyalty and protection. I thought of you as a younger brother," Berell pleaded.

"And I thought of you as my older brother. You have never received less than my respect and adoration until now, Berell, and now you have received my complete disdain and disappointment." Rian's voice was shaking in his fury.

Tears began to streak down Berell's face. "I have disappointed you, Rian? Of all the things I have done before, this is what disappoints you?" He took a deep breath at the other man's sad nod and visibly calmed back down. "I have my mind again. I promise I will not fight back or run away if you untie me."

The other scout just shook his head. "Tell me why I should allow you any leniency, Berell, when you just attacked Elaraine, even after you told Orin you would look after her. You looked Orin in the eye and swore to him you would protect her, and you should owe him more loyalty than me after he saved your father's life in the last war."

It took him a while to answer. Elaraine and Rian could see the battle raging in the man: was he going to betray a promise to someone he loved or was he going to obey the orders he vowed to abide by years before? In either case, his word would have been given in vain and Elaraine would wager her last coin that Berell was a man who believed that his word meant everything. Just as Rian was about to just go ahead and take the man to Prince Shep for his judgment and condemnation, Berell shuddered and groaned, his decision having been made.

"I know whose pin it is," he ground out harshly. He looked crestfallen, and Elaraine almost felt sorry for him. "At least... I know whose it might be. I'm sure there are a lot more out there than just one."

"Explain."

"I haven't seen it in years, Rian. I really haven't. For all I know, he's realigned himself with Swennia, but, years ago, he vowed allegiance to the Rischiak royalty. He said there were others. He said there were many others. He said they operated in secret. He said I would have to choose sides one day, too."

"Whose is it?"

Elaraine could tell Rian was making a considerable effort to remain stolid in front of his friend and mentor. He was gritting his teeth and shaking with the exertion of his effort. His frustration was starting to get the better of him. She knew that he would spare Berell, that his threats were idle yet necessary. Berell was shaking his head.

"Please, Rian, don't make me tell you." But he received a squeeze to his throat and a prick with the dagger to his belly. He began to sob. "Fine, fine, I'll tell you," he gasped. "My younger brother, Aundreal. He went to the Rischiak queen with your brother, Simiar. Our fathers made them, Aundreal said. I found him trying to hide the pin when he returned. He said that the borderland nobles were changing their loyalties, that Father was going to give Aundreal the seat in his fortress when he died and that your father was promising Simiar the same. That's all I know. I swear it!"

Rian released his grip on Berell, who slid to the ground in complete anguish. He looked at Elaraine, his face gone white. He sheathed his dagger and walked over to the woman slowly.

"Gods help me for what I have done," Berell sobbed as he slid down the tree.

"Yes, the gods will need to help you, you traitor!" Rian yelled, spinning toward the prostrate man. "But do you know who will need help more than you, you fool?" Berell looked up at him. "The troops who are going to be trapped between the enemy from abroad and the enemy from home. Brother will be fighting brother, fathers against sons, and you worry about

Aundreal and your father learning that you betrayed their trust? You are weak, Berell. And to think I looked up to you. You were my hero, Berell! And now I have to go and turn you over to Prince Shep and then I have to turn in your family, my family, and every borderland noble for questioning! If anything happens, I will hold you entirely accountable." He dropped to the ground, leaning against a tree, his head in his hands. "It makes me really want to hate you, Berell, but I find myself unable to. I thought of you like my brother," he cried out. He was silent for a few minutes, calming himself. "What a time we live in," he said to no one in particular, "when a son must betray his own family and fight against them. When noble families rise and rebel against their king and country."

"Swennia is falling apart," Elaraine whispered down to him. "Can we still win when our own people are against us?"

"Do you not understand, Elaraine Hedri? Think about your own family history. You, of all people, should know that in times of war, we have something to fight for besides just a king's whim. You should know that we are doomed to fail. It has already begun and there is nothing one woman and one scout can do to stop it," Berell spoke up for the last time before Rian stood up, walked over to him, and with one punch knocked him into unconsciousness.

He looked over his shoulder at Elaraine. "Elaraine Hedri," he whispered. "We need a plan."

She looked at Berell and a chill ran down her spine. "We have to tell the prince."

Rian rubbed his face with his shaky hands. "That could kill every person I care about."

"Everybody back in camp could die, too." She put a hand on his shoulder. "The prince protected us. Can't he protect your family, too?"

"Simiar causes more trouble than I can ever clean up."

Elaraine knelt beside him and they remained silent, lost in their own thoughts. Elaraine took the pin from her tunic and spun it in her hands as she studied it. She lost herself in the details of the artistry while Rian collected himself and Berell lay unconscious.

It took a long time for Rian and Berell to be in any condition to return to the prince's troops. Elaraine knew Orin would be worried, but she could not bring herself to just leave Berell and Rian. She was surprised, however, that no one had been sent to fetch her. The sun was beginning to set when Rian finally got to his feet and went over to Berell, who was still prostrate on the ground in his grief. The younger scout sat back down next to his woebegone friend and patted him hesitantly on the back before turning away once again.

"Berell, this is not the end of the world. At best, Prince Shep will forgive you. At worst, he will send you back to the capital to his father and your family will lose its title the day the king condemns you. You were not actually the one to betray the Swennian crown, so let us hope for the best, all right?"

Berell slumped further to the ground. "No, I may not have been the one to betray the crown, but I allowed the betrayal to happen, and we all know that the king does not distinguish between the two. My life is surely forfeit."

Rian sighed. "Berell, you are truly an idiot. For this to get to the king, Prince Shep has to tell him and send you there. After all these years of faithful service, do you honestly believe that he would condemn you so easily?"

"Rian is right, Berell," Elaraine spoke up. "Prince Shep is more likely to be angry over your breaking curfew than protecting your family. He has a family and would be able to relate to your loyalty."

It took many more moments for anything to happen. The two men stayed sitting on the ground and Elaraine began to lean on a tree. Finally, Rian broke the standstill. He stood and wiped off the dirt from his leggings and tunic. He put a hand under Berell's arm and dragged the man to his feet. When Berell was eye-to-eye with the younger scout, he straightened himself to his full height, a kind of steely resolve finally coming over him that Rian seemed to silently understand.

Elaraine could only shake her head at the day's events, wishing fervently that she had never found that cloak pin. Only hours before, her life had been so much simpler. Within those few hours she had been accepted into a group and then destroyed that group. The enemy was mainly outside of Swennian borders and fellow Swennians had been friends at the beginning of the day. But now she could see that the war was closer to home than she had ever supposed it to be. Brothers were being pitted against one another in a dangerous game. Fathers and sons were at war and houses were tumbling with their switching loyalties. And in the middle of this controversy were two crowns.

She could feel herself growing angry as the three of them made their way to where they supposed the main army to be. She walked behind Rian and Berell and she hated that Rian had to keep Berell so close, out of fear of an escape. She wondered in what kind of world a mentor should be restrained for questioning by his apprentice. While she knew that this was a necessary evil in this case, she could only feel her blood boiling over at the situation.

It took over an hour to find the encampment. The army was quiet and no fires were lit. Rian and Berell tried to teach her a little more about signs as they went along to break the tension but they soon gave up. The tension had only multiplied as a result.

Orin was the first person Elaraine could accurately distinguish in the crowd. A few scouts were wandering here and there. Because scouts just do not wander aimlessly, Elaraine knew they were all on edge, nervous about what was taking Rian and Berell so long. Undoubtedly, the news of Elaraine not having returned at the designated hour had spread, causing more suspension in the group than had it only been a couple of tardy scouts known for their antics.

The trio slowed their pace down considerably at the sight of the camp. They could all feel the burden of truth that lay before them. They were all wondering how to break the news of internal treachery to the prince and what would happen to Berell when the prince found out.

Orin spotted them before anyone else had and started to make his way towards them. He was walking fast and deliberately. He was furious, and Elaraine knew it. Their father used to walk that way when he was at his maddest. He was a man on a mission. Elaraine girded her loins for his shouting and screaming, preparing herself for the onslaught of fear-borne anger. She was ready for that. She would take the yelling without complaint. After all, she deserved it after the worry she put him through when she did not arrive at the army when she had said she would. Orin had had hours to stew and brew over what he was going to say to her, on exactly how to express his turmoil.

Hot on Orin's heels were Nox and Dayn. From what she could tell, the two men were turning a dark shade of red and their fists were balled tightly at their sides. The sight almost made her want to laugh. Almost. It was the imposing figure in front of them that forbade her from letting out the laughter that was threatening to escape her when she saw her friends. It was true that she had never seen them so angry, but, then again, she had never seen men so red before either. They were so bug-eyed that they looked like they were choking. They had their arms crossed over their chests and were ready for an argument.

What happened, however, surprised her. Her brother embraced her without saying a word. He just held her for a few moments before she hugged him back and the reality that she was there set in. He pushed her away to arm's length and fed her to the wolves behind him.

"You know what I'll say and it would only be a waste of breath," he said. "Dayn and Nox were talking all afternoon about what they would do when you finally showed up, and I've decided it would be far better to just hand you over to them." He glanced up and saw Rian holding onto a ready-to-bolt Berell. He motioned for them to follow him. "We'll be with Prince Shep if things get out of hand," he shouted to Andell, who was emerging from his tent nearby.

Andell gave him a nod and a wave as he strapped on his boots. "I'll watch them for you!" he shouted back.

Elaraine crossed her own arms and glared at her friends defiantly. "Bring it."

And she got it. Both men let their rage and worry run free. Elaraine merely let a song play again and again in her head, tuning out their shouts. She watched Andell from between their shoulders. He was sharpening his sword while keeping an eye on the two men before her. Suddenly, he was looking directly at her and she noticed an eerie silence surrounding her.

"Elaraine!" Nox snapped. "Elaraine! Are you even listening to us?"

"Sure I am!" she snapped back at him. "How could I not?"

"Then answer Dayn!"

She had been caught. She had not been expecting any questions, only ire-filled statements. She heaved a sigh and threw her hands in the air.

"Well, I would if I knew what he asked!"

Andell fell off his seat laughing and more eyes were being drawn to the scene. Elaraine could feel herself blush at the attention, but Nox and Dayn were unabashed. Dayn was snapping his fingers in front of her face to draw her attention back to him.

"Hey! Don't lose me now!" he yelled. "I asked you where in the world you were all afternoon! You were supposed to be back hours ago!"

"I was with Rian and Berell! Where else would I have been?"

Nox glared at her. "He means where, exactly, were you, and not with who."

She pointed behind her in the direction they had come from. "We were a long way away from here in that direction between oaks, maples, and hickory trees."

"And what were you doing between those oaks, maples, and hickory trees?" Dayn said through a clenched jaw.

She shrugged and dug her boot toe in the dirt. "We were talking."

"'Talking'?" Nox sounded incredulous. "You were 'talking'?" Elaraine nodded. "And what, if I may be so bold to ask, was so important that you had to talk about it and not come back to the main army as you were ordered to do and had promised to do? What was so important that you found it necessary to make us worry?"

"You'll find out soon enough, and it's not my business to tell you."

Dayn was the first to explode in anger once again. He clenched and unclenched his hands into fists. "Then whose job is it to tell us?"

"Prince Shep. Who else's job would it be?"

She tried to move past him but was stopped by a set of hands on her shoulders. She easily could have shaken off Nox's hands but she stopped dead in her tracks. She looked up at him, an eyebrow raised, her body beginning to tense.

"Nox," she said slowly, "just what do you think you're doing?"

"We're not done talking yet!" He was back to shouting.

She began to laugh. "Oh, we're not, are we?" She stepped closer to him. "Then allow me to talk." Nox took a step back, allowed her to turn towards him, and then reapplied his grip as she poked a finger into his chest. "First of all, I don't owe either one of you an explanation of my whereabouts. That is between me, Rian, Berell, and Prince Shep. Second of all, if anyone is going to yell at me and embarrass me, that's the responsibility of my brother, not his cronies. Thirdly, I put up with you and Dayn yelling at me out of consideration of you two being like brothers to me and I took that you must have been worried into consideration. But enough is enough." Nox was starting to get angry again and his grip was tightening on her shoulders. She poked him again. "You don't have the right to put your hands on me and you're hurting me!" She glared up at Nox when he did not release his grip. "Now, I'm going to tell you what we're going to do. You are going to take your hands off of me before I put my boot up your rear end until it shakes hands with your brain and I am going to go sit outside Prince Shep's tent until a verdict is reached on what was discussed between those trees." Nox's hands did not leave her shoulders. She laughed wryly and tried to heave her shoulders out of his grasp. "Did you not just hear me, Nox? Get your hands off me!"

Nox only looked back at her, refusing to move his hands from her. She only grinned in satisfaction when she first hit him. His grip did not loosen, however, and she went down with him. They rolled around in the dirt for a few minutes, Nox refusing to let go and Elaraine refusing to quit wrestling until he did. After a while, she got the upper hand when she head butted him. He got a bloody nose and had to let go of one of her shoulders to stop the flow. She managed to get his other hand off her easily and kicked him over to his stomach. The crowd around them had grown quiet. Her boot was on his backside to make good on her threat when a cough from behind her startled her.

Prince Shep was leaning against a nearby tent post with Orin right beside him. Prince Shep looked amused as he lounged there with his arms folded across his chest. Elaraine looked around. Men were surrounding her and Nox in a loose ring, and Andell was on his feet by Dayn, holding the younger man back from their fight. She still had her foot on Nox's backside.

"May I ask why you are standing on Nox there?" Prince Shep asked flippantly.

She shrugged. "I told him that if he didn't take his hands off me my boot would enter his rear end and shake hands with his brain. I am in the process of making good on that promise."

Prince Shep frowned. "He had his hands on you?" He looked over at Orin, who was cracking his knuckles. "Orin, I will leave this one up to you. It looks like she has taken fairly good care of the situation, though. He is bloody and down. On the other hand, she is your little sister and I would not blame you at all if you wanted to take matters into your own hands. No one here would blame you either." He pulled Orin over and whispered something in his ear. Orin nodded and moved away. "So, which will it be?"

Orin frowned. "I think Elaraine has taken care of herself but I'd like to give Nox a warning, man-to-man, if I may?"

Prince Shep nodded his consent and Orin slowly, and calmly, made his way over to where Nox was laying. He lifted his little sister's foot off Nox, placed it back on the ground with a pat, and hefted the young man to his feet. Orin lifted Nox so his feet were off the ground and they were looking eye-to-eye.

In a voice calm and clear, Orin spelled the situation out for Nox. "If you ever even think of laying a finger on Elaraine again, she won't have the chance to make you snivel like a little girl because I will have already killed you, do you understand?" When Nox did not answer him, Orin shook him. "I said, 'do you understand?'!"

Nox nodded, still holding his nose. "Yes!"

Orin let him go and Nox landed in a heap at his feet. "I'm so glad we understand each other."

Orin walked back to where the prince was leaning and retook his place at the prince's side without saying another word. Prince Shep waved Elaraine over to follow him as he turned to walk back to his tent, with Andell in tow. Elaraine caught up with her brother and leaned in to talk to him so the others could not hear.

"Thank you for letting what I did be the end of it, Orin," she said gratefully.

He looked down at her and frowned. "What else was I supposed to do but let that be the end of it, little sister?" He patted her shoulder. "If I had stepped in any more than I did, you would have had an awfully hard time getting any respect at all from the men. But hear me when I say that if he does it again, I'm not going to care if you'll lose the men's respect or not."

Elaraine nodded and looked around her. When she saw that no one was looking, she gave him a brief hug and a whispered "thank you" before she followed the line of people entering the prince's tent.

Berell was in the corner looking forlorn but he was untied. Rian had his head bowed and was sitting near him silently. Everyone filed past the young scout without disturbing him. Elaraine wanted to reach out and hug him in his distress but knew that it would neither be appreciated nor understood. Ranci was waiting at the center of the tent for the prince to return, ignoring the two men already in the tent with her, but she looked up when the group Elaraine was with entered.

"I heard that our young Miss Elaraine got herself into some more trouble," she grinned.

"Nothing I couldn't handle," the young woman returned. "But I think Orin wanted to break everything on Nox that I didn't."

"I can't blame him," Prince Shep said, his joviality gone. "But back to the business at hand." His hand gesture encompassed the entire tent. "I don't like this at all." Everyone sat as he began to pace, describing everything that had been relayed to him by Rian and Berell. When he was finished with the telling, he stopped pacing and sighed. "First of all, Elaraine, you should have reported back to me immediately, but I understand why you didn't. I'm glad you stayed in case Rian needed help. As it is, I don't think Berell is much of a threat. Not as much as his family is anyway."

"Can we rely upon this man as a credible source of this treason?" Ranci asked, indicating Berell with a toss of her head. "If his own brother and father are lords and doing this, what is there to stop a high-ranking scout from doing the same? Or he could just be creating a ploy to keep his rightful title from being passed on to his brother."

Orin just shook his head. "I don't believe someone involved in this treason would have spoken to me as quickly as he did. And he did turn in his family, which must be the hardest thing a person can face. And he's a man I have known for years. I can see him protecting his family and their secrets but I don't see him creating a story to inherit a title he never wanted anyway. He used to tell me he wanted Aundreal to have the title in his stead."

Elaraine looked at her brother. "There are worse things you can do besides turning in your family."

He frowned. "That's beside the point right now, Elaraine. My point is, I think Berell is still loyal, and he's been faithful so far. He has always been faithful to Swennia."

Prince Shep nodded and sat down with everyone else. "I agree." He held up a hand to stop Andell from interrupting him. "I'm not saying he will have as many freedoms as he did before, but he is a valuable scout. I'll assign Rian and Berell new partners in the morning, and Berell will be with two other scouts until we return to the capital after this war. It is neither my wish nor duty to condemn him without absolute proof he participated in his family's treason. But word shall be sent to the king about what has been said of the noble families being traitors."

Elaraine looked up as she heard a tin topple over. Rian was standing now and looking stricken. A glance at Berell told her he was thinking the same thing as Rian.

"With all due respect, Your Highness, but Berell has been my partner since I was an apprentice. I beg you not to give us new partners! I shall be more than happy to be on the same restrictions as Berell if it will keep us together!" the scout cried out.

Prince Shep nodded, understanding Rian's distress. "An hour ago you were leading him into camp tied with a belt thinking he may be a traitor. Now you wish to remain his partner. And you would have me believe you did not know Simiar and your father were plotting against Swennia?"

Rian bowed his head. "I did not know. If I had, would I have led Berell back here tied? I could have helped Berell convince Elaraine the cloak pin wasn't important. My family is in trouble now, too. Instead, I did not know and I brought him to you tied with my belt. I performed the duty I swore to do, sire. It does not mean I do not still think of Berell like I would my brother and it does not make me love my country less."

"Your loyalty is commendable, Rian, and perhaps not misplaced. But Berell trained you well and you are needed out front with the others. Aron was injured last week and is having difficulties being so far away from our healers in camp, so I will pair him with Berell and another scout for now and you will be paired up with his partner, Konor. Is that all right for the time being?"

The scout resigned himself to the situation before him. "Yes, Prince Shep. That will be fine." He squared his shoulders proudly. "If I may be excused, sire, I would like to—"

Prince Shep held up a hand. "No excuses, Rian. I understand that you want to leave, and you have permission to go and be idle if that is what you wish to do."

Rian bowed and left hastily, leaving behind him a sullen group. Everyone was silent for a few moments, collecting their thoughts. Andell was the first one to speak and break the silence.

"How do we send the news back to the king?" he asked, voicing the question on everyone's mind.

"What about sending Konor and Rian back to the capital?" Elaraine asked. "Rian knows the story and with Konor he wouldn't be going alone."

Prince Shep frowned at the suggestion. "We need more scouts than we have already. What about a foot soldier? We have plenty, and one or two can be spared."

"I recommend against it, Your Highness. Foot soldiers would deliver the message too late and are likely to stop at the next pub they reach to refresh their gullets and forget their missions all together. Besides, they would not relay the message correctly," Orin advised.

The debate raged on, some favoring scouts despite there not being many in the ranks of men and others recommended a couple of the men on horses, but all agreed that the news had to be taken back to the king. Elaraine eventually fell out of the debate, deciding she did not know enough of these matters to make an informed decision like the others.

"Scouts are out of the question, the men on horseback cannot be spared if we meet Rischiaks before their return, and no one else is fast enough," Ranci spoke up.

Prince Shep turned to her. "So who do you recommend?"

The woman shrugged. "I recommend that no one go. We are being sent to wage war. Let the king learn of internal affairs in his own time and, for all we truly know, this rebellion may never actually come to fruition, and what can the king do without hard evidence anyway? All we have is the word of a scout that his brother and a few others betrayed the crown. All this he mostly learned second or third hand. What he says his brother told him could have been merely a younger brother trying to impress his older brother." She placed a hand on the prince's shoulder. "We need to press on to the border, Prince Shep. We are wasting precious time every second we waste on this issue."

The prince looked over at Elaraine, who was fiddling with a lock of hair that had fallen in front of her face, quite content to have been forgotten. "Elaraine, what do you suggest we do?"

She jerked her head up. "Prince Shep, I'm not qualified to be able to have an opinion on this."

"Yet I value it."

"But I have none to give."

"Even a simpleton would have an opinion." He sighed when she continued to hesitate. "It is merely an opinion you are giving me. I will take it into consideration when I make my decision."

She thought about it carefully for a minute before she let the hair fall from between her fingers to land between her eyes as she answered. "I believe Ranci is right and we need to press on to the border. The enemy is not going to wait because we want to debate on whether there is actually a rebellion being planned. When we get to the border, maybe a preventative measure can be taken to make sure we aren't overwhelmed by our own people, but the king's spies will learn of the treason soon anyway, especially if that is what those strange tracks were from last night."

He thought about it for a while longer, but at last Prince Shep nodded and stood. He walked out the tent flap and to the soldier standing guard just outside his tent. A horn sounded and the camp began to break down. Orin frowned and Elaraine could not help but feel the excitement growing in the pit of her stomach. They were going to press on. Despite the evening enveloping them quickly, they needed to move a bit further before they stopped for the night in lieu of the latest find. They needed to go a bit further from where the pin had been found and a bit further from those tracks that still worried them from the night before in order for them to rest feeling safer.

Chapter Sixteen

They rode hard that evening, not stopping for rest or food, to the point of utter exhaustion. When they would give the horses a break by walking them instead, they still kept a grueling pace. Anyone who walked would stumble over all the fallen limbs, roots, and rocks on the forest floor. The foot soldiers in the far rear were having difficulty keeping up with those on horseback. More than once, Elaraine swooned in her saddle from lack of sleep, only to be caught by Andell or her brother. Dayn and Nox were keeping their distance since the earlier spectacle that had been made. Nox's pride had been bruised in more than one way. Ranci was keeping a close eye on her son and had given up her position riding next to the prince to do so. Prince Shep rode at the head of the columns. Nobody spoke to him, and he seemed content to be left alone. Even if someone had tried to make conversation with the man, he was too far gone in his thoughts to have heard them anyway.

Eventually dawn broke over the horizon, sending rays of sunlight to try to brighten the troops' gloomy thoughts and warm their tired bodies, but it didn't seem to help in either aspect. No one had been overly thrilled at the prospect of riding all day and then riding all night, and their clothes grew increasingly damp as they rode through plants covered in morning dew. The way Orin explained the hard trek to Elaraine to put her in a slightly better mood was that the sooner they got to the border, the less time they would have to spend in the saddle. She told him it didn't help her at all to think of it that way and suggested that he should pass that word along to all the people grumbling behind them, but he just laughed in response. After hours upon hours of riding, however, not even the idea of not riding anymore could cheer the woman up because whenever she would walk Tix she would inevitably trip and stumble. The way she saw it, they were spending the same amount of time in the saddle as they would have if they would have taken their time, just more of it was being spent in the saddle all at once.

An hour after dawn, the column came to a wide river, and Prince Shep called them to a long-awaited halt. They were to refill their water skins, grab a bite to eat from the wagons behind them, and then try to ford the river. It was a meager break, but it was welcomed without complaint. Foot soldiers were scrambling frantically to find horsemen willing to take them across the water or were trying to find any spare inch in the wagons where they could fit. Many of the men could not swim and to these men the river looked less like refreshment and more like a grave. Indeed, the swift current would take a man who could not swim well under the water to his doom. Besides, walking the rest of the day in soggy clothing sounded like a day of extreme chafing to even those who were going to be staying dry, so whoever could carry an extra man would.

Elaraine found a man she had seen struggling earlier in the day and offered him a seat on her horse with her. He was not too keen on the idea at first but did not argue with her too much when no one else was making him a similar offer. After all, the man was a little too big for most of the men to share a horse with, even though his brown cloak told them he deserved that respect as a scout and as a noble. So, after a while of quiet refusals from other horsemen, he approached her and accepted her offer.

The food wagons entered the water first, men holding on to the rims of them for dear life, praying for safe passage. Next went the healers' wagons with a couple of mounted men on either side of them to help keep those men who could not find a ride across the water from washing away in the current. Last went the horsemen, urging their horses to swim across as fast and as hard as they could, each with an extra man mounted with them.

Elaraine's horse was fighting her on the crossing. Tix did not want to go into the water and then struggled the entire swim over under the extra weight. The scout behind her cleared his throat nervously many times and finally resigned himself to make a conversation with her to take his mind off of Tix's crossing.

"I hear you are to join the scouts," he said simply and expressionlessly, not one to start long conversations and feeling uncomfortable with his sudden impulse to do so. He bumped into her trying to tighten his cloak. "I am sorry about that."

"It's fine." She nodded, focusing on guiding Tix through the water. "That was the plan, anyway. I do not know if I will still be allowed to after yesterday... what with not reporting back on time and all. But it would be an honor to be a scout."

She felt the man shrug. "Prince Shep might have been displeased that you did not return when he told you to, but from what Rian told me you are quite the quick learner. He said he has never seen someone take to the job as quickly as you did, and that matters more to the prince than disobeying his orders once or twice, though I highly recommend you limit yourself on the number of times you do so. If you can do the job and complete the mission, that is what matters to the prince the most. He would not commend your abilities if he was going to take you away from the scouts."

Elaraine was beaming from the compliment as they finally reached the shoreline. "Thank you," is all she could think to say as he slid unceremoniously from behind her.

He grunted and held a hand up to her. "I am sorry for not introducing myself to you earlier, milady, but I am Konor, and I thank you for your generous ride across the river."

She took his hand and shook it. "I was more than happy to offer it." She paused and frowned. "Konor, please call me 'Elaraine.'"

"You wish for no title, but I tell you, Elaraine, I agree with what the men say: you are a finer woman than any I have ever known. You are a lady and ought to be treated as such." He bowed low to her as Orin rode to her side. "If you will kindly excuse me, Elaraine, I need to find my brother before we begin again and then I must meet with Rian."

Elaraine watched as Konor walked away, satisfied that Rian would have a good new partner. Dayn and Nox rode up beside her, having dropped off their passengers with their respective groups. They followed her gaze to the big man leaving her company.

"Isn't he too tall to be a scout?" Nox scoffed. "Here I was thinking that a good scout should be short, skinny, and dirty. It would be so much harder to blend into one's surroundings and be as large as he is."

Orin muttered something under his breath as he wheeled his horse away to get away from the argument he knew would be coming.

Elaraine did not even bother looking at Nox. "Are you saying that I'm 'short, skinny, and dirty,' Nox?"

He realized his blunder immediately and sighed. "No. I was only talking about the men."

"Neither Berell nor Rian are 'short, skinny, and dirty.' I can't really say that any of the others are either. Konor is just tall."

"Doesn't that make it hard for him to hide?"

"No harder than it would be for you to hide with that ego of yours," Elaraine retorted as she spun Tix around to find Orin.

Her brother was milling around with the foot soldiers refilling their water skins, looking bored. Tix picked his footing carefully as they made their way over to him, afraid to fall back into the water from the slick bank. Orin had just drawn a design in the mud when Elaraine finally got to him. With men darting to and fro in front of Tix, the short distance to her brother had seemed to take forever.

"Hey there, little sister," he said without looking up at her. "I'm glad you made it across all right. Some of the horses decided they didn't want to come across with their riders."

"Tix didn't like it, but he sucked it up, found a shred of courage, and came over anyway," she grunted as she dismounted. "What's the matter? You look upset."

Orin threw the stick he was using into the river. "You shouldn't have advised Prince Shep as you did. Word should have been sent back to the King."

"He asked for my opinion and I gave it to him, just like you said I should."

"When the prince asks you for your opinion, he wants good advice, not what your opinion really is. He asked you for your opinion more out of some misguided attempt at respect than to hear what you had to say."

Elaraine bristled at his tone. "But I really think that it was best that we hurry and get to the border. And in the end it is his decision whose advice he follows."

"The king deserves to know."

"Who would have been sent?"

That gave Orin pause. "I don't know. I know you're probably right, but I can't shake the feeling that we aren't doing the right thing by not telling the king. When he finds out this was withheld from him, he will be furious with everyone involved in the decision, and that's something you and I can't afford right now."

"Prince Shep knows what he's doing, so give him some credit. He's your friend. Has he steered you wrong before?"

"No, and neither did his brother. But this word of treason is disturbing, and the crown deserves to know."

"Do you honestly believe I do not know that? Orin, I struggled with it all day yesterday! I had to watch a grown man fall apart over the decision of whether to betray his family or the prince he serves. And Rian knew the ramifications as well. His family will be under suspicion, too. If we thought the king shouldn't know what we had found, we would have let Berell go. Now, please, brother, step off your mighty high horse and treat me decently, like your little sister that I am!" she pleaded. "You cannot tell me to do something one day and when I do, change your mind because it's not what you would have said!"

He clenched his hand into a fist and closed his eyes. "I'm sorry, Elaraine. Between not knowing anything about where Moraiah and Josi are and this campaign, my patience and intelligence is wearing awfully thin. But I can't shake the feeling that we should have sent someone... that they should know what is happening!"

"And they will, Orin," Andell butted in. "But not from us. He has spies to learn this kind of news, and I guarantee you that he already knows everything there is to know about this. Give your sister a little credit for her advice." He slapped Elaraine on the back. "But we are being called up to talk with Prince Shep and a few of the scouts."

"Should I go fetch Ranci?" Orin stood and stretched.

"No. Prince Shep wants this to be just us four." He paused. "Well, sort of. A few of the scouts are going to be there as well, which is why he wants this to be a smaller council than before— without Ranci, Dayn and Nox present."

Elaraine and Orin led their horses over to where Prince Shep was sitting on a small fallen oak tree. Andell was walking briskly with a sense of urgency in his step. They did not talk as they wove their way through the crowd. Enough talking was about to happen at the council. Prince Shep motioned for them to sit next to him without glancing at them as they came upon him. Instead, he was peering into the foliage, watching a pair of scouts struggling to wrangle something to the ground. Elaraine stood up after she had sat and followed his gaze and had started watching the two men, too, when she felt a tug on her wrist lowering her back to sitting next to the prince. Orin was seated on Prince Shep's other side, and Andell was going to help the scouts.

"What is it?" Elaraine asked, breaking the uncomfortable silence and fidgeting as she fought the urge to stand back up to get a better view, but the prince's hand on her wrist kept her sitting where she was.

"I'm not exactly sure," the prince whispered as what they were fighting with let out a loud howl. "I have only been getting brief glimpses of it every now and then when it tries to get away. But I do know that those scouts wish a council with me over whatever it is they are fighting with over there."

"I think I know what it is." Orin grimaced as one of the scouts cried out and started to curse what they were wrangling. "No, not 'think.' I know what it is. It's a timber wolf."

"A timber wolf?" Elaraine looked across the prince at him skeptically. "How are you sure?"

He laughed wryly. "Well, it's black, looks almost like a dog, fast, howls, from what I hear has been seen ambushing its prey, and has unbelievable strength. It was only natural for me to call it what it is: a timber wolf. Though even at that, this must be a giant timber wolf for the scouts to be having this much trouble subduing it."

"Seems simple enough to identify," Prince Shep agreed, "but then the question arises as to what it's doing in these parts. They aren't native to Swennia. They are only native to southern Rischiak."

"I haven't seen them since the last war. The Rischiaks use them in their army, making short work of horsemen. The horses are so weighed down and surrounded by men that the horses have a hard time trying to get away from them. But I'm sure of it. That," Orin pointed, "is a timber wolf."

"So we come back to the questions of why it is this far away from the border."

"Only one thing comes to mind, and I'd really rather not even think about that."

The prince nodded slowly. "My thoughts exactly, but, at the same time, we would have gotten word from the border if that was the case."

Elaraine raised a hand. "I'm not understanding you here."

"What we think," Prince Shep explained patiently, "is that the troops at the border were overrun. If this wolf is from the Rischiak army, that means they are close and that means they got past the border."

"But that's not possible! Could that wolf not just be the offspring of a wolf used during the last war? Maybe a timber wolf escaped the Rischiaks back then."

The two men stared at her for a moment before shaking their heads at her naïveté. Prince Shep could not help but smile, though, and he patted her hand as he let go of her wrist. Andell was yelling for one of the scouts to give him more rope.

"I don't think it's possible that this wolf is from the last war. There would have at least been rumors of wolves being seen. Unfortunately, however, it is quite possible that our troops were overrun. The troops at the border would have been very outnumbered if the Rischiaks have crossed the border. If we do not get there in time, if this wolf is not an indication of what has happened already, then our men at the border very well could be overrun soon."

"Prince Arlun would never let that happen," Andell yelled back over to them. "He has a brilliant military mind!"

"He may be brilliant, but my brother cannot withstand an army so overwhelmingly large without aid!" Prince Shep yelled back. "We need to get there sooner rather than later, so how is it going over there? Do you almost have that thing under control yet?"

"Almost have it, sir!" a scout yelled over his shoulder. "He sure is giving us quite the fight!"

A few more minutes went by, filled with cries from the scouts and Andell and howls from the wolf. The fight was moving closer and closer to the three sitting on the log, and Orin was growing more and more impatient with the whole ordeal. He heaved a sigh and went to help them, unable to sit still any longer. The prince stood and began to pace until he, too, went to join the men, ordering Elaraine to stay where she was. Soon, the wolf was tied by all four of its paws to a sturdy oak tree, and the men were trying to dust off their clothes.

Orin had been thrown in the mud a couple of times and looked exhausted. One of the scouts had a deep scratch across his face, and the other was favoring a gash in the shape of a claw mark on his left shoulder. Prince Shep looked mussed, but better than the others. Andell had some cuts and bruises but was smiling when he came back over to Elaraine.

"Gave us quite the fight, he did!" he laughed. "I haven't had such a good fight since the last war! Almost makes me want to get to this war faster! The feeling was unbelievable."

"He's a wily old man, this one," Prince Shep chuckled as he clapped his hand on Andell's shoulder. "It does a prince proud to have him for a soldier, I tell you!"

The other men shared a hearty laugh while Orin just bristled and licked his wounds and dignity. A healer was called for to tend to the scouts after they held their council with Prince Shep. Andell sat down nearly on top of Elaraine in his haste to sit down after his excitement had worn off. The two other men squeezed in on the log with them and waited for the exhausted scouts to begin their tale.

"For the love of everything, men, tell us!" Andell could not contain his impatient curiosity any longer as the scouts continued to shuffle their feet about speaking.

"My lord, the enemy is on the move!" the smaller of the scouts gasped out.

"Yes, yes, no surprise there, but is there any new news beyond that? What do you know about that wolf?" Prince Shep said excitedly.

"We do not really know," the other scout said. "We found it after we crossed this river yesterday... that is why we could not report back last night as we were ordered to do."

"It had a purple collar on when we found it, but it was torn off when we were trying to catch it," the smaller scout said.

"Purple? A wolf from the Rischiak crown?" Orin scratched his head and rubbed his chin. "That would be a new development."

"The queen is known to keep them regularly," the prince reminded him. "And from all accounts they are quite the loyal spies for her."

"Spies?" Elaraine interjected. "They cannot speak and cannot report back. What good could they possibly be at spying?"

"They collect evidence from the enemy," the smaller scout explained. "They are quiet and sneak into a camp. It is quite easily done. Men must sleep, after all. Then they are trained to pick up equipment, like a sheath or cloak, and from that the queen can tell who is encamped nearby."

Andell had stood and was examining the wolf closely. "I am afraid I must respectfully disagree with you. This wolf is no scout." He started to point to different aspects of the wolf. "The pads of his feet are not overly worn, and a wolf his age, as a spy, would have feet greatly worn down and calloused. His fur is neither matted nor dirty. His ears are not ragged. He still has his tail. Scout wolves have docked tails. And he attacked us out of fear. I do not believe he was trained as a scout. I do not believe he is an animal meant to be roaming as he was. Someone is missing this wolf, or they very soon will be."

Orin and the prince walked over to where Andell was standing and started to examine the animal for themselves. It gave a defiant growl every now and then under their inspection. The men pointed different things out for themselves and would nod and grunt their agreement occasionally.

Finally, the prince slapped his friend on the back, but without the joviality that he usually used. "I am afraid you may be right, Andell. This wolf does look like a pet. And we only know of one person who keeps wolves as pets."

"But a royal pet? Here in the wilderness of Swennia?" the scouts said in unison. "But that would mean—"

"I am afraid so. This wolf has been pampered all its life. Look at it. He is too old to just be starting his spy work. Andell is right: there is no sign he has ever fought before and his tail would have been docked if he was a scout. No, this wolf is a pet of the queen. The purple collar confirms it." Prince Shep slapped himself on the forehead. "How could I be so dense? I should have figured it out when I heard about the collar! No spy wolf wears a collar!"

"What do we do now, your Highness?" Orin asked, sitting down next to his sister. "Do we continue on our path or do we head back to the capital? Either way, we must decide quickly."

The prince looked pained at having to make the decision. He began to pace, muttering to himself, weighing the cost of his choices. The scouts excused themselves to have the healer look at their injuries. Prince Shep did not even notice them leaving. After a few tense minutes, he spun on his heel to look at the man sitting by Elaraine.

"What do you think, Orin? I need your advice!" The prince sounded desperate. "Neither choice is a good one. I will lose too many men no matter which way I choose."

Orin stood and laid a hand on his friend's shoulder. "Prince Shep," he said gently, "you are a brave man and a good leader. Your men will follow you no matter where you decide to lead them." He gestured at the men milling about. "Do you not see the power you hold over them? You could swear allegiance to the Rischiak crown and defect to Rischiak, and all the men here would follow you without question or hesitation. You fear their deaths when they do not. If they feared death, they would not have become soldiers. They would not follow you so blindly wherever you go. Compassion is a virtue, my prince, but in this you need to lose it for a minute and make a decision using the facts you know about the situation at hand. Base it, not on the number of dead or your feelings, but on facts and outcomes as you have always done."

Elaraine felt uncomfortable sitting there between the friends, and Andell was shuffling his feet in the background looking everywhere but at Orin and Prince Shep. Both Andell and Elaraine were finding it difficult to see the prince struggling like he was to make the decision. The internal battle he was dealing with made him seem too human for them, too vulnerable.

"Prince Shep," Andell stuttered after a long silence in the group, "Orin is right. Not a man here would not follow where you go. They will do what you say and will never question you. You have their allegiance beyond their deaths. They will not blame you for whatever might happen, if that is what is holding you back."

The stricken man shook his head. "No, that is not the problem. The problem is that I do not want them to follow me this time." He took a deep breath and calmed himself. "I see it now. I see it with perfect clarity. This mission is a fool's errand. The campaign was doomed from the start. My father became too comfortable on the throne he does not move from. And my brother strives too hard to be the perfect heir and does not dare disagree with anything the king says. We were blind to the true enemy." He kicked the ground. "All of my life, I grew up believing the enemy lay beyond our borders, but that is not where the true enemy is. No. The true enemy was here, in Swennia. The true enemy has always been us."

Orin backed away and gestured to his liege respectfully. "I understand all of this, sire, but a decision still must be made. Do we return to the capital or do we press on to the border?"

The prince's eyes looked void of life when he finally replied. "We ride on. We cannot look back now. If it is our time to die, let it be like the heroes the men are, not like the animals the enemy wants us to be." He ran a shaky hand through his hair. "We will ride hard, with no rest unless I say we are to rest, and we will get there in five days, but we need to push ourselves harder so long as the weather is with us."

With that, he walked away with the weight of the world seeming to rest squarely on his shoulders. Men parted silently before him, not knowing what it was that had their leader sullen and despondent. Seeing him like that disheartened the men, yet they drew strength from the fact that he was bearing the entire burden like the leader and hero he was. But they could all see it when he looked up and his sad gaze would meet theirs: most would not be going home.

Chapter Seventeen

The pace the prince had set when they were all ready to set out once again was even more grueling than before they had crossed the river. Men were quickly falling out of line in the rear and the healers' wagons were filling rapidly with men who were too exhausted to walk another step or could not keep up with the men on horseback. Elaraine thought that Andell and Orin were ready to leave the men behind and ride ahead if they would have been allowed to, based on the impatient looks they kept throwing over their shoulders at the men, but she also knew that the prince would never abandon those loyal to him. Prince Shep didn't speak to anyone for the first full day after the council about the timber wolf. Many of the horsemen tried to speak with the man and all failed miserably, having to return to their column without receiving a word in return.

Elaraine felt sorry for the man. She could not even imagine the burden he must feel every morning he woke up just being a prince, let alone having the responsibility of having the fate of hundreds of lives in his hands. It was a job and responsibility she did not envy. Dayn and Nox had grown bold enough to ride beside her once again, and she was grudgingly grateful for their company. At least they were people she could talk to whenever they could bring themselves to break the solemn mood the prince had cast over everybody.

Ranci was the brooding member of the group for quite a while. She resented the fact that she had not been invited to the last council, even though, as she admitted to Elaraine, she understood why the exclusion had been made. She told the younger woman that she was content with the decision that had been made, despite the fact her counsel had been deemed unnecessary. She maintained that having been informed a meeting was occurring in the first place would have eased her discontent. She rode behind Orin and Andell, not quite ready to take back her spot next to the prince.

Mumblings of discontent made their way up to the ears of the head of the columns after a full day's march. Andell tried to squash them, but he soon gave up his attempts. After all, he harbored the same complaints; why not let them be voiced? They were not hurting anybody. He was hungry, tired, and needed to refill his water skin. While they noticed the complaints soured Prince Shep's mood even further, Andell and Orin did not silence the men. Andell would not have admitted it to the prince, but he agreed wholeheartedly with the men. The pace they were keeping was insane. No one talked of turning back to the capital, however, so Orin and Andell were content knowing the men's loyalty remained true to their leader.

They did not break for their midday meal, let alone for sleep. An order came down the line early on that any meals eaten until the rest would be taken in the saddle or while walking. The rations were slim as it was, let alone trying to find something to eat in their saddlebags that could be eaten in the saddle without any preparation. Elaraine found some stale bread and some dry berries in one of her bags that she shared with Orin, who only seemed to have dry meat in his bag, which he in turn shared with her. The only rest they got from the saddle was when they were letting their horses' backs rest by leading them, when they stopped to let the horses eat and drink, or when they themselves had to answer the call of nature.

The second day saw a torrential rain, but the pace slowed only minutely. The horses were finding it more difficult to find footing on the muddy forest path. Orin, Andell, and Ranci all recommended a slower pace on that second day, but all were turned back to the main column with a negative answer. Prince Shep was not to be deterred from his goal of reaching the border in five days. He responded to concerns about the horses saying that if a horse fell the rider would just have to walk like the rest of the men in his company. Before the timber wolf had been caught and their plans had been changed, the army had been expected to reach the border in ten days, not five. Elaraine could not see how the pace could be endured.

The first true rest was called after three days of the breakneck speed. Dawn broke seeing the army dismounting and setting up camp. The horses all seemed to heave sighs of relief as they were unsaddled and groomed. They consumed their grain quickly, and the men could not get to the small creek nearby without squeezing through the herd of horses gathered there. Elaraine felt guilty as she watched Tix eat. He was a strong horse and she was lighter than the men, and he looked dead on his feet. But he had carried her without fail even when she managed to close her eyes for a few sparse moments in the saddle. She knew she was lucky to have him. Everyone was still tending to their horses when she finished. She gave Tix a loving pat to his neck and he whinnied at her touch before she moved away to find herself a good place to rest.

Elaraine had never been so grateful to sleep on a boulder. Orin cooked them a quick meal of a bird he shot down earlier in the day and some dried berries. It may not have been fancy, but they could not have cared less. It was not stale bread, and they were not moving while they ate, so they thought the meal fit for a king. After he filled their water skins, Orin settled in next to her.

"How many more days of this?" his sister yawned. "I don't know how much longer I'll be able to keep up and the foot soldiers are falling more and more behind."

Orin just shook his head. "Too many days are left to keep this speed up. The men have to have some energy left or they won't be of any use in a battle. But the prince is right: we need to get to his brother sooner rather than later."

"But wouldn't we have been getting there soon enough? Did you have to do this at the last border war?" Nox joined in, lifting Elaraine's head as he settled down behind her. He laid her head back down on his stomach. "Is that better?"

"Much... thank you," she muttered as she stretched to find a more comfortable position.

"I don't remember it being like this at all. This isn't like the last war, Nox. There are so many more factors here that we didn't have before," Orin whispered as some of the men filed past them, "like that timber wolf, rumors of the nobles turning against us, and where this invasion is supposed to take place. I mean... why would the Rischiaks pick such a horrible place to cross the border? Why would they pick the low ground and a river crossing?"

"Maybe it's not supposed to make sense," Elaraine slurred, Nox's steady breathing lulling her to sleep. "Maybe the confusion is just a different kind of weapon: while we're confused, they're not."

She heard a few surprised mutterings from Orin as he scrambled up, but she was too tired to care. Nox promised to wake her up when it was time to leave, his voice sounding very far away. She could only nod as her dream began to roll in.

She could not remember her whole dream, and most of it happened in a blur anyway. She knew that in it Orin was walking away from her, leaving her behind on a hill, despite her crying out for him to stay with her. She ran after him, trying to catch him, but her tears obscured her vision and she fell over a body, losing him. She stood and looked around. Dayn and Nox were lying at her feet, spewing blood and reaching for Prince Shep's shield. As she bent down to help them, they coughed and blood spattered over her face. Andell and Prince Shep were nowhere in sight. She was standing on a field of slaughter and looking at the spot where she had seen Orin disappear. The next thing she knew, Ranci was approaching her from where Orin had disappeared into the mists, an eerie smile plastered on her pale face. Without warning, she turned into her ghostly form from Elaraine's other dream.

She did not know what immediately led to that point, and she did not know what happened afterwards. She could feel herself thrashing in her sleep, trying to get away from Ranci, desperate to wake up but unable to do so. The ghost of Ranci passed through her like it had in her other dream, leaving Elaraine terrified once again.

The next thing she knew, she was waking up screaming with Nox holding her down. Orin was calling her name over and over again. Her forehead was drenched in a cold sweat, and her palms felt clammy against the arm she was holding. She felt as though she had just run a few miles instead of just having woken up. There was a calloused hand under her chin that began to gently pat her cheek when she opened her eyes.

"Elaraine? Elaraine! Elaraine, are you all right?" Orin was asking her repeatedly. He felt her forehead when she did not answer him right away. "Please, little sister, just answer me and I'll quit worrying."

She struggled to nod but opted for clearing her throat instead when the hand on her face would not let her move her head. "I'm all right," she rasped, her throat dry from the screaming. "Just a bad dream."

"You were screaming," Nox said shakily. "You were screaming, crying, thrashing—"

"It was pretty awful," Orin agreed. "I haven't heard you scream like that since that dream you had in the Dungeons Ussal. I think some of the men are pretty shaken up from hearing you." He laughed wryly. "We had to run them off when they came over to see what was happening. We thought seeing a score of men with swords drawn when you woke up might scare you more than you already were."

Scenes of the dream came back to her: the blood, the shield, Orin leaving, and she would never forget Ranci flying towards her like she did in every dream. They merged with the dream she had been having since the

Dungeons Ussal, creating one large nightmare. The look of hate that Ranci had before she would fly at Elaraine may have terrified her the most, if she hadn't seen her friends dead in her dream. Her hands began to tremble from the exertion of fighting back more screams and tears. The arm she was holding moved as the torso it belonged to hovered over her. Prince Shep's gaze held hers no matter how hard she tried to avert her bleary eyes, ashamed of herself for him seeing her in such a panicked state.

"Do you remember anything about the dream?" he prompted softly. "I always find that I feel better after I talk about it and I'm all ears to hear about yours. Why don't you tell me everything and then maybe you will feel well enough to sleep a little more."

She thought about the wisdom of telling him versus not telling him. She thought it silly, telling a man about a nightmare, so she opted for a lie. She shook her head and let go of his arm hurriedly when she realized she was still holding onto him.

"No... I only know that it was bad," she whispered so low that the men had to strain to hear her. She tried to smile but she knew they could see through the feeble attempt. "I'm fine now, though. Really. It was only a dream, like you said. It wasn't real. None of that can actually happen, so I shouldn't worry. It must have been from not getting much sleep these past couple of days. It's sure good to be awake."

"It should be!" Dayn scoffed from her feet. "It took us forever to get you to wake up!"

She flashed him a startled look when she realized he was there with them, but she quickly regained her composure. "Oh, well, I was really tired."

Orin grunted as Prince Shep removed his hand from her face and sat back on his heels. He looked grim. Nox and Dayn stood up and went off to get something to eat before they were ordered to remount. After Elaraine's screaming it was unlikely anyone in their vicinity would be able to rest anymore that day so they knew they ought to just keep travelling and pushing onward.

"I will let this go for now," the prince said gravely, "but I still want to talk about this dream soon." He looked up at Orin. "And the other one you had that upset you so much that Orin mentioned." He stood and dusted off his leggings.

Elaraine frowned and tried to sit up, but her brother kept her lying down with hands on her shoulders. "Why?"

"Let's just say that I believe in the power of a dream. Sometimes, your mind is trying to tell you something that you refuse to acknowledge when you're awake. If you keep having bad dreams that cause this to happen, where you scream in terror and agony, then you need to tell someone, and I would be interested in helping you. Besides, it is not a suggestion that you tell me. It is an order."

"He didn't want to be a soldier at first," Orin whispered to her as the prince walked away. "The way his father treated him... well, let's just say that it made him quit his studies when he was young so he could become a soldier. He had always wanted to be a scholar. But he needed to escape that place." He let her sit up slowly and offered her a full water skin. "I think you interest him." He paused. "In a purely intellectual way, of course."

She accepted the water gratefully. "He must be bored if I interest him," she muttered, taking another healthy swig from the water skin. "I just find his curiosity mildly odd. 'The power of a dream'? You must admit that it sounds ridiculous. There is no power in dreams! They are not real!"

"Dreams often reveal things we cannot normally see," her brother argued. "And let him have his fun. He is only asking you to tell him what it is you dream about that scares you so badly. It's harmless, don't you think? And it may make him feel better if someone confides something like that in him."

"It's personal!" she spat back at him. "It's absolutely none of his business!"

"You told me about the last dream," he said a little too reasonably for her liking. "Wasn't that dream personal as well?"

"Well, yes, but that's different! You're my brother and I'm allowed to tell you and it still remain personal! Telling someone who is not blood makes it public, and these are not dreams I want to be made public!"

"I wish you could hear yourself, Elaraine. You sound like a testy child. Just tell him and be done with it. He'll only order you if you don't volunteer it when he asks, so just save yourselves both some trouble and tell him." Orin was starting to get exasperated and his sister knew it. "He will not tell anyone anything you confide in him. I trust him with our lives. I think you can trust him with a couple of dreams."

"But I can't remember it. I told you that already."

"We all know that you lied. You are a horrible liar, and I'm afraid that that is probably what prompted his request to discuss it. You piqued his interest, Elaraine. That was your own fault."

He moved away to refill the water skin she had drained. She hung her head between her knees and wrung her hands. Her nightmare had made her even more tired than she had been before. She could feel her eyelids getting heavy once again and tried to fight it. She was more than thankful for the order that came down the line at midday, only a short while after she had woken up, from Prince Shep calling for the remount and the move out of the camp. At least if she were in a saddle, she knew it would be nearly impossible for her to fall asleep like that.

Orin helped her to her feet and led her over to an already saddled Tix. The gelding looked rested and was ready to go. He snorted at her when she scratched his nose for a minute.

"You're doing good, boy!" she told him softly. "I'm sorry it's been so hard for you, but we don't have much longer to go. Only a couple more days to go and then we'll be at the border and we can rest for a little while. Can you hang in there for me?" He tossed his head. "Good boy! I knew you could!"

Dayn helped her into the saddle after she failed at getting her leg over Tix a couple of times. He did not say a word to her about her trouble. He understood her exhaustion because he was feeling it, too. She rode between Nox and Dayn, talking to them and trying to get herself into a better mood, pretending that a short time before she had not been having a nightmare.

The pace was just as tough as it had been before, if not harder. Weary bodies clung to the saddles and wobbled on tired feet. Prince Shep had gone back to his unsociable state, and no one bothered to approach him this time.

As dusk approached once again, the hope was raised that maybe the prince would call another halt. But after good stopping place after good stopping place was passed without the order for a rest, their hopes were dashed and a dark gloom settled over the exhausted men. Elaraine was swaying in her saddle, unable to stay awake and unable to sleep. A couple of times she caught herself starting to slip in her saddle. She saw the men beside her exchange glances before steering the three horses out of the column.

"What are you doing?" she argued as they dismounted beside her. "We need to stay in line!"

"We won't be able to stay in line when you fall off your horse and get trampled!" Dayn grunted, moving his saddle bags onto Tix. "Now, please dismount." He moved to tie Nox's saddle bags down behind his on Elaraine's horse with some rope.

She raised an eyebrow at him suspiciously. "Why?"

"She is sure dense when she is tired," Nox laughed, reaching up to grasp her waist.

"What do you think you're doing?" Orin yelled as he galloped back to stop beside them. He glared at Nox's hands still holding his sister's waist. "You're supposed to stay in line!"

Nox dropped his arms to his sides immediately. "We're trying to make it so Elaraine can sleep. She was about to fall off her horse!" he said defensively, but backing away from the woman at the same time. "We weren't doing anything to hurt her and we were about to rejoin the line!"

Orin eyed his sister closely, taking in the circles around her eyes and the loosely held reins in her hands. He sighed, muttering something unintelligible to himself, and rubbed his face with his hands as his horse danced under him impatiently. At last, he looked down at them.

"So what's this idea you two were hatching?" he said slowly.

"I can stay awake, Orin," Elaraine promised. "I just need to hold out until the prince makes us walk again. I just need the exercise to get my blood flowing again."

"You look ready to keel over any minute," her brother answered softly. "Admit it, you need some sleep. You didn't really rest earlier, and we don't need you falling and breaking your neck."

She nodded and shrugged, giving up, knowing that they were all right. She did need sleep. She needed it desperately. She and Orin looked at the other two, who were still preparing to carry out their idea.

"She's going to take turns riding between us," Dayn volunteered to tell them. "Tix can carry the bags, and we'll switch her between us so our horses won't get too tired too quickly, but it's the only way to make sure she doesn't fall off."

"We'll be able to keep up," Nox added. "And we'll only be holding her waist to keep her on the horse," he said quickly when his eyes met Orin's sudden glare.

Orin nodded and lowered his voice. "Fine, but hurry up and get back in the column before Prince Shep snaps back to reality. If he sees you three back here fooling around and trying to get this to work, he'll have all our heads!"

Orin kicked his horse back into a gallop to catch back up to his spot by Andell, throwing a glance over his shoulder to make sure that they were still working quickly to get their plan off the ground. Elaraine knew they were right. She would fall off Tix if she fell asleep, and this was the only way she could figure out to get some rest as well. She decided, however, that when Dayn and Nox needed to rest, she would return the favor.

Nox held her steady as Dayn hefted himself back onto his horse. Dayn held his arms down to help Elaraine up onto his horse as Nox went to the bags to fetch some lengths of rope. Dayn held onto her so she would not fall while Nox strapped her legs and her waist to his, making it easier for Dayn to hold onto her and harder for her to fall off. Nox explained to her when she first objected to the rope that when she fell asleep, she would go limp and that it would be too difficult for Dayn to ride and help keep her upright with just an arm on her waist for too long.

When he was done, Nox wished her sweet dreams and went over to his horse. He mounted with ease and steered his mount over to Tix, who was waiting patiently where they had left him. Nox took Tix's reins and the three of them caught back up to the column pretty quickly. When they fell back in behind Ranci, Andell, and Orin, Orin cast a look over his shoulder to see how it had worked and could not suppress a smile when he saw that his sister was already nodding off to sleep.

Elaraine was not awake when Andell noticed her tied to Dayn. She was not awake when Andell would laugh at the difficulty Dayn would have when their path would change and she would start to slide off, bringing him with her. And she stayed asleep when she was transferred over to Nox's saddle.

Andell and Orin helped the two other men in the transfer because she had, indeed, gone limp in her slumber, and they had to make the transfer while riding. She did not know how long she slept, but it was a welcomed and dreamless sleep. When she finally woke up, she felt more rested than she had in a long time.

She noticed immediately that the smell of the person she was tied to was different from Dayn and Nox, or even Orin. It did not sit well with her, this being tied up to someone other than those three. She quickly amended that thought. Andell was like a guardian to her and she would have trusted him to not let her fall while she rested. She looked at the bridle to see who it was she rode with. The crest on the bridle told her who it was before he spoke, and she knew that her assumption that it was Andell was wrong.

"Finally awake?" he laughed. "Well, it's about time!"

"How did I get here? Wasn't I back there?" she yawned, looking around him for Tix, only to see a lot of faces smiling back at her. She did not find the situation at all amusing. She promised herself that that would be the last time she participated so willingly in one of Dayn and Nox's plots without setting a lot of ground rules first. Dayn and Nox waved at her and started laughing when she shot them a glare.

"Well, you had been passed around to just about every horseman here before I noticed what was going on, and I decided that I ought to take a turn, too. After all, it is my fault the pace is so hard and you are not used to it," Prince Shep explained. "But we are only a couple more hours' ride to the border, so you might as well try and sleep some more if you would like. Leo, here, is more than capable of carrying both of us until then."

She shook her head. "It's all right, sire. I'm all slept out."

"All right. Then," he said firmly, steering Leo around a large walnut tree, "why don't we talk about these dreams you've been having?"

Chapter Eighteen

She took a deep breath so she would not snap at the man sharing his saddle with her. It really was not any of his business, but Orin was right in that it was only telling him her dreams, not anything more than that. So she recounted her dreams without any more prompting. She told him every detail she could remember because she got tired of him interrupting her to ask her questions. He really wanted her to go into extra detail about his shield on the battlefield in her latest nightmare. He had to tell her a few times to slow down her telling when she got too carried away and started speaking so fast that she would stutter, but retelling the dreams made her feel the same emotions she had felt while she was in the nightmare. She would just sigh and tell him again what she had just said, taking extra care to pronounce each word slowly. When she was done telling him about her nightmares and answering every question he threw her way, she took a deep breath and was surprised at how much better she felt at having told him everything.

"And you say that in each dream Ranci turned into a ghost?" he asked for the tenth time.

"Yes," she sighed. "And then I wake up screaming."

"Hmm."

He was quiet for quite a while, leaving Elaraine wondering what in the world he meant by 'hmm.' She was happy by the respite she received from his questioning, but at the same time, she really wished he had left the conversation with something more substantial than just a grunt. She could not take it any longer.

"All right, I give up!" she almost yelled. "You quiz me for an hour and then all you have to say is 'hmm' and then you fall into this pensive silence and, if I might say so, it is rather unnerving when all you have to say at the end of all that is 'hmm!'"

She could feel him silently laugh behind her. "I have no idea what your dreams mean," he admitted. "But I find them interesting. Would you mind terribly if I asked you about them more often?"

She sighed. "Have you not heard about them enough for a lifetime?"

"Not just these dreams, Elaraine! I mean your dreams in general. If I were to analyze your dreams, I am sure I would find you to be an absolute enigma."

"An 'enigma'?" She hated how she was quickly becoming less irritated with the man but could not resist the good mood sweeping over her. "I've been called many things in my life, but I think I actually like the sound of that one!"

They talked the rest of the trip, forgetting for a time that social differences should have kept them from acting so familiar with each other. He adamantly refused to let her return to riding Tix. Elaraine forgot to use his title a few times, but Prince Shep did not care or correct her. It gave him a chance to feel more human for once without the pomp of his title. Somehow, Elaraine was always the one to do that for him. He could laugh, be angry, or be sad, and she did not make him feel any weaker for it. He welcomed these times when they could just forget about the war, even if it was only for a few minutes.

Behind them, things were another matter. Ranci could not stop smiling while the men within ear shot were appalled. Even Orin felt like shaking his little sister. He was happy his sister was happy, but was annoyed with who she was happy with. Nox and Dayn were turning a little green and refused to acknowledge the happy scene before them. Andell was the only one of the men who did not seem to mind. He noticed how, when Elaraine was around, Prince Shep acted more human and would put down his defenses.

But the happy time could not last forever, especially only a happy conversation. They could have carried on in that way for hours had they been given the opportunity. But when an arrow came slicing through the air to pierce a nearby tree, the good conversation abruptly ended and chaos ensued.

Andell and Prince Shep tried to keep the troops in formation as confusion and fear swept along the columns. Orin was focused on a point in the distance, a smallish figure running pell-mell away from the lines of soldiers. In hot pursuit of the figure were two men in royal blue tunics, gaining fast on their quarry. Orin spurred his horse into action and drew his sword. He flew by his sister without a backward glance, his only thought on the figure trying to get away. Prince Shep was on his heels after quickly putting Elaraine on the ground and was doing his utmost to catch up with

Orin. Orin was too set on his mission to be caught by any of the other horsemen now left in the columns. The prince did not catch Orin until Orin drew his sword.

Elaraine watched as her brother leaned down in the saddle, wielding his blade like a baton as he chased after the now-fleeing pursuers. The small figure stumbled in front of the prince's stallion as Prince Shep reined in for a quick stop. Elaraine watched as the green-cloaked man looked up at the prince and slowly sank to the forest floor. Prince Shep was off his horse in the blink of an eye, trying to support the man. He called for Andell, who hurried to his prince's side to help him.

A grim-looking Orin was coming back, leading his horse and wiping his blade off in some large ferns he was walking by. Attached to his saddle, Elaraine could see a blue cloth flapping, and it did not take her long to think of what it was. Andell and Prince Shep had lifted the man onto Andell's saddle and he was leading his horse back as well, falling into careful step with Orin. Prince Shep was the last to follow, having needed to collect himself before rejoining everybody.

Orin took his place by his sister and was silent while the healers examined Rian. He was severely injured, a cut to the side of his head and the way he was holding his arm was not a good sign. His tunic was matted and sticky with blood from an arrow deeply embedded in his side. As fast as the healers worked, Rian's prognosis was still not good. Even Elaraine could tell the healers were having to race to save Rian's life. Elaraine did not think his skin was a healthy color. He was turning an odd shade of yellow-green that she had never seen before. Orin just stayed silent until the head healer finally managed to get the bleeding under control enough to get him into one of their wagons.

"I thought it was Moraiah," he finally whispered, so low that Elaraine could barely hear him. "I saw someone small trying to run... it's been haunting my dreams, you know. I keep thinking that Moraiah and Josi are out there running from something. Why else would they not have reached the capital when we did?"

"They probably just got held up, Orin," Elaraine tried to soothe her brother. "Moraiah and Josi can take care of themselves. You made sure of that. So just trust that they got delayed, arrived after we left, and are safe. Until you hear differently, that's what you have to believe. You'll go mad, otherwise."

He turned away and sheathed his sword. "I suppose I should mean no offense with this, little sister, but I do not expect you to understand how I feel right now. Your family is not with you because you fled when you had to. My family is not with me because of war."

"You're right, Orin, our situations are very much different. We both may have made choices that led us to where we are now without our families, but do you know what the difference is?" She calmed herself down when she realized her voice was beginning to rise. "The difference is that Moraiah and Josi love you, and my husband saw me as a servant. My husband truly did not love me, while your family worships you. You have all the love in the world and are breaking apart at the seams because of no news. I understand, Orin, I do. But maybe in this case, no news is good news."

She went to join Dayn and Nox, who were still fuming about the earlier scene they had watched with Prince Shep speaking to Elaraine. They tried to ignore her, but their hearts eventually gave way when they saw she was mad and upset.

Nox slapped her on the back. "Cheer up, Elaraine. You and Orin fight all the time."

"I'm not mad at Orin," she corrected sourly. "I'm mad at everything right now. I mean, if it weren't for the war, Orin would be back home with his family and happy. If it weren't for the war, Rian wouldn't be teetering on death's door."

"And if it weren't for the war, you would probably be dead by now. The only reason the king let you go so easily was because he is too busy thinking about the war. Otherwise, I doubt you'd be pouting around here right now. Plus, Orin and his family wouldn't be back home, remember? He would be on the run like before, all of us roaming and trying to avoid being caught or seen. So stop sulking and accept the world as it is: a bad place."

She turned to him. "Is the world truly a bad place or is it the people that make it bad?"

Nox just stared at her blankly. Dayn laughed and clapped his friend on the back.

"I do believe that that was too deep for our Nox here," Dayn managed to spurt out between laughs.

That made her smile faintly. "Well, anyway, I'm going to let Orin be for a little while. I don't think my hanging onto him like I did when we were younger is helping him that much. He needs room to think about all that's happening."

"Actually, we tend to disagree," Dayn said, finally sobering. "We've discussed this and Nox and I agree. It is not you who are hanging onto Orin, but it is Orin who is hanging onto you."

"It's not just Orin, either," Ranci joined the discussion. "I think there are quite a few other men here who are hanging onto you. You do not seem to be hanging onto any of them. They seem to be finding solace in your kindness."

Dayn blushed as he glared at his mother. "Woman, why are you here? This was a private conversation."

"If it was so private, why is it everyone around you can hear it? And did I teach you to be so disrespectful of women?" She smacked him upside his head. "Well? Did I? Is that anyway to talk to your mother?" She turned away from him with a dramatic flourish. "If I'd known you were going to be like this, I never would have endured that entire day of labor for you to be born. I never would have made sure you were raised with plenty of food and shelter, or made the clothes on your back. I wouldn't have tried to get Elaraine to marry you after her marriage fell apart...."

"Mother!" Dayn yelled frantically at her, earning many a snicker from the eavesdropping troops. "Please... stop talking... right now!"

She sighed and patted his shoulder. "Well, at least you said 'please,' son." She was laughing as she walked away.

"That woman!" he gritted as he watched her merry retreat. He shook his head a few times in exasperation. "What were we talking about again?"

Nox was drawing a blank as he stared blankly at Ranci as she walked away. "I have absolutely no idea...."

Elaraine tuned them out as she just turned around. She found them more nonsensical than usual. Orin was sulking at the edge of the forest talking to Andell and Prince Shep, and she started to walk toward them. The men motioned her over when they saw her hesitant approach. Orin just kept shaking his head and making large gestures with his hands at the prince. The prince looked none too happy either, but his jaw was set in resignation, and he held Tix's reins in a tight fist. Andell looked worried, chewing his bottom lip and rubbing the stubble on his chin. She quirked an eyebrow at them as she came upon them but remained silent, afraid of what the trouble might be.

"We need you to ride ahead and warn the rest of the army," Andell told her when she reached them. "Until Rian wakes up, we won't know exactly what happened, but those Rischiak foot soldiers aren't here for their own amusement or to help us."

It took her a few seconds to answer. While she hated the idea of leaving these three men behind for any length of time, she knew her duty came before family and other obligations. Besides, she could prove herself to Orin if she went and succeeded.

"I understand," she nodded.

"Now, don't fight us on this," Orin growled, apparently giving up his battle with the prince. "I don't want you to go, either, but—"

"Orin, I already said I would do it! Catch up with the conversation, big brother!"

He only glared at her as Prince Shep cut in. "Tell my brother what we saw happen to Rian and he'll understand. Tell him we're going to dig in here until we know what's going on. I am not going to move us another inch until we know what is happening further along the trail. Luckily, Orin got the men who got Rian, but we haven't heard from the other scouts yet and we don't know what is going on out there. I'm not about to take the men anywhere until we know where the Rischiaks are. I cannot afford to lose half of my men in an ambush if there is one out there. But you ride there and straight back, with no sight-seeing, Elaraine. And don't speak to anyone else about this. You are only to tell Prince Arlun."

She nodded, committing what he told her to memory. "Is there anything else you want me to tell Prince Arlun?"

He shook his head and held the reins out to her. "Just tell him that we will reinforce him when we can but that we are in trouble here, too."

She nodded and accepted Tix's reins from the prince. "What happens if you get attacked before I get back?"

"Elaraine, don't worry about that. Just do your duty and don't fail," Andell said softly. He laid a heavy hand on her shoulder. "If you always worry about what might happen, you're blind to what is actually happening and won't do anything at all."

"But what's happening is that we're under attack here, so it's not like this is a blind possibility, Andell!" She turned to the prince. "How will I find you if you are attacked? Will you not retreat somewhere?"

"Elaraine, Berell taught you how to scout, did he not? And growing up in Gegernen, you must have known a lot of those skills already. Just use what he taught you. You may have only gone with the scouts once, but you should have absorbed enough information in that one lesson to be able to find us anywhere if what you were raised knowing isn't enough! We're a bunch of bumbling and grumbling men, for crying out loud! How hard could that search possibly be? Now take Nox and Dayn with you."

Andell called for the two men to join them and Nox and Dayn started over with their horses in tow.

"But I can help if I stay here! Send Nox or Dayn, but why send all three of us? Isn't every person needed if something happens here?"

"One woman will not turn the tide of this war, Elaraine," Prince Shep said after a few moments. "If we get attacked, we get attacked. Take Dayn and Nox and get on your way. Mind everything I have said."

She hung her head but had to agree with him. How could only one person change the outcome of a war? And certainly no woman, who had never had formal training in battle skills before, could. And how could she possibly argue further with the prince? She felt dejected and rejected at being told to leave them.

Orin grabbed her before she could turn away. He held her tightly like he might not ever see her again. She could feel him shaking. "Elaraine," he whispered harshly in her ear, "go there and straight back. Only speak with Prince Arlun and his advisers. Do not go exploring around that camp. Promise me?" He tightened his grip when she did not answer him right away.

"Orin, please, let me go." She tried to push him away but his grasp would not loosen.

"I can tell that if you don't promise me then you won't heed what I say this time. You've always been curious about everything but you can't be this time! Now... you've always kept your word, and I'm really counting on it this time. Promise me!"

"Big brother, you're going to leave bruises at this rate! Please... let go of me!"

"You have to promise me before I let you go."

The look in his eyes was dangerous. She had not seen that glare since she broke one of his toys when they were children. He was always very gentle with her and he had very rarely gotten into such a foul mood, especially around her. While she did not want to, she nodded her consent and he let her go, although she could tell he was probably more in loathe doing so than she was in agreeing to what he had said. She stood in front of him for a couple of moments before finally turning away.

"I don't know what got into you, Orin, but I'm a grown woman. I understand the necessity for speed, I do. There was no need to remind me like that. And there was no need to act like that," she said at last, refusing to blurt out all the words she wished she could. She wished she could scream at him, shake him, ask him why he was always so protective of her, and tell him he needed to let her be independent for once, but she knew that would never go over well and would likely get her the opposite of what she wanted.

She mounted Tix in resignation and galloped away from Prince Shep, Andell, and her brother, the sounds of Nox's and Dayn's horses' hooves thundering in her ears after her. She could still see the fear, anger, and sadness in her brother's eyes when she closed her eyes to blink away her tears. She kicked Tix into a fast run, trying to drown out her brother's words and trying not to figure out what he meant by them.

"Elaraine! Slow down!" Dayn yelled after her. "The horses can't keep this pace for that long!"

She did not listen. She kept on, Tix straining after a while to keep running. Swennian horses had unbelievable stamina and endurance but after such a long week, the horses were starting to show fatigue. The marches had been long day after day and it was beginning to wear his legs down. Nox was catching her, and while she tried to spur her horse on, it was easy for him to grab her reins and slow them all down.

"Elaraine!" he was yelling. "Why didn't you answer us?"

"It's not his place," she mumbled. "It's not his place to tell me that, make me promise that."

"You're still upset about that?" Nox seemed flabbergasted. "Elaraine, he says those things and does those things because he's your brother and he loves you. That's all. You always take Orin too seriously. Get over it! Get your head out of where the sun doesn't shine and get back to business!"

"You don't wonder one little bit why he doesn't want me to look around? Why every time someone so much as mentions the main army, he tenses up and becomes quiet? He always gets quiet when they are talked about, even when we still lived in Gegernen. He didn't use to be this way. He's always been protective of me, but never like this. He's never hurt me before." Her fingers ran along her tunic where she could feel the bruises forming. "That's what bothers me. If he hurt me trying to keep me from exploring that camp, then what is there that could hurt me or I shouldn't see?"

"It's probably just because it's an army camp. It's disgusting, and you're bound to see things he deems you too innocent to see. And he probably gets anxious because he remembers the last war. That's all. Now, can we please try and save our horses and just walk for a little while? You wore us all out back there."

"He's never done that before," she grumbled as she dismounted. "And he's not my father. But both he and Prince Shep were acting oddly. They both told me I'm only supposed to talk to Prince Arlun and not to look around. They acted like there's something there that I'm not supposed to know about. But, then, why send me if that's the case?"

"We're the most expendable people there and that is why we have been sent," Dayn offered, trying desperately to end the conversation. "Now, Elaraine, we're both begging you to stop talking about it and to stop thinking about it. You're a grown woman moping around like a small child. It is not a flattering suit for you."

She hung her head. "I know, but it's just so aggravating. I know I've grown since I left the Dungeons Ussal, but, at the same time, it's like he's treating me more and more like a child the closer we get to this camp and I want to know why! I've seen battle. I've killed men! I do not need to be coddled and I do not need to be hidden away from all the horrors this life has to offer. After all, it's not like my life is unmarred right now as it is." The look the two men exchanged did not go unnoticed. "You two know!" she accused, waggling a finger at them and stopped walking. "You know why they are worried about sending me!"

Nox shrugged as he continued walking. "So what if we do? We've already told you what he told us and you won't listen."

"I'm getting a headache. You two give me a headache. Do you mind if we go the rest of the way in peace and quiet?" Dayn begged, pinching the bridge of his nose. "Travelling with you two is going to make me deaf and old."

Chapter Nineteen

The rest of the long trip was made in an uncomfortable silence through the night. They trudged through the mud, sliding everywhere, until they reached a plateau overlooking a long, flat plain. Tents were everywhere before them, dispersed haphazardly before a large creek. The plain seemed filled with tents. A few soldiers were beginning to mill about in the predawn hours, and a couple of fires were lit in the center, where Elaraine guessed the healers and their tents to be based on the wagons nearby.

"There are so many more people than I expected there to be!" she said in awe. "The way everyone was talking, the army was nowhere near big enough!"

"It isn't anywhere near big enough," Dayn said roughly. "We need at least twice as many men, but we have none to spare. The Rischiaks will be much larger than this. The last war really put a strain on the number of veteran men we had anyways. Unless there's a miracle—"

"That's enough, Dayn," Nox said coolly. "There's no call for that kind of talk." He turned to the woman. "But he's right. We don't have nearly enough people."

"So you silence me but then you go and say the exact same thing I do?" Dayn growled. "Kind of a double standard you have there, don't you think?"

"There's a difference in what we said, my friend. It's all in the tone. I said it calmly and without emotion while you said it like the world's end was close at hand and like you had been spat upon. No double standard has been created here."

Elaraine just shook her head as she remounted and began to nudge Tix toward the tent city. "You two really annoy me sometimes. You know that, right?"

They continued to argue behind her, but she was too focused on trying to find Prince Arlun's tent to pay them much attention. As the men of the camp woke up, she found more and more curious eyes drawn in her direction. As the rows between tents became narrower, they were forced to leave their horses tied near a wagon.

It did not take them long to find Prince Arlun's tent, considering the maze of tents they had to navigate to get there. The standards in the center of the encampment served as a good beacon for them to follow, and Prince Arlun's was right next to them with a guard at the tent flap. Elaraine thought of Prince Shep's tent, guard-less and standard-less. Unless you saw it being set up you never would have known a prince slept there.

The guard straightened and watched them carefully as they approached. Nox saw his hand tighten on the hilt of his sword and pointed it out to his companions with a gesture. The guard looked grim and sounded even grimmer when he hailed them.

"Halt! No one is to approach this tent until Prince Arlun awakes! What is your business here?" he growled.

"Prince Shep sent us," Dayn spoke up when he realized Elaraine had lost her confident drive now that they were finally there and would very likely remain mute while being yelled at. "He sends news of Rischiak movements that needs to be conveyed to Prince Arlun immediately."

"Prince Arlun is asleep," the guard repeated, trying to dismiss them. "Come back in a few hours."

"You don't understand—" Dayn started, but was cut off by the guard.

"No, I think it is you who doesn't understand. You see, Prince Arlun knows all about the Rischiak movements, making your news a repeat of what he has already heard. On top of that, he only went to bed for the first time in days a couple of hours ago." He lowered his voice and leaned toward them slightly, motioning for them to do the same. "Have you ever seen Prince Arlun when he is that sleep deprived?" He watched as the three shook their heads. "Well, the man has a temper in the best of his moods. When he hasn't gotten any sleep, he's—"

"Worse than a bear," a new voice interrupted the guard.

The guard spun around, his eyes becoming large and frightened. Elaraine looked and saw a bedraggled head peering through the tent flap at them. His sandy hair was mussed and the bags under his eyes betrayed his desperate need for sleep. He was tall, his head towering well over the guard's when he stood up and stretched as he emerged from the tent. He was well-dressed despite having just been woken up from his sleep, and the way he held himself spoke volumes of what he thought of himself, Elaraine thought.

"Drake, I could have sworn," Prince Arlun continued sternly as he met and matched Elaraine's gaze, "that you were under orders to let messengers in to see me immediately."

"But you also ordered me to not let anyone enter your tent until you were awake," Drake said defensively. "When you're telling me two different things, what do you expect to happen?"

It occurred to Elaraine that Drake was to Prince Arlun as Andell was to Prince Shep. She was sure that the imposing, albeit tired, figure before her would not let just any of his men speak to him or about him as Drake did without severe repercussions. The man he let do so must have a special relationship with him, because Prince Arlun's temperamental reputation preceded him. He may have looked calm and good-natured on the outside, but there was a tenseness about him that gave Elaraine the impression that he was ready to attack anyone for anything at any time. He put her defenses up with his continued stare, and her mind became frenzied as she tried to remember her message for him. Instead, an image of an angry bear wearing Prince Arlun's clothes assaulted her thoughts.

Prince Arlun was looking at her expectantly, eyebrows raised and frowning. Then he sighed and took a few steps towards her. He snapped his fingers in front of her face. "Hello! Did you hear me?"

She shook her head to stop her daydreams of a rampaging prince-bear. "No, sire. I'm sorry." She bowed deeply before him, much to everyone's surprise, even her own. "I am afraid I became slightly distracted for a moment. It will not happen again."

She could smell brandy hanging in the air when he chuckled lightly and approached her. He ruffled her hair, much to her dismay. She tried tying the now flying locks of hair back in place as he stepped back, but the slight breeze was blowing just hard enough to make it nearly impossible. She gave up after a few moments and tried to ignore the wisps of hair flying in front of her face. Prince Arlun was giving her a quirky and lopsided smirk.

"No wonder my brother puts up with you, Elaraine Hedri. You really are quite amusing." He leaned into her and dropped his voice to a whisper. "You do not need to bow to me like that. We are comrades in arms and, while it is respectful in court, it is not necessary to bow to a comrade at battle. Besides, ladies are meant to curtsy, and I am too tired to return any formalities."

She straightened slightly and blinked in surprise. "I'm sorry, sire."

Nox leaned over to her as Prince Arlun opened the tent for them to enter. "Remain as courteous as you were. He may just be trying to get you into trouble and I think he is more than a little drunk. He is not reputed to be nice, but he is reputed to be sly and manipulative. I think we should trust the rumors until we observe differently."

He beckoned them into the tent after telling her to stop apologizing, that it really was all right. He pulled the slow-to-move Nox through the tent opening with a "You're letting all the warm air out!" Then he sat back down on the bed and stretched out.

"Please forgive me. Drake was correct, I am afraid. I have not slept in days and it is beginning to show. So please give me your report as thoroughly and quickly as you can before I drift back off to sleep. I may not wake up for days as it is." He yawned widely and closed his eyes. "Miss Hedri, report," he repeated when she hesitated. "I'm not used to having to ask twice for something to happen and I find it rather tiresome." He opened one eye and narrowed it at her. "Don't make me ask a third time." He closed his eye again.

She couldn't stop thinking about how different the two brothers were. "Prince Shep wants me to inform you that one of our scouts, Rian Periborin, has been attacked by Rischiaks. My brother, Orin, killed the men who were chasing Rian, but Prince Shep says that he cannot be here as soon as he had originally planned because he isn't going to move from where he is until he knows where the Rischiaks are and what they're doing there."

"Have the other scouts not told him what they have found?" Prince Arlun asked with his eyes still closed.

"No, sire. That is the problem. None of the other scouts had returned as of our leaving to come here."

"No news whatsoever?"

"No, sire. That's one of the reasons Prince Shep sent us ahead to report to you. He doesn't know what's in wait for him and he doesn't want to risk an ambush."

"But you three made it through these supposed enemy lines without detection?"

"Yes, sire."

"And you three are inexperienced commoners and my brother is very experienced and has had the best training royalty can buy. He's being cowardly and over careful."

Prince Arlun was silent for a few minutes. His eyes were closed, and Elaraine was afraid he had fallen asleep while mulling the situation over. All she could think about was getting back to her brother and Prince Shep. Every second of silence made her more and more uneasy. She jumped when he finally gave her the orders she had been told to wait for.

"Tell Prince Shep that he is to continue here without delay. I have not heard of Rischiaks moving around behind our lines. It is hard to believe that they are doing so. I have the best scouts in the army at my disposal and they have not found anything. It was probably just a few boys with the same color uniform on as the Rischiaks playing." He looked at Elaraine closely before adding, "Boys do that, you know. They play. They do not know when to be serious or when something is a bad idea." He cleared his throat and closed his eyes again.

"I don't think, sire, that Prince Shep is willing to take the chance that it was just boys playing. He wants his men to make it here in one piece."

"Are you implying that I do not care for the safety of his men, Ms. Hedri?" His eyes snapped open and he sat up. He stood and his head nearly touched the top of the tent.

She sighed heavily and resisted the urge to roll her eyes. "No, sire, I just—"

He walked up to her and stood inches from her face, the smell of the brandy now strong and making her uneasy. "Ms. Hedri, what uniform does it look like I'm wearing?"

"Sire—"

"That's right." He patted her head, his condescension oozing into the act. "I'm a prince, while you are a mere commoner. My brother is just a prince, who is unworthy of even that title, while I am the Crown Prince. If you report back to him and he decides not to follow my orders, kindly remind him of the fact that he has no say in this matter. He was an unwanted and useless spare prince, and I know his place, even if he does not. Tell him I expect him here by tomorrow evening before the sun sets. If he is not here by then, he will face my wrath. Am I understood?"

She did not know how the conversation had turned into such a defensive battle so quickly. She felt bullied and helpless to do anything as she just stood there looking up at him. She wanted to yell in Prince Shep's defense, but her tongue and mouth would not move.

"I asked you a question, Ms. Hedri, and I do believe I have already asked you to be prompt in your answers, as I am still not in the habit of having to ask multiple times. But I shall ask you once more because you are new to the niceties of decorum: am I understood?"

She looked at him for a minute to calm herself before she replied. "Yes, sire."

He looked at her for a moment more before shoving her through the tent flap with Nox and Dayn close behind her. "If you understood so well, then why are you not leaving and going back? My brother is on a deadline, you know."

Elaraine turned on her heel without further comment and proceeded into the rows upon rows of tents, too angry to pay attention to where she was going. Nox and Dayn were content to let her work out her anger on her own, staying behind her and letting her continue in silence. After a while, Elaraine realized they were headed nowhere near where they had left their horses and sat down on a log in defeat. Nox and Dayn sat on either side of her and exchanged a look over her head.

"He shouldn't have said those things about Prince Shep," she grumbled. "At least Prince Shep cares about what happens to his men. Prince Arlun just wants to exert his authority... the stupid narcissist. He isn't half the leader... or man... that Prince Shep is."

Nox patted her back. "It's a benefit of being a Crown Prince, I suppose. But look on the bright side, Elaraine. At least Prince Shep is humble and doesn't act like that. If he was the Crown Prince, who knows how he'd act... he might have been just like Prince Arlun."

"It still doesn't give him the right to just dismiss everything Prince Shep has to say. He's not back there getting attacked!"

"You're right, he's here facing an attack. The future of our nation is on his shoulders and he is facing the biggest battle of our time. Hopefully, it will be the last for generations to come. It's his job to make sure everything that needs taken care of gets done when it's supposed to be done. Throwing around his title should be expected. I think he's handling the pressure well considering what he's facing. History will not remember that you or I were here, but it will always remember that Prince Arlun was here."

She just looked up from her knees and glared at him. She grumbled under her breath as Dayn stood up, protesting as he caught hold of her hand.

Dayn just laughed and pulled her back to her feet. "I hate to tell you this, but you are just a commoner like the rest of us even if you do deserve to be so much more. He. Outranks. You. Fact of life. Forever. Move on."

Elaraine punched him in the shoulder. "There're other ways to do it than just being rude. Prince Shep outranks me, too, but he is at least civil about it. I was only trying to deliver a message. Don't get me wrong. I can understand that he can pull rank and I respect the rank he has. But it was unnecessary to phrase it like he did, and there wasn't any need in speaking like that about Prince Shep. And he was drunk!"

"It's his prerogative, Elaraine. If he's off duty he can drink. He is, after all, the leader of the army. And the Crown Prince. I'm quite sure those two things give him the freedom to deviate from just about every kind of propriety there is."

"I'm still just the messenger, not the maker of the message. If he and his brother are not on good terms or are having a power struggle, there is no reason to take it out on me. I only said what Prince Shep told me to."

"Yes, and the messenger is also the killer of his best friend and cousin, remember? You're lucky he didn't just kill you. He knows who you are. So just be thankful he only pulled rank. After all, it was friendly enough until he did throw his title around, so at least we know he has an open mind."

"You're beginning to sound a lot like Orin."

"Well... that's bad news to hear. I'm going to have to tell your brother I need some space! Maybe I should start hanging around Andell more and get a little wiser. Or maybe Prince Shep. Maybe he can teach me how to win you over so easily."

"Dayn, be quiet. They're just friends. He just looks after her like Orin does... like a big brother or something like that," Nox growled.

Dayn put his palms out to Nox. "Calm down! I was just saying that he really knows how to calm Elaraine down. Or, if you haven't noticed, she's been a lot happier than she used to be. And it's not because of Orin, you or me."

"Maybe she was already getting better and it just happened to coincide with meeting the prince. Did you ever consider that? Why does he have to be credited with her being calmer and braver and happier and more outgoing and—"

"I get the idea, Nox, and I understand what you're saying, but I don't believe in coincidences. At least there's an authority figure besides Orin she can respect now."

Elaraine glared at the two men. "I'm right here, you know. And it's not because of anybody in particular. I've just had to grow up a lot more recently. Going to war changes people... except for you two. You two are still the silliest men I've ever had to meet and put up with."

She was smiling as she walked away, knowing she had gotten under their skin. They were grumbling behind her back about how they had grown up and were wondering why she had not seen it. She did not know why, but those two always gave her an extra little bounce in her step when they tried to make her feel better. Knowing that they cared when they did not have to made her feel loved, and she loved them in turn. They were her brothers when Orin was not there, and she always felt safe when they were around. Of course, that also meant they never left her side, but that gave Orin peace of mind, so she was willing to put up with most of their little annoyances. Not to say she was always patient about those annoyances, but she tried.

Thinking of the two men at her side was giving her a headache. She knew that they at least seemed to like her more than she did them and that was a perplexing situation for her. She had no idea what to say for them to finally move on with their lives, but their jealousy over her friendship with Prince Shep was ridiculous to her. But she knew they realized she occasionally wished there was a chance for it to be more than just a friendship. She realized that Nox and Dayn had a right to be jealous. All they craved was her heart, and that was directed away from them. And she surmised that it always would be that way. She tried not to, but when she compared her two friends with Prince Shep she realized that they never even stood a chance. They would always only be her pseudo-brothers.

At the same time, there was her real brother, whose heart was being torn between searching for his family and staying with the army to fight for his king and Swennia. It was a decision he had never thought he would have to make. He always tried to keep those he loved as far from harm's way as possible, often putting himself in danger to do so.

Oh, Orin, she thought, *how ironic! You always tried to keep me away from fights and here I am in the middle of the biggest one in many a year. That alone should give you a heart attack, big brother!*

The woman found it mildly troubling when she realized how little she thought of her own family. Her husband had been pushed to the far recesses of her mind in the recent months, and she felt assuredly ashamed for that. He was still her husband, after all, and she felt she must have liked him at some point in their marriage.

Elaraine's good mood was quickly souring again. She began to dwell more and more on Prince Arlun's sudden attitude change and the allegiance she had to Prince Shep. She had to respect Prince Arlun, but something about him disturbed and frightened her, though she could not quite put her finger on what it was about him that made her feel so uneasy. Something in his eyes told her he was dangerous even though he had acted kindly towards her at the beginning of their meeting.

Elaraine was so deeply lost in her thoughts that she was not paying close enough attention to where she was going and ran into a log pile by a fire pit. She cursed softly at the pain in her toes and watched the logs start rolling and stop a few feet away when they hit a tent pole. She could hear the occupant of the tent grumbling about being awakened, but she was too busy trying to hide her embarrassment from anyone who might have actually seen the incident to care about having woken the person up. Instantly, Nox and Dayn were at her side trying to usher her away from the scene. She was arguing that she didn't need their help, so it took the trio a while to realize that the occupant of the tent had come out and was watching them all very closely.

They were all surprised when a throat cleared and a voice that was decidedly feminine, said: "You know, I thought you'd at least be more graceful than that, Elaraine. After all, my little sister should have at least gotten some of the grace I did."

It took a while for anyone to speak. The tall woman sighed and heaved herself away from the post, making her way over the silent and frozen friends. She tied her hair as she came towards them. She shoved Nox and Dayn aside.

"You really should be more careful and watch where you're going," she told Elaraine softly.

Elaraine bristled at the reproach from the stranger. "I have a lot on my mind, so excuse me for trying to think and straighten everything out."

The woman looked at her and pushed Elaraine's loose hair behind an ear. "You have absolutely no idea who I am, do you?"

Elaraine shook her head, recoiling from the touch. "No. And I do not appreciate being scolded by a stranger, so, if you'll excuse me, I'll be leaving now."

The woman frowned and looked at her closely. "But I already told you a few moments ago... we're sisters, Elaraine."

Chapter Twenty

Dayn was eyeing the strange woman warily as he went back to Elaraine's side. He started to dust her off before she swatted his efforts away. "Elaraine, let's get going. You know how Orin will be if we're gone for what he might deem too long."

"He'll be angry as it is if he finds out that we walked around the encampment like we did. He and Prince Shep told us not to go exploring," Nox reminded her, trying to guide her away.

"And it will be our skins that get tanned, not yours."

The woman laughed. "What? Orin is still playing the overprotective brother? He was doing that to me a long time ago. I finally had to tell him that he was just my little brother and to stop or I would put him in his place in front of his friends. He left me alone after that." She shrugged. "But I suppose I'm not all that surprised you seem so lost right now. We weren't ever supposed to meet, but how am I supposed to just let my little sister stumble her way through the camp and not do anything? Orin should have at least told you there was the possibility of our meeting. Did he not?" She waited for any indication she had even been heard and only shrugged again when she did not receive an answer. "Well, that's not surprising either. After all, we're half-siblings and never really got along."

"So, Orin is your half-brother?" Elaraine asked distantly. "Not your whole brother?" She shook her head as she snapped herself out of it. "Wait a second! I don't have an older sister. I don't know if you even know Orin, so leave us all alone and go back to bed. I'm sorry for waking you up, but we'd better be going now. Our camp is quite a distance from here."

The woman nodded, still grinning. "Fine, but do me a favor?"

"Will it get us away from you sooner?"

She nodded and stood up. "Tell Orin that Jonnie said hello. He'll know who I am."

Without saying another word to the three visitors, Jonnie stretched and walked back to her tent, securing the tent flap tight behind her. Three pairs of eyes stared after her before falling back onto each other. Nox was the first to break the uncomfortable silence they had fallen into.

"I have no idea what just happened, or who that was. But I don't think we should tell Orin her message. You never promised to deliver it, so it's not like you would be letting her down or anything. I think we should just leave now and pretend that this last little encounter never actually happened. After all, if she was a woman Orin doesn't want you to know, he really will skin Dayn and me."

"No he wouldn't," Elaraine said as they steered her back to their horses. "He'd just be mad at me because I went exploring when he told me not to and I promised him I wouldn't." She was quiet for a minute as they continued on their way. "I think Nox is right. Let's not tell Orin about our little misadventure just now."

The two men agreed as they walked along with her. They were all soon restored to their good spirits, the encounter with the strange woman and the hard feelings towards Prince Arlun forgotten for the moment. All Elaraine could think about was getting back to her brother and Prince Shep.

The ride back to Prince Shep's troops was uneventful and swift. They had to spend the night in the forest but they arrived in the morning. Their original message delivered, a great weight had been lifted from their shoulders. All they had to do right then was to return and report back, giving the prince his brother's painfully direct response. They were stopped by scouts long before they reached their comrades.

"Berell? I thought Prince Shep said you weren't allowed to leave camp! You were under lock and key when we left," Elaraine said as the man moved into their path from behind a large beech tree.

"Rian is not doing well," Berell said, refusing to meet her kind gaze. "Prince Shep needs as many scouts as he can get."

"We weren't gone that long, Berell, and he had enough scouts when we left," Dayn jumped in.

Berell did not answer him but instead walked up to Elaraine and held a hand up to her. "Elaraine, I don't want to be the one to tell you, but I think you need to hear it from a friend. Will you please come with me for a few moments?"

Elaraine just stared at his hand. "Berell—"

"Don't go, Elaraine," Dayn almost begged. "We already know he's a traitor. I don't trust him."

"I don't either," Nox was sure to add.

"Berell, what's this about?" she asked.

His hand dropped back to his side and he looked mildly defeated. "Elaraine, there's nothing for you back at camp. Turn tail now and run back home where you belong."

"What are you talking about?" She grabbed her reins tighter and started to steer Tix away, but was stopped by the man on the ground grabbing the saddle. "Berell, I have to go to Prince Shep and deliver a message and then I need to talk to Orin."

"No, Elaraine." He hung his head and leaned against Tix. He mumbled something into the horse's shoulder.

"What was that?"

"Elaraine... Orin ...he— he went out a few hours after you left on a patrol. He's not back yet."

"That's fine, I'll just report to Prince Shep while I wait."

"Okay, I must admit that I did not make myself completely clear just now." He sighed and looked up at her. "Prince Shep is not there either."

"Where is Prince Shep?"

"He took Andell and some other men to look for Orin."

"Why would they need to look for Orin?" Then it suddenly dawned on her and she felt sick to her stomach. She swooned in her saddle and Berell caught her as she began to fall. "Oh. Oh no. No, no, no, no, no." She looked at Berell. "Please tell me this is just another one of your lies. Where's Orin?"

"Elaraine, if I knew where your brother was, I would tell you. I swear I would. I am not so cruel as to lie to you about this. No one knows where he is. He was really upset and Prince Shep told him to take someone with him but he refused. He was only supposed to be gone a couple of hours but he still has not returned."

"But Orin always returns."

"That would be the reason why everyone is worried."

"You don't understand, Berell. Orin always returns. So if he hasn't returned then that means—"

Dayn reached over to her and pulled her onto his horse. "Don't panic yet, Elaraine. Let's just get to camp and see what's going on there. For all we know Berell hasn't gotten news of their return yet."

He steered his own mount toward camp, bypassing Berell, who was still holding onto Tix's reins like they were lifelines. Nox told Berell to take Tix to the camp before following his friends. Elaraine tried to think positively as they passed by other scouts looking for trails and signs of Orin or the Rischiaks like Berell had been. All she could think of was how Orin never just disappeared without a reason. Something had to have happened to Orin and she knew it in the pit of her stomach.

Her friends tried to comfort and reassure her as their ride came to an end. She did not pay attention to them. Her mind was trapped in its own scared, little world. She was terrified of going to the camp and her brother not being there like he had said he would be. But nothing could have prepared her for the condition the camp was actually in.

The camp was in a strange chaos, and the prince was nowhere to be found. Men were running around sharpening spears and swords, polishing shields, and fixing their armor. New strips of leather were being attached over the vulnerable armor points. But while there was all this activity, there was hardly any talking amongst the men. Whenever they passed someone, they would look up from their duties and watch them pass by, the worry written all over their faces. They all knew Orin and they had all been friends. And now their friend was gone, leaving in his absence a younger sister that they needed to watch out for. Everyone knew Elaraine could take care of herself, but if Orin returned and she did not have someone to watch over her or if something had happened to her, he would be unhappy, thereby making them unhappy. Besides, they felt it was their duty to watch after Elaraine.

Elaraine felt unnerved by the gazes cast in her direction. The three friends found the whole scene eerie and it only reinforced the pain in Elaraine's chest about her brother's inexplicable disappearance. Perhaps Prince Shep would have been able to shed some light upon the matter but he and Andell were both gone, just as Berell had told them. She felt lost without them there.

Ranci was waiting for them outside of Dayn's tent. He dismounted and helped Elaraine down. Nox was quick to join them. Ranci refused to meet their gazes as she sat on the makeshift bench. It was the only time Elaraine had ever seen her acting nervous, which really did not help matters.

"She already knows, Mother," Dayn almost whispered. "There's no need to hide it."

Ranci's eyes were filled with tears and grabbed Elaraine's hand. "He was taken, Elaraine. We don't know how. But please don't worry. Prince Shep and Andell are out there looking for him."

The panic was starting again, but she slowly pulled her hand away. "But it was Orin. He wouldn't just let someone take him, Ranci, which means there had to have been a fight, which means someone is hurt. And if Orin is not here and he is gone, then that means that whoever was hurt was him. So don't tell me not to worry. It's my brother who is missing." She closed her eyes as the tears began to flow. "It's Orin, Ranci. He's the only family I have left who can and does acknowledge I exist and cares." She buried her head in Dayn's proffered chest as she let out a heart-wrenching sob. "It's Orin."

"Wait for Prince Shep to return," Nox cooed, smoothing her hair. "We'll know whether or not to panic when he gets back."

Elaraine could only cry into Dayn's tunic. The past two days had been a whirlwind of emotions. They had only been away for one night and so many things had changed. She had begun to feel safe and secure again the closer she had gotten to the camp because that was where Orin and Prince Shep were. Now her security net was gone.

She had tried to hide her insecurities behind a mask, tried to be strong for her friends and her brother. But on the inside she was only a quivering puddle of fear. Dayn and Nox had always known it and had played along with her charade. Orin and Prince Shep chose to overlook her fear and had tried to push her beyond it.

Eventually Elaraine cried herself to sleep. Her tent was set up far away from where they now were so Dayn laid her to rest on his cot. Ranci never left her side. She was utterly exhausted, emotionally and physically, but her rest was not peaceful. A few hours after falling asleep she woke up screaming and had to be held down.

She thrashed under the weight as she tried to escape her nightmare. When she opened her eyes, she was staring up into familiar and friendly eyes. They seemed sympathetic as they gazed back at her. When she wiped away her tears, Prince Shep's tears fell upon her. He sat back after she settled down.

"I'm so sorry, Elaraine. I tried to find him; I really did. But there wasn't any trace of him at all." He wrung his hands and stared at the ground. "We aren't going to give up looking, and I don't like having to give you this order given the circumstances, but you are to stay here and not go exploring like I know you are wont to do. You are not to go looking for him."

"Are you really trying to keep me away from trying to find Orin?" She sat up slowly and gritted her teeth against the swelling anger. "Sire, that is not fair."

"Life isn't fair, Elaraine, and right now I can't afford to be either. If there wasn't a war, maybe things would be different. But there is, and so they aren't." He stood up and walked to the tent flap. "Elaraine, I promise you that I will find him. But I can't find him if I have to worry about you getting hurt too, so stay here."

With that, he left a dumbfounded and angry Elaraine sitting in the tent. She lay back down and tried to clear her mind so she could get some much-needed rest. Prince Shep was looking for her brother, which was all that mattered to her in her tired state. She knew she would be useless to Orin as she was, but at least he had friends that could help him. She would be eternally grateful for that, too. The medicine she felt on her ankle was starting to help that pain, but it would still be a little while before she could walk without help.

She slept much better that time. She dreamt of laughing along the riverbank when she and Orin were children. He was so much older than her, being a child from one of their father's earlier marriages. Their father had remarried a couple of times but eventually remarried Orin's mother and they had had Elaraine. Her father was the only person in Gegernen to have ever remarried after separating from his wife. But her father was not from

Gegernen, so it was hardly a scandal at the time.

Orin only ever treated her like she was a child. But she really did not mind. At least she knew that when he treated her like that that he cared about her. And when he was overprotective, she felt safe. Her friends in the camp would do that for her right now. She could only pray that wherever Orin was, he had someone doing the same thing for him.

It was dawn when she next awoke. Every muscle in her body hurt. She was too stressed to think straight and she raced out of the tent to see if there had been any news about Orin in the night. She found Prince Shep conversing with Ranci by a small and crackling fire. Neither of them looked happy to see her walking around so early in the morning.

"Elaraine." Ranci nodded in greeting. "You should be resting. If you push yourself too hard right now, you're liable to collapse. Dayn and Nox already delivered the report from Prince Arlun, and some messengers from Prince Arlun's camp arrived last night approving our waiting until we know what is happening here before joining them," Ranci advised.

"Not until Orin comes back," the young woman said as she sat down with them. "I need to know he's safe before I rest again."

The prince had grown quiet when he had noticed Elaraine's arrival. He remained silent as the two women talked and eventually excused himself to return to his tent. Andell soon joined them and maintained an air of silence.

"Andell, please talk to me," she almost begged. "Prince Shep won't tell me anything except that I have to stay here and not help in the search, but can't someone at least tell me what's going on? Prince Arlun wants us to be joining his army and that means leaving my brother behind, which I'm not ready to accept. I need to know what's going on."

Andell sighed and rubbed his temples. "What have you been told so far?"

"Not much. Just that he went out for patrol alone and never returned."

He nodded slowly and then sighed. "A couple of scouts from Prince Arlun's army joined us yesterday morning right after you left. They said that there was Rischiak movement all around us. Orin was worried about you three and decided to check the reports for himself. He headed south and he never came back. We waited a few hours, but after so long without news, we decided no news was bad news because Orin always comes back and reports in."

Elaraine nodded, the sinking feeling in her stomach slowly subsiding as she learned the story. "Go on, please, Andell."

Andell sped on. "We all know your brother, Elaraine, and we knew that when he said that he would be back in a couple of hours, that's exactly what he meant. But we gave him more time than that because we didn't know if he was hurt or lost or something along those lines." Elaraine nodded again. "When the deadline passed, Prince Shep deployed everyone with even the slightest scouting experience and we set off to try and find him. We found where there had been a struggle only a short distance from the boundary of the camp. There was only a small amount of blood in that clearing, Elaraine. It was not enough to say someone had been more than just hurt there, and there weren't any signs of where they all went after that. We went in every direction. We searched everywhere. We just can't find any sign of anything." He finally looked sideways at her. "It's like he just disappeared, Elaraine."

"Prince Shep is beside himself," Ranci added. "He feels like he is failing you. He truly does not know what to do to make things right."

Elaraine was torn between her duty to her prince and her duty to her brother. On the one hand, Prince Shep had ordered her not to go looking for Orin and she had agreed. But now that she had rested she was starting to think of ways to get Orin back. She would be in trouble either way but she just would not be able to live with herself should she just abandon Orin to the search of the scouts. Her mind was decided, and she resigned herself to the decision that if she did what she was planning to do, she would be on her own. She would have to face the unknown by herself. And she would have to accept the consequences on her own. Ranci poked her side, making her jump and jarring her from her thoughts.

"I know that look," the woman warned Elaraine, "and don't you think of doing it. You have no business doing that." Elaraine only blinked at her. "And don't pretend you don't know what I'm talking about."

"Ranci, if I am guessing correctly then I assume you think I'll disobey the prince's orders. Why would I not have the right to? It's not his brother who disappeared. It was mine." Elaraine stood up and dusted herself off. "I think if anyone were to have the right to do what it is you're talking about, then it would be me, would it not?"

Andell and Ranci just stared after her as she made her way to her own tent to try and relax the pain away. She would give the men until the end of the day to find Orin, but if Orin had not been found by the deadline then all promises were off and she would get her brother back by herself.

She collapsed onto Dayn's cot, barely able to bring herself to pull a blanket over herself.

A little more rest, she told herself. *A little more rest and I'll be all right. A little more rest and I can find Orin.*

She stayed there staring at the ceiling of the tent and listening to the sounds of the camp to try to fall back asleep. A horseman had just arrived and she could hear the clacking of the horse hooves on the ground as they walked past her tent. She frowned when they paused before the opening but relaxed when they continued along their way. She was not in the mood for a visitor.

She knew what had been done to Orin. Deep down she knew the answer. He had been taken. He would have been able to fight a few Rischiaks and come back, but the fact that he did not return, in her mind at least, was proof he had been overwhelmed and had been taken away.

Voices were coming from outside her tent. Prince Shep was arguing with Andell and it jerked Elaraine from her thoughts.

"Oh, stop it," a woman spoke up. "Arguing is not going to get my brother back here any faster. I know you're tired. I'm tired. We're all tired! But stop bickering for two minutes so we can figure out what to do next. We have to find Orin. But right now our most important responsibility is Elaraine's safety. What precautions have been taken so she doesn't go after Orin herself?"

"We have assigned someone to follow—"

Someone hushed Andell and Prince Shep poked his head inside her tent. She feigned sleep until he pulled his head back outside.

"It's fine. She's asleep," Prince Shep reported.

"As I was saying," Andell continued, sounding more than a little annoyed, "we've assigned someone to follow her. She'd reject a guard if we told her."

"If they targeted Orin specifically, then they could also come after Elaraine," the woman prompted.

"Yes... which is why we are having her followed, Jonnie." The prince sounded tired as he snapped at her.

Elaraine frowned and pushed the blanket away towards the end of the bed, hoping that hearing of two women named 'Jonnie' in the army within the same day was merely a coincidence. She did not like the idea of being followed any more than she did the idea of having to be guarded. The ground was cold and damp under her feet as she padded her way closer to the tent flap.

"It's not good enough. She's new to the army, she doesn't know how to fight, she's naïve, and she's alone except for two dunces who follow her around like lovesick puppies." The woman's voice was rising. "My little sister has to be protected! I just got her back and I can't lose her again!"

Elaraine was looking through the gap made by the tent flap. The woman Prince Shep had called "Jonnie" was the same woman from the main army's camp. Elaraine gasped softly and backed away at the realization, but not before three heads spun to see her.

Chapter Twenty-One

Elaraine raced back to the cot, hoping to pretend to be asleep well enough that they might just think that they had seen something that wasn't there. She knew it was a false hope but it was the only chance she had to avoid complete and utter humiliation in the situation. Just as she was pulling the blanket back over herself, however, Prince Shep was at her side glowering down at her.

"You've started eavesdropping?" he asked at last.

Elaraine blinked up at him. "It's not really 'eavesdropping' when you are talking very loudly outside my tent and I can hear it all anyway. I just wanted to see what was going on and to tell you to go away," she lied.

He saw right through it. "Couldn't you have yelled out like a normal person would have?"

"Well... yes... but what if I woke other people up?"

"It's well past the time when everyone should be awake and it's still not right to not say anything if you can hear a private conversation. So, what's your next excuse?"

She grinned. "I was sleepwalking?"

He was not amused in the slightest. "Uh-huh... well, this is what we're going to do. You're not going to eavesdrop anymore. You're going to stay in this tent until I come back."

"You can't make me do that!" she said as she jumped back up to her feet.

"I am a prince, so, yes, I can make you do just that." He spun on his heel and walked out of the tent, leaving Elaraine in his wake. He returned a few moments later with Jonnie behind him. "You have a visitor," is all he said before leaving again.

The two women stood there for a long time considering each other. Elaraine went back and sat on the cot and left the other woman standing by the tent flap.

Jonnie cleared her throat. "It's hard to believe we're related when you act like that. I should have stayed and helped raise you to be stronger than this."

"It's hard not to act like this when you are kept in the dark," Elaraine answered.

"Other people don't rule your actions. Only you do."

"Don't preach to me over responsibility. You're the one who left. You're the one who never came back. You're the one who decided not to be a sister."

"I had to."

"There's no such thing as 'having' to do something. If you look hard enough, there's always another option."

"This being said by the girl who killed someone in a pub. Besides, you don't understand my situation," Jonnie scoffed.

"I can't understand what I don't know. I don't know you so why do you expect me to understand you?"

Jonnie sat next to Elaraine, only to have Elaraine move to the other end of the cot. "Do you even want to try?"

"No offense, Jonnie, but until a day ago, I didn't even know you were my sister. I've always known Orin was my brother and right now he's missing. I'll worry about understanding you after he's back safe and sound."

The older woman nodded slowly. "That's fair." She turned to face Elaraine and gripped the younger woman's shoulders tightly. "I need to tell you some things first before you hear them around the camp now that I'm here. I didn't leave home the way I did because I wanted to. I thought there were bigger and better things for me out in the world than what Gegernen could provide. I was never meant to stay in that village. I was meant for more than that. The army has given me a way to do that. And even though I wasn't there, it doesn't mean I didn't care or that I wasn't watching over you. I'm the first woman ever to join the army and it's created resentment amongst the men and—"

"Jonnie, don't start off by thinking I'll form my judgments based upon what others say. I'll make them off what you do. If you want to tell me your life story, fine. But do so after Orin is found. You obviously care about him if you got here so quickly, so why don't you go out and find him?"

"I can't."

"Why not?"

"I'm not trained to find him. Technically speaking, I'm neither a scout nor a tracker. I am partnered with a scout, but that's only because that is the only place they could think to place me after they discovered I was a woman. I am more of a guard for my partner. While he tries to teach me how to be a scout, the lessons are wasted on me, as I did not even listen to our father when he was trying to teach me those things. But my partner keeps trying to teach me despite years of my failing to learn the lessons. I would only get lost and I would never find my way back to camp without my partner. I would never be able to find Orin."

"So why won't they let me go? I have skills that can help."

"You're not really a warrior, Elaraine. You're just a woman who got out of a bad situation and fights because she must. You wouldn't be able to defend yourself out there if you had to, and the scouts are spread so thin anyway, with Rian hurt and Berell needing to be watched. Prince Shep can't afford to team anyone up with you. The best way for you to help everyone find Orin is for you to stay put so no energy has to be put into finding you too."

"Orin would never have given up on me so easily. I cannot give up on him, either."

Jonnie cocked an eyebrow at her. "Who said anything about you giving up on him?"

Then she left without saying another word. Elaraine took a long time making up her mind as to what she should do. Finally, she decided she knew loyalty to her brother before she knew loyalty to Swennia or the prince. She got ready to break her promise.

She packed light, only taking her sword and a small knife. She would stop by the food stores for some bread before she left but after that she would be on her way to find Orin. She only hoped she did not get caught trying to leave the camp. If she got caught, she knew there would be no way to sneak back out because neither Jonnie nor Prince Shep would let her be by herself until Orin was found.

She waited until dusk fell to leave. But it was still more difficult than she expected trying to get out of the camp. It seemed everywhere Elaraine turned there were men milling around blocking her way from getting out without being seen. A few times she would dive behind a tent only to have to rush behind another as someone would turn and start going towards her new spot.

She was about to go find Nox to convince him to help her when there was a shout at the other end of the camp. Fires were immediately extinguished and tents were knocked over in the chaos that followed. Men ran everywhere and Elaraine made it to the edge of the camp when she heard the beginnings of steel hitting steel. She did not dare look over her shoulder to see what was happening. She was only grateful for the distraction as she sprinted in the direction she had heard Orin had gone.

It only took a couple of minutes for her to register the footsteps behind her. The noise of the skirmish behind her masked it until she was far enough away to hear the forest night life. Whoever was following her was keeping pace with her, stopping whenever she stopped and speeding up at the same time she did. It was the heaviness of the other person's tread that gave them away. Eventually her lungs felt like they were going to burst and she was forced to slow her pace to a walk. When her follower continued his pursuit, Elaraine began to feel panicked and she walked a little faster, being careful to avoid stepping on the dark shadows that resembled tree branches. Whoever it was seemed to sense her fear because he started to pay less attention to keeping quiet. He started to break twigs and go through brush as he chased her and he fell out of her pace.

Overhead she heard a bird cry but she kept her eyes on her path ahead as she hurried on. When she heard the flap of wings near her head, she turned with a jerk in time to see a falcon fly away with a small rodent in its talons. She watched in morbid fascination as the bird soared away, her pursuer forgotten for a few seconds. But then her thoughts jarred her back into the purpose at hand. To find Orin before he was killed was the thought that spurred her on, making her forget about the falcon.

She soon found the path left by Orin and his abductors. The last rays of the sun for the day shone upon the trail and gave Elaraine hope. As she walked around the area she could tell there had been quite a shuffle. Branches were lying broken on the forest floor with drops of blood here and there, tree trunks had sword strikes scarring them, and a discharged arrow was embedded in an old elm tree.

She did not stay long at the site because she knew she was still being pursued. She could not hear them but she could feel their presence lurking in the shadows. She made a cursory investigation and followed the trail as far and as quickly as she could before nightfall.

With the coming of night, she knew she would have to abandon her cause in the darkness and wait for the dawn. She found a small rock outcropping that would keep the wind off her and would hide her from whoever had been following her. She had not heard whoever it had been for hours, but her instinct told her they were still out there somewhere, near at hand. When she peered deeper into the woods the hairs on her neck would stand on end and a shiver would go up her spine. Without realizing it, she fell asleep huddled against the boulders.

She awoke at daybreak, the morning frost soaking through her leggings and tunic. She stretched and yawned as she opened her eyes, jumping up when she saw Nox and Dayn glowering down at her.

"What are you doing here?" she yelled, trying to get her heart to slow back down.

"Well, shall we ignore the fact that you were to be confined to the tent and you are somehow here? Or shall we ignore the fact that you came out here alone, tracking a raid party that overtook Orin? Take your pick because I will only ignore one for the time being," Nox said through his gritted teeth, his fists clenched tightly and his knuckles turning white.

Elaraine shrank back against the boulder at his tone. "Um... can we ignore the one about my being here alone?"

"Fine," Dayn forced out evenly. "Prince Shep ordered you to stay in the tent, did he not?" Elaraine nodded. "And Jonnie said the same thing, did she not?" Elaraine nodded. "And instead of staying behind at the camp yesterday and helping us when we were attacked, you slipped out past the sentinels and came out here alone to find Orin without telling anyone, didn't you?"

"I thought you were going to ignore the 'alone' one!"

"That was Nox, not me." Dayn stormed over to her and began to shake her. "What were you thinking? You could have been killed! Did that ever, even once, cross your thick skull?"

"You have no idea how worried everyone is because of you!" Nox yelled, finally losing his thinly veiled temper. "Prince Shep thinks you've been captured by the same people who captured Orin! He's out looking for you himself! Rian is so worried that he's even looking for you despite his wounds. They are even talking about letting Berell scout without a partner because they were too stretched for people to find one person, let alone two, on top of doing their scouting duties! You're lucky Dayn tracked you yesterday instead of Rian or Prince Shep! You're also lucky I was the first one he found after you settled in for the night and he ran back to get someone."

"You don't have to yell! I know it was a stupid thing to do! But if it had been your brother that had been taken, what would you have done?" Elaraine shot back. "You would have done the same thing I did and not thought twice! Admit it!"

"Talking to you doesn't work! Jonnie and the prince tried talking to you, remember? Maybe yelling is what a certain woman needs to understand that the world is a dangerous place for the innocent and the sooner she learns it the better off everyone will be! Stop hiding behind your anger and your hurt like they are a shield!"

"Orin would be the first one to yell at you, too, if he knew you were doing this!" Dayn somehow managed to insert into their shouting match. "It would kill him if he knew it, and we all know it."

"He's the only one who's defended me. He always helped me when we were little. He was the one who beat the bullies away and kept me out of trouble. Risking my life for him now is the least I can do," Elaraine sobbed, falling to her knees as Dayn finally relaxed his grip on her arms.

The men watched as Elaraine sobbed herself to exhaustion. When no more tears could fall, Elaraine looked up at her friends, and their hearts broke at her salt-stained cheeks and hopeless look. The men looked at each other, trying to decide what to do. They looked back at her when she tugged on their tunics to get their attention.

"I can't give up on looking for him! Not until I find him or his body.

Please... help me!" she begged through her hiccups.

Dayn and Nox looked back at each other and sighed. They knew it was pointless to argue with her. If they hauled her back to the camp, it would have been with her kicking and screaming and with her ultimately sneaking away again. But, on the other hand, the camp was in turmoil with two people to look for and leaving to go with Elaraine like that would have meant four missing people for them to contend with.

"I'll go back and tell the prince and Jonnie what's going on. They won't be happy, but it's better than them being left in the dark about everything," Dayn finally sighed. "But if I were you, Elaraine, I'd be ready for a storm when, or if, I returned to the camp. The prince will have every right to try you for desertion. Whether or not he will use that right is up in the air, but he'll be angry enough to disregard all other feelings at this point and just let his wrath loose."

"I'm afraid all three of you will have to go back to camp," an awfully familiar voice said from behind the rock outcropping, making them all jump at the sound. His gaze never left Elaraine's as he came into view. "For, you see, if only Dayn returns to report all this to me, as heartrending a story as it is, there is not a place on earth any of you can hide that would protect you from the wrath Dayn was so kind to mention. I am not forgiving to those who try to deceive me or go against me."

Dayn was the first one to regain his senses at the sudden appearance of the prince. "Prince Shep, we can't just throw her over our shoulders and take her back with us!" Dayn protested. "You know how she is... she would only leave again, and this way there's someone with her who can protect her. I was going to go back to tell you. We know it's not exactly ideal, but—"

The prince spun on him. "What part of the plan is 'ideal,' Dayn? Please, tell me, because I would sure like to know! One woman, or even one woman and one man, are not enough to get Orin back, no matter how good their cause. I told you three to remain in the camp because I said I would handle it and I was handling it how it should have been from the start. So, none of this is ideal, Dayn. None of it... especially not the part where you're going to risk your lives to do this. Losing one man was enough, but to lose three or four is..." he waved his arm around, trying to think of the right words.

"Intolerable?" Nox suggested tentatively, but the only answer he received was a glare and a growl from Prince Shep.

The prince walked back around the boulder and they could hear him muttering angrily. The three friends could only look at each other. Finally, the prince grew silent and the friends held their breath.

Prince Shep rounded the outcropping and glowered down at Elaraine. "You disobeyed me. I'm not only the commanding officer of this army but your prince. My word is law. Give me one good reason I should let you go or let you return to the camp at all." he hissed through tightly clenched teeth.

The woman was quiet for a moment before she answered, and when she did answer, the men had to strain to hear her, her voice was so quiet and haggard. "Prince Shep, I never wanted to join the army. I was given to your army by the king. I fought with you because of the children, not because I wanted this kind of life. All I really want is to have a quiet life in peace. But if my being in the army is required of me to pay for what I have done, so be it. I will live that kind of life as best I can. But isn't one of the reasons people join the army to protect their family? Orin is a part of my family, and the army did not help him. He's my brother. If I don't try to save him, then what good am I? My life already doesn't amount to much, but if I give up on my brother, it will amount to nothing. I know why you're mad, but," she met his glare, "I would do it again in a heartbeat to save him."

The prince was silent for a while, thinking about what she had said. He sighed and let his arms drop to his sides in defeat. "If it was for anyone other than Orin, Elaraine, I would turn you loose here and now, forgetting about friendship and everything else. I can't have my subordinates undermining my authority by acting against my direct orders, do you understand?"

Elaraine nodded. "I'm—"

Prince Shep raised a hand to cut her off. "I do not want to hear that you're sorry or that you'll never do it again. You need to understand that what you did was wrong. I won't stop you from going because you've made it this far and tracked them farther than Rian or any of the other trackers and scouts could. But let me make this clear: if this had been for Dayn, or Nox, or even Andell, you would have been sent before my brother or father for desertion. Do you understand?"

Elaraine nodded, her gaze not meeting his. "Yes, Prince Shep, I understand."

"You left us like a coward when we were under attack, and I do not allow cowards in my camp. Now, fortunately for you, you left to save someone, and I heard you were already leaving when it started so you're not really a coward, and the men don't think of you that way, either. But instead of talking with me on this issue, you acted on your own." He turned to the two men. "And as for you two... trying to keep this whole venture a secret... then plotting to join with her on it... don't get me started on it because it makes me so angry I could thrash you." He started to pace to let some of his pent-up frustration loose. "So now I am left with three people who are willing to go to the ends of the earth to save their friend and brother. When this is over, I want to forget this ever happened and move on." He sighed and looked at the rosy clouds above. There were many long moments of silence. "Orin saved my life once," he said at last. "It's time to return the favor."

With that, he turned on his heel and continued to follow the trail that Elaraine had been following the night before. It only took a moment before the other three fell in behind him, having to first shake their shock of his having joined them without punishing them in any way. The party remained silent except to discuss the tracks from time to time, and even those discussions were few and far between. At midday they stopped to rest for a spell at a small river they were going to have to cross to pick up the trail again.

"Do you think we're getting any closer to them?" Nox panted as he tried to catch his breath.

"They were moving fast to start with but their tracks lately have been more labored. I think they had to slow down. But we are still far behind them." The prince dug a rock from the toe of his boot. "How these little pebbles always end up in my boot, I have no idea. It doesn't matter how high my boot comes on my leg or anything! But always in the toe of my boots...." he started mumbling to himself.

"Prince Shep," Elaraine finally spoke for the first time since they set out, "do you think Orin is alive?"

The man looked at her as he shoved his foot back into his boot. "If I thought he was dead I wouldn't have come with you. Why waste time on a pointless venture searching for a dead man?"

He watched as she lowered her eyes back to the ground. He let her drown in her own thoughts for a while before he decided to put her to some ease. He walked over to her and laid a gentle hand upon her shoulder, and she looked up at him with watery eyes. He knelt beside her and tucked a lock of her hair back behind her ear as some tears began to fall again. He wiped their path away with his sleeve.

"Elaraine, you're his sister. You know the answer to that question better than anyone. Do you, in your heart, feel that your brother is dead?" She shook her head vehemently. "Then there you go." He stood back up and dusted off his leggings and tunic. "Well, as good as that break was, we need to get going if we're ever going to catch them."

He set back out on their path, the other three obediently falling in line behind him, looking for the best place to ford the river. They were completely unaware of the eyes watching them from the other side.

Chapter Twenty-Two

The small group swam the river uneventfully, albeit slowly, and picked up the trail they had been following soon after they reached the far bank. The sun was starting to hide behind the dark clouds that were rolling in. Leaves began to flit across the trail as the wind picked up. They started to hurry along the path so that they would not lose it in the oncoming storm. A couple of times Elaraine would stop and look around her, unable to shake a steadily growing feeling of dread. Her frequent stops drew the attention of her companions and for a while they let her stop without comment, but it became evident her apprehension was slowing them down.

"For the love of...Elaraine! What in the world do you keep stopping to look around for? The tracks go forward!" Dayn finally snapped.

"I feel like we're being watched. The little hairs on the back of my neck keep prickling," she murmured as she looked behind her once more. "It's unnerving."

"It's just your imagination," Prince Shep said confidently as he crouched by the trail once more in the fading light. "If we were being followed, why haven't they attacked us by now? They have had ample opportunities."

"I don't know, but that is what is worrying me." She whirled as a twig snapped behind her. "Whatever is watching us is just out there lurking."

Nox laughed and gave her shoulder a conciliatory pat while he spun her around slowly on their heels. "There, there, Ela. See? There is absolutely nothing to—"

Nox stopped speaking mid-sentence as he was turning them around. Elaraine looked up to see what had cut him off only to see their path blocked by an armed guard of Rischiaks. Their blue cloaks were waving silently behind them in the winds of the coming storm.

"Nox," she choked out, "please tell me you were not about to say we had nothing to worry about."

Prince Shep was still crouched on the ground but his hand was making its way slowly to his hunting knife in his boot as he stared up at the Rischiaks. The head guard stepped forward and unsheathed his sword. The sound of the sword scraping along the sheath stung the air.

"Oh, I wouldn't do that, Prince," the head guard growled as he slithered his sword along the prince's neck. "You're on Rischiak land now. I wouldn't do anything stupid if I were you."

Prince Shep let his arm fall. "This is not Rischiak land. This land belongs to my father and my brother and you are not welcome here. Rischiak scum is not welcome in Swennia."

"The losers always say that," the guard answered as his men moved to disarm Dayn, Nox, and Elaraine. "It seems to our queen that, seeing how she has the upper hand in this region, it is her land and you are the scum who are not welcome on Rischiak land."

"Then I suppose we are at an impasse."

The guard threw his head back and laughed. "I don't think so, Prince." He took the prince's knife and unbuckled Prince Shep's sword belt. "You see, if you are not armed, you don't have much of a say in what happens here." He turned back to his men. "The queen is waiting. Take them back to her."

As the head guard moved away from them, his men approached with burlap sacks. Dayn and Nox went to stand in front of Elaraine. Nox pulled her to stand directly behind him.

"Elaraine, go. Make a run for it," he whispered urgently as the guardsmen continued to advance, shoving her slightly away from him. "Get back to camp and get help."

"It's too far away, she'll never make it!" Dayn groaned as the guards put a sack over the prince's head and when the prince began to struggle in their custody they punched him in the head. He went limp immediately and a guard threw him over a shoulder. The other guards started to stalk towards the three of them. "There's too many of them and we won't be able to hold them all off long enough to help her."

"Maybe they'll take us to Orin," Elaraine choked out as the men got closer.

"Oh, that's wonderful. Well, at least they may take us to Orin!" Nox whispered sarcastically. "What good can we be to him if we're in the same position he is? He's probably locked up!" He began to crouch into a defensive stance as the guardsmen began to encircle the trio.

"We got out of the Dungeons Ussal! They are fortified and guarded."

"Did you forget I was actually on the outside of that prison helping you? If we're all locked up an escape is considerably harder." Nox punched the nearest guard as the ring got closer. Then he turned and shoved her away from them. "Now, try to run!"

She never got the chance because just as she was turning to try to break out of the circle a guard grabbed her by the throat and lifted her from the ground. Dayn spun towards her as she cried out and got a fist in his jaw. Before she blacked out from the lack of air, she saw a guard put a bag over Dayn's head and heft him over a shoulder to be hauled away and three guards pin Nox to the ground. Nox thrashing and yelling at her were the last things she knew before her world went black.

When Elaraine finally woke up it was dark and the storm had finally broken forth with all its fury. She was leaning slightly against the trunk of the tree that was sheltering them. Its boughs were trying to touch the ground with the force of the wind shrieking by them. The tree creaked under the pressure of the storm.

Nearby, the Rischiak guards had built a fire and were eating and drinking under a larger, more stable tree. She managed to sit up a little more against the trunk to see Dayn, Nox, and Prince Shep still unconscious and laying next to her. Her throat and head were both throbbing and it took a concerted effort not to cough to alert their captors that she was awake. Her vision blurred and she had to close her eyes for a minute to clear everything again.

She saw Prince Shep stir and he let out a low moan. His hand went to his head as he groaned again and kicked his feet out. As he tried to sit up, she stuck her foot out against him to stop him from moving around too much so he wouldn't alert the Rischiaks. He flailed out weakly against her.

"Shh, Prince Shep," she said softly over the wind, letting the wind help carry her voice to him. "If you move then they'll know we're awake. They may separate us!"

"My head!" he ground out. "It feels like it's splitting in two!"

"You took a fist to the temple."

"Did I get a hit in?" he asked sounding hopeful.

"No. One hit and you went down. They carried you off before they got the rest of us."

"Where are we?" He went to remove the sack from his head but stopped when she kicked him. "I want to see where we are! Stop kicking at me."

"If you remove it, they'll know you are awake!"

"Do you have one?"

"No."

"Why not?"

"How am I supposed to know? Do I look like a Rischiak guard to you?"

"You don't look like anything with this sack on my head." He sighed heavily and resigned himself to his condition, settling back down. "How did they take the rest of you?"

"Dayn was punched too. I blacked out in a stranglehold so I don't know how we got here or how Nox was taken. But the odds were not in his favor the last time I saw him."

"Are you okay?!" His voice rose into a loud growl that she feared the guards would hear, but the storm covered it.

"Yes, I'm fine. Just a little sore."

He settled back down. "Are Dayn and Nox here too?"

"They're still unconscious next to you. You almost kicked Dayn a few moments ago."

He was quiet for a while and she was afraid he had gone unconscious again. She watched the Rischiaks eat and drink around their fire. Their tree was close to the ones she and her friends were under but far enough away that she couldn't hear what they were saying. The wind was just too loud. Finally, the prince broke the silence.

"Elaraine, is there any way you can get away?" She remained silent. "Elaraine?" He sounded worried.

She sighed in resignation. "Even if I could escape right now, where would I go? I don't know where we are. And if that guard is right, then this side of the river is not Swennian land anymore but belongs to the Rischiaks. Who would help me? How would I find my way back to you with help?"

"I didn't say anything about getting help. If even one of us can get away, they need to!"

"I'm not leaving you three and I am not leaving the search for Orin." She looked out the corner of her eye when she noticed a distinct drop in the amount of activity coming from the Rischiaks. Some of them seemed to be on alert. "Prince, don't talk until I do, understand?"

He nodded and she closed her eyes when she saw two of the Rischiaks stand up and walk towards them. She heard them stop near her but then nobody moved. Elaraine prayed that Nox and Dayn remained unconscious until the Rischiaks left again.

"Think they're still out?" she heard a Rischiak say, followed by what sounded like a kick into Prince Shep's stomach if the small puff of a groan he gave was any indication.

She was thankful the storm was too loud for the Rischiaks to have heard him. One of them started poking her face. She swallowed her disgust and soon the poking stopped, only to be replaced by a strong hand around her throat. The hand continued to tighten but she refused to open her eyes. The voices around her started sounding like she was down a well when the hand finally released its hold.

"If they're not then they are good at faking," the other Rischiak replied. "Not many people could get kicked like that and not move."

She heard them rustling around with the burlap sacks covering her friends' faces.

"There! Now we'll see if they're awake or not."

There was a long stretch of silence and then she heard a muttered "She looks like Orin."

Elaraine felt her heart skip a beat with the knowledge that these Rischiaks had seen Orin. Maybe she would see him soon after all. It became harder for her to keep up the farce of being unconscious.

"I wonder what she'll say when she sees him."

Her heart dropped as she heard them walk away. Her mind went directly to the worst possible scenarios. Did they mean Orin was dead? Were they torturing him? She opened her eyes after what seemed like an hour of silence to see Prince Shep looking up at her.

"It will be okay," he mouthed at her as a bolt of lightning flashed across the sky.

"How do you know?" she whispered, fighting back the oncoming tears for the tenth time that day.

"I don't. But I know Orin."

"At least they've seen him," Dayn groaned from where he lay.

"How long have you been awake?" Nox asked from Elaraine's other side.

"How long have both of you been awake?" Prince Shep ground out.

"I've been awake since before Elaraine woke up. It doesn't take a genius to realize being silent is the best policy when you have a sack on your head."

"Same," Dayn groaned again. "My head is killing me! It feels like I was hit with a rock."

"What do we do from here?"

"They've seen Orin, so they must know where he is."

"Do you think they'll take us where he is?" Elaraine asked, glad to know that everyone was awake now.

"It doesn't make sense to not take us where they have him. It's best to keep all the prisoners in one location," the prince chimed in. "Strategically speaking, of course."

"What happens when we get there?"

"We don't even know where 'there' is. Let's not worry about that until we get our bearings on wherever that is, okay? We can only worry about one thing at a time at this point."

It was hours before the storm subsided. They all laid in silence with their own thoughts and troubles. The Rischiaks drank and ate until late into the night. Occasionally, a guard would come over to check on them and they would close their eyes and remain absolutely still, not yet daring to show they were awake. But once the Rischiak left they would assure one another that they were still all right.

Eventually most of the Rischiaks went to sleep, leaving only a single guard awake to keep an eye on everything. The silence of the night was broken only by logs breaking on the fire and an occasional owl hooting in the distance. None of the prisoners slept that night. After the guard had changed twice, Elaraine could see the sun begin to break over the horizon and knew that soon they would be on their way again. Every minute that passed she felt an urgency to get to Orin, but her hands were literally tied and she was of no use to him alone against the Rischiak army. She was coming to doubt if they could save him with just the four of them.

Soon the head guard woke up and ate his breakfast with the rest of the guards. They grumbled and complained as they went about their business. Then he made his way over to their small group. He hovered over them for a long moment before breaking the silence.

"Okay, Swennians. Let's get one thing straight. I know you are awake. I know you've been awake for a while. We didn't hit you hard enough for you to still be unconscious and you aren't dead. We aren't going to kill you unless you misbehave and make our job difficult. The prince, as he knows, is worth more to us alive than dead. The rest of you are extraneous and I will not hesitate to make sure you are no longer a problem. Now get up and get in a line. It's time to move on. We are expected somewhere."

He turned on his heel and left. Elaraine opened her eyes to see her friends looking up at her. They were frowning and all of them showed their lack of rest on their faces.

"I guess it's time to be awake and get up," she shrugged as she stood, her hands tied in front of her helping her balance as she righted herself. "There's no point in faking it anymore. If they kill us for lagging right now then I really will never see Orin again."

"Elaraine, are you all right?" Dayn whispered as he struggled to his feet, too. It was hard for him to balance righting himself with his hands tied behind his back like the others'.

She put a hand to her throat and felt instantaneous pain. "I am better off with bruises than with a slit throat. Let's get going."

His gaze fell to her arms where the handprints where Orin had shaken her were still visible. "I am sorry, Elaraine. I am sorry you got caught up in any of this. You should still be safe and sound with Ranci and me in the woods. Or at least be in Gegernen enjoying a quiet life. I should have kept them from being able to find you when you were hiding. Then they wouldn't have taken you away and you wouldn't have gone to the Dungeons Ussal and you wouldn't have escaped, becoming a fugitive again...."

"Dayn, stop it." Nox interrupted Dayn's tirade. "There are a lot of would-have-beens and should-have-beens, but the fact is that we're here now and so is she. We can't change the past, so we have to protect her future. We need to get Elaraine and Prince Shep back to Swennia safe and sound. That comes before finding Orin."

"But—" Elaraine started.

"No, Elaraine!" Dayn interrupted her. "He's right. If need be, he and I will continue on for Orin but somehow you and Prince Shep need to get out and get home."

They helped Prince Shep to his feet when he kept falling back down to the ground in his effort to stand up. When he was on his feet he teetered for a minute before stabilizing his stance. They made their way to the Rischiak line slowly, looking for a way to escape and finding none that didn't end with them being caught immediately.

They were put into a line and marched all day under the hot sun. Occasionally they were allowed to take a short break for water and a piece of bread. Elaraine was exhausted and grit her teeth against the pain. The past few days of following the trail had worn her out already and the forced march was faster than she could handle for such an extended period of time.

On one of their breaks, however, Prince Shep and Nox told her they had seen signs of the original trail they had been following, making her dampened spirits soar. That they were still on the right trail despite being captives and the strong storm the night before not having wiped out all traces of Orin's trail gave Elaraine hope that she would see her brother again. Dayn remained silent the entire day, even going so far as to avoid all possible contact with them. He sat apart from them on breaks and never looked in their direction, refusing to make eye contact.

"He feels guilty," Nox told her, following her gaze as she ate a piece of bread when they finally stopped for the day. "He blames everything that has happened to you so far on himself. He blames himself for Worrin and I taking you from Ranci's cottage that day."

"He shouldn't. It all started long before I met him, because of something I did." She swallowed the dry bread and looked back at Dayn. "He blames himself for everything in the world. He is too young to believe he carries the world on his shoulders."

"The world rests on the shoulders of the young," Prince Shep chimed in. "It is the young who wage wars and are diplomats. It is the young who are forced to marry for land unifications and peace. It is the young who sow the fields and harvest the crops. It is the young who hunt for meat to put on the dinner table. Dayn is feeling the weight as he should. He is not much younger than we are, after all, and we feel the weight on our shoulders as well."

"In this he should not feel guilty. In this he is utterly blameless."

"You will never convince him of his innocence."

They spent another sleepless night under the stars. Elaraine was just thankful that it was not raining. She heard a wolf howling to the moon shortly after the second watch began and her heart felt at one with the mournful cry. She was left in silence to think on her past and how she had reached this point in her life. Dayn could blame himself, but it would not change the fact that she had killed a man and set these events into motion. She was able to see clearly how it had changed the lives of those around her as well.

The day came early for the weary prisoners. The sun had not yet fully risen when a guard came to rouse them from their thoughts to get them ready to go once again. They were given a chance to take care of nature and eat a sliver of dry bread. Elaraine was washing her meager meal down with a swig of water when Nox nudged her elbow and pointed in the distance. She could see tents encamped upon a hill with tendrils of smoke rising from between them. The camp was not yet awake. Beyond the tents was a large stone wall with flags waving from the balustrades on top of the stonework.

"It used to be an old outpost of ours," Prince Shep confided as he followed their gaze. "I did my training here. In the winter they have a horrible wolf problem. Five years ago, my brother had a new outpost built three leagues north of here. He decided this outpost was too in the open to withstand attack by the Rischiaks. He had ordered this outpost be burned to the ground."

"It seems his orders were disobeyed," Dayn said wryly. "He left the Rischiaks an abandoned outpost ready to be occupied. It is like he said 'Why, hello, enemy! I hope you'll be comfortable here!'"

Not another word was said as they were shuffled through the woods in the direction of the encampment and the outpost beyond. Elaraine's legs felt like they could give out at any time. That this was the last day and so close to the end, whatever that end may be, gave her the strength to keep going. She would stumble occasionally but one of her friends would help her regain her footing. Dayn was reluctant to touch her but couldn't stand to see her fall.

"Dayn, I blame you for nothing," she whispered to him once when he caught her and she watched as his face crumpled.

"You may not blame me, but that does not ease the guilt I feel," he whispered back, still refusing to meet her gaze. "I cannot protect you as I wish to or should. I am only half a man."

They wound their way through the encampment around midday. Rischiaks came from their duties to sneer and throw taunts their way. Elaraine felt her face heat and turn red. She gripped her hands into fists the whole way, biting her tongue until they finally reached the gates to the outpost. She could hear her friends swearing about the embarrassment of having to have gone through the encampment behind her.

"I could swear some of those soldiers looked familiar," Prince Shep ground out. "Some of them I remember from training grounds in Swennia." He spat on the ground and cursed again. "Traitors. They went to help the scum."

Elaraine kept her eyes on the gate in front of her as the head guard called for it to be opened. She had long suspected there had to have been traitors in Swennia for the Rischiaks to have made it as far into the border as they had, so she let Prince Shep wallow in his own revelations. Men scrambled along the roofline to carry out the head guard's orders. Her friends grew silent as the first latch on the other side of the thick gate could be heard being thrown open. As the wooden doors were opened with the whine of wear and age, her jaw dropped and then she cursed loudly at what she saw.

Chapter Twenty-Three

When the gate had finally opened all the way, Elaraine's friends fell silent as well, before a whole new set of cursing started from Elaraine and Nox. Standing in front of them with an armed guard at her back was Moraiah. She stood tall and proud with a silver crown perched on top of her head and a string of light blue sapphires was wrapped around her neck. Josi stood close by her side, a hand on his sword. He constantly thumbed the large aquamarine stone on the hilt. Elaraine thought he had aged significantly since she had seen him last. The day she had been found with Ranci and Dayn and taken back into Gegernen seemed a lifetime ago. A timber wolf paced in the courtyard tied to a tether. Josi jumped whenever the large animal would let out an occasional soft growl.

"Who is it?" Prince Shep whispered in Nox's ear. "You obviously know her to be talking like that."

As Moraiah and Josi walked toward their group, Elaraine snapped out of her shock. She clenched her fists as the reality of Moraiah's betrayal washed over her.

"It's Orin's wife and son," Elaraine answered for him. "It's Moraiah."

"I knew she looked familiar," Prince Shep whispered. "The years have aged her."

"Quiet!" the head guard bellowed. "Show deference to the Queen of Rischiak and bow your heads."

"She's not our queen," Nox retorted. "I bow only to the Crown of Swennia."

"Bow your head before you have no head to bow!" Josi yelled from where he stood by his mother. "She will be Queen of Swennia soon enough and she deserves your gratitude for not having you killed outright."

"Where is Orin, Moraiah?" Elaraine pled. She gestured to encompass the encampment and the outpost. "What is going on?"

Steel gray eyes met hers. "They blamed us, Elaraine. They blamed us and sentenced us. For what? Swennian law? Swennian law is laughable. In Rischiak women can fight back to defend themselves. When they sentenced you based on what your husband had said I knew it was time to go home. I thought Josi would be safer in Swennia while I fought for the crown to be returned to me," she looked lovingly at her son, "but he followed me and helped me get it from my younger sister. She was easier to convince than I thought she would have been. My brother is fighting Swennia so he was not a bother." She took a long breath. "Now, the Crown Prince ordered you to bow your head, so I recommend you do just that!" Four heads ducked slightly. "That was not a bow!"

"It's all you're getting!" Nox shrilled back at her. "How could you betray us like this?"

"Betrayal is an easy thing when you think one of the most precious things in the world has been taken from you. I thought Orin was dead," she screamed. A sad smile crossed her face but it was gone so quickly Elaraine thought she may have imagined it. When she spoke again, her voice was softer. "But you saved him. And then he was going to leave me again to fight for the Swennian law that condemned him, his wife, and sister. But now he will be back at my side forever."

Elaraine felt a frantic tremor go through her. "You mean he's not here?"

"Of course he's not here. I would not have my beloved so close to the battlefield. He will never be close to battle again. He is nearby but he will be safe from you."

Elaraine didn't miss the sidelong glance Josi gave his mother. "Josi, is your father all right?"

He looked her way in surprise and then glanced around nervously. "Of course he is! Why wouldn't he be? But like my mother said, he is not here."

"Was that his choice or your mother's?" Prince Shep piped in. "Your father is a good man; he would not like to be away from his country in its time of need."

"He doesn't like being away from me either!" Moraiah shrilled. She turned to the guards. "Take them below. I will see to them later when they are more agreeable to what I will have to say." She sneered at them. "Be sure to make them comfortable. We don't want our guests to say we did not treat them well."

With a flourish of her gown, Moraiah and her entourage went back into the inner buildings of the outpost. Elaraine watched the retreating figures in confusion. No one moved for a while, not even the guards. Finally, when Moraiah was out of sight, one of the guards took her roughly by the elbow and led her to a set of stairs leading below the stone wall. She could hear her friends crunching the dry grass behind her.

They were led down a narrow passageway lit by torches at random intervals. It was dark, dank, and smelled of mold. They could hear rustling in the darkness that made Elaraine suspect rats would be their neighbors and the idea made her skin crawl. Elaraine was tossed into a tiny cell with iron bars for a door. It reminded her of the Dungeons Ussal. Across from her Prince Shep, Nox, and Dayn were tossed unceremoniously into a cell that looked slightly larger than hers and were locked in. When the guards left, so did the light.

Elaraine pushed up against a wall near the door and sat with her thoughts. She could hear the men across from her trying to get comfortable but every so often they would give a grunt when one of the others would step on them. Finally they quieted and they all listened for signs of the outside world.

"Did you know Moraiah was Rischiak?" Prince Shep asked to no one in particular.

Elaraine ignored the question. Apparently Dayn and Nox took the same attitude because the prince had to repeat the question three more times, steadily getting louder with each asking.

Elaraine finally gave in. "When the last war ended, Orin returned with Moraiah as a bride. He said he had met her in a hospital along the borderlands. We never questioned him on whether she was Swennian or Rischiak. We just assumed she would be Swennian."

"She was darker than we were, but we just assumed it was because she was from the southern borderland and Gegernen is so far north," Nox joined in. "If Orin said she was loyal to Swennia then we believed him."

"They would talk of returning closer to her home every now and then," Elaraine whispered so lowly they had to strain to hear her, "but it never amounted to much beyond talk. Moraiah would always change her mind a few days before they were to leave."

"Do you think Orin knew?" the prince asked.

"That she's Rischiak or that she's a queen?" Elaraine choked out as there was a sudden flurry of activity in the rear of her cell.

"Either. Both. I don't know." The prince was sounding frustrated. "Orin was one of my best men! If he can do this, then I would not put it past anyone to do it, too."

"Orin is loyal to the Swennian crown. If he knew she was Rischiak or that she's a queen he never told me so you will have to ask him when we find him."

"Are you seriously considering still looking for him?" Dayn said heatedly. "His wife is a queen! The Queen of Rischiak! Do you think he'll really want to return to the northern lands to eke out a living as a farmer in Swennia?"

"I think he'll want to return to his family and his country."

"His family is Rischiak."

To that Elaraine had no answer. Had Orin known about Moraiah? The question of where his loyalty lay had never before entered anyone's heads. But here they were worried that his loyalties had shifted due to marriage. Could it be possible? Could his love for Moraiah outweigh the love he felt for his home and country? For her, their parents, and their siblings?

Elaraine didn't know how long they waited in silence before they heard footsteps coming down the corridor. The footsteps were heavy and measured. They could hear keys clanking as the footsteps came closer. Shadows formed as a torch began to round a corner.

Elaraine jumped to her feet as the torch illuminated the bearer. "Orin!"

Orin stood before her in a clean dark blue tunic. There were guards behind him that Elaraine recognized from the encampment. Orin glowered down at her.

"What made you foolish enough to try to follow me?" He said in a slow and steady voice that Elaraine had come long before to know accompanied

254

his trying to control his temper.

"To get you back safely," she stammered.

"That isn't your job."

"No, my job is to keep my family safe."

"That's my job. That's not your job."

"You were gone and unable to do your job."

"Not by choice."

"So you are willing to defect and turn into a traitor for your wife?" Prince Shep chimed in from the other cell. "That's not like you, Orin. At least it's not like the Orin I knew."

Orin's face twisted in pain but kept his gaze on his sister's forehead. "Moraiah...needs my help. And so long as she has Josi here, here is where I need to remain." He sighed and ran a hand through his hair. "I swear, when they took me, I had no idea what she was. Then, when I got here...." He looked Elaraine in the eyes and her heart crumpled with the plea she saw written there. "Please, Elaraine. Please believe me. Jonnie told me something about Moraiah years ago and I didn't believe her. I should have. I should have listened to her. If I had maybe everything, even this war, could have been avoided."

"What did Jonnie tell you?"

Orin sighed and began to pace. "She said that Moraiah would go into the woods at night when I was asleep, that she would say words that weren't in our language, and that she would send letters to the borderland even though she had told me she had no connections there." He stopped pacing. "But when I asked Moraiah about it she said she was writing to her friends and that living in the borderland you had to know more than one language. It made sense, so I left it alone. It all makes sense that she lied now." He spun to look at the prince. "My prince, is this war because I married Moraiah? If it is, I'll never forgive myself."

"If it is, then it is her fault, not yours," Prince Shep answered.

"My friends are dying."

"You men from the northern lands need to come to terms with the fact that not everything bad that happens is your fault," the prince sighed. "Elaraine being here is not Dayn's fault and this war is not your fault, Orin. Things happen. This war was a long time coming. Your arrest was probably just the final tick in the tally for war in Moraiah's mind." He sighed heavily before standing straight and squaring his shoulder. "But, Orin, you tell me right now where your loyalties lie."

Orin closed his eyes and groaned. "I am utterly torn. My allegiance is to my country, but this is my family. Prince Shep, I cannot leave my family. Nor will I fight against you."

"You are choosing exile?"

"I am choosing to live with my family. If that means I am exiled, then so be it." He inserted a key into the lock of the men's cell and his voice grew hard. "Moraiah wants to see all of you now. While you will not be in chains, you will not be able to break free. Do not mistake my kindness for charity. If you try to escape while you are in my custody, I will still have to chase you down and catch you." He opened their door and let them out. He looked down at Elaraine when he turned to her cell. "Elaraine, I am sorry. I did not know about Moraiah and now that I do know, I cannot just abandon Josi."

"So the Rischiaks took you against your will?" she whispered.

"Of course it was against my will!"

"I followed you. I disobeyed orders to find you. I feared you were dead. I thought I was coming to find a corpse, but what I find is a Queen's Consort. The enemy queen's consort is my brother." Her eyes welled with tears. "And the whole time I was searching for you, praying for you, you've known. You've known the truth about Moraiah. And you knew people would search for you because you're Orin Hedri. Dalun Shrevelt's killing made it so I have no country. I was sent to war with the king hoping I would be killed so his problem would disappear. My allegiance was to you, Orin."

"And now?"

She looked at her friends, who were watching her expectantly. "Orin, I do not believe exile is meant for me. Swennia may not want me, but neither will Rischiak. Where then can I turn? You sent no word back of your safety. Dayn, Nox, and Prince Shep protected me, guarded me, followed me, and trusted me. They comforted me when I thought I had lost you."

Orin's jaw and fists flexed. "So where are you turning?"

She looked at him sharply. "Honestly, Orin, I don't know. And how can you ask me what I will do when a few hours ago I thought you were still loyal to the same crown I was following. So you better be telling me the complete truth about what happened."

Orin did not say another word as he unlocked her cell and she walked into the passageway where the others were already waiting in a line. She joined the line behind Dayn, but Dayn turned around and pulled her to stand between him and Nox. When she looked up at him quizzically he just shook his head back at her and looked straight ahead again. In a way it comforted her to be surrounded by her friends.

The guards leading them to Moraiah had brought more torches than when they took them to the prison to begin with so Elaraine and her companions could see from whence they came more easily. All the other cells were empty, but there were definite signs of rats. Elaraine shivered. She hated rats. Being alone in a cell in the coming night did not sit well with her if there were rats down there, too. As they passed a cell with a lot of rustling beyond the bars without a person inside, she gave a visible shudder. Dayn's hand landed on her arm.

"It'll be okay, Elaraine," he whispered. "The rats won't get you."

Elaraine ignored the meaningful look Nox gave her brother at the word 'rats.' The party of prisoners and guards were silent but for their footfalls shuffling along the damp stones through the passageway. It seemed a longer walk to Elaraine than it had before but eventually they reached the narrow stairway they had used hours before to get to the cells. Elaraine braced herself for sunlight but was surprised to see it was already night when they emerged. By the way her friends acted, she could tell they were surprised at the darkness as well. They kept looking around at the many stars decorating the sky. There wasn't a cloud to be seen and the stars twinkled merrily in their ignorance of the problems below them.

"It's pretty, isn't it?" Orin murmured next to Elaraine. "You'd never realize we were prisoners with such a beautiful sight to see."

No one answered Orin. He led the way to a small stone building in the middle of the courtyard. A dim light was glowing and flickering through a window and, as they drew nearer, Elaraine could see shadows of people playing against the walls. No sounds came from the building until Orin raised his hand to knock. Before he could, a scuffle came from behind the door and it squealed open to show Josi and Moraiah in the building. Moraiah was sitting at a short table playing with a small white kitten and Josi was standing behind her, one hand on the hilt of his sword, still playing with the aquamarine stone. The small squire that had opened the door bowed as the newcomers entered and was then dismissed from the building with a single glance from Moraiah, as were the guards that had brought them from the dungeon.

The seven of them were left alone and for a while no one spoke. They just stared at each other unblinkingly. The small kitten would mewl and wind its way between Moraiah's fingers as she continued to play with it without watching it. Josi kept his gaze on his father and Orin remained behind the small party.

"Prince Shep, I am afraid you and your party are not welcome near this place," Moraiah said at last, turning her attention back to the kitten on the table.

"We didn't want to come here either, so I would have to say we are nearly even on that score," the prince ground out.

"Come now, prince, don't be coy," she laughed. "We both know you were coming for Orin."

"If we had known it was his wife who had him, we would not have searched for him."

"Such loyalty to a commoner, Prince Shep. It is heartwarming."

"I reward loyalty with loyalty." Prince Shep glanced at Orin. "I reward cowardice and betrayal with death." Elaraine couldn't be sure if that sound behind her was Orin groaning. "Why are you doing this, Moraiah? Call the Rischiaks away and we will leave the border alone as well. We can end this here and now, you and me. We can avoid this war starting tonight."

"You answer to your brother and your father, so I am afraid I cannot take your word that hostilities will end long enough for my family and me to cross the border safely," she said rising from her seat, coddling the kitten to her chest tightly. "Why should I stop my men from killing Swennians when Swennians do not mind abandoning their own anyway? The more men my people kill the less men you will have to kill later when they abandon you."

"Orin went to the dungeons to protect you."

"He went to the dungeons to protect everybody. You said you reward loyalty with loyalty, did you not? No one has been more loyal to the current royal house than Orin and you rewarded him with torture while your cousin was corrupt and you refused to do anything about it. You let him thrive and believe himself invincible. It is because of you and your brother that Dalun Shrevelt is dead. It is not the fault of Elaraine, Orin, or I. When the ruling house becomes corrupt, it is time for an external party to overthrow it, is it not? It is inevitable that it will be so."

"It is not that simple."

"Unfortunately for you, it seems to me to be just that simple. Unfortunately for me, I have no way to get word to your brother for him to know our demands. Our party headed to his palace was killed on their way to talk to him. The faster an envoy gets there the better for everyone involved. So I will make this simple. Nox and Dayn will return to your brother and tell him what I have said. Prince Shep and Elaraine will remain here. When the king sends word of his acceptance of my rule, Prince Shep will be released and Elaraine will accompany my family back to Rischiak. You will not have to bother with this family anymore."

"Why not send just Nox and one of your men? You could ensure the message is passed correctly, then."

"We both know that your brother would kill my man before he enters the camp. Then where am I left? The message is not passed on and I am stuck here in an ancient fortress that is crumbling around me with prisoners I do not want to have. This is no place to raise the future king of Rischiak." She laid a hand on Josi's shoulder and the kitten meandered to Josi's shoulder and perched there as if it were a bird. "We need to head home. I have been gone from my people for far too long. They need leadership these days. They grew weak from Swennian oppression at the border and my sister dismantled much of the army."

"If we do this...if we go," Nox choked out, "then no harm will come to Elaraine or the prince?"

She looked at Nox and sniffed. "You have my word."

"Some good that will do us," Dayn snarled and then grunted when Nox elbowed his stomach.

"How will we get back to you? We wouldn't even know how to find the people we left to track Orin!"

"You don't need to go back to them. You need to get to Prince Arlun's camp. That is south. So go south. When you are sent back, this is north. So come north. It's not that hard," Josi said shortly. "You can always ask the peasants for directions."

"On foot this could take weeks."

"Then it will take weeks. At least it won't take forever." Moraiah drew out, her voice becoming whimsical as she took a seat on the table.

"And in our absence you will not harm the prince or Elaraine?"

"Nox, if you stayed you wouldn't be able to protect us, anyway," Elaraine kept an eye on her nephew as she saw him become tense. "It is better if at least you and Dayn leave. At least we could say half of our party is fine and well somewhere."

Nox looked down at her and looped an arm loosely around her shoulders. "What if something happens?"

"Something can happen any day, Nox, with or without you by my side." She laughed wryly trying to lighten the mood of the room slightly. "At least in this we have a decision. Go and come back with help and an answer. That is what you can do to save Prince Shep and me."

"Even if they bring help," Moraiah said from her perch where she was watching their brief exchange, "you will not benefit as you think you will. You will be coming with Josi, Orin, and I to Rischiak."

"Swennia is still my home."

"Home is where your family is. We are your family. And we are headed south. You are blinded by kind faces and words if you still want to stay here and that is very foolish of you." She snapped her fingers and the guards returned. "Take Elaraine and the prince back to their cells. Nox and Dayn will be leaving to go to Prince Arlun's camp. Send a guard with them so they will get to the Swennian line without harm." She stared at Nox and

Dayn. "After all, it would be such a pity if these two were to come to harm before their assignment had been completed, would it not? But tell him to return as soon as they reach the line. He is not to wait for their return trip."

As Elaraine was led bodily from the building, she cast a gaze over her shoulder. Beyond Prince Shep being led behind her Nox and Dayn were staring after them, their jaws clenched and eyes full of worry.

Chapter Twenty-Four

Elaraine and Prince Shep didn't talk on their way back to their cells. Elaraine shuddered when the door slammed shut with a clang in her face and she heard a scurry of movement behind her. With a single torch hanging on the wall down the small corridor, Elaraine could make out the silhouette of Prince Shep against his cell door looking over at her. The distant flicker kept her from seeing his face, but his shadow was braced against the iron bars. The two of them stared at each other's shadows for what seemed to Elaraine to be hours.

The scurry of movement behind Elaraine kept getting louder and closer to her. She tried to move closer to the bars to escape her furry roommates, but she was already pressed as far as she could against the bars and she could not squeeze her body between the bars. When something brushed against her leg, she let out a loud, shrill scream and started to flail, trying to kick the animal away from her.

"Elaraine, they won't hurt you," Prince Shep tried to soothe her from across the hall. "Acting crazy will only get them riled and then you could really have a big problem."

"They will bite me," Elaraine whispered back hoarsely.

"Anything can bite you, but you aren't afraid of everything, are you?" The prince sighed and moved away from his bars for a moment. "We need more light. They may stay away from the light."

"The torch is down the hall," was her gloomy reply.

"You give up on things too easily, Elaraine. Where's your faith that things will get better?" He reappeared at his bars and she could feel his glare in the dim light. "Thinking so gloomily will only bring you gloom."

"Are you always thinking about happiness and sunshine?"

"I try to. Sometimes it's hard, but I still try."

"And that outlook still landed you exactly where the person who thinks gloomily is. You are in the same prison I am."

"But I am not screaming about the rats. I did not look back at Nox and Dayn like I thought that was the last time I'd ever see them."

"I screamed about a rat that touched me. And it may be the last time I see Nox and Dayn." Elaraine started to pace in her small cell, making sure to keep one shoulder brushing against the iron-barred door to stay as far away from the rats as she was physically able. "You heard Moraiah. When Nox and Dayn get word to your brother and he withdraws, which he will because you are here as a prisoner with the enemy, Moraiah will take me back to her kingdom."

"Don't you want to go? You wouldn't have to be afraid of being put to death for murdering my cousin anymore. You would be with your family. It sounds like you would find the situation ideal."

"Some of my family. And Rischiak isn't my home."

"Ah, Jonnie. That is true. Jonnie would be staying here. But you don't know her as well as you do Orin, so why should her remaining in Swennia be holding you back from going to Rischiak with Orin? Like I said, you could be a lot safer there than here if you survive this war."

"Prince Shep, I killed Dalun Shrevelt. I will pay for what I did. I did it and it was against the law— I will pay the price. And I obviously don't know Orin that well if I thought he would never leave Swennia or abandon the loyalty to his prince."

"Family is a tricky thing. Just when you start thinking you understand them, they change the rules on you. Something happens and they completely change. It is hard to determine if you have ever truly known someone. You can hope you know them the best you are able and to be there if they ever change back to the way they were before. But understanding them totally is nearly impossible. You need to trust him more because you are his sister. Let other people judge him and pass their judgments on his actions."

"You talk like you actually have experience with this kind of thing."

"Just because I'm a prince doesn't mean I don't have family problems like anyone else. After all, why do you think I'm here to begin with? As the second prince, not the Crown Prince, I am the working dog in the family. But out here, away from the capital, I am my own man. Well, as much as I can be, anyway. I eat what everyone else eats, I wear what everyone else wears, and I sleep in a tent like everyone else sleeps in. I am a 'regular' man. The difference is my title, so I have a command and a reputation to keep. But I rely on men like Andell and Orin to help me with that job. I have had to study people a great deal in order to lead them well."

"But as a prince you are privileged. You never want for anything. You can snap your fingers and have the world served to you."

"I want for much and receive what I do not want. I never wanted to be a king, so thankfully I am the second-born son. I am glad my brother is the Crown Prince. Being a prince is burdensome. With my father...the way he is...my brother is basically the king now without the crown. All I must do is live my life and stay alive in case I am needed to take the throne before my brother can produce his own heir. That is not much of a life if that is all you are good for: being a replacement." Elaraine saw him shake his head several times. "No, I never wanted my title. I never wanted to be a member of the royal family. Don't get me wrong, I am loyal to my family. But if I were able to choose my occupation, I think I would rather be a regular soldier or a farmer. I want to make a decision that does not involve whether a mass of people die or not."

"It would be a big sacrifice to make to live in poverty like you want to. You are too good a diplomat and liaison to be a field worker or a regular soldier."

She watched as he visibly sighed and slouched. "I will never know either way which life would be best. They are merely dreams. They are unattainable dreams doomed to die before their birth." He moved away from his bars and Elaraine heard rustling. He let out a long, drawn out mournful sigh. "Good night, Elaraine."

Prince Shep did not say another word that night and neither did Elaraine. Not long after the prince retired for the evening, the torch down the corridor sputtered out and died, leaving Elaraine in complete darkness with the rats and her thoughts. Elaraine did not sleep that night, afraid that the rats would gnaw on her in her slumber. She could hear the prince moving in his cell every once in a while, but whether he was awake or just moving in his sleep, she could not tell. She wished he would talk to her, but that was not to be.

With the morning came a small tankard of water and a piece of hard bread. The two prisoners mumbled a greeting to each other at their cell doors before the prince retreated deeper into his cell as the guard with the torch walked away. Elaraine wanted to call him back to the bars to have that interaction, but she sensed tension in the air and was not comfortable in breaking the silence between them. The rats with her were quieting down and Elaraine felt like giving in to her exhaustion and sleep, but whenever she started to crouch to start to lie down, she would hear another rustle or a scratch behind her and she would bolt back upright and stare beyond her bars again. She focused on nothing but her thoughts, and her thoughts were not happy ones to have. Her mind swirled between thoughts of Orin, of the Rischiaks, of Nox and Dayn, of Jonnie, of her parents, of how to get away from there with Prince Shep, and what she would do if Nox and Dayn returned. Her mind refused to quiet down enough for her to sleep.

"If you never sleep and only think, you won't be in any condition for what happens after this," Prince Shep finally said, breaking the silence and scaring Elaraine out of her endless cycle of thinking.

"For all you know I've been sleeping when you have slept." Elaraine snapped. She didn't know why she was being snarky with him after wanting for hours upon hours for him to talk to her, but at the moment she resented his trying to parent her. She was at her wit's end and needed to talk, not sleep. "Besides, it's not like you've been keeping tabs on me to know if I've slept or not."

"Have you?" He sounded skeptical.

Elaraine hesitated and then let out a resigned sigh. "No, I haven't. My mind won't let me sleep."

"So it's your mind now and not the rats?"

"The rats aren't helping the situation any, but it is really just my mind that is keeping me awake at this point. I think the rats are getting used to my being here and are leaving me alone."

He was silent for a few moments. "How big is your tunic? Can you tuck your arms and head into it?"

Elaraine tugged her tunic to check the amount of room. She had lost weight since they had left the capital. The long journey had taken its toll. "Yes, I think so."

"Your leggings will protect your legs. Tuck your head and arms into your tunic. The rats will have less to gnaw on if you hide exposed flesh. If you just close your eyes then I am sure your mind will quiet down eventually and let you sleep." There followed a short silence that allowed Elaraine to cringe and shudder at the thought of rats gnawing on her. "You need the sleep, Elaraine. Don't make me order you to go to sleep. When the time comes to leave, if you're not fit to go, I will have to leave you behind. And I will not think twice about leaving you."

She heard the prince shift in his cell as she mulled over her options for just a moment longer before deciding Prince Shep was right. She sat with her back against the wall and her side against the iron bars. She pulled her arms in her tunic next to her chest and tucked her head through the head hole of her tunic. She pulled her legs beneath her and tried to make herself relax. While she was still uncomfortable with the idea of sleeping among rats, exhaustion overrode her anxiety and she was soon lost to the world to her dreams and nightmares.

Elaraine would wake up needing to shift her weight. Out of the corner of her eye she would sometimes be able to make out Prince Shep's shadow silhouetted against the bars of his cell. Every time she woke up, Elaraine was thankful that the rats were evidently staying at bay and she would fall back to sleep quickly.

At long last, slumber would not retake her and she struggled back to her feet. She realized that what had finally awoken her was the screech of a door's hinges. She heard steady footfalls coming down the corridor toward her and Prince Shep. A torch light drew nearer and soon she was being given her daily meal of water and stale bread. With the meager food and rest she had gotten, Elaraine's mind had cleared somewhat and she felt she had more energy. The rest gave her the presence of mind to process recent events and come to terms with what had happened to her and her friends. She was pleasantly surprised that the guard had left the torch in a holder near their cells. She could see the prince at his cell bars clearly now. He looked tired and in dire need of grooming, but she was sure she looked the same way.

With her meal quickly out of the way, she stood and stretched her back and popped out the kinks. While the sleep had relaxed her, she had grown stiff in the hours she had slept. She was surprised and relieved not to hear rats moving about her and she felt herself relax even more. Her yawn was cut short by Prince Shep clearing his throat.

"Orin came by last night," he said. "Nox and Dayn made it to the border between the Rischiaks and our army. There they disappeared. He doesn't know what happened to them after that, but they at least made it safely to that point. He thought you would like to know, but you were asleep and he didn't want to wake you up." Elaraine nodded and looked at the floor. "He also had a guard get rid of the rats in your cell, so you may want to make sure all those breadcrumbs are not in your cell or you will attract more rats. Don't rub his face in his kindness by attracting more rats for the guards to have to deal with soon. Besides, I really don't want them migrating over here to where I'll have to deal with them. My rats are already huge monsters."

Prince Shep turned around and backed deeper into the darkness of his cell. The torch threw his shadow on the cell walls around him. When he came back, he had a bundle of cloth and a loaf of bread under his arm. He looked at her for a moment, his expression unreadable.

"Are you feeling better now?" he asked, kneeling on the ground and messing with his shoes.

"Yes, I think the tunic trick to stay away from the rats helped a lot," Elaraine admitted, giving credit where it was due.

"I am glad to hear it," he grunted.

Elaraine watched him fiddle around with his shoes and the small bundle for a while. Something about his countenance told her that whatever he was doing was not meant to be talked about, but at long last her curiosity got the better of her. He was acting too oddly for it not to be asked about in some way. When he put the bread in the cloth bundle, she broke the silence with a soft whisper.

"Prince Shep, is your foot okay?"

"It is fine, thanks," he grunted again as he stood. She heard his knee pop as he righted himself. "Elaraine, I'm afraid this will not be as exciting as how Orin and Nox have said you left the Dungeons Ussal, but Orin found a way to get us out of here," he whispered as he inserted a key into the lock of his cell. When he stepped out and got to her cell he stopped. "He is loyal, Elaraine. He's loyal to me and he's loyal to you. But he's also loyal to his wife and son. He's a torn man. We have to accept this of Orin. I will accept this if you can. For now, this is all he can do for us. But we have to go while we can."

Elaraine nodded and swallowed the emotional lump in her throat at her brother's possible sacrifice at helping them escape. When she stepped from her cell, Prince Shep grabbed his small bundle and led her down the corridor where the guards came from with their food. More torches were lit to light their way of escape and she surmised it was Orin's doing. As the prince led her up the uneven stone stairs, it occurred to her that that day in the building with the meeting with Moraiah could have been her last time seeing him. If he went to Rischiak with Moraiah and Josi, it would be infinitely more difficult to get to him again and Moraiah was certainly not acting like she would ever let him leave her again.

It was night when they walked outside. Elaraine wondered how long they had been down in the subterranean prison. She had not seen the sunlight since they were first brought to the Rischiak encampment. Prince Shep took a moment to get his bearings and checked a piece of a scroll from his waistband. He silently led the way, trusting that Elaraine would obediently follow behind him, which she did.

The bright light of the moon lit their way through the encampment. They would hide behind the nearest tent when they heard or saw a Rischiak come near them. When the danger passed by, they would continue on towards the woods that seemed to beckon them with its trees with outstretched boughs, like sentinels calling them to safety.

They were nearly to the far edge of the encampment when they were finally spotted by a hidden guard. A shout of alarm was raised throughout the camp and soon the prince and Elaraine were running pell-mell toward the woods, knowing their best chance was to lose the enemy in the dark woods while their armed enemy pursued them in full force. Elaraine glanced over her shoulder once to see the Rischiak weaponry glistening in the moonlight and reflecting the flames of the fires. She stumbled as she looked behind her in a hole she didn't see. The prince skidded to a stop and grabbed her arm, pulling her behind him as he ran as fast as he could to the safety of the woods.

As they passed the boundary between the woods and the clearing, Elaraine felt relief that they just needed to find a good hiding place to survive and stay out of the prison they had just escaped. Her leg was aching from her stumble but the fear of their pursuers spurred her on. The prince seemed tireless as he continued to pull her along. The only sign he was tired was his labored breathing, but he never slowed down or let her go. Elaraine was thankful for his hold on her because she felt if he had not had that hold on her she would have lost him long before. Her energy was ebbing quickly.

They passed many rock outcroppings that would have hidden them but would not have been safe if the Rischiaks had taken the time to search them for the two fugitives. The shouts were getting closer behind them and Elaraine wondered how much longer they could keep ahead of their pursuers. Elaraine saw a strange-shaped outcropping ahead of them. It was shaped like fingers clawing their way out from the earth. Beyond this outcropping was a wide river they could hear as they ran. Prince Shep ran right into the river, pulling Elaraine along behind him. When they landed in the water, he pulled her to him. He held her close as they began to float down the fast-moving river and away from their pursuers.

The icy river stung Elaraine. Her leg began to ache in earnest and she could feel it begin to cramp. She knew if it cramped completely she may not be able to stay afloat, so she began an easy kick, scraping against the bottom of the river sporadically and occasionally her foot would get caught on a rock, holding them back a moment. The prince kept pulling her on and kept her close to him despite her kicking. The cries faded into the distance and they both relaxed a little. When the river widened around a bend, Prince Shep pulled her toward the bank. As she put weight on her legs again, she stumbled and fell all the way back into the river. She tried again with the same result. The prince had to lift her from the water. He tied his small bundle to his belt and tossed her over one shoulder. He carried her, despite her protests, until he found a safe-looking clearing only a short distance from the river.

He sat her down on one of the rocks and untied his bundle. Elaraine rolled up her leggings to see her right leg in the moonlight. It was stinging and tingling at the same time. Her knee was so swollen she could barely push the fabric over it. She gasped as Prince Shep gently pulled off her boots. She could feel something warm running down from ankle to her foot. The moonlight illuminated the clearing enough where she could see the blood coming from a hole in her ankle.

"Elaraine," Prince Shep choked out with a shaking voice. "Elaraine, stay here while I go get some water to clean this." He grabbed a leather pouch from the bundle and he handed her a small knife. "Use this only if you have to," he said before turning and walking away.

She watched as he disappeared into the woods, clutching the knife tightly in her hands. It hadn't taken them long to reach the clearing the first time with her weighing him down, so she didn't expect it to take him as long as it did for him to return. He was silent as he emptied the leather pouch slowly on her ankle. She gritted her teeth and scraped her nails and fists against the rock in agony but she did not cry out. She didn't notice when his hands began to shake because she was too absorbed in her own pain. When he had finally poured all the water and stopped moving altogether, she took a few deep breaths to collect herself. He didn't meet her gaze as she looked down at where he knelt before her.

"Is it bad?" She asked at last, knowing the answer.

She had seen a bone in that cut when her boot had been removed. The pale moonlight had made the bone look extraordinarily ghastly. When the prince didn't answer her right away, Elaraine tried to move away from him to look at it more closely and take care of it herself, but he gently grabbed her calf and wouldn't let her move away. He was careful not to jostle her ankle as he moved her back to where she had been sitting.

"I'm sorry, Elaraine. I'm so, so sorry." His voice was shaky, but she knew he wasn't crying. "I shouldn't have brought you with me on this escape. You were not ready and now you are hurt. I could have sent help for you when I got back to the army."

"By then I could have been in Rischiak. If I go to Rischiak, against my will or no, we both know my life becomes forfeit in Swennia. Your father and Prince Arlun would not listen to whether I was forced to go or not and I would automatically be labeled a traitor. I am glad you brought me. At least now I have a fighting chance to survive."

"But now you're hurt. I don't know how we'll get you back to the army this way. You won't be able to walk and I won't be able to leave you."

"Prince Shep, even if you were to leave me here, I would be better off than if I went to Rischiak." She took a deep breath and braced herself. "And you should leave me here. They will find us here if we wait too long past day break. We both know Moraiah will be sending people out to search for us. You mean too much to her plans for her to just let you escape and I cannot be the means to which she catches you. Either you leave me here right now and keep going and I will crawl off somewhere and take care of myself or we patch my leg up the best we can and then hobble our way to the army and forget about how long it may take us."

"Elaraine, I am no healer. I cannot fix a broken ankle. And if I set it wrong you may never walk correctly again. Your knee is swollen. I don't know how to fix it. If the knee is damaged, even if I splint your ankle correctly you won't be able to walk. I would have to splint your entire leg. I cannot do that so you would have to endure your knee as long as you possibly could, despite any agony you would feel." He looked up at her and she could see water in his eyes, making her uncomfortable. She wished the moonlight was not out for the first time that night. "But I won't leave you. I can't leave you hurt here alone. If I leave, animals will come, the Rischiaks will come, and I will not be able to find you again because they will take you away or they will... they will—" He cut himself off with a choke and escaped into himself for a moment to collect himself again.

Elaraine could hear an owl hoot overhead, the shadow crossing in front of the moon before continuing to fly into the distance. Insects chirped around them as their silence dragged on. Elaraine said nothing when the prince stood and walked into the trees near them. She leaned back onto her elbows to gaze up at the light of the moon, ignoring the pain in her knee and ankle. She wondered if the prince would leave her, but the thought of him doing so did not cause hard feelings to flare, which surprised her. In fact, she found herself wishing he would so he could save himself.

She did not look up when he returned and started rustling the items he had brought back with him. He sat on the ground and she sat up when he gingerly placed her ankle in his lap. He tore the bottom of his tunic into long strips and placed those beside him. He took two wide sticks he had placed beside him and asked for the knife she still held. She handed it to him and watched as he whittled a side of each stick flat and then tested them for splinters. He then whittled the four other sticks beside him in the same way. The last four sticks were longer than the first two. He put the knife back into a small sheath and put it safely in the top of his boot. He took some bracing breaths.

"I wish I had some ale," he murmured. "It would help the both of us get through this."

Without another word between the two of them, he wrapped a strip of the tunic around her still-bleeding ankle and then took her foot and calf in firm hands before gently moving the foot back into place. As Prince Shep grit his teeth as he tried to help her, he and the moon were the only things that heard Elaraine as she screamed her pain in the pale moon light.

Chapter Twenty-Five

The prince did not stall trying to splint Elaraine's injuries. His hands shook as he tried to calm her down as he worked. She was in so much pain she saw bright lights and her screams silenced the insects and birds in the forest. Tears streamed down her face unabashedly and a couple of times the prince had to stop to wipe his own face. Sooner than she thought he would, but not sooner than she had hoped, the prince finished his work and her leg was splinted with the sticks and strips of his tunic covering the salve he had made and rubbed into her ankle wound. The splints were not sturdy but would hopefully work until they could get her to a healer.

The prince seemed shaken as he walked away from her towards the river again to rinse his bloodied hands. He returned a while later, sand still on his knees from where he had knelt on the riverbank. The pain in Elaraine's leg had dulled to a bad ache again and he helped her from the rock to the ground so she could sleep. He promised her he would wake her up so she could take a turn at watch, but he never did.

At daybreak he woke her up and helped her to her feet. He gave her a small chunk of bread from the loaf she had seen the night before. It was a welcome meal, but not enough to satisfy her hunger. She wanted to ask Prince Shep for some more, but she could not bring herself to ask. She knew the loaf would need to be rationed. With no way to hunt for food, they would have to rely on the vegetation, though edible plants were not guaranteed to be found in these unknown lands.

The prince turned to watch her attempt to hobble to the edge of the clearing after him as they departed their camp spot. A deep frown crossed his face and furrowed his brow. He had tied the small bundle back on his waist before she reached him and without a word he picked her up and threw her over a shoulder again. When he looped an arm around her to keep her steady, he was careful not to put pressure on her injured leg. She vehemently protested the arrangement, but he shushed her as he continued into the woods.

"Just for a little while, Elaraine," he said softly. "Let your leg rest a little while longer. If you overexert yourself now so close to Moraiah and her horde we may never make it back to our army. While I am able, let me help you."

She stopped squirming and resigned herself to being carried during their flight. She knew he was right, so she decided not to argue too much. The silence between them was becoming all too common in recent days and it was finally becoming unnerving for her, but she did not know how to break it.

"What are you thinking about?" Prince Shep asked her, breaking the silence for her.

"That the silence between us was finally no longer a good thing," she answered. "Why have our conversations become strained lately?"

He grew quiet and the silence stretched on between them once more, so Elaraine was surprised when he finally spoke again. "How is your leg feeling?"

"It aches, but why did you change the conversation?"

"I don't like it when you get hurt."

"I will be fine. It all just needs to be set by a healer when we can manage to get that done."

He sighed and shifted her weight on his shoulder. "No, you don't understand. The thought of your getting hurt drove me from my position as the leader of the army to find you. Seeing you actually get hurt... hurt me, too. You are a dangerous woman for me, Elaraine. You distract me from what is the best thing to do and what is the right thing to do. I fear one day I may give up my duty completely to keep you safe, and I cannot do that."

"A prince should do his duty and not be so impulsive."

"And now you understand why you are so dangerous. You cause a dutiful prince to become impulsive. When I try to distance myself from that danger, I am drawn back despite all of my intentions."

"So is the silence you impose the distance that you seek?"

"I do not seek it as much as need it."

She thought for a while. "You do not need me to tell you. The smart and dutiful thing you should have done this morning or last night would have been to leave me, you know. I will only slow down your escape."

"And yet here I am hauling you around like a sack of grain!" He laughed so hard she shook on his shoulder. He was oblivious to her gritting her teeth and clenching her hands into fists to hide the pain the sudden jostle caused her. "So, I am obviously not as smart or dutiful as people think I am. It is a good thing I can fool everyone so well!"

She smiled in reply, knowing he would not see it, making her a little sad despite herself. "If the king or your brother were to see you hauling me around like this, they would say you have lowered yourself to a position too far below that of a royal and you would never get another good posting."

"Then I would be where I have wanted to be since the day I was born," he said somberly. "But my father will not leave the comfort of the palace to get his hands dirty in a war he insists upon continuing or to find me. He will remain oblivious to the true horrors of war by staying safely behind the palace walls in all his frippery. No one can even remember why the Rischiaks and the Swennians cannot get along. No one even knows how this war started. My father and brother will not listen to any of their advisors about ending it. They only look for glory." He shook his head. "So here we are in a war."

She refused to let the silence re-enter their friendship. "Why do you think the war started?"

"Me, personally? Land. Isn't it always land?" His laugh was wry. "But there is nothing I can do about the war. I cannot make deals with Moraiah without approval from the King or from my brother. I follow orders despite my title. The second son of a king does not wield much power in matters of State without a word of consent from the King or from my brother. If I am told by them to go to war, then to war I go and I do not question their authority in these manners. My grievances remain locked tightly in my head."

"You have peasant status after all," she said without thinking. As soon as the words were out of her mouth, she wanted to slap herself as she felt him tense beneath her.

"Within my family, yes. To them, I am nothing but a peasant."

"I am sorry I said that, my prince. Please forgive me." She felt shame wash over her for what she had said and the strained tone it had caused in his reply.

He walked in silence for a few moments as he shifted her weight again. "For now it is just you and I, so let us rid ourselves of titles and just be honest with one another, shall we? You don't have to ask forgiveness for having spoken so plainly the truth to me just now. After all, it is a rather obvious truth. But when we return to our people, I would ask the respect of my station be returned."

"Of course! But I am still sorry. I did not mean to hurt you with what I said. Whether it was the truth or not, I spoke without thinking."

There was another short pause between the two of them while he considered his answer. "Would it make you feel better if your apology were to be accepted? Would that make you stop apologizing?" he asked as he stepped over a fallen log carefully, grasping her legs a little tighter as he did so.

"Yes, I would. I do not want what I said to cause another strain between us. I do not want you saying my tongue is dangerous, too, when you already think everything else about me is." She groaned as her ankle was jostled a little bit as he had to strain his stride to cross a decent-sized rock.

"Then it is forgiven," he said as lightly as he could. "And let us forget it was ever said."

"Thank you."

"Do not speak of it anymore," he said a little sharply, but checked his tone quickly. "To help pass the time, why don't you tell me about your childhood? I would like to hear of a childhood outside of a palace's walls."

"It is not as interesting as you would like to think it would be."

"Amuse me and tell me anyway."

So she did. She talked for hours about her getting into trouble playing jokes on Orin. He laughed whole-heartedly when she told him about the time she smacked Orin on the back of his head, making him angry, and when he turned to chase her he lost his footing and fell into a pile of horse manure she was supposed to have shoveled. She talked of the very few memories she could bring up of Jonnie now that her sister's face had shaken the memories out of hiding. Prince Shep asked her about her parents and what they would make the kids eat and their jobs. She spent a long time talking about the times Orin was gone to war and when he had brought Moraiah back with him. She talked about Josi growing up and the jokes he would play on her. Orin had told her it was payback for the jokes she had played on him while they were growing up. He listened in subdued silence as she talked and shed tears about when she had killed Dalun and her time hiding with Ranci and Dayn.

When mid-day arrived, they finally stopped for a break. As soon as Elaraine was off his shoulder and sitting on the ground, Prince Shep stretched for a long time before falling to the ground to rest. Elaraine felt bad that he was so tired, but she knew he wouldn't have let her walk to that point if she had begged. She was surprised at how far they had travelled so far that day despite his obvious exhaustion. Clouds were starting to move in to cover the sky. The heavily foliaged trees had kept them in the shade away from the sun's heat all day, but the storm clouds were making the forest darker very quickly.

For lunch they each ate another small piece of bread, a piece smaller than they had eaten at breakfast. Elaraine resolved to talk less on the next leg of their trip and look more for edible plants and berries from her upside-down perch. The bread would not last another day with two people eating from it three times a day, even if the pieces were too small to satisfy their hunger. It humbled her to know that the prince risked everything to make sure she made it back to the army safely, going so far as to carry her across his back, straining his endurance early in their journey despite not knowing how long it would take them to make it back to the Swennian army. It was not lost on her that he risked his very life to save hers by staying with her.

After a long rest, Prince Shep once again picked her up, this time with her on his back, her arms wrapped around his shoulder and his hands holding her legs to his sides. This strained her knee horribly and her ankle moved too much for comfort, but she endured it, believing it was more comfortable for him to have her this way. They stopped once when she saw some blueberries they could eat, but from then until dusk Prince Shep told her of his childhood and they did not stop. It surprised her how candidly he spoke of being an illegitimate prince. He had not been born within the palace at all, but in exile with his mother in the very village she had met him. He talked about his teachers and military training. He would talk about fancy balls and meeting with the kings and queens of other lands. He talked of his parents wanting him to marry a princess, so he ran away from the palace and had been sent to become a soldier as a punishment upon his return. While he had laughed often at her tales, she laughed little at his.

She had always blindly envied the wealth and the leisure she imagined the royal children had growing up, but she realized listening to him that even wealthy and privileged children have their problems. Even if she had had to work her entire life and it had not been easy, she had been loved and had laughed as a child. His stories rarely involved his family being happy, having fun, or being proud of him. She inwardly grieved for his lost childhood. He had been forced to face the responsibility of his position early in his life as his father decided the princes need to enter the court life and be public figures when they were still young. He had been forced to leave his mother, to be adopted by his stepmother, when his brother Arlun had become so ill the palace healers thought he would not live. It amazed her that he did not speak bitterly of his upbringing. He seemed to talk about it as though he were merely living the life he had been given, trying to make the best of it. She admired the strength with which he walked through life and still managed to be caring, honorable, and just. She did not realize that the silence had settled back over them until she heard him ask her what she was thinking about.

"Just listening as you talk. Absorbing the details of the childhood of the privileged."

"Is it what you thought it was?"

"Was mine what you thought it was?"

"No."

"Dreams are often better than the reality, aren't they?"

He laughed. "In your case, with as many jokes as you played on Orin in your youth, I think the reality was better. I cannot imagine doing that to the man without retribution and I am a prince!"

"Being his sister definitely has had its advantages, though there was the occasional retribution. But it was hard, too, because any man that came to see me had to meet him first. I didn't see many men after they met my brother."

"But one man made it through," the prince said, suddenly sobering.

"But that doesn't make him a good man. He tricked my parents, my brother and I and I quickly came to regret marrying him. I am honestly relieved to be rid of his company."

"I'm sorry. How did he die?"

"He didn't die. When I was being taken away to the Dungeons Ussal, he was living happily with the woman he was flaunting around Gegernen. At least he finally started to go out in public with her. While we were together, he was merely sneaking away to see her. Well, he thought he was being secret about the whole affair, but the entire village knew about it."

"So you are still married but you no longer see each other?"

"We wordlessly agreed to go our separate ways. He can now live with the other woman and I can do as I wish. His taking a mistress dissolved any true marriage we may have had."

"But you will not remarry?"

"As long as one of us lives, no. I will still follow the law when it comes to my marriage. But I suppose he believes I may have died in the prison, so he very well may be married to two women right now." She shrugged away the sadness the thought of her husband's indifference always brought her. "And it matters not because I do not plan to ever see him again anyway."

"Do you ever wish to remarry?"

"I do not plan to break my marriage vows. I am still married. Until one or the other of us dies, I will remain true to my vow. And I do not wish to make the same mistake twice. If it were to ever happen, he would need to be the opposite of my husband and we would have to truly love each other. And you, Prince Shep? Do you ever wish to marry?"

He let a short sigh escape. "For now, just call me 'Shep.' I lowered myself to your social status until we return to the army, remember? And yes, I will marry. It is my duty to marry. It will probably be a marriage for political gain for my father or for my brother. I would like to marry a woman I could love but, ultimately, I await their decision on the matter. For all I know, the decision has already been made."

"I hope for your sake it is a woman who can capture your heart," Elaraine said as she allowed herself to fall asleep on his back as he continued to carry her.

"But what if my heart has already been captured?" she heard him whisper softly just before she lost herself to the dreams she knew would be better than the reality.

The sun was still out when she woke up, but they had stopped again. She was lying on the ground next to Prince Shep on her side. The splints digging down into her healthy leg had awakened her. He was sitting and looking up at the clouds above them while he absentmindedly picked at blades of grass.

"Good evening!" he said without looking down at her. "I needed another break, I'm sorry."

"Don't be sorry, P—," she was cut off by his sharp look and corrected herself quickly, "Shep." He nodded and turned his gaze back to the sky. "I'm sorry to be so useless." Her leg was feeling slightly better as she started to softly rub it. "If you want to go a little further today, I think I can make it on my own, but we'll need to go a little slower than you have been walking."

He shook his head and smiled down at her and swatted her hand away from rubbing her leg. "Elaraine, your leg is still not good. I can see the swelling through your leggings." He turned his gaze back towards the sky and plucked another piece of grass. "Let us wait another day before you try walking. The salve I put on your ankle should be helping it heal by then."

"We aren't making good time with you carrying me, are we?" She grunted as she sat up and dusted part of her tunic to get grass and dirt off of herself. "I am only slowing you down."

He shrugged and lay down in the grass, still looking up at the clouds. "We are doing better than if we were still in Moraiah's dungeon, and that is what matters. Let us stop thinking about slowing each other down or that we are obstacles to each other's progress. I am not leaving you and you are not leaving me, I know, so we are in this together." He closed his eyes for a long moment before looking over at her. "And I think we'll stay here until morning. It is a secure-looking area and I do not know if we will find a better or equal spot in the short time before dusk. If we both rest tonight, I am sure we will make better time tomorrow. We will share watch tonight. I need to sleep tonight."

She frowned and sighed at his answer before starting to dig in her pockets. Elaraine produced the berries they had picked earlier in the day and piled most of them on the prince's chest. She ate the small ration she kept for herself and watched as he picked at his berries until they were eventually all devoured. His eyes never left the clouds.

"Shep," she said hesitantly and he shifted his attention towards her. "Why do you keep looking up at the sky?" She looked skyward as she asked him and then looked back over at him.

He chewed his bottom lip a moment and she watched as a look of deep concern crossed over his face. He spoke so quietly she had to strain to hear him at first until his voice started to rise in excitement. "These past couple of days, from searching for you and Orin to today... this is the freest I have felt in a very long time... maybe since before I was sent for by my father when Arlun was so sick. I have answered only to myself for this short time. I made the decisions and it had nothing to do with orders from people above me. And I can't bring myself, at the moment, to think about the restrictions I will face once again when we reach the army. I heard birds singing while you were sleeping and I needed to just sit here for a while and listen to the freedom I wish I could have forever." He looked over at her with pleading eyes. "Please... please forgive my selfishness just this once, Elaraine. I want to delay our flight just by a couple of extra hours. I want to be free just a little while longer. I don't think at this point that we are still being followed because they honestly would have caught us by now. And it helps you as well! It can give you some more time to recover so you may be able to walk a little on your own tomorrow. I know it hurts you to be carried as well. I know you were fighting the pain this afternoon. But it also means that it will take longer to get you to a healer. My mind is torn about what to do. I wish to lower myself to this level for a little while more, but if you need to press on, then we will press on."

It took her a few moments to respond. "Shep, I have had the freedom you seek. If this delay will help you get through your future of servitude to your family, I will not stand in your way of experiencing it. I cannot begrudge you this. But keep in mind that your responsibilities are unavoidable. You cannot run away from them at this point in your life and you have always known that. You are a good man and a good prince. And do not ever consider wanting this freedom to be lowering yourself. I do not consider myself to be lower in station for having had it and neither should you."

"It is a freedom I am not meant to have. I am not meant to carry a woman on my back. I am not meant to wander lost in the woods. My father and my brother would say that these things are meant for a peasant. And despite our circumstances, I am enjoying every moment."

"Your father and your brother are not here to judge you. And your carrying me is not a proud moment for me either, if it makes you feel any better. I am unaccustomed to having to rely on someone else like this and I do not particularly enjoy having to be so dependent."

"It may not be a proud moment for you to be carried this way, but my ability to help you get to safety is a proud moment for me. It is a moment of pride I do not have often." He flung an arm across his face. "A few times today I considered not even returning to the army. I wanted to go any other direction than the right direction."

"Few people actually run towards their duty when it pertains to war, I believe."

He nodded and then turned on his side towards her, propping his head in a hand. His face became animated and slightly desperate. "Elaraine, beyond this fleeing from Moraiah and the Rischiaks, when we are alone from now on, will you please just call me Shep and treat me more as a friend, like you do now? It may be a way for me to retain my sanity when my duty, inevitably, becomes too much for me to handle."

His eyes were pleading with her and she could not find it in her heart to deny his request. She had misgivings about his request, but she just nodded and she heard him release a sigh of relief. He and Elaraine both looked at the sky and watched a flock of birds cross their lines of vision.

Elaraine lay back down beside him and thought about how much the prince had to have lowered himself from his royal status to have carried her all this way. The level of kindness shown by a royal to a commoner as he had shown her had previously been unfathomable to her. These thoughts surrounded her and soon she was napping again. She was determined to give her prince a full night's sleep by taking all the watches as he had done the night before, but to do that she needed to rest now. She felt a need to help him in some small way to repay some of his kindness.

Chapter Twenty-Six

Elaraine kept watch all night and she was able to let Prince Shep get the sleep he desperately needed. She could tell he was utterly exhausted and his light break down the day before only reinforced that fact in her mind. He was angry with her for not having woken him up before dawn to take his turn on watch, but she diffused some of his anger when she told him friends do each other favors. That word, "friend," seemed to be a magical word to his ears as he visibly relaxed and his face returned to its normal hue from an angry red.

Her leg was feeling much better given the extra rest. The prince examined her injuries before they continued. He changed the wrappings he had put around her ankle to stop the blood. Her ankle was not bleeding much anymore but it would still need to be bandaged for a while longer to at least keep it clean. He said he would rinse the used bandages to be able to reuse them if they were able to find a stream or a river as he shoved the used bandages in his belt.

He did not argue with her when she started to hobble as they continued on their way, which she was thankful for. He let her shuffle along for a while, following behind her and only lending a hand when he felt she was struggling. They were not making good time, but Elaraine felt good in that she was not physically weighing him down. He needed a physical break as much as she needed it the day before.

They had only travelled an hour or so before Elaraine needed to stop for a quick rest. Her leg was aching and she needed to get off of it for a few minutes. The prince did not say anything against the break, but his glances up and down their trail told Elaraine he was anxious to keep going. This confused Elaraine as the day before he was almost begging her to have more time for his freedom and now he was visibly impatient to keep moving. She also knew, however, that if he carried her they would have been making better time than they were. He did not stop moving around the rock she was perched on as she rested. He sometimes looked like he was searching for food, but it did not disguise his angst. He would clear his throat as he rounded the rock and twisted his hands occasionally.

He allowed her to continue on by herself for the next hour after the break without an argument. They talked occasionally but they generally kept to themselves, allowing Elaraine to conserve a little energy and concentrate on trying to walk more quickly than she was. Every now and then she would cast a glance over her shoulder and would catch the prince with a disapproving frown on his face. When he would notice her looking the frown would disappear and he would attempt to give her an encouraging smile, but the frown did not disappear from her mind.

The stop-and-go every hour routine continued until it was time to break for their mid-day meal. By then there was a shooting pain radiating from her ankle to her knee to her hip. She was ready to stop for the day but she knew they had not covered a fourth of what they needed to. The terrain had been rough for a person with an injured leg. There had been large rocks and fallen trees to cross and go around. There had been a large stream with a rocky bottom and sandy shores that she had found extremely difficult to get across. The bottom of the river would not allow her to shuffle across as she had been doing in the woods. She would have landed face-first into the water if it hadn't been for Shep being there to catch her.

At the mid-day meal of berries and mushrooms they had picked along the way, Elaraine could tell the prince wanted to talk to her but was stalling having the conversation. As the last berry in her hand was swallowed, the prince cleared his throat and coughed and she turned her attention to him. He wiped his hands on his leggings.

"Elaraine, I think I need to carry you the rest of the distance today. We need to travel a lot farther before we can call it a day."

She nodded. "I know. I was just trying to give you a break from yesterday. We cannot make it back to Rian, Andell, Jonnie, and everyone else with you carrying me every day. You will be too exhausted to continue in just a day or two if you were to keep doing what you have been doing." She stretched her good leg. "So why don't we agree that in the mornings I walk and after mid-day you carry me?"

He seemed to deflate when the tension left him. "You are not going to fight me on this decision?" He sounded very surprised.

"Why would I fight you when the solution is a simple matter of common sense?"

"Because you have before, including on simple matters involving common sense," he said with a smile. "But carrying you on my back like yesterday afternoon was more difficult than throwing you over my shoulder, so I am afraid we may have to start with you over my shoulder. I know it is not comfortable, but maybe tomorrow when we make up some time we lost today I can carry you the other way."

"It was more comfortable on your shoulder, actually," she said as he knelt before her so she could lay across his shoulder, "because my leg was jostled less this way than when I was on your back."

"Good to know," he laughed as he stood up and started walking again.

"Shep, earlier when we were walking, why were you frowning so much?" she couldn't help but ask.

He took a deep breath and released it slowly. "You were in pain and trying to hobble on anyway. It was painful to watch. That is all."

"Why didn't you say something if it was that bad?"

"Because it would have been pretty useless, wouldn't it?"

His question did not need an answer and they both knew it. They continued on in amiable silence. They would hear the occasional animal running through the underbrush and the songs of birds coming from branches overhead. The time passed more quickly than Elaraine expected. Soon the shadows were becoming longer on the forest floor and sunset was fast approaching.

The prince chose a spot near a small creek for their campsite. They hadn't found any new food in the afternoon trek, so they ate the last two pieces of bread next to the water. After they ate, the prince undressed Elaraine's injuries and rinsed her ankle in the crisp running water. The cold water felt good on her ankle as it helped to numb her leg before he started to re-splint and redress her injuries. Her ankle and knee were very swollen and her ankle was barely bleeding now beyond the scab, but the area around it was hot and swollen. Elaraine knew it was becoming infected without the treatment of a healer, but there was nothing either of them could do about it at the moment. She did not want to add to his worries, but looking at the prince's face she could see the worry there plainly.

As he gingerly prodded the red and hot area around her ankle, Elaraine could not help but flinch. She refused to voice the pain, though, when he prodded a particularly sensitive spot. He finished as quickly as he could, but her foot stung horribly and she felt light-headed from the pain by the time the last bandage had been tied holding the splint in place again. They did not talk for a few moments after he had finished and sat down next to her on the bank of the creek. He filled the small leather pouch with water and reattached it to his waist.

"It looks worse," he said.

"It just looks bad."

"We need to get you to a healer. Or at least someone who can do better than I can."

"We can only go so fast and we both know it." She lay down amongst the rocks and closed her eyes. "I'll take second watch," was all she said before she fell asleep.

The prince woke her up to take the second watch, which she did happily. She was relieved the watches were going as smoothly as they were. She heard nothing but animals moving about her and nothing ever came near them, not even to drink from the creek. That there had not been any sign of pursuit surprised her, but she supposed that two escaped prisoners were of not much consequence considering she and the prince did not have much of an idea of where they were, which only delayed a battle with the Rischiaks and that played into Moraiah's favor. Elaraine hated that their escape probably only served to help her sister-in-law.

At daybreak, she woke the prince back up to start on their way. He refused to let her walk that morning, however. The sight of her ankle had changed his mind about their earlier agreement, angering Elaraine but she was unable to voice that anger to him. The prince attempted a few times that morning to start conversations with her, but after a while he seemed to sense that it was not the time to talk with her because she was not happy. He stopped when he saw some berries they could eat later and again when he caught sight of some mushrooms. He stumbled from fatigue occasionally but would press on wordlessly and without any complaint.

A light breeze picked up shortly after mid-day, chilling them both. The storm two days before had missed them, but Elaraine didn't think they would be that lucky as the wind became stronger. Through his sweaty clothes, the prince began to shiver, jostling Elaraine more than he meant to. He apologized every time he felt her flinch. Elaraine strained her neck to look up at the sky and could see some dark clouds through the leaves. Within a few minutes the breeze had picked up into a significant wind and it was pressing against them. Elaraine could feel the prince begin to strain more beneath her and it worried her.

"Shep, we need to find cover," she said, her own teeth starting to chatter in the cold wind.

"We need to try to push on farther today," he replied through gritted teeth.

A low rumble could be heard in the distance and the wind got even stronger. The prince pressed on farther as fast as he could, but Elaraine could feel him shaking and growing weaker.

"Shep, we have to find a place to stop and very soon," she insisted. "We can't make it much farther and this storm is not going to wait for us to find an ideal spot to wait for it to pass."

"But there isn't a place here at all!" She could hear a hint of desperation in his voice. "I can't see a place ahead that will shelter us."

She looked up and saw behind them a large hole in the back of a tree they had just passed. It was not ideal by her standards because it was not a significantly large hole and would only protect them from rain coming from a direction opposite that that the wind was coming, but it was better than nothing. She tapped the prince on his other shoulder and told him to turn around. When he turned, he saw the hole as well and sighed.

He hauled her over to the tree and placed her gently inside, trying to wedge her as far into a corner as he could but he had to remove the splint on her knee to bend her knee so he could maneuver her in the tight space. Then he wedged himself into the hole. He grunted and left the hole soon after and took his tunic off. When he wedged himself back into the tree, he managed to find large splinters to hang the tunic on over the hole to help shield them from the imminent rain.

The two of them barely fit in that hole and the thunder rumbled ever closer to them. They could hear the rain start to pelt the leaves around them. Some of the moisture came into the hole they were hiding in, but the tunic kept the worst of it away with the prince holding it in place from the inside.

Elaraine's knee was in excruciating pain but she refused to mention it to her friend. Her ankle was beginning to rage in pain as well from the strain it was in trying to take stress from her knee. She gritted her teeth and endured the pain as the storm raged outside the tree. The prince rearranged his seating and pulled her legs to rest over his and returned to his task of holding the tunic in place. Her leg and ankle immediately started feeling better.

The storm raged for a long time. The prince dug from a pouch at his waist some of the berries he had found earlier and told Elaraine to eat and rest while she could. She closed her eyes but did not sleep. The thunder would wake her every time she came close to sleep. Water was coming in the tree and the two of them were shaking from the cold. Elaraine could see things beyond the tunic whirling about in the wind. The lightning flashes were coming quickly, one right after another, and the thunder was nearly synchronous with the lightning.

The prince patted her good leg at one point and murmured a few times, "It will be over soon. It will all be over soon."

She did not doubt him but she still could not rest. She finally gave up on resting and took a hold of the side of the tunic nearest her so the prince could relax a little. He seemed surprised, but he did not question her. He gave her a small smile and leaned back against the inside of the tree. Some gusts of wind nearly pulled the tunic out of their grasps and Elaraine had to hold tightly onto her side of the tunic to make sure it stayed in place and inside the tree.

They stayed in the tree for hours as the storm raged around them. When lightning illuminated the hole they were in, Elaraine could see her royal companion sleeping, wedged tightly in his corner, an edge of his tunic clutched tightly in one fist, his other hand lying gently on her leg. Elaraine could not sleep no matter how hard she tried. Thunder shook the tree and the lightning kept her alert. For the longest time the storm seemed to just hover over them, unleashing its wrath on the two fugitives. The frightened animals had long since stopped running past the tree looking for shelter of their own. Now nothing moved outside unless the wind made it move.

When the storm seemed like it was moving away, Elaraine let herself finally relax. She found a more comfortable position and studied her companion once again. The prince remained still and sleeping, so Elaraine let her eyes close as well. Soon the storm was forgotten as she succumbed to sleep.

It seemed like only seconds before the prince was shaking her gently awake. She shoved his shaking hand away with a grunt and tried to return to sleep, but the pushing on her became more urgent. She cracked one eye open at Prince Shep and realized he was not even looking at her. He was looking into the face of a stranger whose head was poked through the tunic door and was looking at them very intently. Elaraine was awake in an instant. She remembered the prince had the small knife in his boot, but it would not be possible for him to reach it at all in their position, let alone to do so without the stranger noticing the movement and attacking first.

Prince Shep slid her feet gently but quickly away from his legs as the stranger's hand entered the tree and beckoned them to follow him. As the prince ungracefully crawled outside on the soggy ground, he motioned for her to remain where she was. She removed the tunic from the long splinters and grasped it firmly in her hands. It was completely soaked from the storm and there was a long tear on the back of it.

Elaraine watched as the two men talked, a significant distance between the two of them. Elaraine could see their lips moving but could not hear anything they said. The talk seemed civil enough from her position. After all, the stranger's hand never strayed to the sword he wore sheathed on his hip. The young stranger was not dressed as a soldier, but rather as a poor farmer. Elaraine wondered where he had gotten the sword. They talked for a few moments more and then they both relaxed and shook each other's hands.

Prince Shep turned and walked back to her. He held her hands tightly and helped her maneuver from their shelter. He kept one arm around her waist and the other on her arm as she steadied herself on wobbly joints. Her legs felt incredibly weak and sore and without the knee splint her leg was having problems sustaining any weight at all. She gave him a quizzical look and then gestured toward the newcomer still a short distance from them.

The prince shook his head and told the man to go get his own companion and return. When the man had turned and headed in the direction they themselves had come from with one last look at them. The prince helped her hobble over to a large boulder nearby to rest on so she could work out some of the kinks in her joints.

"His name is Gigoro. He is from around here and does not like Rischiaks so close to his home and family. He says the Rischiaks took his parents away, leaving him with a younger sister to raise. He was leaving home to look for the Swennian army when he saw my army tunic fluttering in the storm, so he left his sister in a cave nearby. He is going to get her now."

"He has a strange name," she grumbled.

"Many sons on the borderlands, like him, take old names that mix Rischiak and Swennian. He will continue on with us."

"Why? We know the Rischiaks are here, so why does he not return home now that he knows that we know? He can go home and eke out a living and raise his sister."

"He cannot return home. Rischiaks have taken up residence in his home and have destroyed all his crops. He says he has nothing to return for. He was left in charge of a very young sister and he wants to get her to the capital and away from here. He says he wants to join the army once he sees her somewhere safe." He dropped to his knees in front of her and tugged on her splints to see how they had weathered the storm and then re-splinted her knee. "We need every man we can at this point, so he will come with us."

"We do not have food or supplies for two more people," she reminded him. "We don't even have enough supplies for us."

"They have their own supplies, so I am afraid we will be the burden to them in that regard." He stood back up and wiped his dirty hands on his leggings. "But we can pick berries and mushrooms for our dinners as we have been. We will be fine until we find more help." He looked around and then dropped to his knees again. He pulled the small knife from his boot and put it in her boot next to the ankle splint. "Just in case," he reassured her as he stood back up, looking slightly self-satisfied. Then he dropped his voice. "But, Elaraine, I did not tell him who I was, so do not call me 'prince' just yet. If this is an elaborate trap to get us back, I want to put as much distance between us and Moraiah's camp as possible. If he was sent to get us, then he will know by now who we are, but if he was not sent to get us and is innocent, he will not know who we are and we can make it back safely and without further incident... I hope...."

Soon Gigoro, with a young girl in tow, rejoined them. They were both covered in mud and the girl clutched a homemade doll tightly to her chest with the hand not clutching her brother's hand. The prince introduced Elaraine to Gigoro and his sister and then Gigoro returned the favor by introducing himself and his sister, Julera, to them. The small girl trembled beneath their gazes and tried to hide behind her brother. Elaraine guessed the girl was eight or nine years old but she was small for her age if she was even that old. Gigoro was young as well. Elaraine thought he was not older than twenty. He was certainly young to be thrust into the role of caregiver for such a young child.

As Elaraine gazed down at her, the girl suddenly dropped her brother's hand and raced towards her. She would have toppled Elaraine over had the prince not been there to brace her against the impact. Elaraine bit back the sudden tears of pain that sprang to her eyes as Julera wrapped her arms around her legs and squeezed tight. When she got her breath back to normal, Elaraine looked down and Julera looked up at her. The girl's eyes overflowed and she buried her head into Elaraine's hip, the small doll still clutched in a tight, little fist. All Elaraine knew to do was to pat the girl's head as she sobbed, the sobs wracking her small body.

Elaraine looked at the two men for help. The prince looked as lost as she felt, his eyes wide as he viewed the scene, and the brother had turned a bright shade of red and had looked away. Since neither of the men were going to help her, she embraced the girl back. She cooed to the girl and patted her head, hoping to calm her down.

They stood like that for a long while, with Elaraine trying to comfort Julera, until Julera grew quiet at long last and then hiccupped. It was a few more minutes before she allowed Elaraine to tilt her head up so she could see the little girl's face. Julera looked up at Elaraine with a runny nose that Elaraine wiped clean with the hem of her tunic and tears staining her face that the prince wiped away with his own damp tunic. Then the girl smiled faintly and gave Elaraine's legs a final and slight hug.

Gigoro quietly suggested they go on their way since everybody was calmer. Julera wordlessly took Elaraine's hand in her own. Elaraine looked at the prince in alarm and bewilderment, wondering how she was supposed to walk at all like this but unwilling to disappoint the girl who was so obviously distraught and scared. Shep just nodded, understanding her dilemma, and looped her arm around his shoulders and looped his arm around her waist. Then they began their slow trek through the woods once more, Gigoro leading the way as Julera held Elaraine's hand tightly and the prince held Elaraine like he was a shield.

Chapter Twenty-Seven

The journey was excruciatingly slow, but none of her companions complained about her pace. Gigoro had noticed her injury early on in their walk. He had started a quicker pace than she could handle and when he looked over his shoulder to see where the rest of them were, he saw Shep supporting her weight in a walk that was half-carried by him. Gigoro found a good resting spot and waited for them to catch him.

Elaraine could feel his gaze analyzing her every movement as she settled on a tree stump to rest her leg. Shep went to confer with Gigoro. When she did not bend her knee and instead felt along the joints, she saw Gigoro turn to Shep and ask something with a nod in her direction. Shep answered him and Gigoro frowned. Then he came over to her and stood in front of her.

"I'm sorry for setting such a hard pace. When Shep helped you out of the tree I thought it was just because you were stiff from having been in there so long that you were moving so painfully. I did not know you were hurt so badly. I am sorry and embarrassed." Gigoro hung his head.

Elaraine could have laughed if she weren't busy trying to catch her breath. "Do not apologize. It is something I should have spoken to you about before we left. I do not want to burden anybody and I feel bad for slowing everyone down."

"How did you hurt your leg?"

She tried to evade telling him the entire truth, remembering what Shep had told her about keeping a lot of who they were a secret. "I was not paying attention to where I was going. I was brought down by a hole in the ground."

"You must have been moving pretty fast to have fallen so hard or not to have noticed the hole in the ground."

She squirmed uncomfortably in her seat. "Well, I was distracted by something and I did not see it. Even a snail could have gotten hurt doing that."

Gigoro nodded and walked away with a final frown at her. Julera came over to Elaraine and started to braid Elaraine's hair while the men built a small fire to make lunch. Luckily, Elaraine thought, the prince had found a large group of bushes with berries on them and edible mushrooms below them. It would not be a meal fit for a palace, but it would be fit enough to eat. Elaraine tried not to cringe whenever Julera would pull a snag out of her hair. The knots seemed innumerable to Elaraine as time wore on, but soon the task was done and she was braiding Julera's hair in her turn and the men were giving them quickly carved spoons to eat the soup with from Gigoro's small pot.

After a short rest, the small company was back on their way again, slowly making their way through the forest. They did not rest anymore, but Elaraine's leg was slowly starting to feel stronger so she did not mind the extra exertion to make up for lost time. The only creatures talking in the forest were the birds. The small group was too involved in their own personal reflections to discuss anything with each other. Perhaps that is how they heard the voices as evening approached.

In the distance, they could hear the shouts of men. Elaraine and the prince looked warily at each other and each said a silent prayer that it was the Swennian army and not the Rischiaks. When Gigoro heard the sounds, he stopped in his tracks and turned to face the other three people.

"Should I go ahead and see who they are? If they are friendly, we could eat more tonight than just berries and mushrooms," Gigoro volunteered. "I know how to not be found in these woods, so they will never know I am there if they are Rischiaks instead of friends."

Nobody said anything, but the prince gave him a silent nod. As Gigoro continued stealthily further into the woods in the direction of the voices, Julera and the prince helped Elaraine to a stump to sit. Julera stood rigidly at Elaraine's side and refused to leave, even when the prince would beckon to her to help him.

"Julera," he called, "Elaraine is fine sitting there by herself, but we need to get a small camp set up in case we need to stay here for the night, so please help me."

The little girl shook her head, whipping her small curls back and forth across her forehead and her eyes widened as she gazed at the trees where her brother had continued on. She sidled closer to Elaraine's side and played nervously with the hem of Elaraine's tunic.

Her voice was as tiny as she was. "Gigoro will be back soon, so we won't camp here, sir. I will keep Elaraine company until he comes back."

Elaraine did not pay much attention to the nervousness of the young girl. Elaraine was still listening to the voices in the distance. They seemed to be getting closer to them. Occasionally, she could hear a shrill whinny of a horse. Elaraine could tell it was an extremely large group of men from the amount of noise coming from them. She worried about Gigoro trying to get close to them undetected.

As the noises got louder and closer, the prince gave up trying to get a small camp started with a drawn-out sigh. Elaraine heard him throw his things down on the ground near her seat. He came over and knelt behind Elaraine. She did not look behind her at him, but he placed a hand gently on her shoulder.

The three of them did not speak as evening and dusk merged. As the stars became visible and the moon rose over the treetops, the pitch of the company of the men rose even more. An individual's yell could be heard over the others every once in a while. They were drawing closer to where the three of them were more quickly than Elaraine had thought they would. She looked behind her at the prince and the frown she saw there told her he was concerned about their approach as well. Julera's eyes were still wide and unblinking as she stared at the path her brother had taken hours earlier.

"Shep," Elaraine finally whispered. But he did not hear her as he was too focused on the sounds of the approaching men. "Shep!" she whispered louder a moment later and repeated herself until he turned almost imperceptibly in her direction. "Shep, can you help me get up and stretch my leg?" she whispered quietly again.

He nodded, his frown deepening slightly. He got to his feet and lifted her to her own feet effortlessly with his hands under her arms. Elaraine grunted slightly as her weight settled onto her injured leg. The discomfort soon passed, with the pain largely emanating from her ankle, pleasantly surprising both Elaraine and the prince. If she gritted her teeth, Elaraine could walk on the leg without help.

Julera moved to accompany them, but Elaraine suggested she sit on the newly vacated stump, telling her to keep watch for them while they walked. The little girl did not seem to like Elaraine's suggestion but took it anyway and sat as the prince led Elaraine a short distance away in a very slow and ginger stroll. Elaraine managed to hobble most of the way on her own.

When they were what Elaraine considered to be a safe distance away from Julera she stopped and pretended to stretch her leg.

"Should Gigoro not have come back by now, Shep?" Elaraine whispered as low as she could and he still hear her so they would not be overheard by the young girl. "The voices and sounds are getting closer by the moment and it seems like a large company of men. They are moving quickly, so I do not think they are just farmers or regular travelers. No one would travel this close to two armies."

"They would have to be soldiers." He agreed and nodded, looking worriedly about them. "Those men are too close for him to have been gone so long just 'looking' to see if they would be friendly to us or not. If I had to guess I would have to say he is with those men now and not just trying to spy on them from afar."

"So, what do we do now? We cannot just leave and take Julera. If he comes back and we are gone we may never find him. And we cannot just leave her here by herself."

"Elaraine, I do not think, at this point, that if he returns he will be alone. Whoever is out there," he nodded in the direction of the voices, "will have surely found him by now and will be coming back with him when they find out from him he was not travelling alone. And, of course, we will not leave her here alone!"

"He may not tell them we are here. We may be kept a secret. I don't think he would risk the enemy getting Julera."

He gave her a sympathetic look and then looked in the direction of the voices again. He shook his head slowly. "Gigoro is no soldier. He is just a very young farmer taking care of his very young sister. He is naïve in the ways of war and strangers. He will tell them he had companions. He may not mention specifics about us, but he will tell them he was not alone. So, people will come."

Elaraine nodded. "Then do we hide? I know we cannot outrun them. They have horses."

"So I hear," he said.

"I know it was obvious to say," she snapped, "but you don't have to be sarcastic!"

"I am sorry for speaking like that to you," he replied softly, fixing his tone. He shifted uncomfortably on his feet, but he did not look at her. He at least sounded contrite.

She nodded, accepting his apology, and bit her tongue for a minute to cool her boiling temper, not forgetting he was her prince. "Then, should we hide, Shep?"

"No." He shook his head slowly and turned his attention fully on her, speaking earnestly but quietly so Julera would not hear him. "No. I think we should go towards the voices ourselves. I think if we were to go there on our own accord, if it is our enemy then they will have mercy on us. If it is our enemy coming this way, we cannot outrun them with your leg like this and now that we have Julera to look after, as well. We could hide, but they will surely find us before too much time has passed." He cast a sad glance at her leg. "And if they are our friends, our going there will only hasten our getting you to a healer to fix your leg correctly. Besides, if they are our friends, we will be able to reunite Julera and Gigoro this evening instead of the young girl wondering for, possibly, days what happened to the only family she has left."

Elaraine could only nod as the prince left her side to go to Julera's. He knelt beside the young girl and spoke to her so lowly that Elaraine could not hear their conversation, but she saw when he told Julera they were going after Gigoro because the young girl became visibly excited, her head and shoulders rising and her attention rapt on Shep. After a few short moments, the two joined Elaraine. The prince knelt before Elaraine and checked her leg and ankle splints once more.

"Elaraine, if I tell you to, you will let me carry you, do you understand? It may serve in our best interests for me to carry you to make us look unaggressive if they are our enemies."

Elaraine nodded and accepted his proffered arm of help and the small party left, following the trail Gigoro had taken. His path was easy to follow, even in the fading sunlight. The broken branches and other foliage would have been a sure sign of his path, even without the deep impressions of his footprints in the still-damp earth from the rain before. Elaraine wondered how he was able to go so silently and still leave such a visible trail.

Just as the forest was being cast into complete darkness, Elaraine could smell the smoke of a fire and could hear conversations around them. She could feel an excited tingle run up her spine and butterflies start to flutter in her stomach in the anticipation of their imminent discovery by the men around them, whom she now knew without a doubt to be soldiers by the constant clinking she could hear from their armor and weaponry. Shep's hand grip around her waist tightened and the arm she was using for support tensed.

"Do you think they are near here?" one voice said. "He said he came from near here."

"Even if they are near," another voice said, "the man and woman he described may not be the prince and Elaraine."

Elaraine could hear the prince inhale a quick breath of air that matched her own. The first voice sounded familiar, though she could not place it in her mind.

"Is the Swennian prince missing, Elaraine?" Julera's little voice whispered through the night air. Elaraine shushed her with a look and a gesture for silence.

"Is it not worth a look anyway? If the woman is as hurt as the boy said she is, they need to be collected anyway. And if it is Elaraine, as it sounds like it is, then it will be the prince who is with her."

"The king said to wait, so we wait," a third voice said. "I want to go, too, Rian, but the king said to wait."

"Nox!" Elaraine whispered. The prince cursed beneath his breath as she began to shout. "Nox! We are over here! Nox! Rian!"

There came a thunder of armor all around them. Water splashed as many men ran through it and torches could be seen weaving through the trees. The torchlight reflected off swords, spears, helmets, and armor. Dozens of men were coming towards them. Shouts rose as the three of them were finally seen by the soldiers.

Julera moved close to Elaraine's side and pressed her head into Elaraine's hip bone as Shep's arm dropped from holding her arm around his shoulders and he held the small knife he had moved to his belt earlier in the day, ready to use it if he had to. His other arm still held her supported upright. Elaraine wrapped an arm loosely around Julera as the girl began to tremble violently and the shouting men were upon them.

As the men surrounded them, Elaraine looked around for the faces of her friends. Some men shoved their way through the crowd, swords drawn and glaring, only to sheath them when they saw who they had surrounded. The Swennian emblems glowed in golden glory around them and Elaraine felt the butterflies in her stomach stop their flight at last. The prince did not relax his stance even as his own men surrounded them.

Finally, a man taller than the rest emerged, the crowd parting to let him pass with ease. The man's blonde hair was pulled into a ponytail that hung between his shoulders. His silver crown encrusted with jewels sat low on his forehead. One hand rested on a long sword sheathed at his hip. His cursory gaze took in the bedraggled group and settled on Shep.

"Prince Shep, your appearance has been truly upsetting to what had been a quiet camp this evening," Prince Arlun said.

"It was not quiet, my brother, for following the sounds your camp made is how we found the camp to begin with," the younger prince drawled slowly. "I have much to tell you and I need to discuss it with you immediately, but Elaraine needs a healer. She was hurt as we were escaping the Rischiaks. While I set her leg as well as I could, it needs a healer as soon as possible or she may not walk normally ever again."

The man nodded and shouted behind him, looking all the while at his brother. "Rian! Nox! Carry Elaraine to the healer's tent."

He turned on his heel and motioned for Prince Shep to follow him as Rian and Nox stepped forward to support her. Elaraine wondered at the lack of brotherly affection between the two princes. Nox and Rian each put one of her arms around their shoulders and when they straightened, she was lifted from her feet by their sheer height. They put their other arms under her legs and carried her through the gathered men. Julera trailed right after them, Elaraine hearing her short strides scurrying to keep up with the men carrying her to the healers.

The men were silent until they had cleared the last ring of the gathered soldiers and were on their own carrying her. They seemed to disregard Julera's presence, never acknowledging her or slowing to ease her stride. The men's steps never faltered in the dark.

"Elaraine, besides your leg, are you all right?" Nox asked her, surprising her into jumping slightly as he broke the silence without warning.

She nodded. "Only my leg is hurt. We were running from the Rischiaks and I was dense, not noticing the hole. I slowed the prince down."

"He did not seem to mind. If he had minded, he would have left you and returned later with help. It is lucky you escaped with a leg hurt as badly as the boy says it is. He said you needed support to walk all day. He was trying to get a small party with a healer to be approved when you started shouting. It was not going well because while he described the two of you and told everyone your names, he did not know the prince was a prince and said he was not with the prince when he was asked. It was becoming a very heated discussion. Dayn and I had similar problems when we found the encampment. The king did not believe what Moraiah had said. Dayn, Rian, and I were going to leave tomorrow morning to find you." The two men shared a glance over her head. "The king had approved our party, with quite a bit of reluctance. But now we do not have to, because you did us a favor and escaped. But, Elaraine, how did you escape the cells at all?"

"Orin. Orin gave the prince the key."

Nox remained silent a moment as they walked. Rian adjusted her weight on his arm. Julera was breathing heavily behind them, trying to keep up with them.

"Elaraine," Dayn huffed as he ran up beside them from the camp. "I heard you came to the camp!" He took in the scene of her being carried. "What happened? Are you all right?"

"I just need to see a healer about my leg. I hurt myself a couple of days ago escaping from Moraiah and the Rischiaks," she said again. "I will be all right, really." She dropped her voice. "How did you get the Crown Prince here so quickly? He was much further south than this when we went to his camp."

Nox nodded to a stump at the outer edge of the camp and he and Rian set her upon it. Rian went a few yards away to stand watch as Nox knelt before her.

"Elaraine, we have some things to tell you. For one, that is no longer the Crown Prince. Prince Arlun is no longer a prince. He is now King Arlun."

"What happened to—?"

"He is alive, but just barely," Dayn whispered, cutting her off. "He has abdicated his throne to King Arlun. The king came to inform his brother himself instead of sending an emissary."

"That is odd... wouldn't sending an emissary have been better right now with the war so close at hand? Should King Arlun not be headed for the capital now?"

"Evidently, and this is just what we have heard," Nox whispered hoarsely, "the new king does not want to just sit on a throne as his father did. The new king wants to be a warrior king as well as a diplomat. He is here to lead the troops himself."

"But then... won't the king be replacing Prince Shep as the leader of the men? What will the prince's duty be?"

"He will be but the second-in-command now. His future position is now undecided in the army as long as the king remains here with his army. But the king has no true military training. While he had been leading a company of men to the border, he did not know how to lead them. The men are grumbling. They want to follow Prince Shep. Prince Shep has been with the men through many battles over the years and cares about his men. With the big battle on the horizon, they want to follow the prince, not the king. I am afraid you have come to a camp with divided loyalties."

"And the men are ready for war," Rian butted in as he rejoined them. "We are here to ride on to the fortress. Dayn and Nox brought news of where the main hub of the enemy is, so that is where we are to march. The king wants to strike them first. Every footman, squire, and experienced warrior has been called upon throughout Swennia to come to this riverbank for the battle."

"Elaraine," Nox coughed. "The king brought many of those men with him when he came. Word had been sent out before he even left the capital on his initial ride south, so they had time to amass."

"That is good news," she whispered. "There are more men now, right?"

"Elaraine," Dayn said in a normal voice sympathetically, reaching for her hand and giving it a gentle squeeze. "Elaraine, Nox is trying to tell you this to give you a warning. The king brought your husband with him when he came."

Footsteps came from behind them and everyone jerked around. Prince Shep stormed into their midst and stopped at Elaraine's side. He swung his fist at a tree and the tree shook at the impact. Julera tiptoed up to the prince and took his large hand in hers. As he looked down at the child he groaned and choked.

"We march to the Rischiaks in the morning. The king wants to be at the fortress by morning in two days. He will not listen to me. He will not listen that the women and children now in the camp need to return home with a guard. He will not listen that we need a plan. Moraiah has a plan," the prince sputtered on uncharacteristically. "Without one in place to stymie hers, we are all doomed." He looked down at Julera and dropped to his knees to embrace her. "Julera," he whispered, pulling away from her slightly. "Julera, you are to stay with Elaraine and Andell from now on," he ordered. "Gigoro will stay safe with me," he promised, embracing her once more. "War is no place for such young people," he cried into her shoulder as he rocked them both.

Chapter Twenty-Eight

Soon after Prince Shep had calmed down, Rian and Nox delivered Elaraine to the healers to be tended to. The prince knew her husband was in the camp and had promised her she would stay as far away from her husband as he could manage. The discontent in the camp was palpable as they had passed through the tents and campfires. The prince did not mention his brother's rise to the throne, nor did he divulge anything further about their discussion.

As the healers reset her ankle and knee, the image of the prince distraught, holding Julera, flashed across her vision, blocking her from feeling some of the pain the healers' wrenching caused her. They praised the initial setting the prince had done under the stressful circumstances, but they did not give Elaraine much hope of using her leg as she had before. They warned her she may always experience some pain and told her she would probably have a limp forever.

As she lay in the healers' tent that night, she could not sleep. The sounds of the camp did not fade, even as night melded with morning and nature itself slept. Dayn and Nox came to get her as camp was ordered to break and pack. They helped a young healer she did not recognize to splint her leg with thick binding and sticks. Her entire leg was splinted and immovable. Her friends carried her to Tix and helped settle her on his back. Her leg made the position difficult and painful, but she gritted her teeth and gripped the reins with white knuckles as her friends mounted their own steeds and joined her.

Elaraine did not see Prince Shep as they started to ride out along the path that they had travelled the previous day. Before long, Gigoro rode alongside her and asked her to take Julera on her horse. With her curt nod, he put his sister behind her and rode on ahead of them. Julera's fingers curled into her belt and held on tightly. Elaraine caught Dayn and Nox casting curious glances her way.

"She is Gigoro's younger sister," she explained as she caught Nox's gaze falling upon them once more. "He is her sole caretaker. When he left their farm, he needed to take her with him. She has stayed by my side since we met them yesterday, except for last night."

"The camp was scary," Julera squeaked behind her. "The men carry weapons everywhere."

Elaraine nodded, her heart aching for what the little girl did not understand about the situation. She patted the little girl's hand at her hip. "Yes, they do, but it is for protection."

"The prince was right last night," Dayn muttered. "The women and children should not be accompanying us." He gestured to Julera. "We are going to be expected to fight and win a battle in addition to protecting innocents."

They rode a while in silence and agreement. Horses whinnied and metal clanked as men grumbled amongst themselves. Occasionally Elaraine could see the regal robes worn by King Arlun at the front of the column, Prince Shep's rich green robe flashing occasionally behind him. They did not stop for a midday meal. Instead, squires rode between the riders dispersing bread and small amounts of fruit. Individual riders would stop to water their horses quickly as they would come to a small creek throughout the day. Elaraine and Julera rode in silence.

"Elaraine," Dayn whispered, "ride close to me for a moment." She steered her horse close to his. "Now get a little ahead of me."

She felt Julera being moved from behind her. She looked frantically behind her to see Dayn taking the girl onto his horse. The girl's head was bobbing in slumber as he settled her in front of him. Julera snuggled into the man's chest as he moved alongside Elaraine again.

"I didn't want her to fall, sleeping behind you like that," he explained as the girl gave a small snore.

Elaraine just nodded, smiling, as they rode on. She recognized landmarks she and the prince had walked by as they rode past. They would be within a stone's throw of Moraiah's camp by nightfall, she knew. King Arlun's two-day time limit had obviously not taken into account the difference between riding horses and healthy travelers versus walking wounded. She knew she had slowed the prince down significantly, but it amazed her just how much now that they were retracing their steps on horseback.

As she had suspected, King Arlun and Prince Shep halted the troops at dusk very close to where Moraiah's troops had been encamped. They were at the rock formation where the prince had first set her leg a few days before. There were deep footprints all over the area. A short tingle went up her spine wondering just how close they had come to being recaptured by the Rischiaks.

Julera had long since woken up and was by then riding with Nox. The man had not been happy with the prospect of having her on his horse, but she was becoming braver around the men and had quickly become attached to Nox. When he had first balked at letting her ride with him, Dayn's laughter had shamed him into relenting. Gigoro came back a few times and it had been decided Julera would remain with Elaraine while her brother prepared for the upcoming battle. Elaraine knew she would not be of much use with her leg as badly injured as it was, so guarding Julera, she felt, was a good job for her to do.

While she was setting up a small tent for herself and Julera, Andell came and sat with them. He grunted from fatigue as he half sat, half fell to the ground. Elaraine sent Julera over with a cup of water to give him and he took it appreciatively and with gusto. He untied and loosened his boots and wiped his face with the hem of his tattered tunic. He watched Elaraine pitch the small tent, making small talk about the day's ride and what had gone on in the camp in her absence.

Elaraine learned a lot from Andell as he sat there. She learned that the men did not approve of the king's presence amongst them. There were grumbles even amongst the most loyal of the warriors in their midst. Many new arrivals to the camp had brought their wives with them, including her own husband. Her husband was making a nuisance of himself, telling anyone who would listen that it was his brother-in-law that had brought this war upon them by marrying Moraiah. Andell did not believe her husband or his new wife knew she was there. All Elaraine could do was bite her lip, but she smiled when Andell spat in disgust when talking about him.

When the tent was finally standing, Elaraine collapsed next to Andell and watched the camp rise around them. One hand stayed on his sword and his eyes never stopped roaming. Elaraine sent Julera to get food from the cooks. The girl skipped away on her errand.

"The prince told me you and I are to stay with Julera," Andell finally said. "I do not want to stay so far away from the battle. My place is with the prince."

Elaraine nodded. "I can remain with Julera. The prince may need you."

He shook his head and sighed. "No, Elaraine. That will not work. He has spoken on this issue. I am to protect you and I will do my duty."

She laughed and punched him playfully. "He just wants the old and infirm far away from the action."

He arched an eyebrow at her. "Would I be the 'old' or the 'infirm'?"

She gestured at her splinted leg. "I am not old, so that makes me the 'infirm.'"

He was still laughing when Julera returned with a small loaf of bread for the three of them to share. They explained to Julera that she was to stay with them throughout the battle and not leave their sight. Elaraine knew Andell was still uncomfortable being away from the prince during the battle, but the thought of his sword guarding the girl eased some of the tension she was feeling. Dayn and Nox came and joined the small group, looking grim. Julera yawned herself to sleep and Andell carried her into the tent to a blanket. He returned to the silent group and sat back down. Without a fire to warm them and illuminate the area, the situation seemed almost surreal to Elaraine.

"We are to be at the front," Nox said. "We asked to stay with you, but we were told to be at the front...beside your husband."

"We will be near the prince, though," Dayn told Andell. "I will watch him for you."

The older man looked grim and nodded. "I would appreciate that, Dayn." He swallowed hard. "It will be his first battle I am not beside him. I am worried about this battle. It feels wrong. We should not have come here. We should let it come to us."

"We will be on their territory."

"Well, technically it is our territory," Nox piped in, only to be slapped upside the head by Dayn. "What?"

"Stop being dense."

"Both of you cut it out," the prince drawled as he joined them, Rian in tow.

"Prince Shep, I thought you had to remain with King Arlun," Andell sputtered at the sudden appearance of his friend and leader.

The prince put a finger to his lips and smiled. "What my brother does not know while he sleeps will not harm him where I am concerned," he said lightly, settling down beside Elaraine. "He cannot keep me from my troops before a battle, after all."

Rian remained standing, looking awkward. The others just stared at him until Nox sighed and reached up to grip Rian's wrist. With one hard yank on his arm, Rian was sitting with them. Elaraine adjusted her leg to make more room for the men. Around them, armor was cleaned and weapons were sharpened. The sounds of talk around them were muffled in hushed tones.

The moon was rising overhead amongst the stars and the clouds. The shadows of birds would block out some of the moon occasionally as they hunted. A woman's laughter broke the fragile quiet of the camp and the prince cursed under his breath.

"Elaraine, I swear I could kill your husband for bringing that woman!" Nox ground out.

A chill gripped her. "You mean to tell me... You mean to tell me that they are the people acting like fools in camp? Do they not know we are too close to the Rischiaks to be making that much noise?"

The prince looked perturbed. "They will give away our presence for sure. Rian, tell them to come here."

Rian stood and left and started to weave through the maze of tents towards the sound of the shrill, feminine laughter. Elaraine started to curse under her own breath. Dayn suddenly stood and took a hold of her arm to pull her to her feet. She looked at him quizzically as he brought her to her feet without a word.

"I did not think you would want to be here when they arrive," he explained as he led her the short distance to the tent where Julera slept. "They will not see you in here in the darkness and then there will be no need for you to feel awkward in front of him and his new wife while the prince talks to them."

She nodded and bit back tears of frustration and appreciation. She let him lower her to the ground in the shadows of the tent. As he left, she could just make out the shadows of three people joining Nox and the others' circle. She heard the prince order them to sit with them and it grated her nerves that they refused to obey him.

"You were to remain silent. We are too near the Rischiaks for me to hear the two of you laughing and making a racket," he said bluntly. "I do not want to hear another sound from your side of camp for the rest of the evening, do you understand?"

"I came with King Arlun," she heard her husband say, disdain dripping from his every word. "I answer to him."

"You are my subject as well," the prince growled, drawing his feet into a crouching position. "And you are threatening the lives of the men I brought with me with your behavior. You were ordered to be silent by King Arlun and me. Now, you will be silent or I will make it so neither of you will utter a word again. Now, go!"

He pointed from where they came and they turned after cursing loudly at him. They walked slowly away, hand in hand. Elaraine waited a moment for them to disappear back into the darkness and for the prince to collect himself before crawling out of the tent to rejoin them. Nox leapt to his feet when he saw her to help her. She reluctantly accepted his help. She was ashamed of her husband. She wanted to apologize to the men for his behavior but she did not know how. Another part of her argued that it was no longer her duty to apologize for him, that she had done that enough for him to last a lifetime. So, instead of apologizing, she remained silent as the group resettled itself into a small circle.

"We will be fighting against Orin, won't we?" she asked at long last, her voice sounding faint and shaky to her own ears.

"If he is on the battlefield in the morning, then, yes, we will be fighting against him," Dayn said, sounding firm.

"I want you to stay back here," the prince butted in, glaring at Dayn. "I do not want you there when the battle reaches its peak. You will protect Julera and make sure the child remains safe. You are in no condition to fight, anyway."

All Elaraine did was nod. She decided not to fight his decision. She did not want to see her brother behind the Rischiak standard leading troops against a prince he had been loyal to only a few short days before. The men talked for hours, but she did not hear another word they said. She kept her head hung until sleep threatened to overtake her where she sat. Andell helped her to the tent this time. He did not say a word to her as he helped her settle on a blanket next to her young charge.

It seemed she had only just barely laid her head down when she was awakened by the sounds of drums and horns ringing in the night. She sat up and scrambled to find her sword and knives. She found them near the entrance of the tent and strapped them on as she shook Julera awake.

Men were racing by her tent, the steel toes of their armor adding its own cadence to the drums and horns. No one shouted, no one cried. Men found their friends and stayed by their sides. Elaraine grabbed Julera by the hand and led her away from the clearing for a hundred yards or so and then handed the child a small knife. Julera could barely hold the knife in both her hands she was shaking so much. She knelt as best she could in the splint to look the scared girl in the eyes.

"Do not use it unless you have to," Elaraine warned. "Stay by my side. Do no wander off. If we are separated, yell my name and I will come running to you as fast as I possibly can."

Julera nodded as Elaraine struggled to regain her feet. She moved the girl behind her and drew her sword. Andell came racing to her side, panting and sweating. He was dressed in armor from the top of his head to his toes and carried a chain link vest in the hand his sword was not clutched in. He threw the vest unceremoniously at her. She thanked him as she shrugged into it. He answered her with a grunt, turning on his heel to look around them.

"Andell? What is going on?"

He shook his head and squinted, trying to see in the dark. "I am not entirely sure," he said at last, still peering into the darkness tensely. "The prince just sent me to find you when the drums started." He looked around quickly. "Where is Julera?"

Julera came around from behind Elaraine and tugged on the bottom of his tunic. "Right here," she murmured softly when he looked down at her. "I'm right here."

He picked her up wordlessly and walked her to a small bunch of brush. Elaraine hobbled after them as well as she could until the glare he threw over his shoulder at her told her to remain where she was. He walked to the center of the brush and placed her down in the middle of it, telling her to stay down and hide until he or Elaraine or one of their friends came to get her. The girl said she understood and Andell patted her head affectionately before coming back to Elaraine.

"I'd tell you to hide, too, if I thought it would do any good at all," he said tensely when he reached her. "But I know before I'd turn around you'd be right back here."

"Yes, I would," she replied wryly.

"But when it all comes to us, you watch yourself. If it gets really bad, and you'll know when that time comes because I may just tell you myself, you get Julera and both of you run for it." He studied her intensely for a moment. "I mean it, Elaraine. The prince will not forgive me if anything were to happen to you. So you get the girl and you run as far and as fast as you can."

Elaraine did not respond to him. She shifted as much weight as she could off her bad leg and looked around the area herself. Her eyes fell on a stump nearby to lean against and sighed as her weight came off her bad leg as she settled against it. She kept a hand on the hilt of her sword as she leaned there uncomfortably. Yells were all around them now and were drawing nearer, but there were no sounds of the clash of steel on steel of battle.

The horns blew desperately once more and the two adults looked at one another. Andell took a deep breath and closed his eyes for a moment to gather himself.

"It is a strange feeling," he murmured, "to be more scared of protecting you two than I would be in the main battle."

She shrugged. "Don't be. I can fight, remember?"

"In battle, the only responsibility I have is to protect myself and guard the prince's back. If I fail there, I really only fail myself. Other people protect the prince besides me. But if I fail here, I fail everything and everyone."

Elaraine just rolled her eyes and looked away. She wasn't as important as Andell was making her sound. A rustle in the brush behind them distracted her.

"Is she safe there from animals?"

Andell looked over his shoulder at where Julera was hiding. "The camp has probably scared most of the animals away. Does she have a knife with her?"

"I gave her one."

He turned his attention back towards the direction of the camp once more. "Then she'll be fine."

They stood in silence. Elaraine tried to stretch her leg but the splints kept her from achieving a full range of motion. She looked around as the first sounds of an actual battle could be heard. The sounds of horses screaming permeated the air with the first sounds of armor and swords meeting.

She and Andell looked at each other and Andell drew his sword and kept it ready at his side. Elaraine drew her sword and kept it by her side as well. Andell called a warning over his shoulder once more at Julera to stay hidden.

"Tighten your splints, Elaraine. If that gets here, you'll need all the support you can get."

She did as he said, quickly tightening her splints, and then turned to him. The question that had been on the tip of her tongue during the night came tumbling out. "Andell, I have to ask you... do you still believe in Orin?"

He wouldn't look at her for a few moments as he mulled the question over in his mind. "Ask me that question again after tonight," he said as the sounds became steadily closer to where they were. "If we see him fighting against us, you will have your answer without having to ask me again."

She could only nod as the first Rischiak came into their small clearing and charged them.

Chapter Twenty-Nine

The Rischiak charged them, howling as he ran towards them and slinging his short sword from side to side. Andell put a hand on Elaraine's arm as she leaned forward from the stump to hold her back and started stepping forward himself. Andell met the enemy's charge in the middle of the small clearing and cut him down quickly, without much effort. He wiped his sword on the fallen man's tunic without a second thought and turned back to Elaraine. A large battle raged near them and was growing closer. As he strode slowly towards her, the pitch of battle heightened but over that clamor they could hear more men coming their way.

Elaraine put as much weight as she dared on her bad leg in front of her so her good leg could support most of her weight and braced herself. She kept the stump behind her as three more Rischiaks entered the clearing, looking around and panting. It took them but a moment to see Elaraine and Andell in the moonlight. When they saw the two Swennians, the Rischiaks ran at them, their weapons drawn and swinging. Andell and Elaraine remained where they were. Two Rischiaks attacked Andell while the third came at Elaraine.

Their swords met in front of her face, the sudden impact zinging up her arm to her shoulder. She adjusted her grasp and held the hilt with both hands as she fought back. She was pushed backwards until the leg she put behind her came in contact with the stump. She pushed off the stump and flung her weight at him, making him stagger back a few steps. She swung her sword back over her shoulder and swung it back at his neck as hard as she could. He fell to his knees with a thud as blood spurt from his neck all over her and the ground. Her stomach churned as he finally fell face-first into the dirt. She looked around for Andell. He was behind her standing over his own attackers and looking at her blankly, his sword was stained red and sweat was running down his brow.

Screams were rising from the encampment along with the sounds of horses and metal on metal. Andell and Elaraine just looked at each other hopelessly. He looked worried and kept sneaking glances toward the camp. Elaraine knew how he felt. Her friends were back there, too.

She shuffled over to him. "Andell, go." The look he gave her was torn. "Julera and I will run like you said if it gets too bad for me to handle alone. I swear it." She shoved on his shoulder to push him in the direction he wanted to go. "Go!"

He shook his head at last and groaned as he removed her hand from him. "I can't. I was told by the prince to stay."

She glared at him and bit her tongue for a moment before returning to her original spot. "Andell, if you come to regret this decision, just know I gave you the chance to leave."

"I would never blame you."

She remained silent as another Rischiak, followed by five of his comrades, entered the clearing running. They did not slow down as the others had as they rushed at Elaraine and Andell. Elaraine felled the leader with relative ease as his arms raised to strike her first. Her sword entered through his armpit into his chest.

The second and third men attacked her together as Andell came to her side. Two more of the men attacked Andell. Elaraine managed to slice the thigh muscle of one of the men as she stumbled backwards once more. The other man kept swinging at her, his sword coming at her in quick and hacking strokes she found difficult to fend off. Sweat was falling from her face and was getting in her eyes. As he raised his arm one last time, she swung out as hard as she could and she felt the initial impact as her sword severed his clothing and continued on into the softness of his belly. She wiped her face and turned to Andell. He was finishing off the second of his attackers. Elaraine looked around and counted. There should have been ten bodies on the ground. Instead, there were nine. She looked around for the sixth man that had come with the latest slew of attackers, but she still only counted nine bodies and the two of them.

She just shook her head and scanned the trees once more before she felt a sinking feeling in the pit of her stomach. She turned to Andell with wide eyes. "Check on Julera, if you would, Andell."

"Why? She's fine." He put his hands on his knees and panted. "Battle is easier. You stay excited. This is just draining, waiting for each attack to come."

"Andell! Stop complaining! Check on Julera!" The panic was starting to creep up her spine.

"I asked 'why.'" He glared up at her at her tone and then lowered it again to continue his panting.

"Ten Rischiaks have attacked us!"

"And?"

"We have only killed nine!"

Andell's head snapped up. He wiped the sweat from his brow with the hem of his tunic and did his own inventory of the clearing before blurting an expletive and racing to where he had hidden the young girl. He called Julera's name as he looked for her.

Elaraine watched anxiously as he searched for her, but when he stood up and kept looking beyond where the brush was, she knew. She knew Julera was gone. She fell back to sitting on the stump. Elaraine trembled as Andell roared as he gave up looking. His chest was heaving and he was hitting his thighs in aggravation. His sword was sheathed, but not entirely. Elaraine's mind was racing through the possibilities of where Julera had gone, but her thoughts always returned to the tenth man.

"Andell, we have to go after her!"

"How?" he said, nearly sobbing. "I cannot leave you and you cannot go after her with your leg."

Elaraine stood and looked around the clearing one last time. "Do not worry about me, Andell. You go after the Rischiak man. The moonlight will light your way well enough. If it was him, he'll not have had time to cover his tracks, so you do not need a tracker. If it was not him, I think she will have gone to find Gigoro. I will go to the camp and tell the prince what is happening." She pushed him away once again and yelled. "Just go! I can take care of myself! Julera can't!"

He nodded and took a steadying breath. "Take care of yourself, Elaraine." He wrapped an arm around her and squeezed for a moment. "I mean it, my friend. Stay safe."

With that he went back to the brush, told her he found a path, and, sword drawn, followed it. Elaraine was left alone in the clearing momentarily. She took her own steadying breath and ignored the pain screaming throughout her leg. She kept her sword in one hand and drew a knife in the other. She hobbled as quickly as she could in the direction of the camp and the terrible sounds of battle.

Only a few yards into the forest she encountered the first signs beyond the clearing that a battle was raging. She hobbled past men, Swennian and Rischiak alike, moaning in pain or pale in death. She wanted so badly to stop and help those in pain, but she could not afford to stop. She told them she would find a healer to be sent to them to help. She tried to ignore the blood streaming to stain everything in the moonlight.

A large fire loomed ahead and she followed its light. Shadows danced around her, playing with her senses. She kept swinging her gaze from side to side, thinking she was seeing an attacker coming at her, but realizing it was only a shadow time and time again. She kept her guard up as she entered the borders of the camp. A horse lay dead between two tents. Near the horse was a slain wolf. As Elaraine crept past the animals, she noticed the horse bore a blanket with a Rischiak emblem. She paused beside it to catch her breath and heard a yell from behind her. She swung halfway around and met her attacker.

His knife sank into her forearm before she could fully react, but as he retreated to see the damage, she took the knife out of her arm, gritted her teeth, and threw the knife back at him with her other arm, sinking the knife deep into his chest. He looked at her in amazement as he fell over and drew a last, shaky breath. Pink foam bubbled from his mouth as he lay there. She watched in morbid fascination a moment before her stomach lurched once more and she lost the meager contents of her stomach on the grass in front of her.

Elaraine sheathed her knife in her boot once more as her knife hand was now unusable. She was relieved she could still move her fingers, but the blood was pouring from the long cut in her arm. The cut was long and deep. In the fire and the moonlight, however, she could not see any bone. She could not stop to wrap it. She wiped her mouth with her good hand and continued on to find the prince and added seeing a healer for herself to her growing list of urgent duties that night. She took one last moment to hope that Andell was faring better than her and had found Julera already.

She had not gone far before she heard her name being screamed. She looked around frantically and saw Nox looking at her with terror in his wide eyes. He screamed something else at her that she could not hear over the din around them.

"Elaraine! Get down!" Another voice screamed at her. As she fell to her face on the grass obediently, she heard the voice scream again. "Nox! Kill him!" The voice repeated the scream two more times, the pitch becoming more desperate each time.

Elaraine looked up to see Nox hurl a short spear over her. Someone gave him another and he threw it, too. He raced at her and grabbed the knife she had sheathed in her boot moments before. She turned to look over her shoulder as he attacked a giant of a Rischiak man. The man's black hair was long and hung to his waist in thick braids. Scars crisscrossed his chest and face. His muscles bulged over the leather straps wrapped around his biceps and calves. Nox, a tall man himself, only came to his shoulder as he rushed him.

The spears Nox had thrown were protruding from his shoulders and the behemoth was still swinging a double-headed axe. Nox dove to the ground in front of him and avoided a swing to the head by the man's axe. Nox reached as far as he could and stabbed the man in the thigh to the knife's hilt and then dragged the knife to the man's knee in a jagged line. The giant still did not slow down and Nox had to start dodging the axe that was being swung downwards at him. Another pair of leather boots entered her line of vision. She heard a yell and saw the giant stagger a few steps before his head landed by Nox's waist with a dull thud and then started to roll towards her. She recoiled as it butted against her boot. The headless body slumped to its knees and then fell sideways to the ground, its gigantic size not diminished at all in death.

Nox got to his feet and dusted his pants. He wiped the knife with the hem of his tunic and came back to Elaraine. He sheathed the knife for her and helped her back to her feet. He dusted off her clothes and then saw her arm. He dragged her between two tents and took off his tunic. He stripped the shirt he wore beneath it and put his tunic back on. He wrapped the shredded shirt around her arm gently but tightly. He looked about them the entire time. When he finished, he sheathed her sword she still clutched tightly for her.

"Where are Andell and Julera?" he asked at last.

"We were fighting some Rischiaks that found us in a clearing near the camp. We had ten attackers total, and we were doing fine, but when we finished off the last wave, we only had nine bodies and no Julera. Andell went after the tenth man to see if he could find Julera. I couldn't go with him as I am, so I came to tell the prince."

He nodded and looked around as a yell sounded near them, but they were still undiscovered. "Are you okay?" He placed his hand on her arm but pulled away like he'd been burned when she flinched. "Besides the arm, are you okay?"

She nodded numbly. "This is worse than before. I have killed before, Nox, and I have been in battle before, but this seems so much worse than before. Nox, I even got sick after I killed one of the Rischiaks!"

He nodded. "Fighting against what may be Orin has made it seem worse for a lot of us."

"Do you really think that's what is making me feel this way?"

He looked at her a moment. "I think you're afraid of seeing Orin wearing the Rischiak emblem and having to fight him." He cupped her face tenderly with a dirty and blood encrusted hand. "I think you're afraid of having to face him. And that's okay, Elaraine. It really is." He dropped his hand and stood up again. "The prince was with me when I killed that behemoth back there. If you need him, you will find him where the battle rages the most. I have to go back to the battle and can't watch over you, so be careful."

"Nox!" she called after him, making him pause a moment. "If you run into a healer, there are a lot of wounded in the forest that need help and I said I would send a healer if I could find one."

He nodded and ran back into the throes of the battle. Elaraine mustered her own courage and followed him back into the main throng. She looked around for a moment, trying to catch sight of her prince. She caught sight of him near the fallen giant, battling three Rischiaks by himself. Dayn and Nox were near his side but unable to help him as they had their own Rischiaks to contend with.

As she raced to them as fast as she could in her splints, she attracted the attention of a group of Rischiaks who gave chase to her. She unsheathed her sword with her good hand and did not slow down her hobbled run. A yell from close behind her sounded and she turned to look, but it was cut off mid-cry by a sword slicing through the man's neck. As the man fell, Elaraine traced the arm holding the sword now behind her. Her eyes widened at the fierce look in Prince Shep's eyes as he attacked the other men following her.

She slew one of the six men and watched in amazement as the prince slew the other five quickly. He turned to her and anger flashed in his eyes.

"What are you doing here? Where is Andell?" he yelled at her, gripping her arm and holding her. When she let out a garbled scream, he released her arm and noticed the blood staining his hand and then saw the makeshift bandage on her arm. "Elaraine, what happened?"

"Someone took Julera. Andell is looking for them."

"What happened to your arm?"

"It's nothing. Nox took care of it."

The prince did not respond as he killed another Rischiak behind her. She, in turn, struck down a Rischiak behind him. They looked at each other a moment. The prince reset his jaw and turned away. He yelled for Dayn and when the man reached their side, the prince commanded him to stay by her side and warned Elaraine to stay with Dayn.

Dayn and Elaraine did not have time to greet each other for as soon as the prince walked away towards Nox the pair was besieged by Rischiaks. It seemed to take forever for them to kill them all and there was no end in sight for the onslaught. Elaraine was beyond exhausted. Dayn's eye was bloodied and swollen and Elaraine doubted she could stand much longer on her leg and her arm was in terrible pain.

As dawn started to break, so did the tide. Fewer Rischiaks were about and healers were able to go around to the wounded without too much fear of being attacked. Nox found them as this tide began to change. As he reached them, he put an arm about Elaraine's waist to help support her. He motioned for Dayn to do the same and they started to help her to the healer's tent despite her protests that there were people in more need of the healers than her.

As they walked slowly across the camp, Nox with his sword still drawn, they had to step across bodies that had piled upon themselves during the battle. She would look down at the faces when they came across the bodies and the moaning men, looking for familiar faces and praying she saw none. She saw a skirt fluttering in the wind nearby and Dayn covered her eyes with his hand. She tried to shake him off but stilled when he told her it was the body of her husband's new wife. Elaraine felt a momentary pang for the woman's slaughter.

"The attack was so sudden," Nox was telling her. "Some of the squires and younger men were by the river watering some horses and saw Rischiaks crossing the river. They raised the alarm, but by then a huge force was crossing. The camp was in a bad spot to begin with. We could only defend ourselves; we couldn't put up a good offensive."

"Did you see Jonnie?" she asked them as they passed another pile of bodies.

"At the beginning, I did," Dayn volunteered.

"I saw her just as I came to find you this morning," Nox told her, reassuring her.

"Gigoro?" she asked next, hoping again Andell had found Julera, but both men shook their heads. "What about... wait! Stop!"

The men stopped and looked at her as she stared down at the ground. Looking up at her with lifeless eyes was Berell, his face twisted in pain, a slash of a sword or knife cutting across his face from his left temple to the right side of his neck. He was reaching away from himself with both arms, Rischiaks on the ground all around him. Dayn bent and closed Berell's eyes.

"I saw it," Dayn said. "He fought them all off until the end. They were around Rian and the prince. Berell saved them."

"Redemption," Nox said simply.

Elaraine had to look away as her tears threatened to flow and they continued on to the healers. A steady stream of wounded was going along with them, many of them also supported by their friends. Elaraine recognized some of the wounded as men she knew. People asked each other about friends and relatives. As they approached the healers' tent, she noticed the line of bodies outside the tent, covered in sheets stained in a splotchy red. Two men were carrying a body out to join his dead comrades. Before they covered his face, Elaraine recognized the dead man as her husband. Unlike with his wife, Elaraine felt no pang in her heart for him. He was covered and she was led into the tent and her friends put her on a spare bed at the direction of a healer.

Dayn and Nox did not leave her side while she was in the healers' tent, but they succumbed to sleep on the ground next to her. A healer covered them with a blanket and moved on. Many more dead and living men exchanged places as Elaraine rested there. Jonnie came to check on her and reassure her she was, indeed, alive and well. She said she was going to join a party to look for Andell and Julera with Gigoro and the prince because the man and young girl had not yet returned and now that the battle had ceased for the moment they could be spared. When Elaraine asked Jonnie about Orin, her sister grew quiet and while she said she had seen Orin during the battle wearing a Rischiak uniform, she refused to disclose more information to Elaraine. Jonnie looked relieved when a healer came to look after Elaraine's arm wound and, before Elaraine could ask more questions, Jonnie left the tent.

The prince came to see her as well to get directions to the clearing she and Andell had been in when they had parted ways. He did not linger with her and he did not ask how she was. He stayed long enough to see some of his men and then he left with Jonnie and Gigoro.

When Nox finally woke up, he sat with her while they waited for her leg to be splinted again. He left for a few moments once to find out what the status of the battle was. When he returned, he sat back down heavily. He kicked at Dayn's legs to wake the other man up. Dayn swatted Nox's legs away but sat up groggily.

"Where is the prince?" Nox asked Elaraine. "We need to get him back here."

"Why? What happened?" Elaraine asked.

"King Arlun called for a meeting with Queen Moraiah."

Dayn sat up straight. "Why?"

"Peace talks. Word around camp is that this battle was too bloody for both Swennia and the Rischiaks. Neither wants it to become a full-fledged war."

Dayn laid back down. "The king can take care of that by himself."

"Well, the king and a guard met with the queen and one of her guards. The queen took Orin as her guard." Dayn and Elaraine sat up. "He recognized Orin and he attacked Orin. Orin's face was split from his ear to his lip. The queen will only talk to Prince Shep now. She is threatening another battle and a war that will wipe out all Swennians. And word is that she will likely declare war either way."

Chapter Thirty

Dayn and Nox raced out of the tent as soon as Elaraine told them where the prince had gone. They caught Rian coming into the tent to see her and took him with them so he could track the small party for them. He wished Elaraine well over his shoulder as Dayn and Nox pulled him from the tent without much explanation.

Elaraine could only lie on the bed and wait to hear news. When she closed her eyes, she saw Berell's lifeless face and it would slowly morph into Orin's. She would open her eyes a moment later, covered in a cold sweat and with a racing heart. The way Nox had heard it, Orin's wound did not sound as severe as Berell's facial wound had been. She could see Berell's skull inside his wound. Orin's face, as she had last seen it, had been so handsome. She was afraid for him, even if he had been with the Rischiaks instead of his own kingdom. Deep down, she could understand his change of allegiance to his wife and son. Orin's devotion had always been, ultimately, to his family, and she had always known that.

A healer came by and redid the splints and wrappings on her leg and ankle. When he was done, Elaraine walked as best as she could back into the main part of the camp. She passed the long line of dead, which had, by that time, become three long lines of dead, and continued to the middle of the camp where the night before Nox and Prince Shep had slain the giant.

Men were piling the Rischiak dead in a large pile at the edge of the forest nearest the river, but the giant's body and head were still where they had fallen, the man's face twisted in a permanent grotesque grin. She stared at the head of the man for a while until she found his scarred face molting into an image of Orin's. The man's scars became her brother's, the man's size became her brother's, and if she closed her eyes, she could just imagine the behemoth dead before her was her brother. She shook her head at the tears forming in her eyes.

Needing to clear her thoughts, she walked to the river's edge and found a flat rock near the river bend. She sat there for a while watching the Rischiaks on their side of the river stack Swennian dead like the Swennians were doing on her side of the river. She pulled her good leg up to her chin and rested there like that. She hugged her leg closer as the pile grew larger. She hoped against reason that Orin would appear on the other side of the river. She sat there for what seemed like ages. Occasionally, one of the Rischiaks would glance up and see her sitting there and then he would continue on with his task.

Around the middle of the day, she decided it was time to return to camp. Everything she passed was in a haze. Nothing came into focus. Her mind registered an occasional tree or person, but she did not know who she passed or where she passed them. She knew when she was in the camp, but she just kept walking. She did not stop walking until she came to the clearing where she and Andell had started the battle.

As her focus came back, she saw that the dead there had not been cleared. She took deep, gulping breaths of air and made her way to her stump. She sat there and gradually her head fell between her knees and she began sobbing. She had taken in all the carnage in the past day and it had finally taken its toll. Her cries came out in loud, heaving sobs.

Her sobs were cut off suddenly when a hand laid itself on her shoulder and gently squeezed. She felt herself jump at the unexpected contact. When she turned to see who it was, she came face-to-face with Andell. Beside him was Julera and behind him were her friends and Jonnie. Julera ran into her outstretched arms and Elaraine's tears fell onto the little girl's hair. Andell patted her arm once more before nodding and walking away.

"Where did you go?" Elaraine asked through her tears. "Julera, why did you leave that brush?"

"I'm sorry!" Julera sobbed back. "I saw the man. I was scared, so I ran! He followed me but Andell found him and saved me. I'm sorry for just running away."

"I'm glad you're safe, Julera," Elaraine said and returned Julera to her brother. "I'm glad they found you."

Gigoro took Julera and they walked away from her. Rian walked past her, too, after telling her he was glad she was up and walking around. Elaraine was left with Jonnie, the prince, Dayn and Nox. The prince was still glowering at her.

"Jonnie," Elaraine said, needing reassurance from her older sister. "Jonnie, Nox said that Orin—."

She nodded. "I know. Nox told us about the meeting already. Prince

Shep says he will take me to the meeting with the queen. When I see Orin, I will let you know how he is, all right?" She also patted Elaraine's arm as she went past her towards the encampment.

The prince told Nox and Dayn to leave them to talk, but they refused. Nox went to stand behind her, placing a hand on her elbow. Dayn did the same on her other side. Elaraine straightened her back and braced herself for the storm it looked like the prince was about to unleash. Prince Shep took a deep breath and clenched his teeth.

"Elaraine, you and Andell should never have separated. You both went against orders," the prince growled. "You are both lucky to have lived. Now, I am going to this meeting with your brother. From this moment until we return to the capital, stay out of my way. I do not want to see either you or Andell."

He stalked past them. While anger roiled in her veins, she felt only one last, solitary tear slide down a cheek with his departure. Dayn and Nox turned her and led her back to the camp to a tent they commandeered and laid her down to rest. Dayn pulled off her boots and propped her feet up on his legs as she lay there. Nox patted her head resting in his lap gently, soothing her into closing her eyes. She was asleep as soon as her eyes closed.

She was awakened by Dayn shaking her urgently in the middle of the night. He was telling her to wake up, that Jonnie had sent word that she was needed. Nox was putting her boots back on her feet and was lacing them as Dayn helped her sit up.

"Come with us!" Nox said excitedly. "You've been summoned to the meeting!"

Elaraine just blinked stupidly as they got her to her feet and started leading her by hand to the riverbank she had left half a day earlier. The night surrounded them, the stars overhead glistening in the dark sky. A small fire could be seen through the trees and raised voices were in an argument nearby. As they came to the riverbank from the trees, Elaraine could see King Arlun, Prince Shep, and Jonnie on one side of the fire. Moraiah, Josi, a guard behind them and a man with a bandaged face sat nearby. Elaraine felt a strangled cry rise in her throat at the sight of her bandaged brother, but Jonnie motioned for her to sit next to her.

"Elaraine," Moraiah said in a gloomy greeting. "I see you made it back to their side safely." Her gaze dropped to her bandaged arm and splinted leg. "Maybe a little worse for the wear, but you made it."

Orin refused to turn in her direction and kept his head down. Elaraine settled stiffly next to Jonnie and the argument resumed.

"We are not surrendering!" Moraiah shouted at King Arlun. "You called this second meeting to discuss terms, not us! Are you mentioning 'surrender' because you want to?"

Prince Shep kept a discreet, steadying hand on his brother as the king shouted back. "You are now outnumbered and we won the battle! Now is the time to discuss conditions for the defeated side's surrender!"

"We have equal dead! My men are ready to resume the battle! We only wish to return home to Rischiak in peace!"

"Then why did you come within Swennian borders?"

"They came to get me, their queen! We are happy in Rischiak. It is you who send armies to the borders to harass us!"

The argument continued in this way for a very long time. Neither royal was making headway in the argument. Elaraine feared another drawing of arms there on the riverbank. She turned to Jonnie.

"Why was I summoned? I cannot do anything here," she whispered.

"Orin and Josi requested to see you. They would not sit still until you were summoned," she whispered back. "Orin may refuse to look at you directly, but the two of them were highly alarmed to learn you had been injured and did not believe us that you were okay."

"Josi, too?"

"Our brother's son does worry for us, even if he does not show it. Moraiah has been raising him to be stoic from the time he was born. A Crown Prince cannot be overly emotional, don't you know?"

The sisters smiled at each other as the argument raged on. Elaraine could not control her yawns after she had been there for a couple of hours, much to the dismay of the prince and the king, who would both cast glares in her direction when one would escape. Dayn poked her in the back really hard until she stopped yawning.

Finally, the prince interrupted the arguing and stood abruptly. Everyone fell silent and all eyes fell upon him.

"I think this is ridiculous!" he shouted. "Moraiah," he turned to the queen, "you and your men will be happy to merely return to Rischiak peacefully and when you return you are content to no longer have hostilities between Rischiak and Swennia. Is that right?" The woman nodded mutely and so he turned to his brother. "King Arlun, you want the Rischiaks off Swennian land, correct?"

"I want them gone and I want them to give their lands to us as part of a surrender agreement."

"Well, you have permanently scarred the queen's husband without provocation, so you have to make a concession or two. You are lucky no one has tried to scar you or me!"

"We are people of honor," Moraiah bristled.

Prince Shep held up a hand asking for her patience. "King Arlun, would you, therefore, concede that because of a dire folly earlier today caused by yourself that the Rischiaks can return to Rischiak in peace and keep their lands?"

"It was not a 'folly!'" the king yelled.

"Orin saved you from that giant I killed with Nox and you attacked him a few short hours later!" the prince yelled back. "Now, concede to those terms before more of your men are killed and your entire army rebels instead of the few dozen who already crossed over that river!"

"I am the king and you are the prince!" the king roared.

"And a king needs an army for power and he does not have power if that army goes to follow the enemy!"

The king seemed to think about what the prince said for a moment and then nodded a nod so small everyone almost missed it. "I will concede, but I want affirmation that no Rischiak will ever step foot on Swennian land again. Ever. Or there shall be a full war between our two kingdoms."

Moraiah gave a nod in return. "You must give those in your camp who want to join us a little while to come to our camp peacefully. Defecting from one country to the next for forever is not a matter to be taken lightly. Give them time to make the decision and do not threaten punishment on them or any of the family they leave behind."

Prince Shep looked between the royals. "It will take time for the official treatise to be written. You and your people will follow us to the Swennian capital with an order of protection for the treaty to be written. Four weeks. You and your people will have four weeks from tomorrow to begin your return to Rischiak to never return and you will have a week beyond that to complete the crossing." He turned between the two royals. "Is this agreement suitable to you both?"

King Arlun nodded reluctantly. Moraiah looked to Orin for the first time that Elaraine saw that evening and he made a minute nod as well. Moraiah also nodded at the agreement. King Arlun and Queen Moraiah shook hands and the two parties made to leave the site.

Orin grasped his wife's arm for a moment and looked at her without a word. She nodded and patted his hand.

"For only a moment. We will be waiting to cross the river with you and Treyl will remain with you to protect you," Moraiah said tenderly and led Josi away from them a short distance, then stood waiting.

Dayn and Nox took their cue to leave Jonnie and Elaraine alone with their brother and left them, throwing a final glance over their shoulders as they entered the woods. King Arlun and Prince Shep left without saying another word to anybody and without another look at the dispersing company. Finally, the siblings were left alone to talk.

"Does it hurt much?" Elaraine asked when her brother still refused to look her in the eyes.

He shook his head. "I could ask the same thing of you, but I am told you are in a lot of pain, Elaraine." They all fell into silence once more. "Do the two of you get along well?"

"It can be a little awkward," Jonnie answered for them both, "but we are going to work through that."

He leaned close to them, making sure to keep his head tilted at the ground. "We won't be given much time, so I have to talk quickly. I am going to Rischiak for Josi. The boy needs to have a father as he grows up. Moraiah already has our parents in the Rischiak camp. We all want the two of you to come with us. 'Forever' is a long time, though. If you come with us, you cannot come back now that this agreement has been reached. It is your decision, and I will respect whatever you decide. If you decide to remain, I want to tell you there will be no hard feelings between us and if you should ever need help here in Swennia I will find a way to return to help you if I can."

He looked them in their faces for the first time that night. His white bandage was stained red in a streak on his face. His expression was as torn as his skin was.

"We love you, too, Orin," Elaraine said. "We will let you know soon if we will come with you."

He nodded and walked away to join his wife and son. Jonnie and Elaraine sat there until Orin and his family were out of sight on the other side of the bank.

"I decided I will go with Orin," Jonnie said suddenly. "I have been shown these past few days that Swennia demands complete, solid loyalty of its people but its loyalty in return is fickle." Elaraine nodded absently. "Dayn and Nox have said they will go where you go." Jonnie studied her. "What, then, would be left for you here?"

An image of the prince as they were fleeing from the Rischiak camp flashed before Elaraine's eyes, his being friendly to her and warming her with only his gaze. Then, an image of his being angry with her earlier in the day replaced the other image. Her brother was marred forever by the temper of his brother.

"My home is wherever those I love are," Elaraine said looking around the area illuminated by the fire. "If Orin, Josi, our parents, and you go to Rischiak, and Nox and Dayn are going to follow me there if I go, then that is where I will go. There would be nothing left for me here."

Jonnie stood up and studied her a moment longer. "Well, you have four weeks to convince yourself of that."

Jonnie helped Elaraine to her feet and hugged her. "I do not need four weeks. I will have nothing here. I will follow my family to Rischiak."

The women walked to camp together. Dayn and Nox met them at the edge of the camp and took Elaraine back to their tent. They sat for a while talking about the agreement that was reached as Nox took her boots off for her. They fell into a companionable silence.

"Elaraine, will you go with Orin?" Dayn finally asked, sounding slightly fearful.

She nodded. "I think so. Once they leave, I will have no one here to call 'family.' My home is where they go."

"If you go, Elaraine, then I will go, too," Dayn said. "My mother has already agreed to go with Moraiah to be an advisor to her so this kind situation can be avoided in the future. But, if you stay, I will stay. I will not leave you alone in this world."

Nox nodded in agreement. "I have no family either way. I will go where you go, too."

Elaraine shook her head. "I can't ask you two to just leave and go with me."

"We never heard you ask us our opinion on the matter or if we would go with you or not," Dayn piped in. "But like we will not let you be alone, we will not be left alone, either."

"We don't want to be left alone, either!" a small voice murmured from outside of the tent before Julera and Gigoro came into the tent to be with them. "We don't want to be left alone in Swennia either."

Gigoro nodded. "I don't relish becoming Rischiak, but Julera has grown attached to you and I cannot raise her without help. If you do not mind helping me with Julera from time to time, would you mind if we went with you as well?"

"Look at all of us! A day ago we were ready to die for Swennia and now we're talking of changing sides!" Elaraine said in near disbelief.

"That is what happens when the ruling family fails you. Their subjects will rebel. The king does not care about us. We were sheep to be massacred on his field of battle for his glory. He would not listen that it was a bad place to camp for the night. He would not listen that it would have been better for us to pick the battlefield and let the Rischiaks come to us. Now our friends lay dead, waiting to be buried in the morning. Swennia lost a lot of good men last night and King Arlun does not care," Nox said bitterly. "Changing sides at this point could not hurt."

"What about Prince Shep?"

"The prince does not rule, he does not control his brother, and, when this war is over, our lives all hang in the balance with King Arlun, not with Prince Shep," Dayn added. "Besides, soon, now that King Arlun has ascended to the throne, he will marry the prince off and then his attention will be turned entirely to domestic pursuits instead of martial pursuits and then we will truly be left in trouble."

The five of them talked for a few more minutes, discussing their upcoming defection. Then they all fell into a deep slumber on the damp ground, ignoring the bugs that would crawl over them. The dawn came all too soon and they set about the sad task of burying the dead. Elaraine made sure to remain out of sight of the prince per his request the previous day.

By noon, King Arlun ordered the camp to break and head back to the capital. The Rischiaks were already there and ready to follow them. They looked warily on as the Swennians fells into long lines to follow their king. Andell rode beside her, having also been banished temporarily from the prince's side. They rode in silence a few hours.

"What are you thinking so deeply about?" Andell asked after a while, catching her staring at the prince's back for the longest time.

"Forever," Elaraine said simply. Softly, she repeated. "I'm thinking of 'forever.'"

Chapter Thirty-One

The four weeks Prince Shep had given the Rischiak camp and those leaving with them had passed quickly for Elaraine. She could hardly believe that the time had come to leave as Orin adjusted her mask for the hundredth time that night as they stood in front of the closed oak doors. Beyond the doors the small party could hear instruments gaily playing and the sounds of laughter floated to the group beyond to grace their ears. Orin's mask was black and covered his entire face, hiding the scar that would have everyone recognizing him. He was flanked by Dayn and Nox, each wearing gray half-masks, revealing only their mouths. The men wore their hair as a gentleman would, short and well-kept. It was so unlike the way their hair had become during the long weeks travelling leading up to that final battle. They wore uniforms of the Swennian army they had kept in good condition during their time in the war. Moraiah had decreed the group would leave for Rischiak at dawn the next morning, so Elaraine would have this one chance to see her friends for the last time.

Elaraine smoothed her white silk dress again. The gold trimming at the edges and the waist had been Julera's idea. Elaraine wished the little girl could be at the ball as well to enjoy a moment in the court, but she and Gigoro were with Moraiah for the disappearance of the four to be less suspicious. If all of Elaraine's friends had left, Moraiah would have sounded an alarm before they had had a chance to leave the encampment that was beyond the capital's walls. Elaraine's mask was white and only hid her forehead, around her eyes and nose, a bold choice considering the decree of the king that Elaraine and her friends would be killed if they ever appeared in his court again, but she held out hope that one man would recognize her and would know that she had at least appeared for a moment before she had disappeared in the morning mist. Her gloves covered her arms to her shoulders, hiding the stab wound scar forming on her forearm. She had always been slow to heal. Her hair was wound tightly and elegantly upon her head, decorated with small white meadow flowers. She wore a sapphire around her neck. She was unused to the heels she wore, but no proper lady wore boots to a ball and tonight she had to at least pretend to be a proper lady.

"Remember," Orin whispered hoarsely, "we have but an hour for you to see him and for us leave. We cannot afford any more time beyond that. If you see him before then, all the better. We will be nearby if you need us."

He stole a few deep breaths before he knocked once on the door to signal a squire on the other side of the door that people were there to be introduced. He led the way and whispered a final reassurance in her ear. "No one has ever seen you in a dress this fine, so no one will know who you are. Do not worry."

She nodded as the door swung open, revealing to them the mirth within. Her heart stopped for a moment and she contemplated running away, but one of her friends behind her had a steady hand on her back pushing her slowly forward. She tried as hard as she could to hide her limp she had from her broken ankle that was still healing, but the harder she tried the more difficult it became, so she stood near the dance floor with her friends and scanned the room as covertly as she could manage.

"Do you see him?" Dayn whispered in her ear as he handed her a cup of water that seemed to sparkle within the crystal cup. She shook her head. "Maybe he has not arrived yet."

"He lives here," Nox snorted in reply as he sipped from a glass of red wine. "It is not like he can say the weather kept him from coming!"

"You aren't making her feel better either," Dayn whispered heatedly at his friend. Elaraine was afraid people around them would start to hear and grasp the conversation. "All you're doing is—"

"Would one of you please dance with me?" she asked as she finally saw him enter the room.

The announcement of his arrival was made and all the people gathered in the ballroom hushed in awe. He made quite the figure in his white uniform with his regal trimmings. His hair was cut neater since he had been in the palace for a while; Elaraine surmised that could be attributed to his brother's will. He wore a mask that was half black and half white. Only his eyes were covered by the disguise, but even if his entire face had been covered, Elaraine would have recognized him anywhere. Her heart ached at the sight of him. He strode boldly and quickly to his seat at the right of his brother's throne. Once he was seated, the music and the laughter started again.

Dayn took her hand and led her slowly to the dance floor. As the music played, he lifted her to stand on his feet. He knew that unless he did this, there would be no way she could make it through the dance. Her leg had never truly recovered. Then he swirled them around the floor. Glances were thrown their way, but Elaraine felt secure in their disguises. Everyone else's masks hid their identities, so she and Dayn were two amongst hundreds of other strangers. She looked at the raised floor with the throne and chairs of honor a couple of times. As their spot in the dancing circle of couples neared the throne, she grew slightly nervous that he would recognize her and announce it publicly. She was both relieved and annoyed as Dayn turned them so she was facing away from the prince as they danced past the throne. As he turned her back to the throne she swore for a moment she caught and held the prince's gaze before he frowned and looked away.

When the dance ended, Dayn escorted her back to their small party and Nox asked her for a dance with a bow. He escorted her back to the dance floor and also lifted her to stand on top of his feet.

"Am I not too heavy for you two when you do that?" she asked, steadying her nerves for the next pass of the throne she knew would inevitably come.

"You have lost too much weight during your time with the Rischiak healers," he grunted as the dance began.

Nox's dance was slower than Dayn's had been. The musicians played a fast ballad but to Elaraine the world seemed to be in slow motion as they neared the throne area. She thought she and the prince had made eye contact again when she passed the throne in Nox's arms when she thought she saw Prince Shep's eyes narrow briefly on her and then he shook his head.

"He recognized you," Nox whispered in her ear as the dance ended and they rejoined their group. "It is time for us to go. You have seen each other."

"Yes, we have. And I did promise we would leave once that had happened." She straightened her back in resolve. "So let us go."

This time Orin stepped forward. "After I have my dance with my sister, we shall go," was his hoarse whisper. It saddened Elaraine that his voice had still not recovered from his yelling in the battle. It did not help his voice to argue with Moraiah nightly, either. He led her to the dance floor and for the third time that night she was lifted to stand on someone's feet. "Will one more pass by him be enough to hold you over for a lifetime, Ela?"

"It will have to be." She tried to sound confident, but her voice trembled in her ears.

He nodded as the music started. As she was turned to see the throne, she knew she had made eye contact with Prince Shep. This time there was no mistaking it. Her heart raced as his eyes widened and she saw his knuckles whiten on his chair's armrests. When her brother spun around with her away from the throne, she felt at peace with her decision and she knew it was time to go. They had stayed too long already. Her brother's and Nox's indulgence with dances beyond Dayn's meant they had stayed too long anyway.

Orin left her as the dance ended to find Dayn and Nox, who were off in the corner talking to a couple of beautiful young ladies. Elaraine just smiled at their attempts at romance and turned her attention back to the dance floor. She gasped loudly and nearly stumbled backward instead.

Prince Shep was before her, a cup of ale in his hand. He silently offered her a drink of it, his eyebrows arching as she fought back her instinct to refuse it. She did not drink, so she knew he was testing her. She smiled and took a sip of the putrid liquid before returning the cup to him, fighting the cough that resulted. He frowned and put the cup on the tray of a nearby squire. He took her hand and, against her protests, took her onto the dance floor for the next dance.

Unlike her brother and friends, he did not lift her onto his feet, and she feared her knee or ankle would buckle beneath her as they started to move. She fought the urge to look at their feet to see what the steps were and instead she could feel a surge of moisture leap to her eyes.

"You looked so graceful when those other men led you around the floor," he whispered gently. "I am sorry if dancing with me embarrasses you. I am afraid I am unused to dancing as well as I have been in the army far too long and away from the polite life of court."

She cleared her throat a bit to hopefully change the pitch of her voice or at the very least make herself sound like she wasn't about to cry. "My prince, I am afraid it is I who should be sorry. My other partners knew of my inability to dance and so lifted me to stand upon their feet. If I looked graceful, it was because they themselves were graceful. I apologize for deceiving you of my ability."

He laughed and lifted her to stand on his immaculately shined shoes. "My lady, I wish you had said something earlier, before suffering the public's scrutiny like that."

"I have suffered more publicly embarrassing events than not knowing how to dance at court, my prince," she said honestly, remembering her public condemnation in Gegernen. His eyes narrowed and she realized her voice was sounding normal once more. "Wh-what I mean is—" she stammered.

He cut her off. "I am afraid your dress and hair are beautiful and perfect this evening, my dear, so the first few steps of our dance are all that can be criticized of you this evening by anyone who has seen you." His smile faded as he looked down at her. "Your leg has not healed," he stated. "I am sorry that I set the bones and joints wrong that night."

They heard a woman in a dancing couple nearby say haughtily and so everyone around them could hear her. "Imagine! She must be trying to woo the prince herself! Doesn't she know he's going to be promised to one of us here? King Arlun said so in his letter to my father inviting me here."

The woman was finally hushed by her companion as he danced them away from the prince and Elaraine against the flow of the other dancers. Elaraine knew she was a bright shade of red and looked at the floor. Elaraine was thankful that the woman had only heard the beginning of what he had said and chose not to acknowledge his statement about her leg, feeling that they had discussed the issue at enough length that he should not still harbor these useless feelings of guilt.

"It is not true, Prince Shep," she said so softly he could barely hear her over the music as he strained to listen. "I do not wish to woo anybody."

"I know," was his gruff reply. When she refused to meet his gaze he lightened his tone. "I think every other woman is here to woo me and my brother, but you mingle with no one and remain aloof with the companions you came with." He sighed when that did not cause a reaction from her and forced her face to tilt up at his. "Please look at me." She did and he gasped before pulling her in close to whisper in her ear. "You may clear your throat to change your voice, you may dress in feminine things and have your hair done like a queen's, but, Elaraine Hedri, you could never truly fool me."

Over his shoulder, she saw her friends and brother on the side of the dance floor looking horrified. Their eyes were wide and while they talked quietly amongst themselves, their eyes did not leave the prince and Elaraine. Nox's knuckles were noticeably white as he grasped a crystal cup. Orin looked almost angry and Dayn had to stop him from walking onto the dance floor. The prince followed her eyes as he turned them around on the dance floor and he scoffed slightly before bending to her ear.

"They are afraid I will expose you to everyone here, you know," the prince said nonchalantly as he spun them around the dance floor. "They don't trust me anymore, do they?"

"If we are caught, your brother will kill us all and the peace between the Rischiaks and the Swennians will be gone forever."

"Then why did you come?" He held her tighter. "Why would you risk all that?"

She swallowed the lump that rose in her throat. "Because, after this, it will be forever."

He held her away from him so he could look at her. He looked at her closely and with obvious surprise. When she met his gaze evenly, his grip on her tightened slightly. "What do you mean?" he said softly between clenched teeth.

"In the morning everyone in the Rischiak camp must go to Rischiak and not come back. You, King Arlun, and Moraiah decided it had to be that way that night by the river. Do you not remember, my prince?"

He nodded. "The Rischiaks must leave, yes. We are at an uneasy peace with them now, but I thought it would be best if they left Swennian land. It is the only way to keep the peace treaty intact."

She took a steadying breath as she prepared to tell him that which she promised herself would remain a secret to him. But when he looked at her with such alarm, she knew she would have no choice but to tell him. "Orin's wife and son are Rischiak. Orin is going to Rischiak with his family. Jonnie decided to stay here, but our parents are going with Orin. My husband is dead. Nox and Dayn decided to go, too, when I made my decision and Moraiah gave them advisor positions in her court. Gigoro and Julera are in the camp as well. Because of a Swennian royal decree, my family and friends will never be allowed to return to our homeland. Your brother will have you a bride soon and then you will be busy here helping the new king. So, what would be left for me here?"

Suddenly his grip on her tightened significantly and his jaw frantically clenched and unclenched. He swallowed a few times and would not look at her. Elaraine felt proud of herself for telling him what she had been so afraid to. She had not told him the secret closest to her heart, but had hinted at it. Now she could leave with a peaceful mind.

When the song ended, she was ready to leave and go to Orin and her friends. Instead of allowing her to leave, the prince kept her held tight to him while the other dancers switched partners or decided to take a short respite. Orin stepped on the floor to collect her, but the music resumed and the prince began to dance with her standing on his feet again.

He looked down at her with what Elaraine had come to know as fear in his eyes and he held her close again. He swallowed deeply a few more times before he was able to whisper to her. "What if I rescind the order? What if I tell my brother that it wouldn't be best for the peace? Then no one has to go anywhere and you can stay here. He owes me a favor for winning the battle of the treaty and winning some battles for him in his campaign. I am sure he would do it with my counsel."

Elaraine winced inwardly at the unspoken plea she detected in his voice. "He will never reverse the decision. It is something we all must accept. So we should just part on the friendliest terms possible. We should not prolong the inevitable goodbye."

"You will leave your homeland?" His voice cracked and raised slightly, but enough that she had to gesture politely for him to quiet down so they would not attract attention to their conversation.

"I will follow my family. In this world, there is nothing more important to me than my family."

"Nothing?" The prince became rigid as he awaited her answer. "What of someone who could become family? Staur is dead. You are free to remarry now."

She laughed lightly and patted his shoulder. "I will keep an eye open for a potential future 'Elaraine Hedri's husband.' He will have to put up with a lot, won't he? I'm too headstrong and independent for most men, am I not?" She tightened her grip on his shoulder and really looked him in the eyes for the first time that night and saw hurt, panic, and desperation. "Soon, you will be married. Soon you will have a lovely princess on your arm and children running about you, and you won't be lonely anymore, Prince Shep. When you are old, you will still be a mighty prince and you will not remember a lowly girl from the country. But when I am old, I will still be a lowly girl from a country village and I will still remember one of the greatest friends... greatest men... I have ever known." She saw Orin right behind him and leaned in to whisper in the prince's ear one last parting message. "Prince Shep, I owe you much. I owe you for saving my life. I owe you for saving Orin's life. I owe you for sparing our lives twice. But, Prince Shep, I owe you for showing me that I am capable of opening my heart to people. I love you."

With that she took Orin's proffered hand and he led her from the stunned prince, who she left standing in the middle of the dance floor, his mouth slightly agape and staring into the space beyond her. She walked as quickly as she could with her brother supporting her. The crowd made way for them as Orin told them she was feeling tired and needed to sit for a moment. Instead of steering her towards a row of benches for the guests of the dance, Orin led her to where Dayn and Nox were waiting anxiously by the door. They were looking over her shoulder, their brows furrowed.

Their expressions made her curious but when she looked over her shoulder at what they were staring at so intently her stomach dropped to her toes. She saw Prince Shep cutting through the crowd towards them like a fish through water, his expression grave. Orin looked, too. As soon as he saw the prince approaching, he grabbed her hand and pulled her through the door with him, Dayn and Nox right behind them.

About The Author

L. T. Clark

L.T. Clark grew up in Georgia, where she spent most of her life. She spent a year teaching English in South Korea after graduating from the University of Georgia. She met her husband in Atlanta and is currently a proud stay-at-home mom to their son and their German Shepherd. She splits nap times between two of her favorite things: writing and baking.

www.ingramcontent.com/pod-product-compliance
Lightning Source LLC
Chambersburg PA
CBHW032141190626
46814CB00005BA/1784